DARK CITY RISING

ALSO BY CL JARVIS

The Edinburgh Doctrines series

The Doctrines of Fire

A Treatise of Air

The Chronicles of Earth

A Codex of Metal

Dark City Rising

DARK CITY RISING

CL JARVIS

PEWTER LYNX PRESS

First published in 2024 by Pewter Lynx Press

ISBN 978-1-7392644-5-1

Copyright © 2024 by CL Jarvis

All characters and events in this publication, other than those clearly in the public domain, are fictitious and any resemblance to real persons, living or dead, is purely coincidental.

All rights reserved.
No part of this book may be reproduced in any form or by any electronic or mechanical means, including information storage and retrieval systems, without written permission from the author, except for the use of brief quotations in a book review.

To the man in London,
whose sly smile I borrowed.

PART I
GLASGOW 1748 TO 1752

"Science is the knowledge of consequences, and dependence of one fact upon another."

— THOMAS HOBBES, THE
LEVIATHAN (1651)

I

GLASGOW

In his naivety, William Cullen once considered the art of arranging a meeting with an aristocrat the most nefarious dark magic in existence.

He met with Francis Leechman in the university tavern most mornings to wet his throat before morning classes. It wasn't meant to be a private conference—it was rare that a student wouldn't stop by the table to speak with one or both professor.

To that end, Leechman positioned them at the central table, between two journeymen and a gaggle of mathematical students. The morning air was ripe with yeasty ale and drying ink.

"Good day, Francis. Any word about...?"

"Yes, yes, your petition." Leechman adjusted his academic robes and cleared his throat. "Sir Thomas isn't going to be much use here."

While Leechman always uttered the unvarnished truth, and rarely concealed anything, Cullen felt it necessary to challenge this statement.

"Are you sure about that, Francis? You told me Sir Thomas would happily introduce me to the earl." Leechman filled yesterday's meeting with reassurances of this fact.

"What I didn't realise was that the sunken business deal between Sir Thomas and Anglesbury fermented considerable ill-will." Leechman set his ale down. "The two men haven't been on cordial terms for months."

"A business deal? I thought it was a failed marriage agreement between their children."

"That's what I meant." Leechman had a way of looking at Cullen as if he were one of his undomesticated students, not a married man with a family of his own. "Knowing Sir Thomas, he's not one to bear a grudge forever, and I'm sure he'll be back on cordial terms with the earl within a couple of years."

Cullen had to laugh. "I'm not waiting three years for the cosmos to re-align on that path of introduction. You know me better than that, Francis."

"Unfortunately, forcing the issue with Sir Thomas will vex him right now."

"Well, if I can't reach Anglesbury through Sir Thomas, who should I approach?"

Leechman grimaced, a sign Cullen was pushing on a nerve and he hoped he'd back off.

The man put Cullen to the mind of a genial cadaver: grey but bright-eyed. His smile was like the cracking of granite through his etched face.

He couldn't deny they were an odd pair. Leechman—a former minister—taught Moral Philosophy for years at Glasgow before Cullen arrived.

Leechman always carried himself with grace through academic dealings. When he chose to lecture in English, his studious and serious bearing meant no one in the university objected to it. Leechman had the gravitas to make English sound as refined as Latin.

Despite this, a little prodding and wine could expose Leechman's sly scepticism of university politics and patronage, which beautifully mirrored Cullen's own. He met Leechman's son first in the classroom, bringing him into acquaintance with the august professor shortly after. As soon as he'd earned Leechman's friendship, Cullen found himself secure in his academic position, protected by the philosopher's approval.

"Maybe the Cumbernauld road isn't your fight, William. Perhaps we can ask one of Anglesbury's surrogates to raise the petition."

"No." Cullen shook his head. "I learned this the hard way in Lanarkshire: if I don't do it, it doesn't get done. His lordship has cause to travel on his roads—even if only in extenuating circumstances—so he knows the state of them. As will the individuals he patronises."

The West Cumbernauld road violently caught his attention the first time he travelled from Glasgow to visit his youngest sister's family. The carriage wheel struck a pothole, causing him to strike his head on the door beam. His wife Anna was five months pregnant at the time with their first child, and Cullen's anxiety led him to berate the driver for careless driving.

"How difficult is it for a dolt like yourself to avoid dangerous ruts and potholes?" he'd shouted.

"Rather difficult, actually," the driver mumbled. Looking at the lumpy condition of the road for the first time, Cullen was forced to agree.

"When you were a pillar of the Hamilton community, of course the condition of the surrounding roads was your business. But your concern these days should be towards your students and academic colleagues, should it not? At least," Leechman hurried to clarify, "That's what the gentry will think."

"Some of my students use that road," Cullen argued. "Their families certainly do. I know I take more charity cases from the countryside into my classroom than most other faculty—more than is sensible, I must admit—but I would have petitioned about the awful turnpikes, even if I was a nobody."

He'd seen the effects of poor roads on enough patient bodies.

Stiff, hunched backs. Ruined hips and knees. His patients didn't waste their breath pleading with Cullen to do anything about such minor problems of course—he was summoned for the fevers, infected wounds and death rattles—but when the patient or their families rose and moved

around their homes, Cullen could see their suffering.

Old Leechman may not help him here, Cullen decided. Approaching the prickly Earl directly was risky—without the proper introductions, he would come across as presumptuous at best, even conceited.

But if he could engineer a chance encounter...

He could surely make Anglesbury care about the problem. Just two minutes of conversation would be enough.

Anglesbury attended the monthly Royal Society dinners. The next dinner was in what, two or three weeks' time? Not ideal, but better than Leechman's timeline—bless his soul—of three years. He busied himself with his ale to conceal a smile.

Back in Hamilton, Cullen was spoiled by village politics. He'd treated the local Duke's stomach complaints shortly after establishing his practice, quickly entered the man's confidence. He liked Cullen's bluff manner of speaking and was happy to facilitate the spending of funds to improve his roads. Now Cullen was operating in unfamiliar domains—roads on the lands of other nobles with more urban sensibilities. They saw his forthrightness as rustic.

Leechman took a sip of ale and cleared his throat. "However, that wasn't the only business I wished to raise with you today..."

Cullen gritted his teeth. This oblique opening signified a trap.

"I received word—from several sources, I might add—about your latest digressions in your chemistry lectures."

It wasn't immediately obvious which digression he was supposed to defend himself against. Fortunately, Leechman was prompt to clarify.

"Did you really describe discussions of the soul as 'unintelligible jargon'?"

"Not in the slightest," Cullen replied. "Your multiple sources would know I merely said any discussion of the location or nature of our immortal soul in the anatomy or medicine classroom would risk descending into unintelligible jargon, and we were better leaving such matters to our brethren in Divinity."

Leechman exhaled.

"Sometimes I wonder, William, if you've overlooked the fact our university maintains warm ties with the General Assembly. Or forgotten our valued university Principal currently serves as the Assembly Moderator. And thus religious matters are treated rather seriously here."

These facts were difficult to miss.

"You know what I meant though, Francis. My students knew what I meant."

"Of course," Leechman spoke confidently, wishing to move past the attribution of concern part of the argument. "Yet it hardly matters what I think, or where my capability to be offended lies."

"Yes, my dear fellow. But if I leave theology to the theologians, shouldn't they leave medicine to the ornery physicians?"

"We've discussed in the past how some of your remarks in the classroom could be interpreted as anti-clerical..."

"...Which isn't the same as being anti-religious."

"Yes, yes. But you were a student here during the John Simson affair. You saw what happened to him." Leechman clicked his tongue in sympathy.

The lucky fool was merely suspended from teaching. Poor Simson. Cullen remembered the old man limping away from the college, eyes welling with tears. This was when the course of future events became self-evident: he knew he'd lose his lecturing rites, but keep his freedom. That was how the university treated a minister giving the Arian doctrines a sympathetic nod.

"I believe you are becoming more sensitive to these matters..."

"Quite right I am!"

"...But I worry you don't understand the consequences of everything you say."

Cullen sighed. He could almost imagine Leechman disliked these conversations as much as he did.

"I've watched England's parliament and church exert a civilising influence on our own kirk, and it gives me great hope we won't face such constraints in the future."

"But you see it in their eyes sometimes, don't you? The disappointment that they've gone four-score years without a blasphemer to hang, or a witch to drown."

"I became convinced early on," Leechman said, ignoring that last remark. "That tolerance of other religions, even the misguided ones, is seen by God as a virtue. This was at odds with the prevailing dogma of my youth. I was very careful in expressing my opinion, though it went against my conscience to project a belief I did not hold, and which is why I preach caution and patience to you. Bringing others to my position required many difficult but tender conversations with my fellow ministers, a lot of prayer and self-counsel. Fortunately, I wasn't the only one having these thoughts; quietly agreeing with the English consensus that toleration is neither a weakness nor a sin."

"But how long did it take you to go from that first spark of conviction, to describing tolerance as a virtue in your classroom without fear of penalty from your superiors?" Since Leechman merely smiled to himself and looked away, Cullen decided to press the point. "Or your explanation of morality as derived from Man and influenced by God, instead of owning its whole provenance to God? Or any of the countless minor quibbles with the consensus General Assembly dogma that would have put you on the bench next to Simson twenty years ago, but which you can safely raise in your classroom without being accused of sympathising with them?"

"I work on God's timeline," Leechman replied. "Which is somewhat slower than Man's." A smile crossed his face, which it usually did when he was being softly ironic. "You expect seismic changes to unfold all at once, William. It's never worked like that."

Cullen didn't necessarily agree with this statement, but he was not so obstinate he couldn't see where his friend was coming from.

"I imagine the medical professors don't have this peculiar problem in Edinburgh or London." This was a point his mind always circled back to.

Leechman laughed lightly. "That is the only aspect of medical education you'd find easier in Edinburgh than Glasgow. The kirk is less involved in the running of Edinburgh's colleges, but that leaves room for other parties to meddle. Trust me, William. You'll make more progress reforming medical education on the west coast."

Cullen had tried to ignore this reality in his future planning.

Leechman leaned forward. "There's plenty of men in Scotland who are on your side, Dr Cullen. They think institutes of learning benefit from freethinking and anti-partisanship. I want to help you reform the system, but I need you to understand the rules and refrain from incautious comments that could offend the wrong people."

Cullen hated following rules as capricious and constricting as this. But he graced his friend with another stiff nod. He wanted to believe this was a friendship of equals, but moments like this made him wonder if Leechman saw this as a teacher-student relationship.

"A pleasure, as always, but I must take my leave, my friend—the world of chemistry waits for no man."

The twin quadrangles of Glasgow University were bordered on two sides by meadows and pastures, adding a sweet freshness to the air that offset the greasy filth of the surrounding city.

On a bright but windy day such as this, scholars fluttered along the main cloister, seeking a little shelter from the elements. Near the entrance, movements slowed as students and faculty alike congregated by the university tavern, enjoying their allocated measures of ale and relaxed discussions of the day's lectures.

People read too much into his flippant remarks, Cullen thought. He enjoyed lecturing at Glasgow, and on a ninety-nine days out of a hundred, he lectured without controversy.

Twenty years ago, he'd have received more than a brief admonishment for his comment on the soul, so he should probably consider himself lucky. Now that his opinion on the matter was public knowledge, perhaps it meant his students wouldn't raise the question with him again.

"Patience, patience…" Cullen muttered, mimicking his friend. It was great that Leechman had a humoral balance suited to waiting; Cullen's blood ran too hot.

On days like today it felt nothing he desired would ever get accomplished, not until he was halfway into the grave, and where was the satisfaction in that? It would be nice if one thing, just one tiny change he desired, could come in a timely manner.

By the time Cullen made it across the Quadrangle, a queue of chemistry students already stretched to his classroom door. Cullen waved them inside. He set up his demonstration equipment before meeting Leechman, and since it was early in the term, he could devote most of the hour to the history of chemistry without expounding the modern state of the art.

"Although metallurgy and wine-making was known in Biblical times, and refined by the Egyptians and Greeks, it is the Arabs who we can first call chemists…"

It hadn't been easy getting his chemistry course attendance to reliable numbers. The students with a gentleman's education dismissed chemistry as no better than alchemy. Students intent on becoming physicians, apothecaries or chirurgeons came to class expecting to learn how to prepare medicinal products. It took a lot of convincing on Cullen's part that he was teaching something different, but that it was a worthwhile pursuit in its own right. Instead of transmuting metals or extracting botanicals, Cullen spoke about the properties of chemical mixtures and the act of heating or cooling substances.

Surveying his domain, Cullen noticed one student scrutinising him with a particular focus. A few days ago, that student hung at the back of the lecture theatre: today he occupied a front row spot, the same silent intensity on his face.

When Cullen concluded the lecture, he wasn't surprised to see this student inch towards him. It was early days in his career, and though he tried to cultivate an approachable personality for the students, many of them had been chastised by previous schoolmasters and lecturers for their youthful natural curiosity. When this student stood up, Cullen saw he was tall and thin, with fine curls of dark brown hair framing a delicate face and soulful eyes. He had an intense gaze, though his hunched posture suggested trepidation.

"Professor Cullen? May I have a word with you?"

The other students trickled out of the room.

"I'd be delighted. Take a seat, Mr...?"

Cullen was still ruminating on the earlier conversation with Leechman, but he cast his mind back to previous chemistry classes, recalling what he knew about the boy.

"Joseph Black."

Yes, a familiar name. The student body wasn't large.

"I need your advice concerning my proposed course of medical study," the young man explained. He had a low voice, with flashes of an Ulster accent.

Cullen rifled through his recollections.

"I understand you are presently studying Arts," Cullen said. This was a reasonable guess, and the young man nodded. "What brings about your interest in medicine?" This wouldn't be the first time a student had jumped ship from arts to medicine, but the leap was made with varying degrees of success.

The young man gave a non-committal shrug.

Cullen raised his eyebrows. Sometimes vague motivation was

better than a steadfast conviction in medical education based upon on the wrong reasons.

"I considered studying medicine at Glasgow when I arrived," he said, when the pause became too much for him to bear. "But in truth, the lecturers bored me. There is so much to learn about man and God's world, but I didn't think I could endure a medical education in pursuit of that."

A knowing smile played over Cullen's lips. "When you chitchat with the other students, Mr Black, do they complain I bore them?"

The serious boy managed to look even more severe. "I don't gossip, Professor Cullen."

"Oh, I didn't mean it as an insult." Cullen was surprised by the vehemence of the denial. "Students naturally exchange a lot of information with their peers, it's currency is it not? Sometimes a bit of romanticism and a flight of fancy helps get you through the day, I find. There's not always a harm in it."

He was usually better at reading students than this. His meaning made clearer, the student relaxed a little.

"I don't want to cause harm, Professor Cullen. That's why I avoid spreading gossip I can't substantiate."

"You're a better man than most, Mr Black."

Plenty of students who hung on the outskirts of the main social cliques, like this boy seemed to, affected disdain for the gossip of their peers. In Cullen's experience, this stance was more borne of jealously than morality: invited into the gossip circles, many would loosen their tongues. That this Joseph Black apparently was given the opportunity to gossip, but declined, was interesting.

"Back to my question, which still stands…"

Black's expression lost some of its affected disengagement. "No, sir—quite the opposite, in fact. Everyone speaks highly of your lecturing style."

That was nice to know.

Sensing his approval, Black continued. "My father is insistent I settle on a profession and focus my studies this year."

Cullen was satisfied that he now understood the matter. A lot of young men came to explore and have fun with their studies, only for their family to break their idleness as the tuition and loans mounted. They resented their fathers' interference and joy-quelling, but fell in line without argument. That this boy's father presented him with a free choice of professions was an unusual laxity.

"Well, Mr Black, you're right that medicine has things to tell us about the natural world, too." He leaned back. "For instance, there is more to chemistry than the mixing of materia medica: I expect my scholars to understand the principles of matter, for I want them to understand why their preparations work on their patients the way they do."

He noticed Black was paying him more attention now—the topic of chemistry particularly interested him, though he seemed to hold back in expressing that interest. There was a general wariness to the boy: he may be one of those who disliked having his feelings exposed.

Caution and restraint were admirable qualities, especially in one so young. Cullen wished he possessed more of both.

"Think on the matter for a while. There's no urgency to decide. But I'm always in need of assistants with my chemical studies."

"I'm afraid I make a weak scholar of chemistry," the boy said with a pinking of his cheeks. "I still can't keep the facts straight in my head. But your offer is very generous."

"Nonsense," said Cullen. "I don't need my natural philosophers fully formed. I'm here to teach you, Mr Black. This chemical apprenticeship can begin from square one."

"It can?" The boy brightened. "Well, that's...very...I mean, thank you."

Given Cullen's current dearth of assistants, he couldn't afford to be anything other than generous, but that seemed impolite to mention.

The boy stared furiously at his knees, trying to repress his excitement. Cullen felt optimistic about this one. "The laboratory is ready when you are, Mr Black. I'm pursuing several lines of inquiry concerning heat and refrigeration, and I would appreciate an extra pair of hands."

Black leaned forward. Cullen realised he'd heard the unspoken 'but' in his last sentence.

"But I am also exploring more...unconventional avenues of philosophical enquiry." Cullen ventured.

Something flashed in Black's eyes.

Cullen paused. He'd spent so many years turning these thoughts over in his head, wishing to share them with the right person, while fearing the consequences of loosening them into the world. He'd come close to sharing his ideas with Leechman, but fear always swallowed him at the last minute, and he was left stuttering onto safer topics.

Yet Leechman felt more of a help than a hinderance on days like this. He said no to everything. He slowed Cullen down. What had Cullen to show for his petition, now months in the making?

The young man in front of him reacted with neither unrestrained excitement nor consternation. He seemed trustworthy. Despite his hesitant manner, Cullen suspected it would take a lot to scandalise him. This risk of him getting overexcited and spilling a secret appeared negligible. Indeed, Black's expression was now thoughtful.

"There are certain theories of elastic nervous fluids generated within the human body...or rather the principle of combustibility when applied to animal heat..." Cullen remembered chemistry was the only medical course Black had taken in his life; he wouldn't understand Cullen's theoretical framework. "...Actually, it's more correct to start with Stahl's phlogiston treatise in the context of the nervous system..." No, that treatise was too advanced and niche.

Black's furrowed brow deepened. Cullen had never considered how he would explain his theory to a neophyte student, because he never thought this was where he'd begin.

Cullen took a deep breath. "I'm sorry, lad. I'm getting ahead of myself. It's probably easiest if I just show you."

Undeterred by his teacher's failure to teach, Black nodded.

Cullen wiped his hand on the sleeve of his academic gown. He glanced around, in case any student or professor had snuck back into the room. The Quadrangle was still.

Cullen balled up both his fists and held them out over the table. This, at least, was a procedure he'd practiced countless times over the past decade. He flicked his middle fingers down his palms.

Like flint against steel, the strike appeared to ignite his hands. Two balls of crimson flames burst from Cullen's palms.

He heard the creak of Black's chair as the young student started. Black's eyes widened and his mouth parted, but while there was shock, there wasn't panic.

"Does it hurt?" Black asked.

"No?" Cullen hadn't expected that to be Black's first question. He squeezed his right hand shut to extinguish the flames. "But..." he reached out and picked up one of his square lecture note cards on the table, and held it over the crimson flames in his left palm. After a second, the corner of his lecture note ignited. Pulling it away, Cullen showed the boy the paper was burning with a yellow flame. He shook it flame out, breathing in the grey curl of smoke rising towards the ceiling.

"That is..." Black stumbled over his thoughts. "That's incredible, Professor Cullen. I'm ashamed to admit this is the first time I've encountered such a display."

Cullen laughed. "You wouldn't have encountered this anywhere else, Mr Black. At least I don't think so. This particular trick is something I've studied in private. I don't think anyone else knows phlogiston-wielding is possible."

And there was its name. Phlogiston-wielding. Cullen had

called it that a thousand times in his head, but this was the first time he'd named it in the presence of someone else. He felt giddy.

"And you're sure it doesn't hurt you, not even in the slightest?" Black persisted, glancing at the charred lecture note between them.

"Well, it's riskier when you start..." Cullen took another deep breath. "I'm getting ahead of myself again, lad. Forgive me. I devote a few hours most afternoons to chemical research in my humble laboratory space. Perhaps we can meet and commence from the beginning?"

2

EDINBURGH

Alexander Monro had perfected the art of walking through Edinburgh without ruining his shoes, or making it obvious that he was measuring his steps to avoid puddles and shit. Safely indoors, he slid out of his over-clogs. A few steps behind him, his colleague John Rutherford was breathily doing the same.

Filthy footwear taken care of, his maid hurried off to prepare the usual glasses of claret for her master and his guest.

They'd made it inside just in time, Monro noted, hearing rain scratch against the window. He'd need a sedan chair for his remaining items of business today.

"I'll ask Marian to bring more candles into the study," he commented, though the room was well lit by the tidy fire. He suspected darker clouds would roll in within the next hour and cast the space into shadow.

"Very good, Alexander," Rutherford agreed, settling himself next to the blaze.

Not a single tight curl of Monro's silvery wig was ever out of place. His cheekbones and brows were sculpted with the same precision, complemented with striking brown eyes. He pursed his lips.

In the daytime, Monro's study was his spot for correspondence and the occasional wealthy patron who desired to meet somewhere less public than a tavern. At night, the room once served as his middle son's bedchamber. Even though his children were full grown, he still caught himself delivering warning knocks on the door before entering at daybreak.

This was just one of the things you tolerated in Edinburgh. The wealthy nobles had their country mansions—they came into the town to play during the winter season, seeing their time in cramped living quarters as nothing more than a game. When they grew tired of it, they could retreat to the Lothians.

Wasn't worth complaining, because Monro's third floor Lawnmarket apartment was one of the more spacious ones in town. His current crop of servants didn't need reminding to sweep cobwebs from the beams or polish the silverware, and it gave the place a harmonious air.

Having friends in high places didn't hurt.

The conversation returned to the topic that had consumed most of their journey here. Rutherford started first. "The Town Council can't be serious about lauding William Cullen."

"Do you think they heard his latest...witticisms?"

"Concerning the soul? I imagine so." Rutherford picked up his proffered glass.

Fortunately, it wasn't the entire town singing Cullen's praises, just that blabbering Bennett. But it rankled Monro all the same.

Monro scratched his chin. "You'd think after the business with David Hume they'd remember to stay away from heretics and atheists. Turns out they're happy to block the first, but welcome the next one in because it suits their present needs—I guess the Councilmen don't want to admit how hypocritical they are when it comes to university appointments."

"It's not even the religious views he espouses that offend me," Rutherford commented. "Though they're bad enough. It's what he says about medicine in the classroom to those students that concern me the most. Which I told the Councilmen." He lapsed into silence.

Shadows filled the room. Rutherford swirled the liquid round his glass.

"Cullen cultivates a certain kind of student. Any illiterate farmhand can approach him to request he waive his course fees; he'll grant the waiver. And then these oafs ask incendiary questions in front of everyone. I can guarantee it wasn't a gentleman who asked about the soul."

"He creates an environment where students feel comfortable asking such questions," Monro said, sipping his claret. "They know he'll entertain any fanciful speculation posed—it's part of his appeal as a teacher."

"I'm sure he thinks it makes him superior to those he sees as the medical traditionalists."

"If he believes that," Monro remarked. "Then I have an acre of land on the Isthmus of Darien I'd like to sell him."

Part of the reason William Cullen occupied so many spirited conversations among the Edinburgh professors was because there wasn't much they could actually do about him.

Monro turned to look at the large portrait occupying pride of place above his study hearth. It showed a round-faced gentleman in brown robes, regarding the viewer with kindly eyes and the hint of a smile. His thinning grey hair hung in gentle curls down to his shoulders.

Rutherford caught Monro staring.

"An heir of Professor Herman Boerhaave, he certainly is not," he said, nodding his head towards the portrait.

"I shudder to think what the late Dr Boerhaave would make of Cullen," Monro agreed. "God rest the man's soul—you wouldn't find a more generous, kind-hearted teacher and physician in all of Leiden. In all of Christendom, I wager. But this William Cullen would erode the patience of saints."

Half a lifetime had passed since Monro and Rutherford journeyed through the medical schools of London, Paris and Leiden, albeit travelling the circuit in opposite direction. Their studies in Leiden under Boerhaave overlapped by half a year.

Monro neither considered Rutherford a friend, nor a rival. But their shared sense of purpose, establishment of an Edinburgh medical school based on Boerhaavian principles, meant they rarely went a day without speaking to each other.

"It's best we utter the name Cullen as little as possible," Monro said. "Turning attention to his teachings is counterproductive. Energy expended into disproving his theories makes them appear worth disproving."

"But still," Rutherford said. "I think we need to do something, or else he'll think we quietly support him." The medical worlds of Glasgow and Edinburgh were porous, and news travelled reliably fast.

Monro had given the subject plenty of thought. "The obvious action is to make sure the faculty has a unified policy of fee waivers. Charity is at the discretion of the professor, naturally. But I think it makes sense to discourage repeat fee waivers. Cullen has an entire circle of charity students who've taken his course for three or more years in a row. He says they can't be expected to master the material in a single sitting, but what it creates is a rabble beholden to him, and soaked in his ideas. The poorest at Edinburgh can have their opportunity to take the course for free once, and if they need to repeat it to gain mastery...well, they can pay for the privilege."

The way the professors saw it, it was cruel to deny talented students who'd fallen on hard times or suffered extenuating circumstances the chance to better themselves. It was just radicals like Cullen who took act of the charity to dangerous extremes. Once you opened the floodgates to the great unwashed, letting them believe they too could become physicians, where would you stop?

"Before I forget..." Rutherford fished an opened letter from his waistcoat pocket. "A minor errand required on behalf of his grace. From a brief perusal, I think this is more your forte than mine…"

Finding Adam Drummond, Deacon of the Incorporation of Surgeons, was a trivial exercise. Monro just need follow the screams.

Strolling through the clipped hedgerows into the palatial Surgeons Hall put Monro to the mind of visiting a country manor. However, once he passed through the front door the smell of congealed blood and decomposing organic matter made it clear this was no genteel estate.

Even if Monro's ears and nose were stoppered, he would have known Drummond was at work from the swarm of apprentices rushing to and from the operating theatre. The ratio of bloodied bandages leaving the room to clean bandages being hurried in indicated Drummond neared the end of his surgical procedure.

Monro kept his outer clogs on whenever he visited the Surgeon's Hall, slowing his pace as he entered the dimly lit theatre.

A few hours after Rutherford made his excuses and left Monro's apartment, the skies cleared. They held into late afternoon, and Monro hoped the walk down Lawnmarket onto the High Street would clear his head. Instead he'd had to slip past an altercation between the Town Guards and a clump of dishevelled men—probably Highlanders, given their broken English. The sight of latent Jacobites conferring made Monro nervous: fortunately, the Town Guard was quick to break up such gatherings.

The Highlanders were shouting something in anger at the Town Guards, but Monro was relieved to see enforcements coming down the street. As he passed, one of the Guards struck a Highlander in the face with the butt of his rifle, sending the man crumpling to the ground.

Monro had many appointments today, otherwise he'd have stopped to check the state of the Highlanders' fractured jaw.

The Surgeon's Hall occupied the furthest southeast corner of Edinburgh, hemmed in on two sides by Flodden Wall. The southern portion of Edinburgh below the Cowgate had always been lightly populated and dedicated to cerebral pursuits: first the site of monasteries—long demolished—now given over to medical education. If Monro followed the southern line of the Flodden Wall a few hundred metres he'd first reach the new Infirmary building, then the Tounis College grounds.

In the operating theatre, Drummond barked orders to his senior apprentices as they fumbled piles of bandages around the patient's lower body.

You couldn't tell from the screams alone—more animal than human—but today's patient was a woman. She was no longer screaming, but continued to twitch. The three hunched boys holding down her limbs seemed to tremble as much as she did, their strength almost worn out.

"Double-check the knot," Drummond was saying. The apprentice cringed.

Looking at the floor ahead of him, Monro saw the patient must have voided her bowels and bladder as soon as she walked into the operating theatre. The scurrying apprentices tried to skip over the worst of the mess and keep their balance doing so. The older trainees didn't appear to care what they stepped in.

"Gilbert and McLaurin—come back here. Help them move the body." Drummond made brief eye contact with Monro, then resumed shouting at the departing figures. "No, we don't need any more bandages in here. Fine, tell Carstares and the others to go straight to the beds."

It must have been months since the shutters were last opened, and the space aired. Monro could smell the rank body odour of the ten teenage apprentices scurrying past him. Part of the reason the ground-floor windows were boarded shut was to reduce the amount of the noise the public could hear from the street.

A clump of crimson sheets littered the floor around Drummond. The patient was almost totally silent—Monro supposed she was too far in shock. The apprentices unceremoniously dumped her on a nearby gurney and hauled her out. Up close, Monro could only see grey flesh and a concentration of rags around her left foot. Or at least, where her left foot once was.

Only Drummond and Monro remained in the room.

"Mr Drummond."

"Make your business quick, Professor Monro. These gut-brained apprentices need me to do everything for them."

Monro did his best not to twitch at his heavy inflection on 'professor.'

"Word from his grace about the Royal Infirmary renovations. He secured a contractor and expects the managers to vote on the proposal next week."

Still towelling his head and face, Drummond snatched the proffered letter from Monro's hand. His wig was tossed on a chair in the corner, alongside his coat. Globules of flesh still hung from Drummond's shorn hair. He rarely bothered to change out of his operating clothes following a procedure, instead buttoning his coat over the mess before walking home.

At sixty, Drummond's eyes were rheumy and his frame curling in on itself. His hands were shaking a little as he prised open the message, though Monro wasn't sure if that was old age or fatigue.

He made a show of reading the letter.

"Where have I heard the name Kincaid before? Ah yes, it's his grace's son-in-law, is it not? Didn't know he was involved in the Holland import business."

Monro kept silent, recognising the sharp edge of sarcasm twisting round.

Having skimmed the note, Drummond tried to thrust the letter back into Monro's hand. "Well, it's not like we have a choice in the matter, so I'm not sure why you're wasting my time showing me this."

"Kincaid is offering us a very favourable rate," Monro said evenly. "But I'm sure there is room for negotiation."

"To see if there's more business he can squeeze out of us? Ha!" Drummond tossed his cloth on the floor and kicked it under the table.

"I don't have time to call upon the other surgeons on the managerial board, so I hope you can convey the contents of the proposal to them." Monro clasped his hands behind his back, refusing to accept the return of his letter.

"This is a damnable charade, Professor Monro, and it's incredible you can act like it's not."

"No, this is called being civilised, Adam. It's how we do things at the medical school."

"I guarantee Kincaid is overcharging us on parts by forty percent."

"Well, then we ask for a discount."

"And what if he says no? Are we allowed to present a competing proposal from another contractor? One who isn't related to your patrons through blood or marriage? I'm sure such men exist—but you wouldn't know that from the lists of *preferred suppliers* they keep dredging up."

Monro sniffed. "These renovations are long-delayed already. Can we really afford to spend months shopping around proposals from lesser contractors? All for a few hundred pounds saved?" Kincaid was a perfectly reasonable choice to complete the work. If anything, Monro viewed his connections as fortuitous. It meant Kincaid wouldn't try and cross them.

Drummond was too highly strung to see these nuances, however. "It's always like this—every time we go through this mockery of due process when it comes to Infirmary funding, admittance of surgeons and renovation work. The outcome is always foreordained and never by the surgeons."

A minuscule smile crawled across Monro's face. "Well, if you wish to withdraw from your Infirmary manager role, I'm sure we could nominate another surgeon in your place. Or does the Incorporation want to try its hand fundraising for a second hospital again?"

Drummond scowled. Being one of the few surgeons permitted access to the Royal Infirmary—the domain of physicians—meant benefiting from increased private practice and the ability to charge eye-watering apprenticeship fees. As he got older, Drummond became more reliant on his army of apprentices and servants to complete his surgical operations and thus stabilise his income. He couldn't afford to quit the Infirmary board.

Sensing his opponent waver, Monro leaned closer. Drummond smelled of raw body odour and the metallic tint of blood. "You know as well as I do, Mr Drummond, that these aren't men you want to cross. The lords don't take well to *disrespectful* remarks."

Drummond cursed. The letter in his hand was already tinged with red-brown fingerprints.

"I hope you enjoy this, Alexander. I'm being sincere, honest to God. I hope that being a glorified caddie for Rutherford and your charming patrons gives you satisfaction in life." Drummond wiped his hands on his breeches. "Goodness knows it looks a miserable existence from my where I'm standing."

The surgeon often resorted to wrapping his barbs in faux concern, especially when he knew he'd lost the argument. This awareness allowed Monro to shrug it off.

"You are right, Mr Drummond," he said smoothly. "This is my calling. I'm here to keep the peace; to maintain harmony between the physicians, surgeons and nobles. Nothing gives me greater satisfaction."

Without him maintaining order, he shuddered to think what a mess this city would be in. Probably no better than Glasgow.

Drummond could only seethe. "Sometimes you act like you never taught in his very room, Alexander. That you're not as much a product of the Incorporation as myself. These days you seem content to pretend you're a physician for one hour of the day, while making hundreds of pounds of teaching surgery and anatomy the next." With that he gathered his belongings and stormed out, the scent of blood and sweat blooming in his wake.

It's jealousy, Monro told himself. Drummond has always possessed a small and petty spirit. It wasn't like he wanted my professorship of anatomy before he was asked to relinquish it.

3

GLASGOW

J oseph Black, reluctant physician and reluctant thief, stood in the centre of the hall and trembled.

He had the tendency to not be good at things, which was why he clung so eagerly to Professor Cullen, who seemed to think he was good at chemistry. But the way Cullen applauded his efforts during their combined phlogiston experiments made the young man think he could be exceptional at something.

"You'll hear sharp tongues complaining that I lack discretion and diplomatic control," Cullen told Black at the start of his apprenticeship. "However, if the natural philosophers of Glasgow plotted the mathematical functions, they'd see the incidence of my incautious remarks have decreased dramatically over my few years at Glasgow."

"Has the magnitude of your alleged remarks also decreased?" Black asked, nervous about an outright agreement that his professor was incautious.

'Prospero' was the nickname his students bestowed upon Cullen this semester, after he commented in an October lecture: "We are such stuff as dreams are made on." Cullen seemed to acquire a new nickname every semester. Last term, he was Julius, after noting his poorly attended class and electing to carry on as Caesar had with his army of one hundred. A few years before that, he was St Francis, after he made some offhand remark about caring for wayward defenceless animals in his capacity as a lecturer.

Black knew Cullen revelled in this banter with his students, and he suspected his professor challenged himself to never receive the same nickname twice. That could only explain the endless literary allusions and distracting metaphors he barraged through when he was supposed to concentrate on medical matters.

"You'll be a fantastic natural philosopher, Mr Black," Cullen laughed. "You are good at keeping track and controlling variables."

Black blushed with delight, though it later occurred to him Cullen had avoided answering his question, perhaps because he didn't know the answer himself.

"The point is, there are some things we need to be discrete about." Cullen ran his hands down his robe. "If the results of our experiments are known before we've developed the proper theoretical groundwork and tested its applications, we risk vilification rather than celebration."

This was surprising.

Espousing such controversial theories went a long way to explaining why Cullen was the most popular professor among the students of Glasgow. His wit and erudition in the classroom accounted for the remainder of his popularity.

"How long do you think until we're ready to publicise our findings, professor?" Black asked.

Cullen frowned and changed the subject.

The secrecy with which Black was asked to track down medical treatises implied there was more at stake than mockery, which Cullen laughingly pointed out he was no stranger to.

"The other faculty and students think I'm primarily concerned with investigating the cause of refrigeration," Cullen told Black. "I don't want them to even suspect I'm pursuing other branches of research."

Hence Black visiting the university library to take out one dissertation on Stahl's phlogiston theories, hidden between a stack of old alchemy papers. And we would have to return in a few days to repeat the exercise until he had accounted for all four books Cullen wished he consult without attracting attention.

Mastering the muscle and digital control necessary to discharge phlogiston proved easy for Black, who could create tiny flames in his palm a week after the experiments.

"You've got a steady hand," Cullen noted. "I think the biggest delay to you mastering this immediately was my poor instruction."

Black smiled diffidently. It was true, though. Cullen could conjure flames in his hand with little thought, and he realised Black's constitution differed slightly from his.

"Like attracts like," Cullen then explained. "Your body can both discharge and absorb phlogiston from its surroundings."

He turned to the candle on his laboratory table. They'd temporarily moved the bottles of chemicals and equipment onto the floor to give them space to move their arms. Cullen also pointed out that the ethers he was using for refrigeration were inflammable.

Cullen raised a finger and beckoned to the candle. Its flame tilted towards him, then vanished.

"This doesn't wildly unbalance your humours?" Black asked.

"I can extinguish the hearth over there, but it's best to discharge the excess phlogiston as quickly as you can."

Black reached forward and pressed his finger to the candlewick. The flame lurched back into existence.

"How rapidly can you discharge or summon phlogiston?" He wondered.

"I was hoping we could experiment on that, since I had trouble timing myself. I think it can be measured in heartbeats."

Hunched over the table and frowning, Black tried to copy

Cullen's beckoning motion and bring the candle flame towards him. This time, it only took a few minutes of instruction.

Assured a candle flame the size of his forefinger couldn't unbalance his body's natural equilibrium, Black pulled the candle flame towards him. When the two men concentrated, they could see the flicker of light tugged from the wick to Black's finger.

Amused, Cullen waited until Black was trying the trick again. As soon as Black beckoned Cullen — who was seated opposite him — beckoned.

"Did you see that, Joe? I think I stole the flame from you."

"We can catch phlogiston in mid-flight?"

"I actually tried it once in my youth and succeeded. I used a bigger ball of fire so I could see what I was doing." He stopped himself from delving further into the story. However, Black seemed unconcerned with the circumstances of his discovery, remaining focussed on the conceit itself.

"It could turn into a fascinating game of tennis," Black finally said.

Cullen clapped his hands together. "You think, lad? Come on —let's try."

Black meant it as a little joke, but and was slightly embarrassed to face Cullen on the opposite side of the laboratory. It wasn't a full tennis court, but there was a little room.

Cullen's hand was already drenched in flames.

"I'm not aiming at you, Joe—just at the wall to your right." The first throws were too slow, the fire dissipated in mid-air. Cullen scribbled some notes, as if it were possible to forget such amazing sights, and tried again with enough force that the ball of phlogiston fire would reach Black's side of the room.

It took a few attempts before Black could tense his nerves just as Cullen's volley came past his fingertips. The fire shot into Black's hand and vanished, with crimson sparks dissipating off Black's body.

"Don't tug so hard, lad." Cullen looked gleeful. "Just enough to hold it for a second, so you can fling it back." Black didn't even think to be annoyed Cullen was giving him instructions on the obvious. Nor did he feel frustrated, which is how he usually felt when he struggled to master something new.

Within twenty minutes, they were playing a crude game of tennis. Black decided not to bother attending his Medical Theory class today. He'd arrived late yesterday, and arriving late a second time would lead to judgemental stares and sarcastic jibes he didn't want. Besides, this was fun, and he couldn't remember the last time he'd felt this rush of happiness.

Cullen wasn't athletic—truth be told, neither was Black—but they managed five consecutive volleys of a phlogiston fireball back and forth before either they dropped it, aimed so badly the other couldn't catch it, or the phlogiston fizzled out.

It was Cullen who broke off the game, because he had patients he needed to call on before sunset.

"Think about what application that could serve, lad," he said as he jammed his hat on. "Goodness knows it seems delightfully useless to me."

Black wanted to surprise his professor by producing a clever application of phlogiston tennis the next time they met. But the exercise in his lodgings that night left him saddened. It could be a defensive art...if there were anyone in the world who would hurl phlogiston at him with malicious intent. Nor could it be a game for students to play late at night once they were thrown out of the tavern. The knowledge was too tightly controlled.

"The young Joseph Black! Though my memory might be failing me." A squat, middle-aged man with a port wine birthmark by his ear emerged from behind a row of books. "Is it yourself?"

"Hello Professor Buchanan," Black said, clutching the books to his chest.

"I'm talking in jest, young man. Though I admit I haven't seen you in my Clinical Medicine class for several months."

"Oh, I apologise," gasped Black, squeezing his books so they wouldn't topple onto the floor. "I should have told you I decided to attend your class next year instead."

Buchanan shrugged, since the guineas had already changed ownership. "I thought you intended to graduate this summer—but it's not like my class is going anywhere."

"Well, I realised I needed more time," Black saw Buchanan's eyes drifting to his books, so in his nervousness he kept talking. "I could benefit from another year, I suppose..."

"Dr Cullen keeping you busy? I can smell sulphur on you from over here, Mr Black!" Buchanan chided with mock severity. "What witchcraft is he making you practise?"

Black's heart sank. Buchanan must have recognised the alchemy books pressed against his chest.

"It's not like that," he protested. "It's just that Professor Cullen says there's chemical wisdom to be gleaned in even the most mystic alchemical texts."

"Don't take everything so personally, Joseph—I didn't mean to offend you or insult Dr Cullen." Buchanan raised his hands in mock surrender. "I have a great respect for Dr Cullen; he's taken the murkiest, most confused scientific art and turned it into something approaching respectability. I'm not sure it will ever be seen as possessing equal to anatomy or botany—their usefulness shines like a beacon and will never tarnish."

"Dr Cullen thinks the chemical arts can be applied to agricultural improvements," Black said. This would be the most Buchanan had heard him say in one setting: he looked taken aback. "He thinks chemical means can improve the soil and reduce wastage."

Buchanan gave a nervous chuckle, his slightly glazed expression suggesting regret at having drawn himself into an argument he had no interest in. "Well, it sounds a little more plausible than getting gold from quicksilver. Certainly less heretical. I best be leaving you to your mystical arts, Mr Black. Try not to get too distracted in pursuit of fool's gold."

"Just because it's not medicine, doesn't mean it isn't important." Black muttered at the departing form.

4

GLASGOW

Persons unfamiliar with Cullen might mistake his early arrival in the College chapel for enthusiasm. In fact, Cullen enjoyed a few minutes in semi-solitude with the smell of the old building: he found the mustiness of old, cool stone soothing. After a few hours crammed with faculty and the students—who tended to skip morning ablutions when dragging themselves to church on Sunday—the comforting aroma was smothered by something hot and stale.

Afterwards, he caught Leechman in the knave, steering him out of the crowds with a tap on the elbow.

"While we wait for Anglesbury and Sir Thomas to cool down..."

"No Francis, I didn't intend to speak to you about that." Cullen coaxed Leechman a few steps further to the left. The murmur of departing parishioners gave them a cloak of privacy. "Did you know David Hume intends to apply for the Glasgow Chair of Logic?"

Leechman cracked a grey smile. "I'm intimately familiar with the situation. I was offered the Philosophy Chair in Edinburgh last spring, and my polite recusal from consideration prompted David to throw his oversized hat into that ring."

Cullen stifled his impatience. He should have known there was more going on behind the scenes than met the eye.

"Well, he obviously didn't get the Edinburgh Chair, or he wouldn't express interest in the Glasgow vacancy." Come to think of it, he vaguely recalled Leechman mentioning the entreaties he'd received from Edinburgh. Leechman said he'd drafted his refusal before the official message arrived, but held onto it for a couple of weeks so as not to seem churlish.

"I find it mildly amusing," Leechman said, with a twinkle in his eyes. "That you would drag me into a conversation about renown atheist David Hume on a Sunday, before we've even exited the chapel." He tipped his head towards the right, where their minister stood in hushed conversation with a deacon.

"Well, blame it on the inquisitive natural philosopher within. Does uttering the name of Hume on consecrated ground bring a righteous thunderbolt down upon me? Why, I'm still standing. Does it mean the Almighty has some limits?"

He could get away with needling Leechman like this. The former minister was used to Cullen's provocations.

"Never assume the lack of immediate divine punishment means you have escaped what is inevitable," Leechman intoned. "After all, 'The wrath of God is like great waters that are dammed for the present,' held back by His mercy and infinite patience."

"Ah, so dammed for the present but damned for the future. That's a little pessimistic for you Francis, isn't it?"

"I suppose this morning's sermon put me in a contemplative mood." Leechman touched Cullen on the arm and they fell in behind the final straggling student parishioners. The students rubbed their eyes and squinted as they trudged out into the overcast skies. They'd probably got a decent nap while the sermon droned on.

"My only advice concerning Hume's posturing is to treat the

whole affair with disinterest," Leechman said, once he was certain they were out of earshot of the ministers. "Ignore it all if you can. The assembly will reject his application out of hand, though they won't miss an opportunity to denounce his heretical writings—more fool them for drawing attention to him."

The university chapel sat a few hundred metres from the main quadrangle. The churchgoers fanned out across the churchyard. Some like Cullen and Leechman were squeezing in a few minutes of acceptable Sabbath business, the others were heel-dragging students who didn't want to return to their dormitories, where they were expected to engage in quiet contemplation and study.

"But quite a lot of rich and influential men admire Hume's teachings."

"It's titillation for bored nobles. I've tutored a few families like that—they don't think greatly about anything. In fact, they rely on men like us to do their thinking for them. It makes them feel daring to say Hume's name, though they don't understand half of what he's talking about."

"Men like Anglesbury," Cullen mused.

Leechman shot Cullen a look.

"You'll do no good playing that kind of desperate game, William. You'll attract attention from the wrong people, and be ignored by everyone else as an embarrassment. Anglesbury does not seriously believe Hume will get appointed to the Logic Chair, and he'll withdraw his pretences of support long before anyone could accuse him of such."

"Well, we don't know there's a chance of a successful election until we try," Cullen insisted. "Francis, you're as opposed to the assembly's meddling in the college as I am, even if we have our own reasons for believing so. And we're far from outliers in our sentiments. Do you really think Hume, as Logic Professor, would be worse than another puffed-up minster?"

Leechman shook his head. "As colourful and outspoken a personality as David is, he wouldn't accomplish anything if appointed to the Chair. The assembly would see to that." They reached the short flight of steps, bringing them to the street outside the university quadrangle. "Have a peaceful Sabbath, William. We send our best wishes to you and yours."

He talks with such certainty about things not yet come to pass, Cullen thought as he watched Leechman disappear into the trickle of parishioners heading home. He doesn't know that's what will happen. Heavens, if he snapped out of inaction for once, maybe something different could happen.

* * *

Cullen was closing his classroom door when he felt a presence in the courtyard behind him.

"Dr Cullen?" asked a bright voice. "I apologise if I'm catching you at an inopportune time."

Cullen turned around to appraise the speaker.

This youth had to be a divinity student. There was a severity to his dress rarely seen among Cullen's medical students. There was also the fact Cullen didn't recognise him. He looked young, with sallow skin and a shock of dark hair.

"Not in the slightest, lad," Cullen replied. "How can I be of assistance?" He would usually invite students to walk with him to his laboratory, or even home if that's where he was going, but something about this student made him uneasy.

"My name's Malcolm Holm," the student explained, rolling through his consonants. "It's a pleasure to finally meet you in person."

Cullen bowed, but glanced around the almost-deserted quadrangle for familiar faces.

"Thank you, Mr Holm. Where do you hail from?"

Holm waved his hand and smiled. "Oh, that isn't important."

Cullen's ill-ease had to be coming from the student himself, then. What was wrong with his posture?

"Perhaps the business can wait for another time, if it's not urgent," Cullen said. "I have a patient to call upon shortly."

In truth, the family of the feverish sailor's wife wasn't expecting to receive him for another hour.

"I was asked to convey a message from my patrons in Edinburgh," Holm continued, refusing to move.

"You're not a student at Glasgow?" Cullen asked. He'd feel less twitchy if he could understand what this was about. Only a few minutes until classes were let out and the quadrangle filled with people.

"I cannot claim that honour," Holm conceded. "My patrons are concerned you're dissatisfied with your current position in Glasgow and expressed an interest in moving your practice to Edinburgh."

"I don't know how they could have heard such a thing," Cullen said, folding his arms. "Given I've expressed no such sentiment." Well, it was true he'd thrown out a few remarks about how an Edinburgh practice could be more profitable for him than his current Glasgow one, but that was casual tavern banter he never uttered in front of anyone too important. How would anyone in Edinburgh learn of those throwaway comments?

Holm smiled again. "Every Scottish academic wishes they were in Edinburgh."

"I wouldn't blame the Aberdonians or St Andreans for such envy. But where is the centre of Scotland's mercantile power? Where does all its commerce flow? Glasgow, not Edinburgh."

"Seeing you in person, you don't strike me as the kind of academic content tutoring mill apprentices and Irish dissidents. You have grander designs."

Cullen's control of his temper was slipping.

"Do you have anything more to offer me than groundless rumours and insults, Mr Holm? Because I wish you to leave."

Holm beamed, like he thought Cullen would never ask.

Now Cullen understood what was strange about Holm's stance. His whole body was coiled, like a viper readying to strike.

"I do, in fact. Keep your heretical teachings here on the west coast. Stay out of Edinburgh if you value the safety of your family."

"Why, you villain!" Cullen brandished his physician cane. "Get out of my university."

If Holm grinned any wider, his face would split in half.

Aware he was being mocked, Cullen swiped at him with his cane. Holm took a step back, laughing.

"How dare you!" Cullen's second swipe caught Holm's shoulder. A small crowd was forming. Holm stepped away from Cullen's onslaught with a leisurely stride, waving away the cane as if it were a fly.

"Professor Cullen!" Cullen should be relieved to hear an authoritative voice behind him, but his rage at Holm dulled all other emotions. There was an edge of fear under his wild slashes with his physician's cane, as he tried to drive Holm away. The young man's laughter was unnatural; an expression of cruel delight at Cullen's impotent fury.

"Detain this ruffian—he is no student!"

As Cullen jabbed, Holm reached out and plucked Cullen's cane from the air. Before he had time to react, Holm tugged it from his grasp, twirled it once, then snapped the cane across his knee. In front of the stunned audience, Holm dropped the fragments and ran out of the Quad.

"Don't let him escape!" yelled Cullen, brandishing his finger at the departing Holm. However, the onlookers seemed as confused as uneasy as him.

Black darted forward and picked up Cullen's broken cane. Holm hadn't quite managed to split it, but the pieces barely held together. Cullen hadn't seen Black join the crowd, and he wondered how much his young apprentice overheard.

"Professor Cullen..." As the rage dissipated, Cullen realised the authoritative voice belonged to the University Principal, Neil Campbell himself. "I think we better move somewhere private..."

The Principal rubbed his eyes. He made no effort to hide his fatigue.

"What are they putting in the tavern ale? Believe it or not, this is the second altercation between a professor and a student I've had to break apart this semester. The first one stemmed from a disagreement over a conjugate verb in the professor's translation of The Iliad that the student swore was misplaced. All told, it led to three black eyes, and one dislocated shoulder. How many weeks are we into the winter term? No, don't answer that."

"But you heard him?" Cullen protested. "The scoundrel had the nerve to threaten me and my family with violence. There was no mistaking it."

"You're telling me he's the first in this university to threaten you with violence, Dr Cullen? Now *that* is shocking."

Cullen rolled his eyes. "Principal Campbell, you know me. I think you're aware I've tripled the size of the chemistry course over these past few years..."

"Yes, and I'm aware Glasgow would not have a medical school were it not for your tireless advocation."

"...And I think you know I wouldn't initiate an altercation without reason. Witnesses can attest I was provoked by that Malcolm Holm, who threatened harm against me if I went to Edinburgh."

The Principal waved his hand to indicate Cullen should stop speaking. He grimaced and rubbed his temples.

"Well, you aren't intending to move to Edinburgh, so I don't see what the problem is."

Cullen's mouth twisted in frustration. The Principal fixed him with a long look.

"Dr Cullen, I'm not blind to the allure Edinburgh holds over medical men. Nor will I pretend Glasgow matches the prestige of the east coast. But I visit Edinburgh often. Their college buildings are falling apart—'ramshackle' is too generous a descriptor for some of them. The city itself is squalid and festering—they're superstitious fisherwoman on the topic of expanding the city beyond its ancient walls, so their city remains a rotten fishbone balanced on a ledge. The medical faculty loathe one other. Their students are rich, pampered and indolent. The only thing Edinburgh has in its favour is its prestige.

"Meanwhile, take a look around us. Our faculty dwellings are the nicest homes in Glasgow—the envy of some East India merchants. We have students flock from the countryside grateful and eager to learn a professional trade. I think we're modernising our education program faster than any university in the world right now. Much credit to you."

The Principal took a moment to scratch under his wig. "That said, Dr Cullen: faculty getting into fights with students doesn't look good to our patrons, and any perceived indulgence of such belligerence on my part could cost me my supporters. I'm fining you fifteen guineas for your conduct, and if such behaviour repeats, I may have to pursue a suspension from teaching."

"You're fining *me*, sir? But this Holm isn't even a student in Glasgow."

"Exactly," sighed the Principal. "So I can't fine or suspend him, can I? Besides, knowing your ample class sizes, fifteen guineas won't make much of a dent in your income."

Black was waiting for Cullen in his laboratory. He hesitated before approaching.

"Don't worry, lad," Cullen said, sinking into his chair. "It's dealt with. I'm not in much trouble."

"I heard some of what was said," Black said, fiddling with his nails. "Is it true you're thinking about moving to Edinburgh?"

"No," Cullen sighed. "Teaching there is not a future I've envisioned for myself."

Black looked unsure. Cullen wondered how confident he actually sounded.

"I heard what that boy said to you. It sounded like a threat on your life."

"Yes, that's how I took it, lad."

Black edged closer. "Is it because of...what we're doing?" He wiggled his fingers for emphasis.

Cullen had been worrying about that. "When I was younger and incautious with my discoveries, there were a few incidents... but there's no way the medical faculty in Edinburgh could have found out about them." At least that's what he tried to assure himself.

"What objection could they have to you as a teacher of chemistry or physic?" Black appeared baffled.

"Sit down, lad. It's hard to explain, but five years ago no one lectured in English. Students came to class expecting to hear the professor recite a prepared document—the same document they read from every year. Students sat, listened, took notes, departed. When I started lecturing in English from abbreviated notes..." Cullen gestured to the pile on his desk. "And updating the notes every year when I learned of new theories, they didn't know what to think. When I started asking the students questions to see if they understood the material, they were stunned. It took several months of coaxing before they realised I genuinely wanted to hear their opinions in the classroom."

"Yes, it's different from my some of arts classes," Black agreed. "But your approach never struck me as dangerous."

"And yet, I designed it to be dangerous, in a way," Cullen mused. "Because now anyone can walk off the street into my lecture theatre and understand what I'm talking about. At least, anyone with a bit of education. As long as they're properly trained, I don't see why any man can't become a physician or surgeon."

Black tilted his head. "I understand your philosophy might worry some individuals. But to resort to that?" He motioned into the Quad. "Is there something else at stake? Because I'm not sure I understand otherwise."

"You and me, Mr Black," Cullen said, shaking his head. "You and me both."

5

GLASGOW

The Philosophical Society met in one of the nicer rooms at the university. At night, the wooden panelling gleamed in the candlelight like mirrors.

Cullen had paid attention—at least he hoped he had—to the speakers. It was business with astronomy being read out. The audience liked astronomy papers; contemplating the cosmos put everyone in a romantic mood and rarely led to contentious debates afterwards. Now thinking about Jupiter's moons, the men circulated to converse with their friends and finish their drinks.

Spying the Earl of Anglesbury speaking with another faculty member, Cullen edged around the room. He tried not to focus too keenly on the pair, in case Leechman saw him and inferred his intentions.

Getting into the same room as the Earl had taken longer than he'd liked. A comedy of errors kept them apart: the Earl was in London, then Cullen was laid low with a head cold, then several months passed where he couldn't get away from work to attend any meetings, then the Society adjourned for the summer. But now they were here.

The Earl appeared bored with his acquaintance—he kept

looking over his shoulder and tapping his feet. Cullen pressed forward. This was the perfect time to intervene. A practical question about Cumbernauld road repairs would be a welcome respite after dry theoretical discourse.

He was clearing his throat when another figure blocked his view; the Earl glancing up with a scornful expression. Cullen thought he'd coughed politely, but now he had to contend with the enormous figure in his way.

"If my capacity for reasoning hasn't extinguished itself—it appears I'm regarding Dr William Cullen."

"You are indeed, my lord." Cullen found his hand cradled by a pair of meaty fists, and a delighted stocky gentleman in an embroidered frock coat and hearty complexion sizing him up. It was rare that someone who already knew his name was this delighted to introduce himself. Seeing the pair in conversation, the Earl yawned and returned the majority of his attention to his oblivious companion.

"Henry Bennett is the name, Dr Cullen, much obliged to meet you. The advantage of getting buffeted west then east as business demands is that there's always the hope I'll be able to attend the Philosophical Society meetings in this august city and chance upon a luminary such as yourself."

Cullen extracted his hand slowly, to avoid causing offence, but his new colleague did not seem to mind.

"Pleasure to meet you, my lord." He was talking to an aristocrat, he could tell by the smooth accent.

"Of course, my life would be much more stimulating if you were in Edinburgh, but I suppose that detracts from the thrill of possibility. Are you a gambler, Dr Cullen?"

"I try not to take risks," Cullen said. That was a complete lie, but it seemed like the right thing to say. "But I enjoy speculating and a gentlemanly game of cards—for honour, never money."

"Quite right, very sensible." Bennett shooed several guests

aside and directed Cullen to a seat in the corner of the room. "I wish I had the patient genius of a man like you."

Cullen had politely ignored Bennett's hint about him moving to Edinburgh, even though he detected no malice in the lord's invitation. But Bennett seemed the kind to overlook avoidance tactics.

"Have you visited the societies of Edinburgh? Is the town to your liking?"

Aristocrats didn't have the same concepts of time mortals like himself were subject to. A man like Bennett could hop in a carriage and set off on the multi-day journey between Edinburgh and Glasgow, with no worries about obligations at home; the world adjusted itself around him. It would take Cullen several weeks of negotiating and preparations to make a similar trip.

"I last graced Edinburgh with my presence as a medical student," Cullen admitted. "Many score years ago."

Following his arts studies at Glasgow, Cullen sought practical experience as a surgeon apprentice and apothecary, which led to only partial fulfilment. He then spent a couple years studying medicine in Edinburgh as part of his transitional period between surgeon and physician. Even then, he couldn't stomach the city long enough to obtain his medical doctorate there: that happened several years later, when he was back in Glasgow.

"Hardly! You're a young man still, Dr Cullen!"

"I find Edinburgh more agreeable than London," Cullen allowed, which wasn't a strong compliment.

"Quite so! London is a chaotic, shocking place." Bennett finished his glass. "But you should consider teaching in Edinburgh, Dr Cullen. In fact, I'm amazed you are still in Glasgow after all these years."

"Glasgow has a fine university, my lord," Cullen said. He didn't bother to explain that he'd build this medical school from the ground up, stretching himself across multiple disciplines to keep it together when they were short on faculty. It was the sort of excuse a pampered man like Bennett would tear to shreds, not realising the sentimentality he attached to such an excuse.

Bennett gave a noise of begrudging agreement.

"If it's a question of patronage, you shouldn't feel embarrassed. You have many friends who will put in a good word for you on the east coast." Bennett tapped his sternum and waggled his eyebrows.

A few hours with Leechman was enough to convince Cullen he was friendless, and could never secure the right patronage connections. Part of that was Leechman's pessimistic and cautious nature: it took him years to cultivate his own supporters. But Cullen thought he made friends quickly. Like this conversation with Lord Bennett, who he'd made the acquaintance of an hour ago?

Leechman had his reasons for his glacial, clinical pace. But surely those reasons didn't hold for everyone?

"I don't think I have many friends in Edinburgh," Cullen said. "I hope you won't think my remark too candid."

Cullen thought about the peculiar, terrifying student who threatened him in the university quadrangle at the start of term. He'd never seen the youth again, though every day his eyes had combed through the students milling around the university. He'd not told Anna about the incident, it would worry her too much, but he'd found himself distracted when walking through the crowded city with her, looking for a menacing glint in the shadows.

Could a stripling that young even be in league with the affluent of Edinburgh?

Bennett grunted and toyed with his glass. He looked annoyed that Cullen reminded him he wasn't the only important man in Edinburgh.

"Brilliant man always attract envious onlookers. You're well above their scurrilous slights."

Cullen reached his hand across the table and beckoned. Lord Bennett pushed his glass over, allowing Cullen to refill it.

"Don't inconvenience yourself for my sake, my Lord." He was sure Bennett was engaged in some harmless flattery—rich men liked to make smart men feel important, because it stoked their ego to know they could affect their intellectual superiors so. Cullen could indulge his idle candlelight entreaties.

"Think nothing of it, Dr Cullen." Lord Bennett sipped the wine. "You should allow your friends to demonstrate their friendliness, and not worry about overextending your favour."

Cullen wasn't going to argue. Lord Bennett spent more time in Edinburgh than he did: he'd know how to navigate its patronage system.

6

GLASGOW

The semester was in full swing, and Cullen barely had room to move his arms when lecturing. It was a small classroom, and in the cold weather students and professor alike bunched onto the side of the room with the hearth.

"Right, a little exercise to prepare our minds. Start by clenching your calves, then your thighs. Move up, clenching every muscle in your body...hold them all for a minute...don't giggle!... now relax. Repeat that cycle again. You feel warmer, right?"

A sufficient amount of blood now worked through his students' limbs and rate of shivering decreased, Cullen turned to the topic of the class.

"Honoured students, you may not believe it—you may not like it, in fact—but you are the future of education in Scotland."

He expected more disavowals, but perhaps the students were too chilly to joke around. The hearth crackled and popped.

"What I mean," Cullen continued, adjusting his robe so the edges didn't flutter so close to the naked flames, "Is that medicine is no longer an arcane study conducted in turrets by the select few. It is open to inquisitive, diligent young men like yourselves who can do honour to a most rewarding profession. The average citizen

49

of Britain distrusts men of medicine…with good reason! They speak in mystic tongues—Latin—and belong to a class of mortals far above the common man. Should one enter your modest dwellings, they'll cover their noses and prod the patient from a safe distance with their cane in 'examination.' Heaven forbid they converse with the patients, and try to put them at ease!"

The hearth continued to crackle. The class stared in rapt attention.

"But the next generation of physicians will be different. They will be capable of conveying their sentiments and diagnoses in plain English. They will come from the same modest towns and villages as their patients. They will be driven by curiosity, enquiry and a healthy skepticism for entrenched dogma." He felt the students' collective chests puff with pride. "I'm proud of you, and what you'll become."

Today's lecture was supposed to pertain to the chemical properties of mixtures, but as soon as Cullen mentioned the sensation of heat emanating from certain mixtures, he decided to take a tour into the nervous system.

"…Right now, hopefully the majority of students are feeling the sensation of heat from the fire on one side of their body, or at least in one extremity. Were you to shuffle too close to the fire you might feel pain, causing you to withdraw your burnt limb. But this begs question—how does your body learn of pain, and decide to take action?"

Sensing one of Professor Cullen's famous diversions, the students nudged one another and hid their grins. Pretending not to notice, Cullen continued.

"If we cut up a body—anyone volunteering? I'll warm the knife first—we'll find a spindly network of nerves running from the head and spine out to the furthest reaches of your fingertips. What I believe these nerves to be powered by is an elastic, subtle fluid conveying sensation and reactions back and forth. This liquid of the nervous system is what wills its owner's muscles to move."

This part of the lecture wasn't controversial—physicians accepted nervous fluid played a role in all theories of the body since Hippocrates. "But how is it willed? My hypothesis is the brain is the orchestrator of the nervous system; controlling perception and volition."

A few of the more engaged students—the ones who always crammed into the front of the lecture—frowned amongst themselves. "I thought nervous sensation transmitted around the body by diffusion from the brain, like water pipes?" one ventured.

"That is what the learned Dr Boerhaave hypothesised," Cullen conceded. He spotted a wave of wrinkled brows. "Since you are knowledgeable where others are not, perhaps you can explain who we're talking about?"

The student, one who never baulked at public oration, nodded quickly.

"The late Herman Boerhaave, the father of physiology, was a Dutch physician and lecturer. He taught at the University of Leiden for thirty years."

"Correct." Cullen eased back into control of the classroom before Fergus really got going. "You will hear Dr Boerhaave's name a lot as you continue your medical students. His discoveries in the fields of botany, physiology and medicine are rightfully celebrated. You'll be expected to be conversant in his medical aphorisms." Cullen bit his tongue before he blurted out the other oft-stated fact about Boerhaave: nearly every physician and anatomist in Britain today studied under him in Leiden. Sometimes it felt like every physician bar one. That aside would take his lecture too far off course.

"However..." Cullen refocussed. "Man is more complex than a watermill. I think even the eminent physician himself would agree. Everything anatomists uncover demonstrates how subtle and complex we are. Which means our brain is surely more than an oversized gland whose sole purpose is to secrete nervous fluid that drips its way around the body."

The students loved it when Cullen deviated from the standard medical doctrines. His medical colleagues, however? They hated it. Even the most tolerant and open-minded ones found his nervous system theories a little embarrassing.

"So why did Dr Boerhaave claim otherwise?" a student asked.

Cullen shrugged. "The great physician was mistaken. All of us can err."

"Surely not you, Dr Cullen," another student called out, loyally. There was general cheering and murmurs of support.

"Oh, I've made my share of mistakes," Cullen said. "It's something I'm honest about with my fellow physicians and when talking to the patient's families. When I don't know things, or I'm wrong, I'm honest about my failings."

"Even to the patients?" echoed someone with a hint of disbelief.

"When consulting with their loved ones, certainly. I leave it to them to intercede with the patients in question in the manner they'd prefer...but I never pretend certainty." Cullen looked around the room at the students. Some were shocked, perhaps dismayed, to hear him admit such things. "Our medical knowledge expands every month. We are blessed to live in a time where scientific progress moves as fast as it does. The theories I teach today may be shown as incorrect tomorrow if anatomists uncover something new. We must learn, teach and practice with humility."

The students murmured in acquiescence.

"This is usually the point in the discussion where Mr Ambrose cracks a witticism," Cullen mused, looking around. "Come on, lad —I'm disappointed by your lack of interruption."

The students shuffled in the chairs and stared at their books.

"He's not here?" Cullen set his notes down. "Ben was setting such a good example of punctuality. I'm sorry he's lapsed before more of you could benefit from it."

"I heard he's fallen sick," piped up someone at the back. "Was holed up in his lodgings."

"What did his physician advise to treat his poor humours?" Cullen asked. It was professional curiosity about how long Ben may be absent, and a concern another fever would sweep through the town.

The boy who'd volunteered the information—whose head could only be seen amongst the crowd in the room—shrugged.

It was possible Ben hadn't seen a doctor at all. He was one of the students Cullen waived tuition fees for.

"He's too sick to leave his rooms? Do you know where the poor fellow is lodging?" Cullen asked.

The lodging's owner—a stooped widow—pointed Cullen to the room on the top floor where Ben stayed. Cullen wasn't a particularly large man, but he needed to inhale and sidestep to reach the final landing. Puddles accumulated on the landing from leaks in the roof, and the building creaked like a ship.

Entering the room, Cullen found Ben un-responsive in his bed. The room smelled of sickness rotting into death. After having got a bit of medication down Ben's throat, Cullen retired to the chair by the window where the air was freshest to finish a couple of letters and plan out a few chemical experiments he could delegate to Black next week. What Cullen thought of as general disorder in the room—saucers and plates scattered around—was, in fact, Ben's attempts to catch rainwater. Rags were stuffed into several walls.

At least he didn't need to wait long. Ben stirred and flopped onto his side.

"Mr Ambrose? It's Dr Cullen." Cullen gave his patient a gentle shake. "Can you tell me how you're feeling?"

"Urrrghhh..."

"I thought of you the other day in class. I was telling the students about Seneca's infamous aphorism..." Cullen chatted on as Ben roused himself. The sickness had wracked Ben's body in short order—his eyes were sunken, and the skin shrunk down across his bones.

"I asked your landlady to prepare a simple beef broth. I don't think she can manage the stairs, so I'll head down and bring it up. After we get some food in you, there's a tincture that should bring down your fever—I'll let some blood if that doesn't work."

By the time he returned, Ben had shuffled himself upright, but looked close to slipping back into a stupor. Cullen got the soup bowl onto Ben's lap and coaxed him into the first spoonful.

"What...why are you here, Professor Cullen?" Ben frowned, unsure if he was in his bed, or if this was a fever dream where he turned up to class only to be force-fed soup by his professor.

"I came as soon as I learned you were sick, lad. Fevers are nasty, but thank God they're usually treatable if caught early."

"...But..."

"What kind of physician-professor would I be if I didn't treat my students?" Cullen asked, baffled.

Ben straightened.

"Don't start on the question of payment again—as far as I'm concerned, that discussion is settled."

"It's not like my family can offer patronage opportunities, and no one doubts your skill as a physician, so they don't require demonstrations. Just...thank you." Ben seemed baffled but hopelessly grateful. Cullen wondered how often his family encountered physicians who entered their dwellings and didn't immediately cast around for proffered coins.

Cullen could predict how his colleagues would react once word got out. Their first reaction would be dismay no doubt— you're saying we should treat our students, in addition to teaching them? How much charity should a man perform before he exhausts his capacity to function in society? Some may volunteer to perform similar duties—others would then follow once popular opinion trailed after him.

It was the same with Latin instruction. Cullen was the second or third professor in the entire university to lecture in English, but within a few years, several of his medical faculty colleagues followed suit. It helped when he delivered a Botany course one summer in Latin, because even Cullen agreed the Latin terminology required to master the botanical arts couldn't be trimmed back. That convinced the skeptics in the medical school that Cullen wasn't mocking them by his use of English, or that he disrespected their approach. They felt safer lowering their defences against him after that summer. Now Botany was the only class taught in Latin, and he heard rumours its current professor would incorporate some conversational English into next semester's course.

* * *

The next morning, Cullen was surprised to find Leechman absent from the tavern. At first he was almost too nauseous with concern to drink his ale—scared his friend had fallen to the same illness as Ben Ambrose.

His relief upon finding Leechman in his classroom—as hale and hearty as possible for the old fellow—was tempered by the suspicion he'd walked into another trap.

"How's that sick student of yours?"

"I'm calling upon Mr Ambrose this afternoon," Cullen said, eyeing his friend. "I expect to find him greatly improved."

"Good. I'm glad you called upon him." Leechman looked sincere. "I was surprised to learn it's apparently not common practice to minister your fallen students here."

"Me too." Cullen, of course, knew word would be on its second lap of Glasgow by the time he got out of bed this morning, but he'd have treated Ben for free even if he was assured no one would hear a word about it. "It's good to remind the students you occasionally know what you're talking about."

His smile was met with a narrower one from Leechman.

Cullen instinctively folded his arms, recognising that instead of lightening the mood, he'd given Leechman his opening for whatever this encounter was really about.

Not for one minute had he believed Leechman would confront him about treating Ben for free. The former minister would never complain about that.

"On the subject of pedagogical instruction..."

Leechman adjusted his robe with mock seriousness, as if he were ascending to the pulpit. "There are several cardinal prescriptions for living a prosperous and virtuous life, though as your inclinations are more...Deist...you may not be aware of them all. The Chosen People abstain from work on the Sabbath. Catholics abstain from meat on Fridays. And physicians, Dr Cullen, abstain from criticising Boerhaave."

Cullen laughed. "The Boerhaavians would have us believe the acquisition of all medical knowledge ceased with Hippocrates. As far as they're concerned, our understanding of the human body is perfect and can only be degraded with further speculation."

He sometimes cursed Leechman's interest in medical matters, even if it didn't run particularly deep. He was depressingly quick to grasp new concepts and followed the rivers of gossip in other academic fields.

"Every respectable medical man in Britain took the pilgrimage to Leiden to receive his education from Dr Boerhaave. Every professor in Edinburgh is his former student. They're right to revere him: every university in the Western world follows the medical curriculum Boerhaave developed at Leiden."

"Every medical man on this island...except me," Cullen commented.

Leechman smiled.

"You had the opportunity to train in Leiden, did you not? But you chose to stay in London. I think the respectable physicians would be sympathetic if pecuniary circumstances or personal tragedy prevented you from training with Dr Boerhaave on the continent. The fact you had the means and refused is like a slap in the face to many. They assume it means you think you're better than Boerhaave, and by extension, them."

A wicked grin split Cullen's face. "Well, I can disabuse you of that accusation, Francis. I know I'm better than them."

"My purpose here isn't to admonish you," Leechman resumed, which drew a scoff from Cullen. "Rather, to extend an olive branch. The university senate..."

Cullen raised a hand. "Please, Francis. Return to admonishing me."

"I've not forgotten your opinion on university committees, William..."

"...That hair-shirts and self-flagellation are a more painless way of bringing sinners closer to God..."

"And yet the student body is growing year-upon-year, and Glasgow needs a better approach to examination scheduling." Leechman was atop the metaphorical pulpit now, brow furrowed in consternation at his wayward flock of one.

Cullen made a terrible acolyte. His opinion on the ongoing scheduling debate—yawning into its fifth semester—was well known.

"I told the Principal and Dean in the last meeting: appoint a single faculty member in each school to coordinate. We don't need extra senate meetings, we don't need to sit down and plan five years' worth of exams at once. It can and should be done with the smallest number of people."

"Both gentlemen heard you, William. The Greek, Latin and Mathematics professors said they need more guidance getting the first round of dates out of their respective schools. The left hand doesn't know what the right is doing, I suspect."

"The eminent, learned philosophers can not figure it out themselves?" Not that Cullen had a high opinion of his Arts colleagues to begin with, it felt edifying to be reminded of their uselessness.

Leechman's hands fluttered, as if he were about to implore his invisible congregation to mend their ways. "Bringing the concerned parties into the same room and talking through the process will probably infuse them with enough self-confidence to act."

"Oh Francis, you know I don't have the patience for that kind of hand-holding." As far as Cullen was concerned, he reserved warm tolerance for his young students. The adults of the college were old enough to manage themselves. "The mathematicians are adopting deliberate helplessness." He'd got sick of repeating himself at the last senate meeting, and the mathematicians became increasingly argumentative, until they seemed ready to declare themselves incapable of holding a quill, just to spite him.

"The Dean appealed to me for assistance because you were the only faculty member to offer a satisfactory solution. This scheduling committee will only take, what, a few hours from you? Most of the schools will go along with your plan with a little coaxing."

Cullen shook his head. "I've said my piece. The other senate members can act...or not." It might do them good to work out something themselves.

For a moment, he dared hope Leechman would drop his mission. Then his friend tilted his head in an attempt to affect innocence.

"You know...the incoming Dean of Students is patronised by Anglesbury. The two have been friends for years, so I hear."

Cullen merely looked.

Leechman tilted his head further, blinking sweetly.

It was typical of Leechman to do this. It made Cullen even more determined to hold his ground. "I won't be swayed, Francis. I'm not doing this for vainglorious university politics, or pity for the mathematicians. No committee is worth the pain."

"If you're determined to ingratiate yourself with the honourable gentleman, William, this seems a more productive course of action than assigning your name to that petition for David Hume in the Logic Chair."

"You can't really think that?" Cullen asked, studying his friend for proof of sincerity. "Francis, Anglesbury's signature was twelve lines down from mine. I sometimes think you believe the *least* direct method of attack to always be the most effective one."

It wasn't as if he was guaranteed an audience with Anglesbury after wrangling this committee. Leechman could be exaggerating the Dean's friendliness with his patron, or maybe the Dean was dangling an empty offer to trick Cullen into doing his dirty work. Besides, there were other ways to get to Anglesbury.

His class was due to start in five minutes, so Leechman left the room shortly after, with nothing more than a plea to think on the matter, or at least consult with his wife.

He didn't need to bother Anna with this nonsense. Only a few more weeks remained until the next Society gathering.

Surprisingly, when Cullen recounted the conversation to Black, his young protégé offered objections.

"Is sitting on a committee for an afternoon really that awful, professor? It sounds like you could achieve two goals at once." Black was smart enough to piece together Cullen's concern over the West Cumbernauld Road from disparate conversations, and he'd listened to at least one vent about the examination scheduling. Or maybe it was more: Cullen never kept track of his vents.

"Ah, I envy the youth of today—their souls unshredded by faculty committee duty." Cullen reset the inflated pig's bladder on the table in front of Black. "They're a waste of time at best. Everyone has to say their piece or they sulk. Most attendees prefer the sound of their own voice to action. I'm sure the scheduling issues will get resolved...eventually...whether or not Dr Cullen is in the room."

Black rested his arm against the table, stretching forward until his fingers almost touched the bladder.

"Still, you always sound so confident and certain, professor. It's hard to imagine anyone would doubt the worth of your ideas."

Cullen recognised his duty as a charming, friendly professor made him the target of hero worship by boys living away from home for the first time. Black wasn't the most idolatrous of his current batch, and he seemed to be growing out of his initial period of awe, so Cullen indulged him.

"Your compliment is well-received, young Black...but many do. It's better not to get caught up in too many of these farces."

Black's expression made it clear he disagreed. But he shrugged and squinted down his arm.

A second later, the bladder shot off the table, smacking against the wall.

"Nicely done. See how you don't need to touch the object to move it?"

Black nodded. Instead of looking pleased, he tried to scrutinise his clavicle.

"Come on, lad. You can speak your mind. I've said it a thousand times and I'll say it a thousand more: I never object to students voicing a disagreement with me, as long as they can justify themselves from the available evidence."

"Well..." Black raised his chin. "I think you should have joined the committee, professor."

When he gave them permission to voice their own theories, some students took delight in the freedom, and began disagreeing with their professor as a matter of principle. Others dared not raise an objection. A few months ago Cullen was sure he'd never hear a squeak of contradiction from young Black. But the boy's growth was surprising.

"I gathered that was your view already. Do you wish to attend the committee in my stead, Mr Black?"

Black giggled.

"No, I'm being serious. If you're of the conviction that action is important, should you not be prepared to act?" Not that students never convinced Cullen to change his mind—he could think of a handful of times where they did—but he encouraged disagreement because it led to teachable moments concerning rhetoric, logic and philosophical nuances. Black hadn't got experienced enough at arguing to prepare himself for Cullen's counter-attacks.

Black's expression faltered, and he rushed to pick up the bladder and set it back on the table.

"I think we should try objects of differing weights and measure how far I can push them with phlogistic force," he said eventually, head buried in his notebook. "With the weight and distances known, we can deduce how much phlogistic force the body can generate, and how far my hand needs to be from the object to induce movement." Since they kept the windows shuttered for privacy, the light in Cullen's laboratory wasn't the brightest, but he recognised a blush spreading across his student's face.

"Good ideas, lad. Let's get to it." Cullen berated himself. The business with Leechman had rattled him more than he'd realised, if he'd pushed Black too far during a pedagogical exercise. Or maybe he'd misjudged the stability of Black's new self-confidence. Cullen tried to clear the atmosphere by changing the subject to the lighter topic of Lord Bennett's entertaining missives, but the boy treated him with a measure of distance for the rest of the day.

7

EDINBURGH

Time spent with Sir Anthony was usually tolerable. The wealthy landowner had the finest wine cellar in Edinburgh, and he took pride in sharing it with guests who appreciated the wares. Monro thought he had a more sophisticated grasp of the French imports than most of the city blue-bloods, which is why he always got a glass.

That said, the encounters rarely lapsed into 'pleasurable.'

"I can understand your concern with the smallpox program, Dr Monro, but rest assured, we have the matter in hand."

"What about the Inner Hebrides?" Monro insisted, resting on the back of the chair. "I received several angry letters from the minister and well-heeled parishioners. My colleague was subject to awful abuse when he visited to discuss the inoculation program."

"That's easy enough to rectify." Sir Anthony poured himself another glass. "His grace the Duke of Castleborough has studied Gaelic translation sigils but found one of the pages marred. He's busying himself unpicking the problem. Within a few months he'll hopefully have a working sigil."

Monro inhaled over the count of five.

"I appreciate his grace's diligence. Pass on my deepest gratitude to him."

Sir Anthony had given a different excuse last time about the Gaelic sigils. Monro was surprised such a sigil was so obscure—he thought a sigil that facilitated translation between the Highlanders and the British would have already found a use before he required it to help calm the objections of Highland priests to inoculation.

"We've had a few hiccups like this since Jacob's father passed away," Sir Anthony explained in the same apologetic but reassuring tone. "He had a few lapses when transmitting his sigil creation steps to his son. Nothing we've not dealt with before."

It was rude to pry into how Sir Anthony's associates guarded their arcane knowledge. All Monro needed to know was individual steps in the sigil creation process were secret to all but one. It prevented one man from assuming too much power.

A Jura parish lost entire families in the smallpox epidemic last season, so his former student told him. You would think it would quell their hostility to lowland physicians but, paradoxically, it sharpened their opposition. It wasn't that the locals knew no English—Monro refused to believe that—but coming from the mouth of a city-bred stranger, it was a declaration of war. A sigil that translated spoken English into Gaelic would solve most of those misunderstandings.

Monro inclined his head. He thought up another compliment for the port his host had given him, and the conversation moved on.

* * *

"Good evening, Malcolm—a pleasure as always to see you."

Rutherford was lying. There was nothing pleasant about a visit from Malcolm Holm.

"Likewise." Holm didn't even wait for Rutherford to invite

him to sit. He made for the chair nearest the table and pulled it closer to the fire. Rutherford's favourite chair.

"Can I get you some claret?" Rutherford asked, shutting the door with care.

"No—but thank you. Maybe a hot chocolate drink, given how chilly it is outside?"

Rutherford sighed and re-opened the door to whisper to his maid.

It was a bad sign when Holm refused alcohol. It meant he was conducting business that evening.

"How are your divinity studies going, Malcolm?" he asked, as a way of delaying what he feared was to come.

"Excellent." Holm smiled. His black curly hair suggested Irish blood, but he spoke with an easy Doric accent, smoothed to suit lowland life. His serene composure and self-assurance might be charming on another youth, but on him it was unnerving.

"No further disagreements with your professors?" Word about Holm reached the medical faculty from many directions.

Holm threw back his head and laughed. "Oh, the divinity professors love arguing with me. They say it keeps their wits fresh."

Rutherford had heard differently. Instead, he ushered the maid back in with a mug of hot chocolate. If Holm noticed how much of his drink the girl was spilling, he didn't say anything. Instead, he treated Rutherford's maid to a similar smile he'd given Rutherford. Trembling, the girl fled.

"I hope you forgive my intrusion upon your time," Holm commented. "The lords asked me to conduct some business on their behalf."

Rutherford poured himself a generous glass of claret. His decanter was almost full of claret, but there still wouldn't be enough of it for tonight.

"How friendly are you with Lord Bennett?" Holm asked, in tones suited to dinner party discussion.

"Lord Bennett? We've always got on well. Why are your

masters displeased with him?" He'd visited a theatre show with the Bennetts and his wife just last month. Lord Bennett was known for his deep booming laugh and lively evening wit. Besides, he thought Lord Bennett practically was a dark practitioner.

"He's been agitating to bring William Cullen to Edinburgh. Telling the Town Council the medical school needs fresh thinkers."

Rutherford was disappointed to see his claret glass empty again. He poured some more.

"Surely if Sir Anthony, Lord Argyle and the like spoke to him, he'd understand how misguided he was?"

"Ah, Lord Bennett's received several friendly cautions and a few frank warnings. It's not like the man, but he is digging his heels in."

"This can't be rectified...?" Rutherford trailed off as Holm shook his head. "Well, I appreciate you warning me, Malcolm. But in this instance, your masters are making a mistake. I've known Henry Bennett for decades. He's outspoken, yes, but he's a solid asset to the political class. It pains me to say it, but I don't think Henry is the only voice calling for Cullen. He's just the loudest." And the most influential.

Holm sipped his chocolate, a picture of untroubled contemplation. Finally, he spoke.

"In fact, you and I may be in agreement here. Conducting business against Lord Bennett himself isn't likely to bring about the outcomes my masters seek, and you'll be relieved to hear they aren't interested in such a move."

Rutherford did his best to hide his relief. Holm smiled again.

"How friendly are you towards Lord Bennett's oldest son?"

The colour leeched from Rutherford's face.

"You mean Donald?"

Holm nodded, the encouraging smile neither leaving his face nor reaching his eyes.

"Donald Bennett's a prized student in my Practice of Physic

class." Rutherford licked his lips, but found his tongue held no moisture. "Malcolm, sir—Donald's an outstanding scholar. Very conscientious youth, he'll be an excellent surgeon when he graduates. He's expected to marry Anne Braithwaite this summer." Rutherford knew he was rambling and tried to calm his mind.

Holm's smile was revealing more and more of his teeth.

"I understand this might be a surprise to you, Dr Rutherford, but I can assure you the lords know what they're doing. You've told me yourself how dangerous Cullen will be if he's invited to Edinburgh. We've spoken about what is happening in Glasgow."

"Donald plays no parts in his father's overtures towards Dr Cullen," Rutherford protested. "I doubt he's even aware of what Lord Bennett is up to, much less voicing support. He's only eighteen."

"I fear a misunderstanding, Dr Rutherford. Lord Bennett has refused to heed my masters' very reasonable warnings. We're left with no choice but to take measures to halt his foolish course of action."

"But..." Rutherford stammered. Did such a disagreement warrant this vicious an act of retribution? Holm tutted and rose to his feet, dropping his chocolate cup carelessly on the floor. Rutherford hung his head. What his masters deemed done was done. He couldn't persuade Holm to change his mind. Holm had no care for money or threats.

"Delicious chocolate, as always. Give my regards to your pretty housemaid." His black coat billowed as he let himself out of the study. Holm was almost out the door when he paused and looked back. "And John, don't trouble yourself over what you might say to the Bennett boy in tomorrow's class. He'll be dead long before then."

* * *

It was a chill night in Edinburgh, a taste of winter brought on northern winds. To the young man seated in his father's study on the Lawnmarket, the cold weather didn't concern him. His servant had stoked the fire in the adjacent bedchamber before retiring to her pallet on the kitchen floor at the back of the apartment, and the young man himself had drawn the shutters closed hours ago. No gusts came through cracks in these windows, but if they did, he would have thick woollen cloaks and blankets to wrap himself in. Failing that, he could rouse the maid and direct her to prepare him a warm drink. But right now he was too engrossed in transcribing his lecture notes to notice how long since he'd last ate or mind the temperature of his surroundings.

Unlike many rich young scholars in this city, Donald Bennett took his medical studies seriously. He found Professor Rutherford's clinical lectures fascinating, even if the professor's delivery of the material was dry and brittle.

He knew the hour must be late, but reminding himself of the time would make him sleepy, and dull his transcription efforts. He wanted to be done with them tonight, so he could re-read his notes before Dr Rutherford's lecture tomorrow. His father would chide him for leaving his studying until so late in the day, but he was on business in Glasgow, dealing with the merchants and shipmasters between departures to North Carolina and India. Judging by his father's most recent letter, tonight was the last night he could get away with such procrastination.

Neither Donald Bennett, nor his family and servants, would have noticed a small mark in the main bedchamber and living space that wasn't there a few days ago. It was located just inches above the floorboard, in the front corner of the room where the dining table sat. If a visitor was invited into the Bennett apartment and offered tea or wine, they would receive it seated in this corner. From a few metres away, the mark might resemble nothing more than a smudge of dirt, scraped from a boot onto the wall. If you knelt and examined it, you'd see it was a collection of circles and intersecting lines, drawn with speed and precision. That there was symbolic intent to the design would be obvious, and if anyone in the Bennett household had observed it, it would have put them at dis-ease. They would have found it easy to wipe off...if they dared touch it.

But the flimsy charcoal marks would have rubbed off with the lightest touch, causing no harm to the erase. By itself, this was a benign marking that did nothing.

Until its sister mark was activated.

While Donald Bennett hunched further over his notes and dragged the candle as close to his face and the paper as he could, the charcoal marking in the adjacent room began to glow like embers. The light that caught on the nearby table and chair legs seemed to flicker, even though the marking stayed still. While the glow did not spread, its brightness increased until it exceeded the light from the hearth.

The glow continued, but now there was a figure standing in front of the marking.

Despite being dropped into this strange room from some-where else, the stranger didn't stagger or flinch. Instead, they glanced around, then pulled their hood lower over their brow. A knife was already in their other hand.

Once the figure—garbed in black, loose-fitting clothes—felt they were adjusted to their new surroundings, they took a few steps away from the still-glowing sigil at their heel. Aside from the front door, there were two doors at the opposite end of the room. The figure ignored the door leading to the kitchen where the maid slept and headed straight for the side room that served as the Bennett's study. The floorboards sighed as the figure moved, but the noise didn't rise above the background crackles of the hearth.

The figure didn't waste time. Their sigil still glowed, but a trained eye would recognise it had dimmed since the figure first materialised. The study door was unlocked, and a gloved hand eased the handle down.

The door swung open. It made a noise as it did, but the figure knew they didn't need to mask their approach anymore. All they needed was to confirm the flash of pale brown hair and slim frame seated behind the door, only just looking up and trying to turn around at the source of the noise interrupting their work.

Donald Bennett wouldn't have had time to see who was behind him. Wouldn't have had time to question, or—if he was really quick-witted—cry for help. One hand had already yanked his head back, the other dragged a serrated knife across his throat.

The spurting blood had barely time to extinguish Donald Bennett's candle; the assassin was already letting the body slump onto the desk, positioning it so it wouldn't immediately crash to the floor. They didn't bother to close the study door as they left, nor did they do much to mask their footfalls as they returned to the sigil.

By the time the assassin crouched down, peeled off his glove and raised his forefinger to the sigil it glowed at a quarter of its initial brightness.

As soon as the assassin's finger touched the sigil, man and dagger vanished. The charcoal lines crumbled to dusty nothing.

Now stillness returned to the cosy apartment, with nothing to be heard but the crackles and groan of the hearth, and the steady patter of Donald Bennett's blood dripping from his father's desk onto the floor.

8

GLASGOW

"If you want to hurt a man, you kill his father. If you want to *destroy* a man, you kill his son," Cullen said quietly.

Black didn't respond. His pale skin was ashen.

Despite sitting only a few metres away, Lord Bennett didn't hear them. Cullen could have shouted his remark in the man's ear, and maybe he wouldn't have heard it then.

Cullen considered it fortunate, in a ghastly way, that the news of Donald Bennett's murder reached him before the boy's distraught father appeared in his classroom. Bennett was near-catatonic, and Cullen shuddered to think how the conversation would have proceeded if he didn't already know about his dead son and tried to work out what ailed him.

"I don't understand how they could do such a thing," Bennett muttered. Cullen wasn't sure if he was referring to the logistics of the murder, or the motivation.

"I'm sorry, my lord," was all Cullen could say. It was all he'd been able to say, ad nauseum, for the past quarter of an hour. It made nothing better, least of all himself.

"Can I get you a glass of wine?" Black asked hastily. He'd been in Cullen's classroom when Bennett stumbled in, and seemed torn between fleeing and trying to assist.

Bennett started, perhaps because he'd never heard Black speak before. Or perhaps because he couldn't comprehend wanting anything pleasurable again.

"I need to leave here," he said, rubbing his tired eyes. "My cousin keeps telling me how lovely Italy is, maybe the fool has a point." Cullen couldn't tell who those remarks were addressed to, or if Bennett even realised anyone was still in the room with him.

"What's on your mind, love?" Anna asked, squeezing his hand.

"Wish I knew," Cullen admitted, nudging the remaining scraps of roast lamb around his plate. Thoughts and emotions swirled in his head, yet he couldn't pin any of them down.

Bennett had left his classroom without prompting, or uttering a word of farewell. He might still be in Glasgow, but for all Cullen knew he boarded the next ship to depart the harbour, or fell from his horse and broke his neck five miles from the university.

The only coherent thing he got out of Bennett was the man's apologetic insistence he "couldn't do this any more." Cullen didn't need elaboration: if the broken Lord Henry Bennett every returned to Edinburgh—and that seemed unlikely—it would only be at his complete abandonment of city politics.

"I heard the dark practitioners in Edinburgh did something like this before," Anna admitted. "There was a rival merchant trading in the West Indies—he made a deal with a local port that would undercut their monopoly on sugar trade from the region. Someone cut his wife's throat while the two of them were in bed—the trader slept through it. They had no idea how anyone could get into their locked Lawnmarket apartment. I'm afraid at the time I dismissed the story as rumours. I thought the husband was covering up his cowardice during a robbery, or denying his own crime of passion. But..." She trailed off.

Cullen pushed his abandoned plate across the table. His youngest started to fuss in the crib, drawing Anna over.

"Who are these men?"

"It's not always clear who is 'in' with the dark practitioners and who is 'out.'" Anna said, jigging the baby on her hip. "Those who are not active supporters tend to congregate on the Edinburgh Town Council, but the distinction doesn't mean a lot, since the dark practitioners make sure enough of their own are also elected to the council to get their way."

Cullen wracked his brains. "That would include men like Lord Samuel Carstaires, Lord Douglas Dunbar, Sir Anthony Grey and Lord Oliver Argyle?"

Most of them were his age or older, but he had no recollection of them from his time in Edinburgh. Students didn't know about these political factions, and he'd never cared to enquire how the town operated.

"Not Carstaires, I don't think," Anna clarified. "The other men, yes. My father always warned me to be wary of Lord Argyle. He's rumoured to be the ringleader."

All this made Edinburgh even less desirable. The Town Council managed academic funding and appointments. Even if it was a mostly neutral ground between these two factions, he didn't like the idea of playing lip service to murderers in the course of his teaching.

"Are there more rumours?" he asked, as Anna fed the baby. She came from the MacDonald clan—her family's influence was concentrated in the Highlands, but she was still more connected to Edinburgh goings-on them him.

Anna shrugged. "If they thought you were a direct threat to them, I imagine it'd be your body they left in a pool of blood, not the poor Bennett lad." She grimaced, but Cullen knew she wasn't the type to descend into feminine hysterics when upset. "I know little about the Bennett family, but I imagine his enemies wanted an excuse to settle several scores at once, most of which weren't connected to you."

"And no one resists them?" Cullen asked.

"They're associated with money more often than blood. Their wealth is Edinburgh's wealth. Scotland's too, I suppose. They propped the country up in the aftermath of the Darien scheme, started our crawl out of that mess, and are the reason we retain any semblance of autonomy from England today. The easiest way to resist them is to stay in Glasgow or Aberdeen, where they don't meddle." Having sated the baby, Anna returned to the table.

"I won't stop what I'm teaching," Cullen blurted out. "Or how I'm teaching it. The medical system must be reformed. They don't want me in Edinburgh? Fine, I won't trouble them. But they can't stop me from teaching in Glasgow."

Was this what had been on his mind? Cullen supposed it was. From Anna's expression, he suspected his wife knew this before he did.

"I know, love. You'll just...be careful, won't you?"

It's your fault the boy is dead, a treacherous voice whispered inside his head. *It's no coincidence Bennett Junior was murdered weeks after his father promised to take up your cause in Edinburgh.*

These dark practitioners had sent a warning to people all over Scotland: this is what happens when you go against us. Cullen was as much a recipient as the others. Well, they could consider him warned.

With a sigh of resignation, Cullen turned over his hand, palm up, so Anna could slide her hand into his.

"I'll do my best, sweetheart."

"And you won't let slip the...other things you're exploring?" His wife's hand froze in place for a second.

As a newlywed, Cullen believed he could keep his phlogiston inquires from his wife. Separating his professional and domestic life. Why would his wife care about laboratory experiments? He was a naïve fool. And too terrible a liar.

"Their ignorance of that kept me alive." It kept us alive, Cullen thought.

His wife understood it was better that there were some things she did not know, and so she never pressed her husband too deeply on what he was trying to accomplish. But she knew enough.

Anna's hand didn't relax. She wet her lips and finally spoke the question that must have been on her mind since hearing of the murder.

"But does that mean you'll cease pursuing your enquiries?"

9
GLASGOW

E stimating he was twenty-five metres from Cullen, Black stopped walking. The two of them were roaming the meadowlands outside the college, and if anyone asked, they were looking for certain plants for their refrigeration project. At least Black thought that was what their excuse would be—his professor seemed to change his mind halfway through the conversation after thinking they'd be collecting samples for his materia medica studies.

"Can you hear me, Joe? Eight multiplied by two."

Cullen's voice didn't enter Black's head through its ears, it appeared directly in his mind. Despite a vigorous wind stirring, rustling the wild grasses between them, Cullen's voice carried as clearly as if they were standing together in the library.

"Sixteen, professor."

In the distance, Cullen raised his hand in a wave of acknowledgment.

"What did Professor Cullen ask you to collect?" This raised voice belonged to another student, making his way over a muddy puddle to reach Black.

"Oh, um..." Cullen had also decided when they were halfway

out the college to invite several other chemistry students to join them on the collection trip, because he thought it would make the two of them seem less suspicious. Now there were three or four other students wandering the pasture, none of whom knew what Cullen and Black were doing.

The student didn't appear to notice Black's confusion, because he kept on walking. "I just hope Professor Cullen didn't want more bluebells because the ones I found are in a patch of brambles, and I'm not enduring any more cuts."

Glancing back towards the college, Black saw Cullen engaged in conversation, his black academic robes whipping in the breeze. No one was paying Black any attention, so he edged further away, curious if Cullen could challenge him with mathematical exercises from fifty metres.

In the weeks after news of Donald Bennett's murder reached Glasgow, Cullen urged Black to focus on their coolant project. No more studying or discussing phlogistic abilities. Black watched his professor shovel several notebooks into the laboratory hearth, a grim expression on his face.

"It's for the best, lad," Cullen told him as he prodded the fire. "It's not worth courting danger."

This avoidance lasted two months. Black came into the laboratory one morning before class and found Cullen scribbling in a fresh notebook. He looked at Black with a dazed expression that made Black wonder how many hours he'd been hunched over his desk. Black didn't need to glance at the notebooks themselves: Cullen's furtive posture told him all he needed to know.

A few days later Cullen told him he believed the connectivity between phlogiston in all living creatures meant men could communicate with each other by thoughts alone.

"Sorry, Joe—ten plus two, divided by two." Cullen's voice interrupted Black when he was still walking.

"Six."

Black kept walking, aiming towards the cracked trunk of a tree left standing on the outskirts of the pasture.

"Did you hear me, Joe? Ten plus two..."

"Six, professor." Black had turned away from Cullen: he realised he needed to focus his thoughts in the direction of his professor. It seemed both participants had to know roughly where the other was for the message to travel.

Their first attempts at proculopathic communication gave Black terrible headaches that sent him to bed at four o'clock in the afternoon. It took a lot of coaxing from Cullen before he submitted to more experiments.

"I only felt a mild throbbing pain in my temple," Cullen said. "I think that means it doesn't have to hurt..."

Now standing at the tree, Black saw his fellow students were clustering around Cullen. Flecks of rain were coming on the wind, and the grey clouds were tinging darker. Cullen's volunteer corps was running low on morale. Cullen waved. Black raised his hand, pretending he'd only explored this far from idle curiosity about the lay of the land.

"Last one, Joe. Are you ready?"

"Yes, professor."

"Well, it seems you can hear me alright, so never mind. I can't remember which numbers we've used, anyway. Come back."

Ultimately, Black let Cullen drag him through these experiments for the same reason Cullen drew up such exercises: the sense that anything was possible.

Men all over Britain, Europe and the Americas were asking themselves the same question: could this be the century we crack open the mysteries of the universe and man?

It seemed like idle fancy a few years ago. Then, Black was a schoolboy in Ulster, hearing about the Jacobite rebellions tearing through his family's homelands. Britain seemed on the verge of collapse into civil war, never more so when he learned the Jacobites had marched up to Edinburgh in September '45, and found the city gates wide open to welcome them.

Now the Highlanders' unrest felt like a thing of the distant past, retreated from Scotland's cities and urban memory.

As Black made his way over the meadows, he saw the botany professor wading out of the college to join Cullen and the students. Laughter blew in Black's direction.

He wondered if this optimism belonged to him and Cullen alone. As a first-year student, Black struggled through the work of Hobbes—not that the philosopher would have wanted him to experience joy. To Hobbes, man was a miserable beast, yoked to Leviathan for his own good. Even with his basest instincts thus reigned in, he still had nothing to look forward to in his "nasty, brutish and short" lifespan.

Picking up Locke's Essay Concerning Human Understanding, Black feared more of the same pessimism. Instead, he found Locke's arguments on knowledge strangely uplifting. Man wasn't born with his fate or knowledge transcribed into his essence: he was a blank slate. There was no predetermined, predefined quantity of knowledge available to a person during his lifespan—could that mean knowledge was limitless?

There was plenty of talk in learned circles—Cullen shared some of his scientific and medical correspondence with Black—but little in the way of consensus. Black thought Cullen would be exposed to a never-ending stream of discoveries that upended the status quo.

What was everyone waiting for?

"Reached the New World, Mr Black?" Cullen called out in jest.

"I suspect not," Black replied with a slight smile. The students didn't consider his wanderings unusual—in fact, they were already departing for the sheltered cloisters.

. . .

"Did Professor McNeill want something from you?" Black asked when the two were alone.

"Same the last time. He fielded rather pointed letters from Professor Alexander Monro concerning my future intentions towards Edinburgh, and wished to give me the courtesy of a warning." Cullen settled in his chair. "Fortunately for the august professor, Edinburgh is the last place I wish to set foot in, and McNeill made that abundantly clear."

Black wondered why Cullen needed to be informed of the letter at all, in that case. "Is he someone important?"

"He certainly thinks of himself that way." Cullen gave his closest approximation of a smirk. "After Dr John Rutherford, Monro is the most important professor among the Edinburgh medical faculty. What Rutherford desires, Monro facilitates into being."

"You don't correspond with Dr Monro personally?"

"Afraid not. I'm not worthy of the time it takes Professor Monro to pen a missive." Cullen frowned. "Technically, he's just a professor, not a doctor. Monro's a surgeon by training: he came up through the Incorporation of Surgeons, doesn't have a medical doctorate."

Black looked closely at Cullen. This was all new information. "You don't like him, professor? Or he doesn't respect you?"

Cullen laughed. "Bit of both, lad. Monro begun his career as Professor of Anatomy through the Incorporation of Surgeons, conducting lectures in their hall. Then rumours spread that Monro was pilfering bodies from Greyfriars and other nearby burial grounds. He denied it—for what it's worth, I believe him—but that didn't calm the public. Nasty riots broke out outside Surgeon's Hall, with a mob threatening to lynch the anatomists for stealing bodies. Monro became terrified for his life.

"The dark practitioners reportedly brokered the arrangement where Monro began lecturing on Tounis College grounds, inaugurating a medical faculty in the process, despite the fact he's not a physician. It was harder to get at Monro inside the university quadrangles, so the mob's hunger was quashed. Monro's been in the service of the dark practitioners ever since."

Black rocked in his chair.

'Dark practitioners' was what Cullen had taken to calling the men behind Don Bennett's murder. The term apparently came from his wife, who'd heard rumours about them, as opposed to being a nickname Cullen made up. No one knew how they did what they did, but there was a whiff of supernatural about them.

"If the dark practitioners had the power to quell a mob uprising, surely the opposite holds true as well?"

Cullen smiled. "You're a careful thinker, lad. There are rumours to that effect in circulation, too. Though if you ever ask Monro, he'll tell you the dark practitioners facilitated his smallpox inoculation program in the Highlands—smoothing out misunderstandings with concerned religious leaders, you know how it goes."

Black nodded. "I suppose the end result is the same."

"Monro and John Rutherford alike; both attentive to the dark practitioners' needs. They're very sympathetic onlookers, if not active participants."

"So Professor Monro dislikes you because of what these dark practitioners tell him?"

Cullen learned forward. "Don't repeat this, but I think it might be the other way around. From what I know of the dark practitioners, they don't care what I say about Boerhaave."

IO

GLASGOW

At the next Philosophical Society meeting neither man, beast nor nature could have stopped Cullen from cornering the Earl of Anglesbury. In allowing Henry Bennett to tempt him with talk of Edinburgh, he'd gotten an innocent boy killed. Cullen had also let Bennett's appeal to his vanity distract him from the good he could achieve in Glasgow.

Helping fix a pothole-plagued road on the outskirts of Glasgow was the least controversial thing he could do. Who did road repairs threaten? No one.

Before the meeting's final applause faded, he was on his feet and leaning over Anglesbury's chair.

"The name's William Cullen, professor of chemistry. Delighted to make your acquaintance, my lord. I wished to share my concern with your lordship about the poor condition of the west Cumbernauld road on the boundary of your estate…"

Anglesbury drew his lips together. "Your medical theories are considered controversial, Dr Cullen."

"Well, you'll be relived to learn tonight's appeal concerns the state of your roads," Cullen responded blithely, biting down a harsher sarcastic inflection.

Anglesbury ignored him.

His temper was going to ruin this opportunity. Cullen pressed his hands into the chair back, using the sensation to ground him. "You may not be aware of this, my lord, but I was one of the academic petitioners wishing to elect David Hume to the Glasgow Logic Chair."

Against all logic, this name-drop had no effect on the lord's hostile stare.

"Supporting the wrong side of the argument seems to be a familiar pattern for you, Dr Cullen."

Now Cullen saw his miscalculation. Anglesbury was a proud man: he'd entertained support of Hume while it was popular to do so, but once the tide turned and the Glasgow Assembly rejected Hume for the chair, he'd quietly distanced himself from the losing side. That particular window of leverage closed for Cullen several months ago.

Before he had time to protest, Anglesbury continued. "I have only the time to build a passing familiarity with the latest medical advances read in the Royal and Philosophical Societies, but I should warn you I heard the name 'Dr Cullen' at a very cursory stage in my hobby-horse, at a juncture one should not desire to hear one's name."

This was not how Cullen imagined the conversation would go. He assumed Anglesbury might object to the cost of repairs, or see a comment upon the state of his roads as a personal slight upon his character. But for him to dismiss Cullen out of hand?

"Forgive my ignorance, my lord, but who is uttering my name and making unflattering aspersions against me?"

"The entirety of the medical faculty of Edinburgh, it appears." Anglesbury smirked.

"Well, the good physicians of Edinburgh are safe from my presence." Cullen internally winced at how flippant he sounded about an affair that destroyed the Bennett family, but if he didn't affect nonchalance he knew his grief and regret would be used against him.

"The knowledge of which brings them much relief," the lord countered.

So the continued unpleasantness stemmed from his medical and teaching theories? Even though he was still in Glasgow?

"I don't wish to challenge your lordship's wisdom," Cullen said, as preamble to doing exactly that. "But the mere reality of teaching at Edinburgh does not mean the venerable professors are correct in every assessment or theoretical position."

Cullen thought the conversation would go poorly if Anglesbury grew bored in his presence. Instead, Anglesbury watched him with pity, which was worse. "Perhaps you're correct, Dr Cullen, but their presence in Edinburgh and yours in Glasgow implies a certain median of correctness above yours, does it not?"

No, it does not, Cullen snarled inside his head. He bowed curtly and left the room.

He made it onto the street and was beckoning a carriage when Leechman finally caught up, still fiddling with his greatcoat buttons.

"You heard that?" Cullen asked, assuming Leechman would answer the affirmative.

"I know you thought you were being helpful, and I wish my own convictions burned half as bright as yours, William...but..."

"You think I'm stupid for accosting Anglesbury without a proper introduction?"

"...Among other things, yes." Leechman tugged his coat closed and stamped his feet. "I think you may have made the road business more onerous than it needs to be."

"Damn them." Cullen could see the irritation mixed with compassion in his old friend's face, which added to his frustration. "Do me a favour and don't pretend we just need wait six more months before trying again. No amount of time will wipe the contempt off that man's face when he looks at me."

Leechman looked at his feet.

"I did everything right, Francis. I was following your advice to the letter, for once in my life, these past few months. I held my tongue in the classroom. I disavowed any rumours about my interest in Edinburgh. I avoided stepping on anyone's toes. It achieved *nothing*."

His friend was one of the few people who knew the true extent Bennett's murder rattled Cullen.

"You kept your family safe," Leechman said gently. "That's the most important thing, William."

Cullen couldn't argue with that. So he didn't. His anger was still burning too hot for him to reflect on the merits of his sacrifice.

"Men like Anglesbury can't see past their own conceits. Tell them a paper was read to the Royal Society with great acclaim and they'll sing its praises without having read a word of it. Tell them a paper that delighted them was greeted with derision by the same Society and they'll rush to condemn it. If you told half those lords a paper was written by a physician from Glasgow, and the other half it came from the pen of an Edinburgh luminary, you know how each half would treat it."

"You should sit in my classroom one afternoon," Leechman replied, with a grey half-smile. "My students generate lively discussion about what constitutes knowledge and knowing. They talk themselves in circles. You could present such a case study."

Accepting Leechman was trying to cheer him up, Cullen exhaled.

"I wanted to believe the Earl of Anglesbury belonged to a malleable minority. Now I suspect he's part of the stubborn majority. It's always about prestige with those men. Even on a topic as benign as roadworks."

"Since the dawn of time, or at least the founding of Oxford," Leechman concurred. "Prestige is something they know and are comfortable with, especially when they know little else."

The two men stood together for a moment in silence, each lost in thought.

II

GLASGOW

An uncomfortable cough pulled Cullen away from his writing.

At the front of his laboratory hovered a tall man.

The appearance of a stranger in his private space sent a jolt of alarm through Cullen. Leechman insisted his conduct *was* improving, and no one could draw ire from his behaviour inside or outside the classroom. Yet for a panicked moment he feared this apparition was another messenger from Edinburgh. And if it was, were they sent to deliver more than a warning?

One second later the edge was taken off his panic. The strangers' confused glances around the room told Cullen this was no scholar, nor did he look ready to deliver threatening news. Although the man's clothing was of a fine quality, it lacked the ostentation of the truly wealthy or fashionable.

As he rose, Cullen tried to deduce what this stranger was doing here then, since he wasn't expecting visitors who matched this man's bearing. He was in his late fifties, greying but still projecting vitality. As he turned, Cullen got a proper look at the man's face. His features were fine, with unusually luminous dark eyes.

Behind him, Black gasped.

Ah, that explained it.

"You must be Dr Cullen," the man ventured. He had a deep, even voice. When he was confident in his surroundings, this man would appear formidable indeed. "It is a pleasure to meet you. I'm John Black."

There was a scuffling noise behind Cullen as Black rushed to his father.

"I was told I'd find Joss here," John continued, turning to look at his son. "And here my boy is."

"Father..." stammered Black.

Cullen observed the pair and tried to make sense of this interaction. He would have expected Black to tell him his father was visiting. The confusion and alarm in Black suggested he was as surprised by this meeting as Cullen.

"Is mother...?"

"Mother sends her regards. Everyone in the family is well. I was simply passing through Glasgow on my way to Aberdeen for the summer, and thought I should call upon you. I arrived this morning. It took a little bit of enquiry before I discerned your whereabouts."

"I didn't know you were going to Aberdeen this summer," Black managed. His pale skin lost what colour it held.

"No. Well, it's not like we were keeping up much of a correspondence these past months."

Black stood mute. There was undeniable reproach in his father's voice, though John Black appeared self-contained in his emotional displays and Cullen couldn't decide how angry the older man might be. Black was certainly scared.

"I'd like to take a brief walk with you, Joss. I'm afraid the acrid smell in here is rather distracting—I don't know how you philosophers can tolerate it. Don't worry: I won't keep you from Professor Cullen too long." Black nodded meekly, fixing his teacher with a pleading, helpless expression.

"Go speak with your father, lad," Cullen said. "He's travelled a long way to see you, I imagine."

"Thank you sir." John Black now focussed his attention on Cullen. "I intend to sup at the Gallowgate tavern around three o'clock. If it's not a trouble, perhaps you would care to join me? I'm interested in making an acquaintance of my son's teachers."

"I'd be delighted," Cullen replied, bowing. The elder Black was maddeningly even in tone, it was impossible to say what his designs or opinions were.

Black scurried out of the laboratory after his father, acting as if he were a decade younger than his present age.

He was gone less than an hour. When Black returned, he seemed shaken, unwilling to talk about what had transpired. Cullen gently persuaded him to leave his experimental work until tomorrow.

The Gallowgate served mediocre mutton chops—it was the kind of public house men from out of town frequented because they didn't know of anywhere better.

John Black, seated in a window booth, greeted Cullen with a small smile and a nod.

"I didn't realise Joseph wasn't replying to your letters," Cullen said as soon as he was seated. "I would have urged him to write had I known. He always spoke fondly of you."

Alone in his laboratory, Cullen had put enough pieces together to work out what might be going on between father and son.

John Black nodded, gazing into the middle distance.

"Joss is a good boy: always dutiful and attentive. He caused very little mischief growing up. But he's always been...unfocussed. Outstanding student when you chide him, naturally good at most things he tries, but it takes a lot of chiding to get to that point."

Cullen remembered his early conversations with Black, where

the boy admitted his father was pressuring him to commit to a trade.

"We don't have any physicians in our immediate family," John continued, eating his chop with measured bites. "But if any of our sons entered the medical profession, Joss seemed the most likely candidate."

A merchant like John Black would live a comfortable life, even when providing for a large family, but his funds would never be infinite. Rich noblemen could afford to pay for years of fruitless education for wayward sons, successful merchants would consider it an investment they'd want returns on.

"I must apologise, sir, for I believed young Joseph had your approval to explore chemistry. I see you feel he was not forthright with you."

Cullen had encouraged Black to complete his degree, but he'd not taken enough medical courses this year to qualify as a doctor. Every year he spent at studying at Glasgow was enabled by his father's purse.

John Black paused to chew on his mutton, ruminating on what to think and say next.

"You have children, Dr Cullen?"

"Yes, sir."

"Good, you know how difficult it can be to see your sons lost in the world. I try to give Joss what he needs to succeed, but I suppose at some point he has to figure out how to make his own way." John Black took a slow sip of ale.

"That said," he continued. "I've never seen Joss so animated as when he tried to explain his chemical research to me this morning. I confess I lack the sophistication to understand it, but I gather he made considerable progress in applying the concept of refrigeration under your tutelage?"

This John Black was a subtle man, Cullen realised. He kept a tight control of his emotions and sought answers in a delicate manner.

"If I may speak with full candour?" Cullen asked. He was allowed a nod. "Joseph is an extraordinary student. I've never seen such deftness of technique, nor originality of thought, in any of my other chemistry students. He is so meticulous, so studious, that I can't help but believe he will change our understanding of natural philosophy entirely."

John Black nodded again, like he already suspected as much. "Forgive my poor insight, Professor Cullen, but what kinds of opportunities in chemistry may be suited to such a young man?"

"That's the problem," sighed Cullen. "He would make a skilful apothecary—I'm sure his insights would serve the preparation of pharmacopeia and other materia medica—but I don't see the other aspects of his personality making for a happy business as a shopkeeper."

John Black shook his head. "I never thought Joss suitable to succeed me in the merchant trade: he's honest in all the wrong ways."

And a man of John Black's quiet ambition wouldn't be content for his son to be a mere vendor of remedies, not after what he'd spent on his education.

"I think your son has the qualities to succeed as a physician," Cullen said carefully. "He has the brains and temperament. With a little application, perhaps."

The calm poise of his father put the young Joseph Black into a new light. Under his nerves and insecurity, could Joseph have inherited some of his father's humours? If he had, Cullen realised Black could do very well for himself in the academic world.

"You have shown me nothing but plain-spoken honesty, Professor Cullen, so I will treat you with the same honour." John Black shovelled the last scrap of chop into his mouth. "You have treated my son with as much care as if he were your own child, and it's remarkable to see how he has flourished in your care. But I worry he has fallen too deep into pursuit of this hobby-horse at the detriment of his medical education. Joss promised me he will be less neglectful of his studies henceforth, and I have no reason to doubt his filial piety. But I'm sceptical of his ability to look out for his own self-interests."

Cullen worried this was where the conversation would end up. He sighed.

"Joss is lucky to have a teacher so attentive to his best interests. One option is for the boy to complete his medical studies in Edinburgh. The quality of education he'll receive there is higher than what he can receive in Glasgow, and there will be more flexibility in his dissertation topic options."

John Black paused, waiting to see how Cullen would react.

"I can only apologise," Cullen sighed. "I can assure you I'll provide more stern guidance to Joseph concerning his studies from here onwards."

His dinner guest nodded slightly to indicate he'd heard what Cullen had said, but didn't want to imply he agreed with Cullen's statement. "I will rest in Glasgow for a few days before continuing on to Aberdeen. We can revisit this matter shortly. You might be better-placed to discuss the situation with Joss than I."

Cullen hated himself for what he'd let happen. He knew what they thought of him in Edinburgh, and how that would affect young Black. But in the quiet, precise manner of John Black, Cullen knew there would come a point where his generosity would stop, and Black would be left without the funds to complete any degree.

* * *

"I suggested Edinburgh to my father, actually," Black said.

Cullen couldn't hide his surprise. "Why in Heaven's name would you do that?"

The morning after his conversation with John Black, he'd been relieved to find the younger Black in his laboratory, setting up the vacuum pump. All sorts of plans had fermented in his mind overnight that he needed to convince his student to follow if he wanted to avoid being sent away from Glasgow.

That Black was already resigned to continuing his education in Edinburgh hadn't surprised Cullen—he saw how deferential the boy was to his father and hoped to gently prompt a rethink—but he was taken aback to learn of Black's guiding role in the decision process.

Black dropped his gaze. "My father wanted to cut funding for my studies altogether. He wasn't angry, but I could see which way his mind was turning. I thought it best to suggest a compromise before he reached that decision."

Cullen's temper was bubbling, but he tried to quell it. He reminded himself that Black would know his father's moods and limits best. If he thought he needed to offer that compromise, he would have good reason. It didn't stop his pride from flaring in defence.

"It's a dark city, Joe. They've threatened me, and they know you're my student."

Black looked hurt. "I tried to do what was best, Dr Cullen. For my family, for my medical studies, for you. It's only for a few years."

"You want to become a physician so badly you'll risk your life in Edinburgh?"

"I thought about the risks and believe they're minimal to myself, provided I'm careful," Black protested.

"You thought through it in the ten minutes you argued with your father about the matter in the Quadrangle?"

Black didn't even look shocked at Cullen's hot remarks, nor did he try to defend himself. He just looked wounded.

I'm now the dog-kicker, Cullen sighed to himself. He took a circuit of the table while Black refocussed on the vacuum pump.

"I'm sorry lad. That was intemperate of me. It's just...oh, when you get past the first rushes of youth, you'll realise there's many decisions you made that you can't unmake. Things you regret either because you did them, or you didn't. At your age, the fear of regret burned into me like irons. Ten years later, I barely remember what the fuss was about over some of those decisions. Life happens and many youthful regret fades. What I'm trying to say, and doing an awful job of it..." He saw Black smile even as he kept his head down "Is that I think your priority should be on your safety. No medical education is worth having your throat cut for. No, you may think I'm exaggerating the risk, since you're not my son. Well, the good professors in the medical school enjoy metaphorically cutting the throats of those they consider outsiders or heretics. Because metaphorically you are my son, in matters of medical doctrine." He paused. "The anatomy schools in London are fine places. Perhaps your father will agree to send you there?"

There was silence while Black screwed a valve shut. Then he raised his face to stare into the fire.

"As I calculated it, Dr Cullen, my becoming a physician or professor will lend credence to your theories. As far as your enemies are concerned, you remain in Glasgow, and my presence in their city doesn't upset their influence or business."

"Of course. Now that lot don't have to waste two days travelling to Glasgow when they need to enact bloody reprisals on me: you're right there."

Black looked ready to stamp his foot. "My father isn't going to fund another semester in Glasgow, he made that clear."

Cullen never thought it would come down to this. He'd promised to protect Black—as with all his students—and to help Black become a physician. Never did he think he'd need to choose which of those promises to break.

The worst part was no matter what John Black said, he'd never supplant the man as the ultimate voice of authority in Joe's life. If he allowed his frustration to run its course he risked estrangement with the boy, when he needed guidance more than ever.

"Alright," he said. Black glanced at him. "I will pray every night that I'm overreacting Joe, and that your presence in Edinburgh isn't going to ruffle anyone's feathers, and that your connection to me isn't strong enough to endanger you. But...I'm going to teach you something. You've learned almost all you can from me, but there's one last thing I *can* teach you..."

* * *

"Just sit in the chair...actually Joseph, would you prefer to lie on the floor?"

"Yes," said a grateful Black, slithering off the chair. "If that's okay with you."

"My knees can just about handle it," Cullen replied. He placed two fingers on Black's wrist. "Don't worry, lad. This aether blast will render you unconscious for a couple of minutes at most, only stinging a little bit. There will be no lasting damage."

The same could not be said for Cullen, who went home with small burn marks at his throat and wrist from where a nervous Black discharged phlogiston as opposed to aether.

"I don't want to kill you," Black kept repeating, helping Cullen apply a poultice under his jabon. "How will I know that's not what I'm doing?"

"You'll know," sighed Cullen, tugging his ruffled shirt sleeves over the incriminating marks. They could be mistaken for chemical burns, at least.

He was teaching Black the single technique he swore he'd never propagate. It conferred too much power upon its practitioner.

Comparatively speaking, phlogiston was the easier element to manipulate. You produced fire. Depending on how your tensed your muscles that fire could stay in your palm, or could fly across the room. Aether, on the other hand, was a spectrum of elements. Light, force, electrical. But the human body was governed by aetherial nervous energy, and manipulating that *kind* of aether gave you control over another human's body.

Rendering someone unconscious—as Cullen was demonstrating on Black—was the most benign application. A tiny flash of light from his fingers and Black's head lolled on the floor.

But a stronger discharge could stop someone's heart. And it wouldn't restart.

Cullen knew this was an option as soon as he realised aetherial manipulation was possible. It was several years before he dared test his hypothesis.

The nervous system understood intent. There had to be more to the control of aethereal incapacitation than simple will on a physiological level, but there wasn't much difference in practice.

Cullen had rendered stray dogs unconscious, but despite girding himself, he'd failed to strike a fatal blow. He told himself it was because he had to entice them into his private laboratory space with table scraps, and they wagged their mangy tails with such enthusiasm when he looked at them.

It was only when one of his brothers-in-law asked him to see if there was anything he could do for a cow undergoing a breach birth, and Cullen realised there wasn't, that the light erupting from his hands was pure white instead of yellow. The calf didn't survive either, but Cullen suspected it was already dead.

Right now, he had to comfort Black, despite being the injured party. Black was so distressed and flustered when he finally knocked out Cullen, he looked ready to cry. Despite his self-preservation instincts and the stinging welts on his wrists yelling at him to quit, Cullen gently coaxed Black into trying again.

"If we stop now, your courage will desert you forever. Try once or twice more now you've got it. In fact, it should be quicker if you target my neck..." Hence the second set of burns.

"I need you to know this technique, Joe. I pray to Our Heavenly Father that you will never need to use it in self-defence...but if those dark practitioners set an assassin on you, you might have seconds to react. There will be no time to reach for a pistol. I need to know you stand a chance of fighting back."

For all his protestations about being safe in Edinburgh, Black nodded quickly. He took a deep breath.

Cullen just had time to see a yellow-tinted light leap from the boy's fingers, before he found himself splayed on the floor again.

"How long was I out, Joe?"

"Seventy-five seconds, professor."

The boy's first tentative effort had knocked him out for all of three, so this was encouraging.

"Good work, lad. Looks like the rest of that poultice will go unused."

Black nodded. Cullen could sense he was done for the day.

After he'd got back on his feet, Cullen turned around slowly until he was looking in what he thought was an easterly direction.

"I've trained you as best I can, Joe. There's little more you can learn from me. I just hope you'll be safe."

PART 2
EDINBURGH 1752 TO 1756

"If we trace the progress of our minds, and with attention observe how it repeats, adds together, and unites its simple ideas received from sensation or reflection, it will lead us farther than at first, perhaps, we should have imagined."

— JOHN LOCKE, AN ESSAY
CONCERNING HUMAN
UNDERSTANDING (1689)

12

EDINBURGH

The door to the basement was jammed shut, its wood swollen from years of dampness. Black tugged at it for a minute until it begrudgingly yielded.

The anatomy theatre beyond was gloomy and oppressive. His eyes were drawn to a thin figure with swirling academic robes at the centre of the room, illuminated by beeswax candles. Behind him, shadows danced across skeletons: some human, others monstrous chimeras. The air was frigid, and an icy wind stung Black's face.

"What do you want?" the figure snapped. "Class doesn't begin until the top of the hour."

That's when Black noticed they stood over a shrouded object on the dissection table. A surgical blade in his hand glinted yellow, then ruby.

"Um, Professor Monro? I'm Joseph Black. I came to present my letter of introduction."

"I know who you are. Can't you see I'm busy?" Monro waved his hand, irritated. "Well, come on then—let's have it."

Black gulped, then took a hesitating step into the enfolding darkness. It had to be a dead body Monro was busy with. Seeing

103

the dead wasn't an unfamiliar experience, but before this he'd only encountered the recently deceased, looking as they had in life. A half-butchered cadaver was something else entirely.

Every footstep on the wooden floorboards released groans and creaks, when Black was trying to make as minimal an impression on the room as he could.

Monro pinched his lips.

"Come on, Mr Black—I don't have all day for this."

What could Black keep his focus on? The irate professor with his piercing eyes or the ghastly cadaver, still half-hidden from view? He held out the crumpled letter like a talisman and took another step forward.

As Black approached the professor, his tremors increased. The more he tried to ignore the cadaver, the more his gaze pulled towards it.

"What in heaven's name is the problem?" Monro thrust out his hand. "Give me the letter."

"It's the dissected body...I'm afraid I'm not used to..." Black protested, then gave up.

He extended the letter as far in front of him as he could, desperate to get the ordeal over with and flee to his lodgings.

Monro's fingertips were just closing around the paper when Black was distracted by a movement on the dissecting table.

From this angle he could finally see the half-exposed corpse of a middle-aged woman, saggy face wrinkled in one ultimate moment of discomfort. The remnants of her shorn hair were lanker than straw, her mouth gaping.

The movement came from her abdomen, below her flat breasts. While her skin was dull as wax, below her ribcage lay something dark and glistening. No, there were many seething things Monro was cutting loose. As Black watched in horror, a portion of the woman's intestines—piled up on her pelvis to allow Monro to pick at what lay beneath—slid onto the table with a wet exhalation. Only now, in these icy conditions, was Black forced to inhale the heavy pall of decay and the rotten contents of the dead woman's stomach.

A fuzzy greyness descended over Black's eyes as the anatomy theatre pirouetted around him.

It seemed like the greyness dropped and rose again instantaneously, and when it did, Black was surprised to find himself no longer standing, but lying on the uneven dais.

"Good heavens…" Monro knelt beside him, loosening Black's cravat. "Oh sir, you weren't lying when you said you had a weak head for dissection."

Black tried to sit up, but Monro eased him back. Floorboard nails dug into his shoulders and neck. "I'd wait a minute if I were you, then rise slowly. You don't want to swoon a second time, do you?"

The blood rushed to Black's cheeks, which he hoped wasn't apparent in the dark light. Monro's lean face regarded him. Black saw the anatomy professor struggling to keep his expression straight.

"Just one glance at the cadaver and you fell like a tree! Quite gracefully, I might add. Here, this damp cloth might help." Not wanting to question where the cloth or water had been before this, Black gingerly patted his forehead.

"I'm sorry, professor," he mumbled, trying not to focus on Monro's quivering mouth.

"Well, it's early in your education, so we may still make a physician of you yet." Monro rose into a crouch and looked towards the door. "My youngest son Sandy promised to stop by before class: he should be here soon to escort you somewhere less perilous."

* * *

Monro could hardly believe it. The reviled champion, Cullen's prized student, fainting upon his first glance at an opened cadaver. Young medical students always fainted or vomited during his dissections, but they usually held out longer than this. Try as he might, it was hard to muster hostility to Cullen's lanky protégé when he was sprawled on his anatomy theatre floor, looking as bashful as a milkmaid.

Black slowly twisted his legs and edged into a seating position, resting his back against the raised seating row behind him. After a pause, he dragged his legs under him. Monro extended his hand and helped Black to his feet, the boy's eyes fixed on his shoe buckles. He looked as if he was about to cry. Monro found this even funnier. He bit the inside of his lips in an attempt to control them.

"You'll have the advantage of your classmates," he added, surprised he felt bad for his amusement. "You aren't the first anatomy student to faint at my feet, and you won't be the last."

* * *

"Father?" A voice coming from the entrance prompted Black to look up, relieved he no longer had to focus on Monro or his dissecting table.

In the doorway stood a big-boned youth, a few years younger than Black. He stood with such relaxed confidence that Black knew this must be Monro Junior.

"If you don't mind Sandy, Mr Joseph Black here is feeling a little queasy. Can you accompany him back to the Yards? There are a few things I need to tell you when you're done."

"No problem," the youth replied. Monro guided Black over to his son.

Black felt steady as long as he concentrated on his feet, and didn't think about what he'd just witnessed.

If Sandy Monro was curious why neither Black nor his father was meeting each other's eyes, or why both were shaking for different reasons, he didn't remark upon the fact. Holding on to the stairwell wall, Black made it to the Yards without incident.

Once he was in the relatively fresh air of the courtyard, he was seized by a coughing fit.

"Everything alright?" Sandy asked. His steady gaze told Black he already possessed some experience with death and gore. It was humiliating that a peer of his could be this talented for the medical profession, while he made an idiot of himself.

"I can't believe I fainted."

As he leaned against the crumbling college walls, all sorts of secondary emotions and thoughts entered Black's head. What was he thinking, showing weakness in front of those dangerous men? What would Cullen say when he learned what happened? How was he supposed to complete his medical dissertation now?

"You're Joseph Black, right? I'm Sandy Monro."

"Honoured to meet you, Sandy." His colleague appeared mildly entertained, but not mocking.

"Do you think you can get back to your lodgings safely?"

"Yes, I'm staying with Mr Russell just around the corner," Black pointed.

"Your cousin, did I hear that?"

"Yes." Black wondered how much the medical faculty had gossiped about him prior to his arrival. And now there would be more gossip.

"Who was that woman?" Black asked. "I thought the first dissection wouldn't begin for several weeks."

"A convicted coin forger," Sandy said with a shrug. "She was sentenced to be hanged, but pleaded her belly a week before the execution date. A midwife inspected her and said she was lying. My father was asked to dissect the body to confirm she wasn't with child."

"It's a bit late now, isn't it?" Black said slowly.

Sandy frowned for a minute, then laughed. "I suppose so. I think my father would have said something when I came in if he'd found proof of a pregnancy. He was exploring her guts when I came in, wasn't he?"

The stench of the anatomy theatre rose back into Black's nostrils, despite sitting in relative freshness of the Yards. He grimaced.

Then he started. "I didn't give Professor Monro his three guineas. I think he received my letter of introduction..." It certainly wasn't on Black's person any more. "But I forgot the course fees."

"I can give them to him now," Sandy said. "If you have the coins. I'm sure my father will want you to call upon him for a proper discussion of your proposed course of studies in the next day or two."

"His anatomy class starts in ten minutes?" Black asked, struggling to figure out how long he'd spent in the murky bowels of the college. It felt like hours.

"Twenty minutes." Sandy regarded Black, seeming to detect his thought patterns. "I suppose you could go home and come back in time for class. I might recommend eating and drinking something if you do. There's a pie seller at the intersection of College Wynd. The ale he sells is drinkable, that's all I can say for it."

"Yes," Black figured he may as well get back into the hellish anatomy theatre before his courage deserted him for good. "That sounds like a good idea. Thank you." After a pause, he handed the guineas in his pocket to Sandy, who took them with a nod. He didn't want to delay the class arranging payment with a man who possessed scant patience for his blunderings.

"Will see you shortly, then," Sandy remarked with a glint.

By the time Black crept back into the theatre, Monro had already begun his preamble to the lecture. Black slipped into the front row, not wanting to draw attention to himself by pushing to the back.

While he imagined his lateness wasn't appreciated, Monro ignored him.

The body was concealed under a stained white sheet. Though his attention was tugged towards it, Black found he could look away. He concentrated on inhaling the scent of a nearby beeswax candle, spluttering in the draught.

"Your first subject for this anatomy course will be your own professor," Monro said, striding towards the students. "Please regard my hands."

One diminutive scholar unleashed a muffled expletive, then mumbled in shame. A few other students frowned and looked uncomfortable.

The candlelight played across Monro's raised hands, throwing into relief how disfigured they were. Thick scarring and discolouration covered the backs of his hands. His fingers were of uneven thickness and curve, as if chunks of his flesh were transposed. Turning his hands inwards, Black could see Monro's palms were in a similar state. As Monro flexed his fingers, Black observed some of them lacked their proper range of movement.

"You will note I always keep a flagon of vinegar on the dissecting table to clean my hands with before and after anatomical demonstrations. When I was your age, I thought such precautions were unnecessary. I was impatient to master my art, and fancied myself invincible." Monro kept his ghastly hands raised as he spoke, as if calling on a higher power to heed him. "Until one day I dissected a diseased lung. I was careless with my surgical technique in other ways—my hands were a mess of cuts and nicks—and both my hands became infected. The infection on my right side spread as far as my shoulder. My surgical mentors warned me I could lose both arms...if not my life. Every inch of my hands and arms, save the thumbs and forefingers, were covered in poultices for several weeks afterwards. I survived, but live with the proof of my hubris every day."

It was some relief when Monro lowered his hands, and they

disappeared into the shadows around his robes. As he looked around the room, most students turned away. Black forced himself to make eye contact. There was no self-pity in Monro's eyes.

"This is serious, hazardous work we perform as anatomist, and it must be conducted without ego. If you learn nothing more from me than this—I will consider my teaching satisfactory."

13

EDINBURGH

The personal meeting with Monro came a few days later, after Black had settled into his lodgings.

He was led by a servant into Monro's airy Lawnmarket apartment, where he found the professor in his study, where he occupied himself most late afternoons. The professor made no mention of what transpired in his anatomy theatre, beyond a polite question about his general health and wellbeing. Black stammered through his answer. While not as snappish as he was upon the first meeting, Monro remained impersonal.

In the natural light of his study, Monro's scarred hands were a lot less distracting. They didn't seem to affect Monro's ability to hold a quill or surgical blade.

"You will have already considered the topic of your medical dissertation, Mr Black..." Monro asked without asking, focussed on making notes in his ledger.

"With the dissertation...I..."

A sudden stabbing pain in his ankle brought his entire chain of thought to a stop.

"Ahhh. I wouldn't move if I were you. That tends to make the situation worse," Monro said, leaning forward with amusement.

Looking down, Black made eye contact with a tortoiseshell cat, who was frozen with his heel in her mouth. Not breaking eye contact, the cat gave Black's foot a few experimental kicks.

"My wife is rather fond of that cat," Monro added, lest Black try to escape his predicament with force.

"A fierce hunter," Black noted. The cat's teeth jabbed underneath his tendon, but the animal wasn't attempting to pierce his skin. "I wouldn't want to be a rodent seeking sanctuary in your apartment." His silk stockings were going to suffer, however.

"Quite," Monro agreed. "This hellish creature is useful for some things. My wife found her as a kitten several years back: someone must have tossed her in the midden heap outside our lands. We heard her crying from several storeys up. I ruined one of my handkerchiefs digging her out. I wanted to drown her, but Isabella took pity on the wretched thing." He shrugged. "Women can be such fanciful creatures—don't marry one if you can avoid it."

The cat tried to fit more of Black's ankle into his mouth, still with a wide-eyed stare and folded back ears.

"I must warn you," Monro said delicately. "You've chosen a rather exciting time to pursue a chemical dissertation. Professors Alston and Whytt have been at each other's throats regarding the properties of lime-water. Both have come to opposing conclusions about the cause of lime-water's causticity. No doubt both men will look to the famed Joseph Black for help determining the true mechanism."

Which would lead to me making the enemy of at least one college professor, thought Black. Possibly both. Alston taught materia medica, Whytt the theory of medicine. Neither specialised in chemistry, but the Chemistry chair Plummer taught the traditional interpretation of the subject—the preparation of pharmaceutical compounds—showing no interest in theoretical research or supervising dissertation students. He fluttered a meaningless smile in Monro's direction. "I will see how I can best serve the field, professor."

Without warning, the cat abandoned her gnawing of Black's leg and took off out of the study, making a noise sounding like a giggle.

"I believe Dr Alston has a modest laboratory in the Infirmary," Monro noted. "Whytt conducts his experimentation at home."

This meant he'd probably need Alston as his dissertation supervisor. Black wasn't sure whether he should call upon Alston or Whytt first, but his overall course of action was now ordained.

* * *

Black left the study with what Monro considered a pleasant degree of trepidation.

Good.

Monro, who had stoked the animosity between Alston and Whytt by relaying rumours the other told him in confidence, doubted Black could emerge from this debate unscathed.

A few days ago, Alston delivered a note to Monro, which included several remarks about the character of Whytt...or at least how Alston perceived it. Monro sent out two notes the next morning: one to Whytt, and the other to a minister seeking Monro's assistance with his bladder stones.

Upon receiving Whytt to confer over a chemistry topic, Monro was therefore called out of his study to speak with his patient. He couldn't be certain Whytt read the missive from Alston that Monro so carelessly left out on his desk, but the distant manner Whytt continued the conversation one he returned implied he had.

It wasn't so much the attack of his character that offended Whytt—for by now he was accustomed to what Alston thought of him—it was the fact Alston made his complaints semi-public. The two professors wouldn't descend to duelling, because Whytt knew better to admit that he'd snuck a glance at another man's private correspondence, but Monro was confident it would prolong their ill-will at least another year.

Hopefully, Cullen's prized student would be too focused on navigating between Scylla and Charybdis to stir up the kind of trouble he and Rutherford feared. Once Mr Black concluded his dissertation research, Monro saw no reason to waste further time provoking the pair.

* * *

If his remaining years in Edinburgh were filled with as much adventure and terror as those first days, Black wasn't sure how he could survive long enough to get a medical degree. He retreated to a modest tavern recommended by his cousin to unwind for a few hours.

What surprised Black most was how worn-out the Tounis College buildings appeared. Built in the reign of King James I, Cullen lamented how draughty and ugly the college was during his brief studies there. Some repairs and extensions took place between then and Black's arrival, but they created a discordant mess of cheap stonework.

Black was sick of Edinburgh as soon as he saw the condition of the illustrious university he was expected to study in, but he was walking with his cousin and couldn't turn around to flee.

Besides—he couldn't afford to infuriate his father, who corresponded regularly with Russell and thus would receive word of his every falter.

Not that Russell appeared to be a strict supervisor. He wasn't much older than Black—though he acted like he was—and found his shyness endearing.

"You always were the quietest Black sibling, Joss."

Russell moved through Edinburgh with easy poise, his manner of speaking honed through business with the rich and powerful.

His surgeon and apothecary businesses were steady, and Black thought his wife and son equally polished.

Black had no idea how anyone could move around a town as cramped and fetid as Edinburgh with poise. He found himself constantly flinching from bodies colliding with him on the High Street, all while fixating on the ground to watch what he was stepping in.

The wood and stone tenements of the High Street put him to mind of decomposing corpses: swollen and distended. In warmer weather he expected some of them to burst. The citizens of Edinburgh seemed undeterred by their precarious living conditions: the High Street was a bright mass of buildings in cheery yellows, reds and blues. Images of hats, shoes and barber blades advertised the wares sold in first and second-floor shops. Street vendors yelled out their wares, but Black could also identify their produce by what littered the streets around them.

Once he entered the tavern, Black was relieved to escape the worst of the noise and clamour. Here was a steady ebb of conversation and a vaguely controlled environment. Outside of his bedchamber, it was the calmest spot he could find in town.

In one corner of the room, crowded around a table that would barely accommodate two men, sat five Africans. Aside from a few glances, no one paid them any attention, nor did they look outwards from their gathering.

They must be servants from various households. Some had the tall and proud bearing of footmen, others perhaps worked in the kitchens. Will the tavern keeper interacted with them civil enough, Black noticed he didn't go out of his way to replenish their bottles the way he did other patrons. But nor did the servants seem interested in rushing through their drinks.

The tallest African must have felt Black staring, because he looked up and held eye contact. He might be the footman attached to Lord Argyle's household—there were only so many families in Edinburgh who could afford black servants. A footman called

Octavius was said to enjoy unusual favour with Argyle. Black could believe he was looking at Octavius, because he felt uncomfortable with the frankness of the man's stare.

Black looked away and refocused on his drink. He didn't want to draw attention to himself.

St Giles' bells chimed. Black thought he missed the first couple of strikes, then tried to decide if it was nine or ten o'clock.

Although everyone seemed deep in conversations, yelled over the fiddler in the centre of the room, a grumbling of discontent rose as the chimes continued.

Men began reaching into their pockets. Coins and snuffboxes clattered onto the table.

Still talking, they unfolded scraps of paper and held them over the nearest candles. A match was passed around.

It had to be ten o'clock, Black realised. The hour that tenement residents could empty their chamberpots into the streets.

A smoky haze settled over the room as the scraps of paper burned. The back of Black's throat stung, and his eyes were watering. A few tavern dwellers glanced at him with mockery or sympathy—having outed himself as a visitor to Edinburgh by his weak reaction.

He could smell it now. Faintly. Creeping. A day's worth of piss and excrement, tossed to earth from hundreds of chamberpots in this wynd alone. In a few hours, cleaners and sweepers would get to work, making the city air tolerable again by the morning, but it would get worse before it got better.

Black coughed. He leaned over the remnants of his ale, but he couldn't taste what he was drinking.

* * *

"And *you* must be Mr Joseph Black," said a jocular voice from the doorway.

It was said in the tones that implied the speaker had encountered multiple individuals in this part of the Infirmary, which Black ruefully decided was the point of the joke.

He'd spent the morning contending with the dilapidated mess that was Alston's laboratory. Most of the glassware was crusted with chemical deposits, possibly from the last century, and Black had no idea how long it would take to scrub and boil clean. He wouldn't endear himself to the Russells bringing this junk home, but he wasn't sure he had a choice.

A more pressing need, given the chill, was to clear the hearth of its ash deposits, knock out whatever birds' nests and dead rats were lodged in the chimney and get some warmth into the room. Which was why the man he suspected was Andrew Plummer, professor of chemistry, found him on his hands and knees, covered in soot.

"I suppose it looks unlikely," Black commented, rising to his feet and wiping the worst of the soot off his hands.

"Well, meaning no disrespect to Charles...but you're less even likely to be a servant," Plummer replied. "I barely have a reason to come down here myself."

Plummer wasn't the first medical faculty member to find an excuse to come peer at the famed Joseph Black from Glasgow; favoured student of the notorious William Cullen. This past week, Black felt less like a student and more like a tiger exhibited in a pleasure garden. Well, maybe not a tiger. More like an exotic, fragile hummingbird.

It was a peculiar change in circumstances, since he was used to being ignored in Glasgow. His affiliation to Cullen gave a cloak of anonymity there. Now the opposite was true.

The times were changing. Quite literally: everyone was getting tripped up over the new Gregorian calendar dates, and whining that King George had stolen half of September with the mandated adjustment. "You didn't receive my money? I paid you on the third of September 1752!" was a tiresome jest by now.

Plummer peered at the rows of affinity tables laid on the table.

"I'd be careful with those, young sir."

"I beg your pardon?" Black assumed he meant being careful not to get the textbook damaged. But the strange, insistent look in Plummer's made him suspect he was missing something.

"Do you pay attention to how those are drawn?" Plummer asked, lowering his voice a fraction. He studied Black's confused face. "How much did Dr Cullen tell you about...what goes on here?"

"These are just chemical shorthand, Professor Plummer," Black said, an uneasy feeling settling on him. "They're for representing elements and the like. Beyond that, they have no further meaning."

Plummer should be familiar with chemical affinity tables, he thought. Cullen said they've been in use ever since he was a young student. He wondered if Plummer suffered from bouts of confusion, because the professor opened and closed his mouth a few times, as if uncertain of what to say in response.

"But do you know what they were derived from, Mr Black? Do you really know?" Plummer shook his head, as if to clear dark thoughts. "I'd be careful if I were you."

14

GLASGOW

The laboratory was more vibrant without young Joseph around. As Cullen slit open a slim letter from his former student, his two apprentices laughed as they distilled a new vat of nitric acid in the corner. Black was such a quiet, studious presence Cullen often forgot he was on in the room. But this term he realised he needed a second replacement for the young chemist, because one neophyte apprentice could manage barely half the work. He supposed these boys were more serious about their medical degrees, so he could hardly upbraid them for laxness in his laboratory. But nonetheless...

Dear Dr Cullen,

I apologise for the delay in responding to your latest message, for my medical studies have consumed most of my waking hours. No more sulphuric fires for this poor scholar, alas! I can manage the dissections tolerably well, and am growing slowly accustomed to handling the unfortunate mortal remains.

Despite their friendliness, Black hadn't yet lost the manner of formal diffidence he used when speaking to a professor. Cullen scanned through the brief update on Black's studies he'd received this morning—his opinions on the Edinburgh professors' lecturing styles, amusing anecdotes about living with his cousin. Three paragraphs in, Cullen found what he was looking for.

It appears our *mutual friends* use a symbol-based language, with a passing similarity to the common chemical affinity table. Perhaps they once came from the same source? Anyway, there is an art to their drawing, which is how their power is conferred upon an object—a kind of calligraphy I suppose, in that one could study the object but unless you replicated its order of constituent strokes, no action would result (or perhaps a different action? I only gleam this from the vaguest hushed generalities and whispered innuendos). I will endeavour to learn more and update you.

I remain as ever.

Your obedient servant, JB

Well, it was a start.

"Joe makes them sound more like dark chymists than anything else." Cullen set a penknife to the lower third of the letter and tossed it in the hearth. There was no sense in keeping a record.

The second letter he broke upon was twice the weight of the first. The writing was cramped and uneven—a sign the writer had fussed over its contents over the course of several days.

Dear Sir,

Your latest message delighted me, and I pondered the feasibility of your linen bleaching proposal for some time. Here are my (wholly inadequate!) thoughts...

Knowing his former student's life might depend on his unassuming conduct, Cullen was playing it safe. No grand ideas, no controversial medical statements in the classroom. To give his imagination a safe outlet, he'd entered a meandering correspondence with a minor noble on the stimulating topic of linen bleaching, with occasional forays into agriculture when the excitement got too much for them.

He met Hugh at a Society meeting before the horrible business with the Bennetts and Anglesbury drove him away from that fora. They'd struck up a conversation because no one else was speaking to them.

"I'm visiting my sister," the man explained. "I have an estate north of Arbroath that keeps me busy."

And what a windswept, desolate pocket of land that turned out to be! Like Cullen, Hugh found Glaswegian intellectual society an ostracising place. His demeanour put Cullen to mind of a windswept tree, clinging to life in the exposed Highlands. They started writing letters as a way to exchange ideas about chemical innovations in linen bleaching, which the noble found a pleasant diversion.

For once in his life, Leechman found no fault with Cullen.

"Hugh of Arbroath?" The silence dragged on so long Cullen feared his friend would unleash a devastating condemnation. But eventually Leechman shrugged. "Never heard of him."

The man held no connection to his enemies in Glasgow or Edinburgh. Although he held a landed title, he was as close to a nobody as such a man could be. He held negligible wealth, and no business ventures anybody in Edinburgh could covet.

Cullen thumbed through the letter. They took turns posing hypotheticals about how to chemically bleach linen. Was there a chemical mixture that would do the job better than sunlight? Cullen rather hoped the answer was no—a tidy resolution would bring this harmless diversion to a close. He could see Hugh had poked some holes in his proposals, and suggested alternative approaches.

Maybe he could persuade one of the lads to run a bleaching

experiment when they had free time? The pair were still giggling in the corner.

15

EDINBURGH

Busy in his laboratory, Black almost missed the spark. Two seconds later and his distillation apparatus was on fire.

"Curse this glassware," Black muttered. He'd a grim premonition the glassware used to distill his ether was faulty: he applied fresh grease onto the joints before applying heat, but fumes must have escaped from somewhere.

A few years ago he'd probably have running screaming from the space, crying for help. Unfortunately, the man he associated most with 'help' in the world chemistry was still in Glasgow. His dissertation supervisor hadn't been down here in months.

First, he moved the bottle of ether off the table, away from the spreading fire. Reduce the risk of anything else igniting.

He always had a bucket of sand nearby, in case of emergencies like this. Black poured the sand over the burning ether, wrapped a cloth around his hand, then swiped the alembic flask from the furnace.

Less than ten seconds after the ether caught fire, the blaze was extinguished. All that was left was a hazy pall as reminder.

"That was impressive." In the doorway stood Sandy Monro, blinking. "Are you alright, Joseph?"

"I suppose…" Black's heart was hammering, but he could feel it slowing back to normal. He felt a little lightheaded. "I don't think we're in danger of a second conflagration."

He expected Sandy to question this statement, asking if he was sure. Instead, Sandy nodded, satisfied with his assessment of the situation.

"You're a braver fellow than me. Cadavers tend not to do anything interesting—certainly not spontaneously combust."

Chemical research never struck Black as particularly courageous, so he shrugged off the compliment. Sandy ambled in the room, wafting smoke away from his face. He helped Black push the windows open further, then pointed towards shards of glass as Black took a broom across the floor.

"How's your chemical research?" Sandy asked, once the mess was tidied up and the bulk of the smoke dissipated. "Is your first scientific blow going to come down against Whytt or Alston?"

"Neither," Black said with good cheer. "I'm investigating the properties of magnesia alba instead. It belongs to the same chemical family as lime-water and behaves similarly, yet receives less attention from the scientific community."

A light dawned in Sandy's eyes. "Ah, that's how you avoid offending your advisor with the wrong discovery while still respecting his research program. Very clever. Did Dr Cullen suggest you investigate magnesia?"

"No," Black fought to hide his annoyance. "This was my idea."

In truth, he'd talked through his idea with Russell until he felt confident enough to approach Alston with this proposed dissertation topic, but he was tired of these insinuations, even when they came from well-meaning allies like Sandy.

Black felt distrusted by the faculty for being an offshoot of Cullen, but every time he deviated from his former professor's philosophies, it was treated by the same professors as personal laxity.

"I don't see much magnesia here," Sandy observed, "just some joinery. I hope your thesis is progressing."

Sandy's recently submitted thesis on the lymphatic system was four times as long as the average Edinburgh doctoral dissertation—submitted after he'd been officially appointed junior professor of anatomy, of course—and rushed to the printers in Paris and Leiden.

"It appears working in Professor Russell's shop has given you a journeyman's preoccupation with weights," Sandy teased. "Although in the world of chemistry, you are only going to short-change yourself with your balances."

"I see things differently," Black began. "Where there is quantification, there is control. If we cannot measure, we cannot understand."

"That sounds dangerously close to Hume's radical empiricism," Sandy noted, a glint in his eyes.

"Well, my friend David uses his empiricism to disprove the existence of everything he cannot see. Were he to inadvertently lose his reading glasses behind his ottoman, after ten minutes of attempted failed retrieval, he would probably conclude his reading glasses never existed. I, on the other hand, wish to prove the existence of a number of things hitherto invisible to the eye and senses."

Sandy folded his arms and leaned against the wall. "Hm, I can see that might become popular."

Regarding his guest, Black thought again how there wasn't much familial resemblance between Monro Junior and his father. Sandy had an amiable countenance and big bones; his father was all sharp edges. A strong nose was all they shared.

Sandy himself laughed over the difference. "I was the perfect image of my father when I was a boy—everybody agrees on that—but guess it couldn't last."

Black felt less envious of the young anatomist when he learned the third son of Alexander Monro wasn't his father's first choice to succeed him to the anatomy chair. Sandy's older brother Donald held that honour until he was seduced by the cacophony of London a few years ago and refused to return north. It was nice, thought Black, to know Sandy was like him in that he still strived to earn his father's esteem.

If Sandy felt any rancour that he was the second-best son, he never showed it. He preferred quiet diligence.

Black assumed Dr Donald Monro shared his father's political gamesmanship, and that was part of his suitability for the university chair. No doubt aware of what fate befell Don Bennett for his father's crimes, Sandy kept out of Monro's dark chymistry dealings and shied away from faculty leadership.

Black suspected part of Sandy's interest in him was he didn't think Black would overwhelm him or threaten his father. Which wasn't flattering, but he needed friends in this city, so resolved to remain courteous.

* * *

"Have you met Dr Francis Aird?" Plummer asked, nodding to the louche, beaming gentleman next to him.

"I don't believe we've had the pleasure," Black said cautiously. He set aside his semi-dismantled furnace and rose to meet his guests. Aird didn't appear daunted by the introduction to a complete stranger: he shook Black's hand vigorously and clasped it within his own.

"Wonderful meeting you, Joseph," he said. To his surprise, Black thought the man—no older than him—might be sincere.

By now, Black had seen more of Plummer than his actual dissertation supervisor.

"Have you had time to consider my terms, Mr Black?"

Of course, Plummer's repeat appearances were less about probing Black's connection to William Cullen, and more about courting him for a laboratory assistantship position of his own.

"Yes," Black said, casting his mind back to the contents of the letter. "We can meet on Thursday morning perhaps?"

Preparing solutions for Plummer's lecture demonstrations sounded like an easy way to earn a couple of extra guineas. Not to mention proving Black's own competence for teaching and demonstrating in the second half of his dissertation.

Plummer looked delighted, as if he'd doubted Black would accept his offer. "Yes, let's do that. Francis has a busy day ahead of him meeting Fairfax and Carstaires, but he insisted he meet the eminent Joseph Black first."

"I imagine that will occupy much of your attention," Black said, glancing at his bubbling distillation apparatus. He could hold a conversation for a few more minutes before he'd have to run back and check it wasn't overheating.

Fairfax and Carstaires were longstanding Town Councilmen, the pair most invested in the running of college. They seemed to conceive the university as their pet project.

Aird laughed. "The pair aren't that bad once you get to know them. We get on fairly well."

Black nodded, feeling the energy sink out of him.

It was silly. He doubted Aird intended to brag, or if Aird thought himself as a rival to Black. But it broke his spirits a little hearing someone succeeding at a task he was ill-suited to.

Black heard Aird's name used in conjunction with him a lot. Aird obtained his doctorate the previous year, but was angling after a faculty appointment. His connection with Rutherford and Plummer meant he was a likely candidate for the same Chairs as Black.

Maybe people thought him simple and naive, but he understood the greasy mechanics of faculty appointments by now. Getting experience as a laboratory assistant was advantageous...but wouldn't get him an appointment if none of the top brass liked him much.

"I'd hate for you to neglect your experiments on my behalf,"

Aird said when he noticed Black's anxious glances. "Is it ether you're distilling? I hear it's a tricky solvent."

"It's hexanes this time." A large bottle labelled 'hexanes' sat in a prominent spot in front of the distillation, but Aird hadn't noticed it. "I hope the rest of your day passes pleasantly, Francis, and I'm sure we'll encounter each other soon."

Aird would be the sort to invite him out for wine in the tavern, with no underhand intentions. He was that kind of clubbable man.

16

EDINBURGH

Rutherford was in his classroom tidying up his books when a footman appeared.

"If you have a minute, Dr Rutherford?"

He was led across the quad to a sedan chair set delicately on the side of the entrance. The other footman took a few respectful steps back. The curtains were pulled back to reveal Lord Argyle, sitting patiently as one would sit in his own dining room.

Rutherford lowered his head to the window.

"Greetings, my lord."

This type of behaviour wasn't unusual. Argyle and men of his class would never call upon a social inferior like Rutherford at his home. But if he was out and about on business and happened to be passing the college, he would at least summon the men inside across several yards to him.

That said, he was used to dealing with Sir Anthony, who cultivated an outsized personality to stand out in cramped, dingy Edinburgh. Lord Argyle was a different beast: self-contained, flinty in countenance and dress. It was a lot harder to deduce what Argyle thought and felt.

The man was now regarding Rutherford as a general might survey an approaching army.

"You've observed Mr Black for some time. Tell me, what do you make of him?"

Nor was it unexpected the lords would only have a trivial question to put to Rutherford, who would have carried his books out with him if he knew this was all that was required.

Rutherford scrunched his nose. "Seems very young. Impressionable. Eager to learn, and quite apt at his studies, but more diffident than usually becomes a gentleman."

Argyle looked thoughtful. "Have you had success...inclining him towards anything?"

"I've not spoken to him often enough, I'm afraid, my lord." Rutherford cleared his throat. "I can try."

Argyle waved a gloved hand. "Don't trouble yourself. I think my friends and I will have an opportunity to view Mr Black in a social situation before long." He pursed his lips. "What of his friendships?"

"He seems agreeable with his peers. He associates with Sandy Monro outside the classroom." Rutherford wanted to cooperate, but he was struggling to answer Argyle's questions about a student he wasn't well acquainted with. Admitting ignorance risked incurring the lord's displeasure, though.

"And women?" Rutherford stared at Argyle in surprise. "Does he seem interested in the fairer sex?"

Rutherford's cheeks itched. "I...I really don't know, my lord."

Argyle stared at Rutherford like he was trying to square unbalanced ledgers. "He's not given to vice and moral weakness, is he?"

"My lord, I've heard nothing that would suggest such a thing." He knew the dark practitioners had the right to make these kinds of enquiries, but he disliked them roping him in. Not that he was eager to defend the young Mr Black, but the boy wasn't much of anything. His activities in Edinburgh to date proved boring to recount.

"Ah, some of these students at the university are like cloistered monks." Argyle appeared to be drawing to the end of his invisible accounting exercise and ending the interrogation. "They are naturally shy when it comes to the fairer sex. We were all like that to some extent once, I suppose."

He tapped the side of his sedan chair abruptly. In his baffled state, Rutherford could only step back and bow.

"I do not wish to keep you here while I pursue idle speculations, Dr Rutherford. You are most patient with my jumbled ramblings."

Rutherford made a series of protestations as the footman resumed their burden that Argyle was neither boring, confusing, nor rambling. At least, whatever the dark practitioners seemed to have planned for the hapless Joseph Black, it wasn't going to involve him.

* * *

Black found Russell in his study, sorting his papers. He hovered in the corner until Russell noticed he had company.

"What ails you, cousin?" Russell's amused expression suggested he didn't consider Black's discomfort anything serious.

"I'm invited to a Season party where a great number of ladies will be presented..." Black began, fumbling for words.

His cousin folded his arms and leaned back in his chair, splaying his legs.

"And you wish to court some of these fine ladies?" he asked, a wicked grin breaking across his face.

"No," protested Black, his rose rising to a wail. "I simply wish to...survive."

Once Russell had stopped laughing long enough to breathe, he reached onto a shelf behind him and pulled out a compact volume.

"*Rules for Conduct by a Gentleman* is as good a place to start as ever. Possession of manners is enough to win you the favour of most ladies, Joss. Look around this city and see what insulting low standard you must rise above."

His cousin made it sound a trifling matter. Black needed to endure his ribbing because there was no one else he could ask for guidance.

"You're doing well already to get an invitation to one of these affairs," Russell noted with a bit more sincerity, since he'd exhausted his initial supply of mockery and wasn't able to get more discomfort out of his naïve relative. "Who sent the invitation?"

"Lord Argyle." Black turned the book over in his hands. It felt disturbingly slim for a discourse on such a weighty, fraught topic.

Russell whistled with a look of genuine admiration. "That's impressive, Joss. Knowing it's the Argyles and their sect, yes, you'll have to tread carefully." He pinched his lower lip between his teeth, as if he wanted to say more. Instead, he looked up with a bright smile. "We can't have you showing up to the gathering in your musty scholars' robes—I might be persuaded to loan you some money for a trip to the tailors, if you promise to help in the back of the apothecary next week."

"That arrangement suits me." Part of Black's accommodation with his Russell's family came with the agreement he'd assist with the running of their apothecary shop. As long as he was left in the storeroom to prepare compounds, Black was happy to oblige.

A smaller stack of books caught Black's eyes on the way out. Russell's collection of textbooks and educational literature took up nearly four walls of the room, but his wife had eked out a shelf at knee height for her own novels. Russell teased his wife over her partiality toward sentimental novels, but Black decided to return to the study when his cousin next departed for the college.

The gentleman philosopher who was ushered into the Argyle's house bore little resemblance to a student. He stood several inches taller thanks to new heeled shoes, with his dark brown hair curled at his jawline and powdered. Russell's wife had loaned Black a thick dark ribbon to tie his queue, and thanks to Russell's recommendations, Black had acquired a navy velvet coat with gold trim around the cuffs.

Like a hawk circling a field mouse from above, Monro watched Black progress from the entrance through the dining room and into the parlour.

Colour flushed across Black's cheeks and he laughed self-consciously with most introductions, but Monro could already see the women found it endearing. Soon, there was a crowd forming around him.

It wasn't long before Argyle, as the host, strode into the room where it seemed most of the energy was gathering.

"Is that young Mr Black? Well met, sir!"

"Good evening, my lord," Black replied. The surrounding conversation faded as the ladies giggled and angled their bodies away. Everyone waited to hear what Argyle would say and do.

"This is your debut in Edinburgh society, Mr Black; as much as my daughter and her graceful companions." There was an appreciative titter, but tingled with nervousness. Black stood up slightly taller, and a silence seemed to settle over his bearing that suggested he was taking the unfolding exchange seriously.

"I would not dream of outshining the ladies on their special night," Black said firmly but with an open expression.

"But you are a celebrity in your own right now, are you not? Unless my esteemed philosopher friends are deceiving me. Do you be fooled by the finery on display tonight—I wager many guests tonight are eager to see a little of your chemical brilliance."

"In mixed company, I fear displays of my scientific expertise are rather coarse." While he had every right to be nervous at the attention on him by one of the most powerful men in Scotland, Black held his ground.

"But surely the learned Joseph Black has scientific displays that are fit for the fairer sex?" There was a greedy glint in Argyle's eyes, though he tried to keep his tone jovial. "Come on, your chemical experiments can't all be dry and tedious."

It's almost like Argyle is expecting Black to do something specific, Monro thought. Like he's trying to bait the young man into doing something he shouldn't. He'd no idea what that could be. Regardless of any hidden meaning, it would look bad if Black snubbed his host another time.

Black bowed his head.

"I wouldn't dream of subjecting the gentlewomen of Edinburgh to my nitrous fires and noxious fumes." He paused. "Perhaps a song would be more conducive?"

* * *

Monro still felt tense. The party had sated its immediate hunger for Joseph Black, who had retired to the relative calm of a sofa with two persistent young ladies. The adults in the room sensibly left them alone to sort themselves out. From the corner of the room Monro hovered, another group of gentleman partially concealing him from watchful eyes.

Margaret Monro appeared at her father's side, lips folded in on themselves.

"You don't wish to join in the sport?" Monro asked, gesturing towards the sofa.

Margaret glared. Monro knew she was too smart to be seen fawning over Black when everyone had the same idea.

"I'll leave tonight's exertion to Miss Viola Dunbar, who made the mistake of bragging to me how she would attempt to overwhelm the scholarly Mr Black. She was positively gleeful when telling me how she would lose her chaperone for said purpose."

"Well, it seems to me..." Monro peered discretely. "That Mr Black is more preoccupied with the equally charming Miss Eleanor, though he is gallantly charming them both."

Margaret looked at her father with pity.

"It is obvious that Miss Viola is the target of Mr Black's affections—by spoiling Miss Eleanor with attention, he inflames the neglected Miss Viola's ardour. Only Miss Viola is oblivious to his tricks."

No woman can make me feel as blind a fool as my own daughter can, Monro reflected with a touch of pride. It had been years since his own courtship of Isabella, and the process seemed a lot less complicated than what youths with their fans went through today. Indeed, the intensity of Miss Dunbar's fan flutters was rising to match the pulse of a hummingbird.

I miscalculated, Monro realised.

"Young men are wont to become fools in the presence of ladies," Monro commented. Margaret nodded politely, because he'd impressed this truth on her many times before. "Mr Black is doing what I do."

"What's that, father?"

"He's listening to them."

Despite his pretences, as a younger man, Monro was tongue-tied around women. But to his amazement, that increased his popularity at balls, because he never interrupted the fairer sex, giving them a cherished opportunity to lead the conversation.

Monro fiddled with his silk gloves. He wasn't good at initiating conversations with strangers, which was why reports of Cullen's gregariousness in upper society rankled him. Sensing his unease, Margaret stayed at his side until he could spot an unengaged acquaintance.

Margaret's marriage into a prominent Highland clan last year was fortuitous. She brokered no complaints about her husband Philip, who appeared an attentive spouse. The couple already had a young son.

Yet it wasn't clear Monro would arrange such a successful union before it fell into place.

Aware of his daughter's beauty and charm, Monro and Isabella agreed to delay her entrance into society for a couple of years to avoid even the pretence of competition with several dark chymists' daughters who were about her age and seeking matches from a limited pool of suitors. Margaret bore the delay with her usual calm humour, though Monro knew she harboured tender feelings for several young gentlemen who now courted dark chymist families. Isabella was anxious further delay would spoil all of Margaret's chances at a good match. Happily, her fears didn't come true.

There were a hundred such scenarios Monro had to dance his family through when it came to the dark chymists. Most of the time, he didn't notice he was doing so.

* * *

Miss Eleanor wore a musk with hints of cedar and nutmeg. Miss Viola's perfume was composed of orange blossom and peach. While both perfumes were delightful on their own, sitting between clouds of the two disorientated Black whenever he turned his head.

"My fair madam, I find only one or two things in this world more alluring than the hunt for undiscovered knowledge." Eleanor blushed, identifying herself as the recipient of his compliment.

Viola Dunbar sighed and tapped the crook of his elbow with her fan. The beauty spot at the corner of her mouth vibrated.

"You would be positively entranced, Mr Black, by my father's library...if you so cared to pay it its proper attention."

"A library, Miss Dunbar? Why I have an utmost appreciation for a finely curated library: they are things of much beauty and charm."

"And if you were desiring undiscovered, secret knowledge..." she continued, a little breathlessly. "Well, my father's library is the envy of philosophers and princes alike."

Ah, thought Black. Now I have something...

17

GLASGOW

"Joe, you did not." Cullen contrived to sound hurt. "I refuse to believe you would do such a thing."

"No young lady's reputations were harmed by my actions," Black said. "I made sure of it."

Cullen stared at the ceiling, entreating the higher powers for... something. Patience? Enlightenment?

He tried again. "That was Viola Dunbar, the daughter of Lord Douglas Dunbar, who you flirted with in a very public manner. I heard she was seen on the High Street the next morning buying a new painted fan, because she broke her old fan the night before through excessive flirting."

"An exaggeration," Black frowned. Like most young men would, he was trying not to look too pleased with himself. "I doubt her wrist was much strained on my behalf."

Black was in Glasgow four days after the society party to visit his friends and Cullen. If he thought he could get ahead of Scotland's cross-country gossip system, he was sorely mistaken.

"And what of Miss Eleanor Dunnald, who you also toyed with? Her family has no connection to the dark chymists."

"A little bit of flirting is no serious thing," Black insisted. "Providing she flirts with no more than one or two unmarried suitors, she'll sustain no damage to her reputation."

The hearth in Cullen's laboratory gave a murmur of disapproval. The candles fluttered as Cullen folded his arms.

"Joe, I can't believe you would do such a thing," Cullen repeated. This wasn't how he expected Black to behave, but it showed how corrupting Edinburgh society could be. This behaviour was a world away from the cautious student he'd taught barely two years ago.

"But it proves we were right! There is a secret library the dark chymists keep their lore. It's not a disparate collection of books, or some other method of preserving their art. It's a library."

"Yes," Cullen waved his hand. "That helps us somewhat. But I forbid you from using Miss Viola to find out more."

"I doubt she knows more than its existence," Black said, sounding neither disappointed nor relieved.

Cullen wasn't sure what he could do with this information. The dark chymists were a disparate force hundreds of miles away. With no divinity students threatening him outside his classes, and no dead noblemen, it seemed they'd won. Cullen remained in Glasgow, circumstances were fixed.

"How are Mrs Cullen and the bairns?" Black asked, adjusting his waistcoat. He'd told Cullen before that his own laboratory was far cooler than what he was used to Glasgow.

"We're all doing well, Joe. I'll pass on your warm wishes."

"Everything going well at the university?"

"Yes. I think I told you I'm teaching Medical Theory this semester as well as Chemistry. It's time-consuming, but no one is waving pitchforks under my window yet."

"What of your practice?" Black asked.

Cullen scratched his head, which was an answer in itself.

"Not as strong as I'd like. There's no shortage of merchants and journeyman, but there isn't a market for more physicians."

"Well, I think you have it easier in Glasgow; there are fewer physicians per person here than in Edinburgh, it seems."

"Yes, you're right lad," Cullen said, deciding to put a stop to the conversation before it became a debate. "I shouldn't complain."

His former pupil regarded him with a quizzical expression for a moment, then shrugged and looked away.

He'd changed a lot in such a short while.

18

EDINBURGH

Following Argyle's society gathering, Black didn't have long to wait for the dark chymists to make their next move. It came in the form of a brief invitation delivered to the Russells. He was requested for dinner at Sir Anthony's.

There was no teasing from his cousin this time.

"We might need to take that coat back to the tailors," he muttered. "I hear deep cuffs have fallen out of favour in Paris."

"I'm sure it will do," Black insisted. "I haven't seen many coats in this season's style around town yet."

Sir Anthony occupied a lavish dwelling at Reid's Court, a stone's throw from Holyrood Abbey at the foot of the Canongate. Stepping into the entrance hall, Black could be forgiven for thinking he was at the Grey's country mansion, instead of their town residence. Hundreds of candles shimmered on the walls and ceiling.

Two servants, one a Highlander, the other an African, took his umbrella and guided him into the dining room, where most of the dark chymists had already congregated. Black braced for hostile glances and frosty silence, but the men beamed at him.

"You found us, Mr Black!" Sir Anthony was on his feet before Black could bow. "Excellent. No, please sit down and let us bring the drinks to you."

Black found himself in the middle of the group of eight men and their spouses, and was immediately beset by enquiries after his health and studies.

Sir Anthony wafted the claret under his nose. "We thought it's about time we sit down with you and talk, gentleman to gentleman. You expect to finish your studies this May, do you not?"

Black couldn't avoid thinking that they chose to seat him down and treat him as a perceived equal after they'd thrown their daughters on him in a failed seduction attempt. It seemed churlish to point that out, though.

He was treated to a generous meal of venison, fish pies and soups, with the nobles charming him in a way that didn't feel heavy-handed enough to make him uncomfortable or for their display to seem contrived. Once their wives were dismissed to the parlour, Argyle opened another bottle of port with a meaningful air, signifying the shift in conversation to more serious concerns. Black noticed Argyle's cuffs were a third the length of the other men in the room.

All the servants made their way out; only Octavius remained. He settled down on a chair beside the door and turned away from the proceedings.

"Loyalty can be a complicated thing, Mr Black." Argyle mused as he handed Black a full glass. "Sometimes we get tugged this way and that by conflicting interests, like a moored boat in a storm. It's understandable that we might get confused about where our loyalties should point."

"A man must adapt to his circumstances," Black said. "And make sure he is not prioritising old and meaningless ties over current realities."

"You are recognised in Edinburgh as a practical man," Sir Anthony said, nodding with a measure of appreciation.

Black had tuned out all of today's lectures, considering what the dark chymists would say to him and how he should respond. While he wasn't sure how they'd couch their intentions, he wasn't surprised by what was being said. "Truth be told, I believe man should keep his own counsel first, and let others conduct their business in the manner they see fit."

"But surely you agree that strong and public loyalty offers its own rewards?" Argyle asked, more intrigued than offended.

"To some I'm sure it does," Black noted, lowering his head to take another sip of port. "I do my best to live without vanities or pretensions, which can easily slip into vice. Quiet dedication is all a man should seek."

Countless times he'd caught his tongue mid-flight, about to ask Monro about the dark chymists, or respond to his hints towards them. But he'd always refrained, because he didn't want word to get out that he was curious about them. Curiosity would attract them as quickly as hostility.

It was a gamble. Black thought that men like Sandy could survive in Edinburgh by professing neutrality and staying out of city politics. But if Sandy had made a secret deal he didn't know about, then he was on dangerous ground.

"It pains me to think you are friendless in this town," Argyle said. "Do you maintain warm relations with Dr Cullen at least? I hear Lord Rothsay was eager to make your acquaintance."

Lord Rothsay was a Town Council loyalist.

"I have great affection for Dr Cullen, but we don't correspond as often as we used to," Black said. "We get caught up in our own lives, as is often the case. I met Lord Rothsay once last winter, but I didn't realise he particularly desired my company."

Subtle nods were exchanged around the table. If Black affected disinterest in the dark chymists, they wanted to assess how close he remained to his former professor or rival factions within Edinburgh.

The dark chymists didn't seem surprised to hear him admit

he'd not written to Cullen often. Perhaps this was information they already held.

There was no change in the room's temperature. Sir Anthony offered to refill Black's glass, Black declined. While glasses kept being emptied, none of the dark chymists were drinking heavily.

When he was excluded from the conversation for a brief second, Black's gaze wandered around the dimly lit room.

"Sir Anthony? That's an incredible chinoiserie vase. I've never seen the like."

The background conversations trailed off.

"I agree," was all Sir Anthony said.

Black felt attention focused on him with intensity for the first time that evening.

"Did you import it directly from China?" he asked.

"No, it was made in Shropshire at my request. I hope that doesn't disappoint you. Would you like to inspect it?"

Notes of conversation drifted back as Black approached the vase. He was not mistaken: it stood as tall as him.

"Are you a chinoiserie collector, Mr Black?"

"One of my brothers has dabbled," Black said vaguely. There was something unnatural about the vase, beyond its size.

Why was the air filling with the taste of phlogiston?

He stood in front of the vassal, with Sir Anthony at his side. There was no mistaking it now—phlogiston was emanating from the vassal.

"I should clarify my interest before I embarrass myself. I've worked closely with several potters to create laboratory equipment for my research and am presenting corresponding with a trader in London regarding a furnace, given how inadequate Dr Plummer's is when it comes to temperature control. I'm not much of an art collector, but I do wonder how you could manufacture such a large vassal." Rising on the balls of his feet, Black glanced inside the vase, which didn't have a lid. "Is that soil to help the vassal stay upright? How curious."

Sir Anthony was regarding Black with a strange expression. Then he beckoned him back towards the table.

"Now I see why you're interested. Fear not, Mr Black. I won't engage you in any unwanted conversation about ceramic fashion trends. But I think there will be points about my vassal I can raise your interest with."

Here was the warning. The dark chymists held knowledge Black lacked. But there was also an invitation: did he want to learn more?

"Did you and Dr Cullen read the works on phlogiston by Dr Stahl? Very thought-provoking."

"I imagine all self-proclaimed philosophers in Britain have read Stahl's works," Black said confidently. "Very few doubt the existence of phlogiston."

"Quite, but the question is of application," grinned Sir Anthony.

These men knew what Cullen knew. But since their understanding of the nervous system was based upon the flawed Boerhaavian model, they wouldn't think Man capable of harnessing phlogiston through his bodily functions. They had no reason to take Cullen's theories of the nervous system seriously—all theory, never an allusion towards application—or draw any conclusions about his hidden doctrine.

At least, Black sorely hoped this was the truth. Feeling the claret buzz through him, he had to appear under-informed.

"I'm embarrassed to admit, but I fear I'm overlooking something obvious. What applications are you concerned with?"

"Well, that vassal you so graciously complimented me on, Mr Black. What if I told you that thanks to the minerals stored within it, this vassal could hold large quantities of phlogiston?"

"That would be incredible," Black blinked. "Is that an application in and of itself?" He had to pretend he didn't know what uses of phlogiston existed.

"Well, it would be of greater use if it could store more phlogiston for longer, or perhaps shrink to fit on a desk without diminishing its storage capacity. It is an invention waiting for an application, I'm afraid. It piques your curiosity, does it not? Perhaps you wish to devote time to developing such improvements?"

"Oh, a wretched scholar such as myself could never give such an important project the intellect and resources it deserves." Black said.

"If it's a question of resources..."

"I meant, unfortunately, my time."

"The most valuable resource of all." Argyle finished. "And so distressingly finite."

"I fear I'm the wrong philosopher for such a task," Black sighed. "It's true that under Dr Cullen's tutelage we explored the properties of coolants, but my research has spilled in so many directions since then it's been impossible for me to follow the field. Given how contested the theories of heat and cooling remain, I've resigned myself to having fallen too far behind current wisdom to keep up." This was a lie, and Black made a mental note to cover his tracks regarding ongoing heat investigations for future security.

"You sound like every other overworked young scholar who escapes the College environs," Sir Anthony laughed. "But I wonder if you've read the latest papers from the Royal Society in London concerning Linnaeus' updated taxonomy of man? Do you incline towards the monogenist or a polygenist stance?"

Black's eye was instantly drawn to Octavius in the corner, who was watching the conversation with disinterest. But he was no longer staring into the middle distance.

"Come on Anthony," Argyle laughed. "The polygenist position is wholly discredited. No one these days believes Africans descended from anyone other than Adam and Eve. The science doesn't support it." He looked at Black apologetically.

Avoiding Octavius' eye, Black shook his head. "No," he said, his voice coming out quieter than he expected. "I'm not familiar with those arguments."

Sir Anthony shrugged; a man deprived of one stimulating after-dinner conversation, but for whom many other topics were available. "They told me you're a philosopher who likes to measure and categorise," he insisted one last time. "In fact, you seem compelled to account for everything."

"A man's measurements are only as good as his instruments and the steadiness of his hand," Black sighed. "That is where I too fall short of perfection."

The conversation gradually wound down from there, though it took the best part of an hour before the other men readied to depart and collected their wives.

"It has been a most pleasant evening making your acquaintance, Mr Black." Argyle bowed stiffly. "I wish you success with your studies."

And so Black was left to trudge up the Canongate back within the city walls. Had he proved a more agreeable guest, he was sure the men would have offered him the use of their sedan chair to speed his journey home.

Black was smart enough to know his limitations. If he professed fealty to the dark chymists, it would be a race against time to see who could take advantage of whom first. Only knowing a fraction of their capabilities, he didn't think he could win that dash. He suspected Cullen would make the same choice he did, albeit in less diplomatic terms.

* * *

The dark chymists left him alone after that, but Black barely noticed their snub. It wasn't that he dived into his final year research, so much as his research rose like a wave and swallowed him whole.

Since he was composing a medical dissertation rather than a chemistry one, Black had finally admitted he'd need to spend some time justifying his magnesia alba investigations to physicians. Hence approaching Monro to ask about its use in treating digestive complaints. Far from dismissing his questions, the professor offered him freedom of his library to research the topic fully.

It was proving a long evening. Monro's cat kept lying on his opened book. Then she smacked his quill onto the floor.

"I hear Dr Plummer wishes to use you as his teaching assistant again next term," Monro remarked, sipping his tea.

Black had heard the same, so he acted nonchalant. "I'm happy to assist him, however I may." He didn't really want another distraction from writing his dissertation, but this one seemed it might pay off.

"You have a fine grasp of Latin and elegant manner of speaking. I was quite impressed with your latest Medical Society speech," Monro commented. "You will make a good lecturer."

"Thank you, professor." Black was immune to this kind of flattery by now. "I think I'd prefer to lecture in English, though."

He felt some trepidation saying this, but it was true.

"It's your own decision, of course." Monro stretched his legs.

"I hope you won't find this question impudent, professor...but when did you stop lecturing in Latin?"

Monro set his saucer down. "I never started." Sensing Black's confusion, he closed his book. "How I came to lecture anatomy in such an unconventional style is an amusing story, though I did not think so at the time.

"We credit my father, Dr John Monro, with laying the foundation for the Edinburgh School of Medicine, though in his lifetime it was little more than a disparate set of enterprising lecturers. Recognising my talent, and natural delight in the subject, my father spared no expense in supporting my medical training. I trained in Leiden and Paris and by the time I was twenty-one, I'd sent several anatomical preparations to my father in Edinburgh. My father joked that during those years abroad, he was more likely to receive a skeleton from me than a letter."

"My father would complain I suffer from a similar failing," Black admitted.

Something flashed in Monro's eyes, but then the sentiment was gone and he settled back into his story.

"By the time I returned to Edinburgh, my father had laid the groundwork for my appointment as professor of anatomy within the Incorporation of Surgeons. I could not ask for a more supportive and encouraging parent; he never withheld his delight at my educational progress and achievements."

Monro looked at Black, perhaps to see if his audience could claim a similar relationship to his father. When Black said nothing, Monro continued.

"At the age of twenty-two, I was scheduled to deliver my first course of anatomy to the surgeons. As was expected of lecturers at that time, I laboured over a Latin discourse for several weeks prior, concerning the union of Boerhaavian and Hippocrenian medical theories. Every sentence I revised into its Platonic ideal.

"Unbeknownst to me, my father, in his excitement, had sung my praises to not only the Incorporation of Surgeons, but the entire body of the College of Physicians and the university. Such was his praise the entirety of all three learning bodies, from student to President, resolved to attend my first lecture and hear this reborn Hippocrates speak.

"You can picture the ensuing tableau: this young anatomist expected an audience of twenty sleepy apprentices, only to enter a room crowded with over a hundred eager souls, among them the most august physicians and surgeons in the country. Seeing me, they erupted into lusty cheers.

"I was terrified. I'd recited my discourse a hundred times that week, committing it to memory as was custom...only for my memory to desert me completely. The room was so poorly lit that I couldn't read my terrible notes. The only thing I could discern in the clamour was my father's beaming face in the front row."

Black shuddered. What Monro described resembled his own nightmares, the only difference being that in his dream-state he often arrived to deliver his first lecture having forgotten to don his breeches.

Savouring the visceral reactions he was provoking in Black, Monro smiled. "Fortunately, my adoring father had set my anatomical preparations in the lecture room for the audience to admire. Not knowing what else to do, I turned to my specimens and began telling the audience about them; discussing their significance and what osteological insights they provided. I set out merely to buy time and calm my mind long enough for the salient points of my discourse to creep back into my head, but seeing how engaged even the president of the Surgeons was with my demonstrations, I quietly abandoned the idea and continued lecturing in the same manner for another hour.

"I couldn't have told you what language was coming out of my mouth during those initial five minutes: could have been Russian or Portuguese for all I knew—not that I can speak either tongue. But in fact it was English.

"I remember clearly once I realised I'd reached the end of my first lecture, I finally dared peek to where my father was sitting. Tears were rolling down his face. I've never seen him so proud." Monro trailed off.

Black resolved to ask Cullen when Leechman and his colleagues began to lecture in English at Glasgow, and if they were aware that Monro had been delivering anatomy lectures in English without notes since 1719.

"And no one considered your lecture style...peculiar?" Black asked carefully, reluctant to draw Monro's attention towards Cullen.

Monro laughed. "Why would they? I taught the material, did I not?"

If Monro didn't see the parallel between his teaching style and the despised Cullen's, Black wouldn't point it out and risk his wrath. Instead, he shrugged, as if he already regretted asking such a stupid question.

19

GLASGOW

Cullen didn't realise a student was in his laboratory until the boy edged next to him.

"Merciful heavens, James!" Cullen exclaimed, almost dropping his quill in shock. "How long have you been standing there?"

"I'm not sure," James replied, staring at his feet. "I didn't mean to startle you, professor."

"Think nothing of it." Cullen pushed back his chair. "I'll consider this my salutary reminder not to squint at papers for too long. What can I do for you?"

James, the Brummie lad, might be angling after an assistantship. He was a solitary figure, preferring to keep to his own company rather than associate his boisterous fellow students. But he liked hanging around Cullen's laboratory, listening to Cullen talk about his studies and travels. In that case, he didn't have any reason for appearing, aside from loneliness.

"It's not important..."

"Well, the unimportant questions are often the most intriguing." Cullen motioned for James to sit. Depending on what he was curious about, Cullen might be able to give the boy a book to consult: with him sitting in the corner, he'd be able to get back to his letters.

Surprisingly, a linen bleaching process he suggested to Hugh last year still held merit. He'd ran a couple of experiments and found an effective bleaching mixture. As Hugh pointed out, the idea still wasn't scaleable, but they'd expended a lot of ink thinking about ways to hone the process to work in an industrial setting.

This winter his friend sounded so melancholy—Cullen couldn't imagine Hugh's barely hospitable estate outside Arbroath held much comfort during those cold months, so he was pleased how excited he sounded about the optimal layout of a linen bleaching works.

But this wasn't an *urgent* correspondence. He could afford to indulge a lonely student.

"You said something in class about aether, then you got interrupted and never finished the point. I, um, just wanted to know more."

"Ah." Cullen took a deep breath. "That."

It was good James and the rest of the class thought he'd been interrupted, or distracted. Better than them knowing he'd lost his nerve and changed the subject.

"You said the nervous system was operated by a kind of aethereal, elastic fluid," James persisted. "Then you started to say that there were other kinds of aether..."

"I did," Cullen conceded. His brain raced. How was he going to explain this away?

Maybe James mistook his professor's sudden reticence for forgetfulness, because he ploughed on.

"I've never heard of aether, you see, and I wondered if I'd misunderstood something, because I wasn't sure what other kinds exist. You haven't discussed nervous fluid in those terms before in class, I don't think—unless it was the Thursday on the second week in November when I was late to class because I got lost looking for the library..."

"No, James. You're right—I haven't talked about nervous system aether in class before." If Cullen didn't interrupt, James would probably end up recounting every class he attended with Cullen and every mention of the nervous system. He had a frightening memory. "My teachings on the nervous system are a little controversial."

That was true...up to a point. The tension between Cullen and the medical establishment was multi-layered: the first layer of contention was that Cullen disagreed with Boerhaave's characterisation of the brain as a gland dripping out nervous fluid.

While the most amiable physician might accept Cullen could differ from accepted theoretical norms and teach his own opinions, the unavoidable contention was when Cullen couldn't seem to shut up about the nervous system. Claiming all maladies and humoral imbalances could be traced back to the nervous system was the truly heretical view.

James still sat there, mild bemusement on his face.

The boy was a terrier when it came to topics that piqued his interest: he'd lock his jaws around something and shake it, refusing to let go. Cullen couldn't wave him away. Nothing short of an explosion in this room would distract him from the subject of aether, and even then it'd only be temporary.

Cullen should never have mentioned 'aether' in the classroom, even as an aside. There was always a student like James eager to pick over his every sentence.

He thought of Black, hammering away at his medical dissertation in Edinburgh. A few years ago, he feared he was sending the young man to his death. Instead, Black thrived. The dark chymists hadn't sunk their claws into him, nor had he done anything to attract their suspicion.

One the Philosophical Society attendees recently enquired after Black, and Cullen realised it had been ages since he'd heard Black described in the context of being Cullen's former student. The connection between them had faded. There was no space to talk about Cullen in the context of Black's latest experimental findings: a new component of air, and the implication that rather than being an element in itself, air was made of several elements.

But what struck Cullen the most: Black never appeared afraid. Cullen envied his courage and quiet conviction.

James opened his mouth.

Cullen raised his hand.

"My theory of the nervous system begins with Newton's universal aether," he began. James settled back into his chair, mollified with knowledge, in comfortable oblivion to the significance of what Cullen was telling him. "Sir Isaac Newton believed aether to be the underlying component of light, heat, and magnetism. Dr Benjamin Franklin's electricity can be classified as another aethereal component."

"So they are all different kinds of aether?" James stared intently at Cullen, loathe to let his state of ignorance continue a moment longer than necessary.

"In a sense," Cullen sighed heavily. He took a breath. "It's more accurate to view them as interconnected flavours of the same universal fluid."

"Heat and light are part of the same thing." James looked at the fire and nodded. "Flames are bright *and* hot."

"You're right, lad."

James nodded again. He tapped the chair arm, departing into his head in search of his next question.

Cullen's heart was pounding, but more from relief than fear.

Talking about the link between light, heat and electricity was safe. The dangerous part was when an eternal questioner like James asked if this meant Man's nervous system was *also* connected to light and heat, and if meant the nervous system had the power to influence its interconnected influences.

Because that was the heart of Cullen's secret.

20

EDINBURGH

He was taking a terrifying leap into the unknown, but what choice did Black have? Passively searching for information about the source of the dark chemists' power had yielded a few clues, but he had so little to show for his three years in Edinburgh. And now that he'd formally declined to align himself with them, Black suspected any casual enquiries would come to naught.

This was why he'd taken to following the dark chymists ringleaders on their dealings around the city. It was boring, exhausting work—they had sedan chairs, he had to walk—but it revealed a few interesting patterns.

There was a tenement building at the southern edge of the Lawnmarket, near St Giles, where the dark chymists often headed to. The building was rumoured to contain an apartment owned by Argyle, but it wasn't his main abode. Nor did he appear to rent it out: there was never candlelight to be seen on that floor after dark.

Could this be where the dark chymists kept their texts?

Cullen wasn't much use. When Black visited Glasgow last August, he seemed uninterested in finding the library, which they'd taken to calling Babylon.

"I don't think we can stop them, Joe. They're a blight on society, but they outnumber us."

Black tried to convince Cullen otherwise, but there was no persuading him. He seemed to have abandoned his desire to move to Edinburgh, even though he seemed stifled in Glasgow. While he'd obtained the grudging respect of many, no one dared to praise him in Edinburgh.

Now the Season was almost at its end. In a few weeks, the first nobles would migrate back to the countryside for the summer, weather permitting. The dark chymists' presence in Edinburgh would become more erratic. Black would also have received his doctorate by then, if he didn't squander his chances.

The timing pressure convinced him he'd need to do more than watch the comings and goings in this particular tenement. He'd have to attempt to get closer.

Which was why when he saw Argyle and Octavius head to the tenement at what was close to a regular time, Black decided to set aside his coffee and follow them. He'd never observed more than one dark chymist at a time go into the tenement, and it seemed safe to presume that wouldn't happen this time.

He was far enough behind that they wouldn't notice him cross the street and enter the stairwell when they were already two or three floors up.

Black jogged up the final turn of stairs. He assumed he'd be confronted with a locked door and be forced to listen through the keyhole, but gave the handle a gentle press, anyway. To his surprise, the handle yielded.

He told himself he'd just peer through the opened door and take in what he could. However, when Black found himself staring into a semi-dark, silent apartment, he decided a step or two inside would be ok. He could still escape at a moment's notice.

It didn't occur to Black to be frightened. He'd followed Argyle into what was otherwise an empty, abandoned apartment. The old man would be no match for him. Not when he fingered Russell's pistol in his pocket.

Black took a few steps into the main room, breathing in the dusty air. He could hear someone walking about on the floor above, as well as voices from further down the stairwell, a joke exchanged in passing. The cool air here reminded him of the college library.

Then a strange note filled his ears. It came from a side room, though the noise quickly expanded to fill the place. Black thought it was a song, but the pitch increased and took on a ringing quality no human voice could achieve.

Finally wrestling the pistol out of his coat, Black took a few tentative steps forward. No one was in the main room—in fact, it was as sparse as a storage room, with no touches of human occupation.

The noise grew and trembled in a way that made Black think whatever it accompanied was reaching its climax. He hurried forward, abandoning caution. Whatever this was, he could ill afford to miss it.

Peering around the corner into the next room, Black saw Argyle standing in front of a man-sized mirror. The mirror's surface shone as if the room was filled with ten chandeliers, which was impossible because there were no lit candles in either room. Next to the mirror stood a pot of equal height. Was Black imagining it or did the pot—painted with a blue and white Oriental fresco—glow?

He'd crept close enough to inhale the scent of phlogiston, acrid in his mouth. While he thought this wasn't the same phlogiston vassal he'd seen at Argyle's dinner party—the decoration was slightly different—he had no doubt that's what he was witnessing in action. He couldn't tell if the noise was coming from the vassal or the mirror.

Regarding himself in the mirror as one would regard a Rocaille fresco, Argyle nodded to himself and stepped forward.

Wait, had he just confused a mirror for a door? Black blinked in confusion as Argyle vanished through the mirror. Even though Black knew intellectually what the dark chymists could accomplish with their arts, his brain still struggled to make sense of what his eyes were telling him, scouring the surroundings for proof of an illusion.

He was about to hurry forward and inspect the mirror from the front when another figure stepped into Black's line of sight.

Black had convinced himself there was no one else in the side room—he'd heard no one—so it was another shock to see Argyle's African footman approach the mirror and stand in front of it. The ringing noise was threatening to split Black's eardrum, taking on more discordant notes and wavers.

The footman was going to step forward and follow Argyle, and Black rocked forward on his feet in anticipation of rushing after them both, when the footman's head snapped around and his eyes locked on Black's.

Black knew he was holding something in his hand, but momentarily forgot it was a loaded pistol. The two men stared at each other for what seemed like several minutes. The African didn't look surprised to find Black watching them. Nor was he afraid or angry.

The footman shook his head imperceptibly at Black.

Don't, is what he seemed to be warning him.

Then he reached out to the wall beside the mirror and traced several rapid criss-crossing lines onto the wooden panel. There were smudged charcoal lines under his finger looking like they'd been there a while. Then the charcoal smudges burst with a blue light, revealing a complex set of circles and lines.

Black was so focused on the glowing lines and their symmetries that it took him a second to notice the African had stepped through the mirror and the ringing noise had stopped.

Emptiness settled on the apartment, and the blue light slowly faded like embers in a dying hearth.

Unsure on his feet, Black craned as far forward as he dared into what was a small room with nothing in it aside from the mirror and clay pot. The mirror was no longer glowing with phantom candles. It now reflected the dusty corner of the room where the footman had been standing.

This had to be the dark chemist's passageway to their secret library. Black couldn't believe how easily he'd uncovered it. He shouldn't remain here, though—the footman had seen him, and there was recognition in his eyes. If he didn't know his name, he'd be able to identify Black to his master on the street. Black would have to send a letter to Cullen tomorrow morning, telling him what'd he seen...

Black was so engrossed in his thoughts, he didn't even notice the blue light from the markings on the wall finally vanish.

Instead, Black turned back towards the door, only for it to have swung closed as he watched Argyle and his footman vanish.

Black tugged the handle. It didn't move.

He jerked the door, thinking it was wedged—though it let him through easily enough—but it wouldn't budge. The door felt locked. Had someone locked the door from outside?

As it transpired, Black didn't have time to panic at the locked door, because an unearthly crash emanating from the building itself overturned his entire world of thoughts.

The floor lurched. Violent jerks interspersed with a continuous rumble beating through the walls and floors.

Black tugged at the door with both hands, the pistol clattering to the floor and skittering as if kicked. The door was immovable. He pounded at it, yelling, but his voice could hardly be heard above the cacophony coming from the building.

It was no use trying to get through that door.

Black paced the parlour, torn between trying to determine where the quakes were coming from and looking to see if the perpetrator was still in the two-room apartment. Tarnished silverware crashed off the shelves; a portrait above the fireplace dropped and cracked. Muffled screams and cries percolated from all sides as inhabitants were shaken awake.

The violent jerks to the fabric of the building weren't letting up, Black realised. In fact, the spasms were coming faster and stronger. He froze in the middle of the room. This wasn't the dark chymists taunting him. This was calculated destruction. The floor bucked, and he stumbled off balance. There were louder, deeper cracks underneath the now-incessant rattles. Whatever dark force set in motion, it was intending to destroy the building.

Black let out an angry, frustrated whimper, unable to summon the necessary thoughts into his head to act. He was trapped five floors off the ground. The shrieks and slam of bodies were now concentrated to his left—the stairwell was jammed with panicked tenants and he doubted they had more than minutes before the building was ripped from its foundations. Even if he could tear the door off its hinges, the stairwell was blocked.

All choices he could muster amounted to certain death. Black turned away from the door. For a moment the noise of crashes and shattering household objects dimmed to nothing, leaving an eerie calm that finally allowed enough thoughts to marshal in his head to come to a decision.

Pushing his feet into the rug and tightening his quadriceps muscles, Black extended an arm towards the window. A blast of phlogiston blew the remaining shards of glass and wooden frames out over the High Street. Black didn't wait for his brain to confirm this, though, he just ran.

No sooner had he started moving than the deepest groan of all rose from the building, drowning out the human wails behind him. Black barely noticed, but he could feel the floor tilt under him as his feet landed, leaving him skidding for balance. Fortunately, by this point, he had enough momentum to keep accelerating.

Black wished his brain worked right now, that he was capable of full cognition. This option also looked like certain death.

Almost.

At least this death came with a slight delay compared with the alternatives. And who knows, he may think of something on the way down.

Black dived out the fifth storey window just as entire the tenement building collapsed.

In the end, it wasn't a plan or idea that saved him: it was his automatic reflex.

As the cobblestones filled his line of sight, Black reached out his hands. A continuous barrage of phlogiston hit the street. The force with which it bounced back against the road was enough to slow Black's fall. The shockwaves from the collapsed building smacked him across the street.

He wasn't sure if he passed out or not. Black found himself lying in the street, dirt and blood oozing out of him. After a few minutes, he realised the street wasn't actually quiet: all sounds were muffled. His body started crawling, once it occurred to Black he could move. The skin on his palms was shredded and raw, perhaps from the fall, perhaps from all the phlogiston he discharged though them. Black felt disconnected from his body: there was a lot of pain, but it didn't seem to belong to him.

A lot of people filled the High Street, running towards the remains of the tenement building. No one noticed him in the dusk, or cared to look closely. Black's head and arms bumped into the wall on the other side of the street, so he stopped trying to crawl.

He'd just rest here awhile.

Evening gave way to nightfall. Bonfires fuelled by debris from the fallen building were lit in the street to give the rescuers some visibility as they dug into the mound of timber and stone where a six-storey tenement once was. Neighbours stood around in useless vigil. Sobs and curses punctuated the night air. A row of bodies was already forming down the slope, neatly ordered. In the dim light, Black couldn't tell if pickpockets or physicians ministered to them.

The collective tragedy unfolding outside their windows distracted many High Street residents from their nightly chamberpot disposal. Still, this close to the ground, Black could smell nothing but excrement and urine. He only noticed the smell now, after what must have been hours lying in a stupor.

After getting out of harm's way, Black had lain in the street, curled under a windowsill overlooking the rubble. The pain took its time re-filling his body, but now he was fully present in the fetid street, watching dead bodies drawn out by torchlight and dropped into the effluence since there was nowhere else for them to go. His thoughts hadn't really joined together, but inarticulate emotions coursed through him.

I should have died.

Where is Dr Cullen?

I want my father.

Why am I alive?

Why are they all dead?

None of this made sense. He'd survived and entire families had perished.

Someone was shivering. He supposed that must be him. He didn't know if it was cold or not, but he supposed he was unlikely to be warm.

Black wondered if he could lie here forever. Let the world keep spinning, night return to day, and just remain inside himself, invisible to the city. No one was looking in his direction, and it was too dark to make him out in the shadows.

Cullen would know what to do. Why did he have to be in Glasgow?

Black decided that he needed the comfort of the Russells more than he needed invisibility. The shock had loosened its grip on his mind enough for him to contemplate standing. It took an eternity to scrabble up the wall and secure his feet under him, and Black was surprised to see it wasn't already morning when looked up at the High Street.

A man standing over the mangled bodies could have been Monro, though Black didn't trust his eyes. Nor did he care. Maybe he wanted to be alone after all.

So he continued his slow trudge downhill. The High Street pyres faded into the blackness of the city.

21

EDINBURGH

In Rutherford's next encounter with the dark practitioners—attending to Sir Anthony's gout, which was flashing up again with the changing weather—he could tell there was an unpleasant undercurrent. The servants avoided eye contact, and his patient spent most of the encounter giving monosyllable responses.

"I would keep your wits about you over the next couple of days," Sir Anthony told him as he was preparing to depart. "There is a bit of unfortunate business we need to focus on, and I'd hate for you to get caught up in it."

"Thank you for telling me," Rutherford said carefully. "I will limit my engagements about town."

He thought he knew what would happen. Monro and he had conferred and pieced together what little they knew to determine Lord Dunbar had fallen from the lordship's graces. It wasn't clear what the cause of this estrangement was—Monro thought secrets were spilled—but Rutherford imagined Holm was sharpening his knives.

"You think they'll come to bloodshed?" Monro asked when they reconvened in his apartment.

After the murder of Don Bennett, Rutherford always found

himself on the pessimistic side when contemplating what the dark practitioners were capable of.

"Nine times out of ten, we don't know what Lord Argyle thinks," he argued. "When they let a note of displeasure slip, it's because they don't feel the need to hide it for much longer."

Monro remained skeptical. "Lord Dunbar sits on the Town Council. Would they really sacrifice their majority?"

"If they considered him enough of a liability? Of course they would. They could force a replacement in without much delay," Rutherford maintained. "They'd only wait a month and a half to get them re-elected. That's when the Council next meets." It seemed to go against the men's instincts for political control, but of course, he only knew a fraction of what they perceived to be at stake.

"The chaos of the Lawnmarket tenement collapse might be good cover for such activities," Monro conceded after a moment's reflection.

Everyone was on edge after the building collapse. Even unflappable Lord Argyle appeared snappish.

While the thought of more slaughter terrified him, Rutherford always hoped they'd suffer casualties in return. They were at their most deadly, but engaging in violence was paradoxically when the dark practitioners seemed the most vulnerable.

* * *

Black didn't know if rage was overcoming his senses, or he really had a shot at finding his target here tonight. He'd only seen him in this tavern once, several years ago. But he had no better ideas, and couldn't concentrate on anything else until he had this conversation. Sure enough, upon descending into the tavern cellar at a similar hour to when he first came in, the corner table was occupied by the same set of servants. He marched over and coughed.

As one, they paused their card game. Octavius nodded to the other African men and rose.

He followed Black for a few paces between the tables, then stopped.

"We need to speak outside."

"No," Octavius replied calmly. "We will speak here."

Octavius' fellow-servants remained seating, but they hadn't resumed their card game. At least one of them was watching Black. Over the clamour of the other tables, Black could hear their silence.

Black recognised Octavius' calculation, and the desire for many eyes on the confrontation. After all, Black wasn't trying to hide his anger. Without witnesses, Black could claim anything he wanted against the African. That wasn't his primary intention, but he didn't want the whole tavern to see him losing his composure against a servant.

They were still pulling bodies out of the Lawnmarket rubble. People who'd visited the site—Black was not one of them—postulated the search would continue into next week. If he appeared shaken and not himself, no one at the university commented upon it.

He could grab Octavius and force him outside, but he suspected his friends would be quick to rush over as soon as he turned physical, even if their involvement made the situation worse for all of them instead of one.

He couldn't let Octavius distract him. "I saw you. I watched your sigil bring down the tenement. Do you even know how many innocent people died?"

"Thirty-two perished instantly," Octavius replied in a level voice. "Five more succumbed to injuries later. Of course I know."

"You don't sound particularly remorseful."

"Indeed. The greatest minds of this age debate the humanity of Africans. They wonder if some exceptional Africans—with nurture in more civilised climates from as early an age as possible—

could attain the full emotional spectrum Europeans enjoy. Am I even capable of remorse for the blood staining my hands? Would a dog feel remorse if its master bade it do the same?"

"You choose to make the mark," Black insisted. "Even though your master wasn't watching." He fought to keep his voice low, so they couldn't be overheard.

"I feel as much remorse as you do, Dr Black. For you followed us into the crowded building and uncovered our secret. You opened a door I closed, you entered a room you were not invited into. Would any deaths have happened if you stayed away?"

Anger surged through Black. How dare this footman make such remarks?

He stepped away from Octavius. Phlogiston was rushing through his nervous system, and he didn't like how close to his skin it felt. He wasn't sure he could control it.

"It would be wrong to kick a dog for the sins of its master," Black said slowly. "But I don't think that little of you." He sensed some remorse within the footman—not as much as was proper— but he understood the consequences of his actions.

"Lord Argyle told me the sigil was for locking the apartment door. Nothing more, nothing less. I don't expect you to believe me, and I have no wish to debate the plausibility or believability of such a remark." A few tavern patrons were watching the pair, but with nothing more than bored curiosity. Black couldn't make it look like a fight was about to ensue.

"That's the sign of a compelling lie," Black said. "It contains a large proportion of truth." He focussed on his breathing, on the feel of cloth against his skin, the press of his right shoe into his small toe.

Taking out his rage on this miserable wretch wouldn't achieve anything productive. Lord Argyle could obtain as many servants as he wished, and instruct them to commit as many atrocities as he saw fit.

"Although it turns out locking the door was the one thing it didn't do." Octavius noted.

Violence against the perpetrator couldn't raise the dead.

"Lord Argyle knew I was following you?"

Octavius shock his head. "We both knew someone followed us. I told him I glimpsed the pursuer in the room, but his face was concealed by a hat and cloak."

"Why?" Black stepped closer, curious. "There's no benefit to you from withholding that information." He assumed Octavius failed to recognise him, which was why he'd not been apprehended afterwards.

"That it was an individual in the employ of the medical faculty was already suspected," Octavius said. "I keep many secrets on behalf of Lord Argyle, but it's rare I can keep a secret of my own."

A form of resistance and revenge, however small.

"I appreciate it," Black said, aware he sounded petulant. "Though I don't imagine you thought I'd be alive to thank you."

Octavius tilted his head. "Memory can be a confusing mistress. The trespasser's likeliness could have returned to me at a later time if circumstances encouraged it. When I saw you walking down the Cowgate a few days later, I decided to avoid such an eventuality."

Octavius believed his sigil failed to lock the door. That's how he reasoned Black escaped unscathed. Of course Octavius wouldn't tell his master that Black escaped, because the fault would be blamed on him for drawing the sigil wrong.

"How will the dark chymists access their library now they've destroyed the entranceway?" he asked. Whatever motivation Octavius had for withholding his identity from Argyle, he could change his mind. Believing Black posed a threat to his life might be enough incentive.

"There is more than one way. Paths can be created. You seem like an intelligent man, Dr Black."

That the only entrance to Babylon was destroyed would be too much to hope for. It didn't stop Black from feeling a flush of disappointment.

"And you seem intelligent enough to know where those entrances are."

Octavius stepped to the side.

"I would not trust the word of an African, Dr Black. We are both child-like fools and unspeakably devious. Neither is a good receptacle for European secrets."

He was still in the service of Argyle, so it was unlikely Octavius knew nothing. But rushing after the dark chymists led to tragedy and ruin. Who knows what new traps the dark chymists had set, especially now they'd sprung one of them?

"I beg you to excuse me, Dr Black. It was my turn to deal, and I fear they're waiting for me instead of playing on." Octavius didn't look ruffled. When he returned to his game, he wouldn't be looking over his shoulder after Black.

"That makes them particularly honourable friends," Black said, stepping back.

"More so than most," Octavius agreed.

22

EDINBURGH

"**Y**ou don't need me standing over you as you prepare these solutions?" Plummer tapped the list with chubby fingers. "You remember how they're all made?"

Black barely needed to glance at the list for confirmation. "Yes, professor."

He'd had a long day, and was ready to be left alone. Doing mindless preparation of chemicals for Plummer's lectures kept the worst of his moods at bay.

"Good." Plummer returned to his desk and picked up his coat. "I'll leave you to it. Honestly, I have a headache coming on and can't have got enough sleep last night. The perks of old age. If you need me, I'll be at home."

"Of course." Black watched Plummer fumble with his coat buttons. "I hope it's not a serious illness, professor." Plummer was usually jovial and sanguine—in the years Black had been in Edinburgh, he couldn't recall the chemistry professor being laid low by illness.

Plummer waved his hand in dismissal of his student's fussing. He seemed to struggle with his overcoat buttons, but headed towards the door without looking back at Black.

Black kept watching. Plummer's breathing sounded strained. Black felt alarm bells ringing, though it wasn't clear what he should be worrying about.

Then Plummer appeared to trip in the middle of the classroom. He stumbled, but kept moving towards the door, reaching out to brush his hand against the wall.

Now Black was on his feet, wordlessly moving behind the professor. Plummer kept huffing and walking, but then he seemed to trip again, and this time the stumble turned into a sway.

Black took the last steps forward at a run. He just managed to catch Plummer before he crumpled to the ground.

* * *

Rutherford promised to call on Monro after treating Plummer. Monro sat in his study tapping his foot, the correspondence on his desk going untouched. When he heard his colleague tramp into the apartment an hour late, he didn't need to turn around to know Plummer's condition was as serious as he'd feared.

"It doesn't look good, Alexander." Rutherford's face was grim. Monro's mouth narrowed to a slit. "I've seen apoplectic fits like this many times before. Even if the patient recovers with most control of his faculties..." Monro let out a noise of grim concurrence. "A second fit is usually months away."

"I've seen similar cases," Monro agreed, taking a sip of wine.

He'd discharged most of his duties in the aftermath of the High Street tenement collapse. Most of the bodies had been recovered, identified and buried. It was a grim business. The state of the mangled corpses reminded him of those from the Battle of Prestonpans. Over a decade had passed since he was called to attend wounded Jacobites and loyalists nine miles outside Edinburgh, but he'd never forget the carnage. He remembered raging at the Jacobite forces for tearing his country apart, praying he'd never see such bloodshed in his homeland again. That the carnage repeated over a decade later in a time of peace didn't comfort him much.

And now Plummer was grievously ill. Bad tidings always came in pairs.

The two professors sat in silence for a while, nursing their cups. There wasn't much more to be said concerning their ailing colleague.

"Aird is really our only choice for the Chemistry chair," Rutherford commented, after sufficient contemplative time had passed.

"Perhaps," agreed Monro, looking out the window.

"Perhaps? Who besides Cullen is even a contender?"

"I was thinking the new Dr Black might be a useful candidate."

Rutherford scoffed. "The boy isn't remotely capable. He's spooked by his own shadow half the time. If we're proposing youngsters, you may as well nominate Sandy."

"Well, in a way, that's my point," Monro said slowly. "I can't imagine Joseph taking on a fraction of the private practice Aird could accumulate. He's not a threat to us, John."

Rutherford hemmed. He took his time coming round to new ideas.

"I don't think Joseph is entirely incapable of teaching—he did an acceptable job covering lectures the last time Plummer was incapacitated. He seems reasonable to work with."

Rutherford laughed. "You can't favour the boy, Alexander? Inviting a disciple of Cullen into the fold is not much better than inviting in the man himself."

"Not in the slightest," Monro said hastily. "But since you mention it, wholeheartedly favouring the disciple might create an opening between disciple and teacher."

"I like the way you're thinking," Rutherford said, leaning forward. "That's very clever, Alexander. The Town Council will discount Black as too inexperienced for the chair, so they'll have no choice but to go for Aird. But not before we've puffed up young Joseph with hopes that the Chair is his for the taking."

* * *

"Fortuitous news has reached me," Monro began, a smile lifting the corner of his mouth.

Black said nothing. He'd stopped by the anatomy theatre to enquire about Plummer's prognosis. He'd received a banal update —no change being the best outcome under the circumstances— before Monro beckoned him closer.

"Concerning who the faculty wishes to appoint to Plummer's Chemistry Chair."

Black remained silent. It looked like he was focussing on his breathing at the expense of everything else.

"Congratulations may soon be in order." Monro's smile widened.

"I thought the Town Council wasn't meeting for another month," Black finally said. He spoke slowly, mulling over his words.

"That's the final seal of approval, true. But the faculty have been rather busy discussing the matter, too."

Black frowned. His expression was maddeningly opaque.

"Surely Dr Francis Aird enjoys greater popularity among the Town Council?"

Monro stretched his fingers.

"I anticipate some back-and-forth, that's true. The councilmen rarely want to make life easy for the medical brethren."

Monro watched the young man, silently willing him to say the name surely at the forefront of his mind. Vexingly, Black refused to indulge him.

"The faculty are unanimous in their support of you," he added. That, at least, was true.

Black remained quiet.

"Well, I shall leave you to your studies and lecture preparation. You're a busy man, these days..."

* * *

A letter from Cullen was waiting on his desk at home. Mrs Russell must have used the opportunity to clear away his empty teacups.

My dear Joe,

Word has reached me of Prof Plummer's unfortunate illness...

Black studied the letter. He set it down. He picked it up again.

Eventually he sharpened his quill, still watching the unfolded letter out of the corner of his eyes. He took his time preparing his writing materials.

Then he changed his mind. He didn't need to respond to the letter today. It could wait a while.

23

GLASGOW

Cullen knew his bad days always had the capacity to get worse, and as soon as he saw Leechman standing in his laboratory, grim-faced, he knew which direction today would go.

"It's the Earl of Hopetoun..." Leechman began, searching Cullen's face to see if he knew what he was talking about. When Cullen continued to look blank, Leechman's grimace deepened, knowing he was the one to break the unwelcome news.

"Sit down," Cullen sighed. "I imagine this won't be a quick discussion."

Leechman looked like he'd prefer to remain standing, but seeing Cullen sink onto a stool, he followed.

"You've met the young earl?" Leechman asked.

Cullen had. He was more familiar with the elder Earl of Hopetoun, who passed away last spring following a period of chronic ill health. His son, who inherited the title, was introduced to Cullen briefly at the Principal's party several years ago.

"Well, he's taken a shine to you," Leechman said, in a tone that indicated this was sombre news. "Has told several of my friends that your teaching innovations are just what Edinburgh needs."

Cullen buried his head in his hand. He knew where this was going.

"This morning I received a letter, informing me he is heading to Edinburgh before everyone disperses for the summer, and will be encouraging the Town Council to consider appointing you to Professor Plummer's chemistry chair."

"Plummer passed away?" Cullen asked, blinking.

"Not yet," Leechman said. "But it's only a matter of time. He suffered another serious apoplexy attack two weeks ago, and it's not clear he'll recover. Your protégé Black is lecturing in Plummer's place while a replacement is decided upon."

"Oh, he is?" Black wasn't the most proactive correspondent, Cullen knew. He imagined he'd hear this news from Black within a few days. It didn't surprise him.

"Word is the faculty favour Dr Black for the chair, but one of Rutherford's former students is also a contender."

"Well, it hardly seems likely the faculty or Town Council will look twice at my name, then." A slurry of relief and disappointment slid through Cullen at this realisation.

"The Earl of Hopetoun thinks otherwise," Leechman said, fidgeting in his seat. "This exact words to my friend before he departed his estate were: 'If I fail to secure Professor Cullen's appointment within my first week in Edinburgh, I'll return with more money.'"

"You told him what happened to Donald Bennett?" Cullen asked, though he knew the question a stupid one. Everyone knew what happened to Donald Bennett.

"Repeatedly, William."

Cullen never dared ask how much his friend knew about the dark chymists. Did he know their practices seemed to derive from early alchemical work? Did he know there was a secret library where they stored their texts? That knowledge felt too dangerous to spread. He could count on one hand how many times they'd mentioned the murder of Don Bennett in the intervening years.

While he frowned, Leechman continued his agitated rant. "I'm far from the only voice dissuading from this. The earl thinks he can outmanoeuvre your opponents."

As an academic who spent hours of his days engrossed in theories, Cullen knew the earl operated from a theoretically sound assumption. The dark chymists and the Town Council were often treated as synonymous, but in reality they were distinct entities, and the dark chymists were by intention the smaller clique that preferred insularity. There were plenty of Edinburgh aristocrats who loathed the dark chymists and didn't go out of their way to assist them or align themselves.

The Hopetouns were one of the most influential Scottish families, and probably had the coins and charisma to persuade enough non-dark chymists burghers to do what they wanted.

But all this rested on the assumption that the dark chymists weren't profoundly threatened by Cullen, and not highly motivated to protect their threatened interest.

"The lad either has rocks in his head, or rocks in his scrotum," Cullen mused.

"It's a combination of both," said Leechman, not even smiling. "He's coming into a sizeable inheritance after the death of his father and clearly wants to make his own mark on Scottish politics. Young enough to think he's invincible, and dares to know better than the generation before."

Cullen knew something of that daring, so he settled on sighing again.

Leechman finally twitched to his feet and began pacing the crowded space.

"You'll have to do something, William. Heavens know I've tried. My friends on both coasts have tried. He'll arrive in Edinburgh within days. You must tell him you don't want to the Chemistry Chair, reject his offer to intercede on your behalf, and pray your letter arrives before he gets himself killed."

"I'll despatch the letter this afternoon," promised Cullen. His lectures were over for the day, and he was sure he could shoo away any students who called upon him in the next hour.

Leechman sagged with relief.

"Excellent, William. I informed you as soon as I heard. I think you still have enough time. If there's any more news, I'll share it with you first." He took off, probably heading toward the nearest glass of claret.

As promised, a few hours later, a messenger was spurring his horse out of Glasgow along the rutted, twisted road east.

However, the sealed letter in his satchel with Cullen's hand-writing on the back was not addressed to the Earl of Hopetoun at his Edinburgh apartment.

It was the fifth or sixth attempt at a letter Cullen wrote at his desk, not counted numerous one-word opening lines he scratched out and rewrote over a tortuous seventy minutes. He thought it would be an easy letter to write to the earl, despite their distant acquaintance, but the words got stuck in his quill.

Finally, after throwing half his vellum roll in the hearth, Cullen gave up trying to write to the Earl of Hopetoun and addressed his next attempt to Dr Joe Black.

He agonised over what to tell his former student. It was of vital urgency he tell Black what the earl intended to do, knowing Black wouldn't need the danger spelled out. In fact, he would probably learn of the Earl's agenda before Cullen's message arrived.

Cullen tried to compose a letter pleading with Black to stop the earl from throwing his patronage around, to empathetically convey Cullen's adamant refusal that the earl risk his life for a Chemistry Chair appointment. To balance flattery and firm disavowal.

Instead, the final attempt at his letter Cullen handed to the messenger was a few lines long, the shortest of all his drafts.

My dear Joe. The Earl of Hopetoun will soon arrive in Edinburgh. Protect him at <u>all</u> costs.

24

EDINBURGH

"I forget what Edinburgh smells like," the earl laughed. "I imagine its yearlong dwellers barely notice it."

"Edinburgh has the capacity to surprise even its loyalest residents," Black said.

They were seated in a coffeehouse next to St Giles cathedral, watching night fall.

Black received Cullen's letter yesterday evening. First thing in the morning, he presented his calling card at the earl's apartment on the High Street. Black was terrified the encounter would go awry, but the earl bade him into the modest quarters with a cheerful wave. He was still in a bandua and turban, and seemed in no rush to change into daytime clothes.

"This is delightful, Dr Black. I hoped I would have the chance to speak with Dr Cullen's most celebrated student before he became a luminary in his own right! I heard about your spectacular dissertation, you know. Pity the poor guests who called upon my estate that week—I fear I talked their ears off, but I couldn't stop thinking about your findings."

Black blushed, which he reflected was a good disguise for his nervousness.

"You flatter me, my lord."

The earl was still waving Black's unopened letter of introduction from Dr Cullen around, but while chatting to Black, he eased it open and scanned its contents. Grateful the earl had offered him coffee, Black focussed on swallowing the noxious brew.

It was clear Cullen wrote to him in a state of great agitation, no doubt afraid of delay. That was probably why—despite urging Black to protect the earl—he hadn't given thought to how a freshly minted doctor like Black might ingratiate himself with one of the richest gentry in Scotland. Given that Cullen already knew the earl, a letter of introduction on Black's behalf would have been a useful inclusion in his packet from Glasgow.

Thus, the letter in the Earl of Hopetoun hands was a forgery. The underlined statement 'at all costs' in Cullen's original note suggested such a necessity. Black, whose rich ink was one of his few luxuries and a clear identifier of his outgoing correspondence, borrowed Russell's inkwell after claiming his own had run dry. He had enough examples of Cullen's correspondence to attempt a replica of his handwriting, which he filled out with the murky dishwater that passed for his cousin's writing ink. Since the earl wasn't a regular correspondent of Cullen, Black gambled he wouldn't notice any inconsistency.

As it was, the earl did little more than skim the letters. He tossed it onto the table with his other papers—the wax seal Black scraped off another letter and re-fixed, clung on long enough—and beamed at his new acquaintance.

"Well, Dr Black, you might not believe it from my present condition, but I have a busy day ahead of me. You've done the stellar work of reminding me that Edinburgh is already out and about, and will not wait for this humble servant. What say we reconvene this evening? There's a lot I wish to speak to you about, and the St Giles' Coffeehouse is a good place for lively debate, even after five o'clock."

Black, who was struggling to figure out a way to bring the

conversation around to the business of Cullen and the dark chymists, could only nod meekly. The earl was a talker: while generous and approachable, he still spoke like a noble who was used to other men falling silent when they heard his voice.

The problem was Black had no idea how the dark chymists would attempt to silence the earl. With Don Bennett, one of their inner circle entered the family apartment as a guest and daub a sigil on the wall, allowing them access later. From what the earl had said, he hadn't entertained anyone in his quarters aside from Black, and he obviously held the dark chymists at arm's length.

Black was relieved the earl understood there was some risk with his business. But the dark chymists didn't have to attack the earl in his apartment.

So he sat with the earl in the coffeehouse—he angled his chair to face the room—and talked. It turned out his experiments on magnesium alba had caught the earl's attention because he had his own ideas about analysing the chemical composition of minerals in the soils around his estate. This was the first time Black had been consulted on chemical matters as if he were some sort of expert, not just a proxy for Cullen.

Not that they could avoid talking about the man, given the earl's stated business in town.

"Dr Cullen consults on industrial topics, does he not?"

"On occasion." Black frowned. He suspected the earl was mistaken, but wracked his memory to see if he could avoid contradicting him. "He mentioned keeping up an exchange with an amateur philosopher, but that was a few years back."

"Really?"

Black had heard only passing references from his former professor, and worried he misremembered.

"I think they discussed linen bleaching at length. It was Hugh...um..."

"Hugh Marr?" The earl slapped the table in delighted shock. "You're telling me Dr Cullen corresponded with *Lord Selkirk?*"

"I apologise my lord, the name isn't familiar..."

"No, he's only assumed that title last year." The earl seemed more tickled with Black's ignorance than annoyed by it. "The man has made a fortune in the past two years with his new linen bleaching plant. Married *considerably* above his station and claimed the new title. He's a little elusive, so people in certain circles were struggling to figure out where he came from. Beyond a poxy plot of land outside Arbroath, I mean. Now you're telling me Dr Cullen advised him on the linen bleaching enterprise?" The earl grinned to himself, realising he was in possession of the hottest morsel of gossip to feed his friends.

"I don't think Dr Cullen intended..." Black began, then gave up.

Because it didn't matter that his former professor never *intended* to advise a random noble how to make a fortune in domestic linen bleaching—something the Scottish economy hitherto lacked—it happened anyway. In trying to keep away from the dark centres of Scottish power, and indulge in kindness towards an otherwise friendless soul, Cullen had inadvertently proved the worst fears of the dark chymists correct.

For the dark chymist circle was composed of mercers with a chokehold on textile trade and manufacture. Up until now, only the richest could dare challenge their monopolies...and most wouldn't, because they knew what those men did to secure their interests. Their dark chymistry was rooted in hidden knowledge of sigils, and their mercantile power depended on similar control of access.

Sitting in a bustling coffeehouse, watching night fall on his city, Black suddenly saw why Cullen was such a threat. He disrupted medicine by bringing in fresh talent from the lower classes, and his chemistry was a brutal leveller of traditional means to affluence. That made him a threat.

The earl noticed none of this, because he was noting how saddened he felt to hear of the recent death of Lord Dunbar, who succumbed to a fever. "His tenement was on the other side of my close. I wonder if his family will sell it?"

While sympathetic to the grieving family, Black's attention fell on the fact that when the Town Council met next week, it would be missing its dark chymist majority for the first time in decades.

"Goodness, is that the hour?" the earl exclaimed as the cathedral bells chimed. "I detained you far longer than I planned." He downed his claret.

"Shall I enquire for a sedan chair?" Black asked, alarmed at the thought of letting the earl out of his sight.

The earl laughed and slapped Black's back as if he'd told a brilliant joke. "By the time that takes you, Doctor, I could have crawled home. I'll just hire a link boy."

Once darkness fell, the street outside most taverns acquired a gaggle of street caddies, willing to escort revellers homes by the light of their lamps for a few pennies.

There was only one such boy loitering outside the Coffeehouse, which made Black nervous for some reason. He was about ten years old, an unremarkable, grubby street child. There was a leanness about his face that suggested he'd already had his share of hard winters. However, his street caddie badge was clearly pinned to his coat breast, and he angled into the light so Black could note the number displayed, without any sign of reluctance.

"Nae trouble, m'Lords," the lad said, puffing out his bony chest. "Come."

The walk down the High Street proceeded ordinarily enough. There weren't many about at this hour. Black tried to monitor every shadow for signs of someone lurking within. Thieves were the least of their concerns, but they were a common threat. In the bubble of the link boy's lamp, it felt like the three of them were adrift in their own universe, infinite darkness stretching around them. Black tried to keep his eyes away from the lamp so he could adjust to the night.

The earl kept up his cheery conversation, a man who had no

reason to fear inconvenience or murderous theft. Black knew his half-answers and grunts were rude, but the Earl was too drunk to notice.

"Watch the ground here, sirs," the lad piped up, steering the gentlemen off the High Street and towards the gaping wynd.

"Oh, we're home already?" the earl exclaimed. "I barely noticed."

"Hmm." The darkness was disorientating, but Black was sure they should have passed a couple more wynds before reaching Marlin's. He'd not had that much to drink, had he? He'd tried to pace himself in the coffeehouse, but his nerves meant his cups kept emptying.

"The boy will see you back to Professor Russell afterwards, Dr Black?...Hey, young fellow..." Black was hesitating and slowing down, but the link boy ahead seemed to be walking faster.

"You!" Black yelled. Not turning around, the link boy broken into a run and swerved round the corner, disappearing into an intersecting wynd.

Black rushed forward, before realising he shouldn't leave the earl behind. By the time he overcome his hesitation and made it to the intersection, he knew pursuit would be futile. The link boy's lamp lay abandoned in front of them, no retreating footsteps to detect.

"This isn't Marlin's Wynd," the earl said. His drunken exuberance was falling away, exposing a core of fear.

It wasn't unheard of for link boys to work in cahoots with thieves, luring wealthy victims into dark closes for a cut of the takings. If the pair were lucky, they'd only lose their purses. Black reached into his coat pocket. He wasn't going to make this difficult for them.

By the light of the lamp, which could extinguish at any minute, the earl was gulping in air. Black assumed he was about to cry for help. That would be the worst thing the rich fool could do.

But then the earl froze.

"Do you hear that?"

It was almost a musical note, rising to fill the wynd. It didn't resemble any instrument Black knew of—a single ringing bell that sounded cold, and bore into his ears. The note swelled and twisted into a disagreeable shriek, and Black's fingers rose towards his ears. The noise came from everywhere. When it stopped after only a few seconds, the echoes kept ringing.

Black pushed the earl back against the wall, casting around for the source of the noise. The wynd remained empty and still. A thieving gang would have no reason to delay once their accomplice left them in this trap. But this noise bore a terrifying resemblance to the unnatural sound the dark chymist's vassal made when it was in action.

The brightness emanating from the abandoned lamp contracted. Already terrified, Black found one fear to cling onto.

Don't let the light go out.

That had to be what their attackers were waiting for, wasn't it?

Terror reached in to Black. With one hand restraining the Earl, Black's other hand extended towards the torch.

He knew he shouldn't do this.

Like he knew he shouldn't forge Cullen's signature and reuse his wax seal.

Like he knew he shouldn't stand between the dark chymists and their target.

And yet, here he was.

Black tensed his right arm. The glow in the oil lamp swelled, taking on a blood-red tint. The flames ferociously clawed at the glass.

"Doctor..."

Black turned and saw it. The shadows a few metres to their right coalescing in odd configurations, seeming to come unstuck from the wall. As Black's brain tried to fit the sight into some category of previously seen thing, he realised the unnatural sight was moving towards them.

"Please, please," the earl moaned, begging for his life.

The movement seemed to accelerate. Black thrust out his hand.

He wasn't sure what he wanted to achieve and had no time to focus properly. What shot out of his hand was a useless mixture of fire and light. But it struck the knot of shadows. With the impact, Black thought the confusing illusion changed to the shape of a man, one hand raised.

Maybe it confused the entity, but it didn't stop it.

Bracing for impact, Black pulled his hands defensively in front of his face and lower body.

Next thing Black knew, he was on the ground, pulling his legs and arms in to protect himself from whatever had knocked him over.

He hadn't time to work out if he was facing a demon or vengeful spirit, but there was something solid bearing down on him. It scratched his left bicep. Black's hand connected with a thin but solid object. His eyes weren't helping him—he couldn't make sense of what he was seeing or not seeing—but when he screwed them shut, it felt like he'd grabbed the wrist of an assailant who was pinning him onto the ground by a knee on his stomach. The assailant was trying to lower his forearm towards Black's body, and Black was doing everything in his power to resist, because he probably wielded a dagger in that arm.

His invisible opponent shifted, and Black found a pressure driving into his throat. His own hand tried to prise it away. That must be the assailant's other forearm on his windpipe.

Black couldn't tell if he was tasting his own blood in his mouth, or the aftertaste of phlogiston, the particularly metallic scent that followed its discharge.

Black's elbows were locked against his sides, but the opponent had the advantage of weight and was scrambling to break his grip.

Despite anticipating his imminent death, it reassured Black that he was fighting a man, not a demon. Why would a spirit act and feel like a mortal? He thought he could hear his attacker panting.

His foe was stronger than him and had at least one weapon.

Come to think of it, why was the assailant trying to kill Black? The Earl of Hopetoun still cowered against the close wall, and with Black on the ground, nothing prevented the assailant from standing up and stabbing the earl before Black had a chance to right himself. Surely if he held out even a few more seconds, his attacker would come to the same conclusion?

That realisation was enough to rally his thoughts and force him to go on the offensive.

Black kicked out where he thought the attacker's shins would be. His foot connected and the pressure on his upper body relented for a second.

That was all Black needed. He drew his hands together and concentrated.

A yellow-white light exploded from his palms, washing against the invisible assailant.

Black was already scrambling to the side, a weight now crushing most of his body. But it didn't feel like an attacker anymore, it felt like a sack of stones.

"Dr Black?"

Hauling himself up the wall, Black leaned on it for balance—or possibly reassurance—and lowered one foot into the space where the assailant had fallen. He was relieved a large, rounded object blocked his foot from touching the ground, though it yielded slightly. He rocked the object to the side with his heel. It moved under his direction, but wasn't moving of its own accord.

A living object wouldn't have survived what he struck it with, but Black wasn't ready to rule this out as a demonic attack.

Steading himself, Black ignited a phlogiston torch in his hand. He didn't care what the Earl of Hopetoun thought.

Was he imagining it, or could he see an outline of a large object at his feet? A kind of shimmer, or change to the texture of the air.

Since many of the dark chymists' arts were reputably temporary—
the sigils holding their power for a few minutes at most—perhaps
this invisibility sigil was wearing off.

Black didn't want to wait around to find out. He certainly
didn't want to touch the body of his attacker.

"Are you alright, my lord?"

The Earl of Hopetoun was backed against the opposite wall of
the wynd, panting. Terror stripped him of reasoning.

"Are you wounded, my lord?"

The earl managed to focus on Black and shook his head. Now
he'd noticed the flames curled around Black's hands he couldn't
look away from them.

There was no sign anyone heard the disturbance, or cared
enough to intervene. The wynd remained empty.

The earl blinked at Black. "Where did you learn to fight?"

Black stared at his companion as if he had forsaken all reason.

"The same place I learned to play the flute, of course."

"But..."

Black was already breaking into a jog. "We need to get out of
here, my lord."

25

EDINBURGH

An aggressive pounding on the door woke the entire Rutherford household. Rutherford had hauled a waistcoat over his nightshirt when his foot-servant reached his bedchamber. The manservant was alert with fright, though his words sounded distant.

"Sir, they say there's no time."

Rutherford didn't need to ask who 'they' were, nor did the servant feel it necessary to tell him.

"Fine, fine." Rutherford tugged a silk turban over his head and wiggled into his breeches. "Get me my coat."

His wife sat up in bed, the sheets pulled protectively around her. She fixed Rutherford with pleading eyes.

"Try to go back to sleep," Rutherford told her gruffly. "I doubt I'll be long." This was a lie, and they both knew it: he had no idea what his patrons sought him for at this hour of the night. It was after one o'clock, surely?

An African footman waited in the stairwell. Rutherford thought the man belonged to the Argyle household. He was not dressed in the gaudy livery Edinburgh aristocrats usually forced their Black footmen to wear, instead dressed in a discrete, dark cloak.

"Follow me, sir."

Rutherford wanted to demand why he was being summoned, but he held his tongue. It was possible the footman hadn't been told.

He was ushered into a carriage manned by servants in similar attire. While everyone treated him with courtesy, a tension in their bodies suggested they had instructions to become discourteous as soon as the situation demanded it.

It was a short but swift ride up the Canongate to the Lawnmarket. Rutherford noticed several red flashes of the Town Guard's uniform, and the way they averted their gaze or drew back into the shadows added to his unease.

He could see the first-floor rooms of Lord Argyle's family were illuminated with candles as he exited the carriage, the only light in a dark street.

Upstairs, the footman bade him through the main bedchamber and kitchen to the storeroom at the back. Despite the candles in the front room, Rutherford realised none of Argyle's family were here.

Several men huddled in the storeroom: the combination of civet musk and body odour told him there was a mixture of nobles and servants in the gloom. It was almost impossible to see more than a metre in front of him without a candle in hand.

"Ah, Dr Rutherford," the voice belonging to Lord Argyle advanced further into the room. "I am sorry to disturb you at such a late hour."

The footman at Rutherford's side coughed politely and held out a small object. Rutherford found his hands closing around a purse swollen with coins.

The dark practitioners weren't subtle in their dealings with people they considered lesser, Rutherford noted. Why waste preamble? Every learned physician in this town recognised a bribe when they were given it.

"It's my honour to assist you," Rutherford murmured, slipping the purse into his coat pocket.

The men in the room stepped aside to let Rutherford through, and for the first time he could see what the candles at the end of the room were concentrated around.

A naked man—modesty protected with scraps of linen—was laid out on the table Lord Argyle used for weighing and accounting his sugar. Rutherford knew he was looking at a corpse before he even took in the man's staring, sightless eyes.

It was Holm.

"What in God's name…?" Rutherford gasped.

"You tell us, Dr Rutherford," Argyle replied. A layer of courtesy was already stripped from his tone. "Malcolm was out on business, didn't report back at the usual time. My men found him face-down in a wynd halfway up the High Street." Argyle didn't have to add that Rutherford's time for providing answers was limited.

Rutherford gave the body a few experimental nudges with his physician's cane.

"He's not been dead more than a few hours since rigor mortis is only starting to set in."

At first glance, Holm's wiry body was unblemished. There were no stab or grapeshot wounds. No ligature marks around his neck. It looked like Holm simply dropped dead.

"Can you turn the body over?"

"You won't find anything on the back," Argyle snapped.

Chastised, Rutherford scrutinised Holm's arms and legs in more detail. Bruises and nicks coated his forearms and shins.

"There are signs of a recent struggle," Rutherford explained. "But this death bears more in common with heart failure than mortal wound."

"Which is impossible," stated another man in the room, who Rutherford didn't recognise.

Rutherford wanted to argue that it wasn't impossible—it wasn't unheard of for weak hearts to afflict families—but the men in this room didn't seem interested in his speculation. In fact, he wondered if they already knew Holm's cause of death and were testing him.

"There are some poisons which kill the victim without trace," Rutherford said. "Perhaps that was what the struggle was about."

"It wasn't," replied a man by the door. He didn't allude as to why.

"I'm afraid, my lords, the cause of death isn't obvious to me." Rutherford looked again at Holm's. He couldn't read the expression on his face, it was a grimace of death that could have resulted from anything. He hesitated, worrying if what he said next would overstep the bounds of his responsibility. "Unless...you believe this is the work of sigils?"

"Our footmen searched his person for signs of a sigil—they finished tearing his clothes apart just before you arrived." Lord Argyle spoke with marginally more patience than he'd deployed in his previous remarks, suggesting a grudging approval of Rutherford's deduction. "No trace."

"What business was he conducting?" Rutherford asked. He regretted asking almost immediately, but Argyle merely clapped his hands.

"Octavius, see if the Duke of Castleborough is ready." The footman murmured acquiescence and headed back into the bedchamber. Rutherford was startled to see a man crouched over the table next to the front windows. He hadn't seen anyone sitting there when he came in.

"Alright, alright..." The figure shuffled to his feet, and made his way into the backroom. Rutherford wasn't familiar with the man, though he moved like an ancient creature.

The Duke came to a stop before Rutherford. "Greetings, good doctor. Please insert this under the unfortunate soul's tongue.

But…" His voice turned into a bark that caused Rutherford to jump. "Don't touch it."

And so a second item was thrust into Rutherford's hands, this one a coin wrapped in a strip of cloth. Rutherford turned it over experimentally. It felt thicker and larger than a guinea. Then it occurred to him the coin could herald some kind of danger if he let his fingers come into contact with it.

The last time he'd spoken to Holm, the youth told him he intended to kill Lord Bennett's son. The dark practitioners achieved their aims: supportive whispers for Cullen faded from Edinburgh like a dying candle for several years. Rutherford was grateful for that reprieve, of course, but he resented the loss of the blameless Bennett boy. Rutherford had once entertained appointing Don to his medical chair upon retirement—it would have been an easy, harmonious handover.

Almost as soon as Holm left his house that night, Rutherford wondered why the dark practitioners bothered to warn him an hour before the deed. They made it clear they didn't care for his opinion, nor did they didn't benefit from appraising him. He suspected it was either a test of his compliance, or Holm enjoyed the cruelty.

And here he was, complicit in further atrocities. Rutherford had no idea what the coin in his hand would do once it was in Holm's mouth, and he dreaded finding out. But he knew he was aiding the dark practitioners.

Holm's jaw would be the first part of his body to seize up in the hours following death. Rutherford wondered if he should pretend he couldn't open Holm's mouth. It would give him the opportunity to smash through Holm's jaw and teeth if the dark practitioners were so desperate for him to accomplish this task. Heavens knew the malevolent creature known as Malcolm Holm deserved worse.

But Rutherford knew any resistance or objection would make

tonight's ordeal longer and more arduous for him. Right now, the hefty purse bumping against his leg promised to make many aspects of his life easier. He'd have a bruise on this thigh by sunrise.

Holm's jaw was stiff, but not unyielding. Rutherford crammed his fingers between Holm's teeth and fumbled for the tongue. He caught a glimpse of the coin in the murky yellow light: bronze or copper, and carved with intricate lines and circles. The earl must have been carving the lines when Rutherford arrived.

It took a few minutes of contorting his hand, but eventually Rutherford was satisfied the coin was under Holm's tongue. He extracted his hand and the cloth as quickly as he could.

"It needs a few minutes to take effect. Please be ready, doctor."

Rutherford wanted to shrink back, but the men in the room were pressing forward. Rutherford wanted to know what he was supposed to be ready for, but found he didn't want to ask.

Holm's mouth was agape, and Rutherford could see the coin glinting. No, that couldn't be right. The coin was glowing too brightly to be reflecting of candlelight.

Rutherford's breath came in hisses, his fingers slimy with sweat. The men around him stood reaction-less, neither concerned nor surprised.

Golden light now poured from Holm's mouth, and a ringing noise grew in Rutherford's ears, like the after-echo from a loud explosion. Now he couldn't look away.

There was a sound like a clash of symbols, and the light was sucked back in to Holm's mouth. As it happened, every candle in the room extinguished.

"Fuckster!" Rutherford couldn't help himself.

Then the figure on the table in front of him began to cough and jerk.

"The coin..." One thought overtaking the others, and stopping him from concentrating on what was happening in front of him, Rutherford reached out and grabbed the shoulders of the man lying there, hauling him upright before he could choke on the coin in his mouth.

The man swayed, and the coughing turned to retching, before Rutherford heard the clunk of the metal landing on the wooden floor.

"The sister-fucking devil..." It was Holm's voice, weak but angry.

Behind Rutherford, servants clamoured to relight the candles.

"I'll kill him," Holm was repeating. "I'll kill them both..."

"Malcolm..." Argyle pushed Rutherford out the way, squeezing Holm's shoulder to focus him.

Rutherford was glad to be dismissed. His brain was only just catching up to what his eyes were telling him. Where a corpse was laid out on the table a minute ago, now there was Holm. Except the corpse *was* Holm. And now he was coughing, cursing, and thrashing around.

"Lord protect me," Rutherford whispered under his breath.

"Dr Rutherford?" The African footman reappeared, another invisible figure now visible. "This way, please."

Rutherford looked around to see if anyone would contradict his dismissal, but no one was paying him any attention. They were all restraining Holm, whispering reassurances to him.

The candles were all re-lit now, and the scene was no less confusing. Instead of a corpse, there was a living man. Maybe it was best the dark practitioners didn't turn around to find Rutherford still here.

As he turned to escape, Rutherford's eye caught the shine of bronze on the floor at his feet. Even with shadows blotting out most illumination, Rutherford could see nothing but a smooth surface.

Whatever sigils were carved on the coin had disappeared.

. . .

Rutherford was trembling by the time he reached the carriage, which hadn't moved from the street. One last glance up told him the lights in the Argyle's front room remained out; onlookers the apartment was still as its neighbours.

"Please," the footman gestured at Rutherford to embark. Nothing about the footman's countenance or tone suggested he was even disconcerted by what he'd witnessed. Rutherford has always viewed African slaves and servants as easily excitable, child-like in their emotions. It was why he thought owning one was more trouble than it was worth. Now he wondered if this footman —Octavius, did Argyle call him?—was too stupid to understand what he'd seen.

"My masters thank you greatly for your services tonight." The footman told him when they arrived at Rutherford's tenement. "You have been and will continue to be handsomely rewarded."

Rutherford wondered if he should protest or demanded explanations. It wasn't clear why the dark practitioners had dragged him into this—he thought his assistance was cursory at best. He didn't want to dwell on what other purposes he fulfilled for the men in that room: the more opaque their reasonings, the worse outcomes he suspected for himself.

"Right." Sleep wouldn't return to him tonight, but Rutherford needed to get behind his own locked doors, as far away from any dark practitioners and their lackeys as possible.

Octavius the footman bowed and let Rutherford make his own way over to the turnpike door.

As his hand rested on the door handle, Rutherford stopped and looked back. In the moonlight he could see the footman still standing beside the horse, with the same polite attentiveness he displayed all night.

"It doesn't bother you?" Rutherford demanded. "What you witnessed tonight?" Seeing the calm African, he became paranoid tonight's events were somehow existing only in his imagination.

Begging for validation from a servant was humiliating, but it would drive him to madness if he let his thoughts fester further.

Octavius chuckled to himself. When he met Rutherford's eye and spoke, some of his affected accent slipped, revealing the more foreign patois underneath.

"Why would I?" he asked in amusement at a joke Rutherford did not understand. "I've seen much worse."

26

EDINBURGH

Black's eyes roamed along the cracks in his bedchamber ceiling. He could hear the Russell's servants chatting quietly in the kitchen below, their work done for the day.

The earl didn't need to be sworn to secrecy—as soon as he recovered his wits, he promised Black he'd keep quiet of his own accord about everything that transpired. Once safe inside, Black had scoured the earl's apartment, examining every surface, deconstructing his bed and clothes cabinet. There was no sign of suspicious markings, and the pale earl immediately agreed not to entertain guests in the space. He was a tall, proud man several years older than Black, but following the attempt on his life, his entire posture slumped towards Black like a chastened child.

The earl clutched Black's forearm as he bid him adieu, staring at Black with a mixture of overwhelming gratitude and fear. No one superior to Black had ever looked at him in this way. He first considered it alarming, then decided it was intoxicating.

Black followed the earl about his business over the next couple of days. The trembling young noble probably wanted to bar himself in his apartment, or flee back to the countryside, but he let anger drive him. He pushed his scheduled appointments earlier in the day, removing the risk he'd be outdoors after dark.

The earl conducted his planned business with aplomb, shaking hands and throwing back impressive quantities of port with nobles across the city. Black diffidently offered the earl a few of his own scribbled calculations about the number of students Cullen could bring to Edinburgh if his class sizes grew at the same rate they were growing in Glasgow, and the annual monetary impact of those additional medical students in the city. The earl worked those financial calculations into every conversation.

He didn't breathe a word of his assassination attempt, and if he continued to fear for his life, he never showed it in public. Black caught the queer, uneasy looks in several men's eyes as they spoke with the earl. A few days ago they would have labelled him a dead man, but the fact he continued to dance through the city suggested a tacit approval of his agenda from the dark chymists, did it not? Or that the earl had somehow already defeated them.

Black assumed the dark chymists would send another warning, or attack the earl again. But they remained silent. They must know someone was assigned to kill the earl, and the fact he survived, killing the assassin in the process, made them deeply uneasy.

Had anyone survived a dark chymist assassination attempt? Black knew better than to ask at such a sensitive juncture, but from what he already knew, the answer was no.

He tried not to think about the late Lord Dunbar. Rumour had it he was 'cleaned up' because of a loose tongue. As far as he knew, his daughter Violet was still alive: married to a noble family in Lancaster with surprising haste last year. Could it be her father belatedly realised she was as much a liability as him, and had tried to get her as far away from Edinburgh as possible?

He reminded himself that if the dark chymists knew he'd discovered the existence of their secret library, he'd probably have joined Lord Dunbar in the earth.

A few pristine sheets of vellum lay on Black's table. They should have transformed into a letter to Cullen by now, but Black struggled to get his thoughts in words. Messengers opened letters all the time to entertain bored tavern patrons on arduous cross-country journeys. He couldn't risk incriminating himself.

None of the Town Council wanted Francis Aird for the Chemistry Chair. Why would they, when Cullen was an option? The faculty hadn't petitioned too hard for Rutherford's former student, assuming there'd be no contest. They'd already voted to nominate Black.

Having seen the earl's performance, Black knew he stood no chance. He'd entertained a brief hope that saving the life of the earl might prompt him to change his loyalties, but the earl's original plan only hardened. Tomorrow the Town Council would meet, and the conclusion was foregone.

* * *

Sir Anthony kept Monro in his hallway for twenty minutes. The floorboards creaked as Monro paced back and forth, a disruptive noise he hoped carried into the man's study.

"Urgent correspondence indeed..." he muttered, pausing to let a scullery maid squeeze past. He heard no voices from the study: as far as he could tell, Sir Anthony was alone.

Never in his decades of service to the dark practitioners had he been treated this rudely. It was a power play.

Minutes before he decided to pound on the study door—politeness be damned—Sir Anthony finally revealed himself.

"Ah, Professor Monro. Sorry to keep you waiting. Please come in."

He didn't even give Monro a chance to accept or decline the apology, just waved him inside to his usual seat. A pair of wine glasses and a bottle were already laid out on his study desk.

"If you'll forgive my impertinence, my lord...what is going on?"

Monro intended to be more circumspect than this. But his legs were sore from standing. Plus, Sir Anthony's placid expression and jovial greeting suggested a measure of deception already in place: indirect questions were liable to be swatted aside.

Sir Anthony didn't look up. "I was thinking of you, Alexander, when my latest shipment of claret arrived last week." He gestured to the bottle. "You'll be my first guest to sample it: I think you're in for a treat."

This was a blatant evasion tactic.

"Thank you, my lord. You didn't need to withhold the claret for my sake."

"Oh, it was no punishment." Sir Anthony poured two generous glasses. Late afternoon daylight cast the study into shadows, making the liquid seem more black than ruby.

"My lord, I don't understand why the Town Council was allowed to approve William Cullen's appointment." Monro fought the urge to take a fortifying sip of claret. He couldn't allow Sir Anthony to steer this conversation. "The faculty were unanimously opposed to his appointment, and I believed—correct me if I'm wrong, my lord—that you and your associations were of a similar inclination."

Sir Anthony nodded along gravely, as if he were taking Monro's concerns seriously.

"I can understand why you might feel dismayed, Alexander. You have our complete trust, but there are some things we cannot divulge, because of how great a risk the information poses if it fell into the wrong hands."

There was a pause. "I understand," Monro said eventually, trying to sound magnanimous.

"Good." Sir Anthony beamed. "How do you like the claret?"

He'd not yet taken a sip.

"It's excellent," Monro lied. "I'm sorry to harp on the subject… but what benefit is there to having William Cullen in Edinburgh? Teaching at the college, no less? In Glasgow he's merely a nuisance: his capacity to cause harm is limited. But bringing him to Edinburgh, the centre of the medical world? You've handed the man a global platform."

Sir Anthony took a swill of claret. Then he frowned.

"Does this claret taste slightly off to you? I'm dreadfully sorry, Alexander: I thought I was handing you a glass of something far superior than…this. What a disappointment." He cleared his throat. "There are certain advantages to having Dr Cullen where we can keep a close eye on him. Maybe a little disruption now prevents a lot of heartache later. I can assure you we've discussed the matter for some time now, and the lords are in agreement about the best way to handle him."

There was no sign Sir Anthony was lying. He spoke with measured ease, the same way he always spoke. To accuse him would sound deranged and dangerously impertinent, so Monro bit his tongue. Yet every instinct told him he was being lied to.

Monro hadn't been at the fateful Town Council meeting, but from rumours swirling later that day, a strange, eerie atmosphere hung over the proceedings. Several dark practitioner loyalists hadn't shown, and the rest stumbled over their words, as if expecting to drop dead at any minute. The only people in the room who seemed calm were the Earl of Hopetoun and Joseph Black, and their assurance unnerved the onlookers even more. The image in Monro's mind was of an unmoored ship idly floating out the harbour, at the mercy of uncharted currents.

After that, his patrons refused to see him. There was no sign of Sir Anthony, Argyle or the others around town. Even Holm vanished from the classroom. It felt like they'd all gone to ground, and Monro was seized by terror. This had never happened before. A whole day later, Sir Anthony sent a note saying that he would meet with Monro at three o'clock. There was still no sign of the others.

"Was there any other business I can help you with?" Sir Anthony asked, setting his glass down and peering at Monro. "I don't want to disrupt your entire day."

"As it happens...I've received word of another smallpox outbreak near Knoydart. It's decimated several villages. I hoped we could use the tragic opportunity to re-attempt the inoculation program."

"Ah, I heard about that outbreak too." Sir Anthony's sigh made Monro's heart sink before he even completed the sentence. "Unfortunately, the Duke of Castleborough ran into an issue reconstructing the Gaelic sigil—water and mould damage to the source grimoires."

"Never mind the Gaelic sigil!" Monro snapped. "We can hire a translator."

Sir Anthony looked genuinely sorry. "It might be time to let the remaining parishes go, professor. Given the current unrest in the Highlands, we can't guarantee the safety of your colleagues."

Monro didn't believe it. He knew the dark practitioners were still lying to him. It didn't matter what those lies were about, or their motivation for lying. All that mattered was they had promised him one thing, and were coming up with reasons to deny him their assistance.

Sir Anthony pretended to shuffle through his papers. "We can end this meeting on a happier note, however. I'm glad you stopped by today. A little bird told me the College of Physicians intends to admit you as a fellow next month."

"I've not heard of this," Monro said warily.

"They will vote on the proposal this Thursday," Sir Anthony continued. "There will be an honorary medical doctorate to accompany this accolade, naturally."

"I'm honoured, my lord," Monro tried to smooth his voice to

sound grateful. "I assume you have a hand in this." The last sentence sounded more like an accusation than a profession of thanks.

"Only to nudge the interested parties in the correct direction. It gives the Physicians great pleasure to reward a man as Christian and upstanding as yourself in both professional and private life. How we wish the city had more men like you...Dr Monro."

Sir Anthony was too accustomed to dealing with Rutherford, who believed blatant falsehoods intended only to stroke the man's ego. The ploy was blindingly obvious to Monro.

Once alone, he bit the skin of his hand. Not deep enough to draw blood, but enough to feel pain.

His masters were content to use and discard him when it suited them. He was a fool to think he could achieve his smallpox inoculation program through their benevolence. And he was already disgusted himself for not resisting their attempt to quiet him like a recalcitrant toddler. Why did it matter if Monro could see their blatant manipulations where Rutherford could not, if the outcome was the same?

"The Lords are serious about bringing in Cullen? The senate could not have made themselves clearer."

Rutherford had been infuriatingly hard to get hold of as well. His excuse—malaise brought on by a draughty bedroom—was at least believable. When he finally appeared in Monro's apartment he looked a little peaky, but shrugged off Monro's concerns.

"I'm feeling my age right now. The wife is out shopping for thicker blankets as we speak."

Despite being sequestered in his apartment for a few days, word reached Rutherford of Cullen's appointment, so Monro didn't have to break the unwelcome news.

"It's rare you'll see the senate so unanimous in their support of one candidate and opposition to the other," concurred Monro. "The Town Council even acknowledged Joseph's nomination, so they can't have misunderstood us."

"Well," Rutherford commented before Monro even sat down. "Goes to show what they think of us." Dark bags under his eyes proved sleep had eluded him for a while.

"The Town Council doesn't think of us at all," Monro complained, massaging his calves. "That's the problem."

He described the mystifying behaviour of Sir Anthony, leaving out the bit about his honorary medical doctorate. Rutherford agreed the behaviour seemed strange, but appeared unwilling to speculate further.

"Is the Earl of Hopetoun secretly affiliated with them? I don't understand why that abrasive pup is dictating terms across the city?"

For a moment, it looked liked Rutherford wanted to say something. His mouth opened slightly, and he took a deep breath. Then he shook his head.

"I'd be astounded if news of Cullen's appointment doesn't send old Plummer to his grave faster than he's already going—I'm told he was spitting fury when he heard. Said the Town Council don't care about his legacy."

"What are we supposed to do? The faculty senate is in uproar, Alexander, but I think you know as well as I the Town Council are unlikely to change their minds."

"No, I suppose it gives them a quiver of satisfaction when they remind us how powerless we are." Monro's tortoiseshell cat strutted into his study, her tail floating above her. She collided with the table leg headfirst—seemingly on purpose—then flopped onto her back. Monro tried to ignore her.

"There's not much we can do without hearing from our patrons at the top. It's arrogance on my part to presume they're not informed of the situation, so I'll wait upon their summons for now." There was a hint of admonishment in Rutherford's tone, that Monro dare question their superiors.

"It has to be one of their games," Monro complained. Usually Rutherford would be the first to agree with his observations, so the fact he dismissed Monro's concerns suggested he was overreacting this time. His cat continued to writhe at his feet, looking at him expectantly. He nudged her with his toe until she took off, trilling. Then he hummed. "You know John, as I'm dwelling on the matter, it occurs to me...we don't have to be passive about this."

"What do you mean, Alexander?"

A prim little smile flashed across Monro's face. "There are plenty of ways we can make it clear to Cullen he's...not welcome in Edinburgh."

It was a tranquil spring night, with just enough darkness to provide concealment in the shadows of the College. Monro waited until he was in the stairwell to the library cellars before lighting a torch. The stillness made him uneasy, but he told himself it would make it easier to hear if anyone—Town Guards, students—were approaching.

He wasn't familiar with this part of the university building, so the steps and underground corridor took a while to navigate.

Finally, after some stumbling and curse words, he found the cellar he wanted. Plummer had given him the keys, no questions asked. Nor had Monro bothered to offer any excuses.

Inside stood rows of large glassware. Chemistry wasn't Monro's area of expertise, but he recognised the distillation apparatus, beakers, and funnels Plummer used to prepare his compounds in the lecture hall. Some of it he'd purchased himself, to replace cracked equipment, but most was inherited from his predecessor, Sinclair. And most of it would be offered to his successor for a nominal fee, as a courtesy.

Well, unless your successor was William Cullen.

Monro grabbed the first row of shelves and gave an experimental tug. As expected, the shelves weren't bolted to the floor.

It was awkward with one hand holding the touch, but Monro heaved. A few grunts later and the shelves tipped. The stillness of the cellar, the college, was destroyed by glass and ceramics shattering into a million pieces.

27

GLASGOW

"**A**ll the laboratory glassware is destroyed? Completely unsalvageable?" Cullen hoped with further clarification the news would make more sense than it currently did.

Leechman shook his head. "I'm sorry, William."

If Plummer's collection was anything like his equipment in Glasgow, Cullen knew it would be custom made. Not only did that make it expensive, but it would take months to commission. He'd be lucky if any replacements arrived in time for the next academic year.

"I know this is Rutherford and Monro's doing. Plummer isn't in the condition to smash bottles."

Leechman made a sympathetic noise. There wasn't more he could do. "I heard the Edinburgh faculty are threatening to block you from the academic senate, since they claim your appointment is unlawful."

Cullen waved his hand. That was the smallest of his concerns. "I'm exchanging letters with Plummer. I think there's a way for everyone to save honour if we both resign and let the faculty re-appoint us as joint chemistry professors, instead of having me replace him."

215

Leechman gave a confused laugh. "That sounds like the sort of meaningless political manoeuvring they get up to in Edinburgh. I barely understand how that makes the situation better, since the Town Council says they want you, and the medical faculty can't oppose them and the outcome isn't going to change. I hear Plummer is doing a little better than expected, but he isn't long for this world."

"I suspect his last surviving years or months will be powered by spite...against me," Cullen said.

His friend's reaction to the news from Edinburgh was surprising. Cullen dreaded Leechman finding out about his appointment to the Chair of Chemistry and impending move east, but his response was oddly muted.

As expected, Leechman grilled him about the contents of his letter to the Earl of Hopetoun. That he believed Cullen's promised disavowal turned out lukewarm was a given. But Cullen's excuses about not recalling its exact contents, how he scribbled it in a state of panic, who's to say how it came across, et cetera, was met with more irritation than exasperation.

Whatever his true feelings, Leechman took refuge in brusque practicalities.

"How's young Joseph taking the developments?"

"He's delighted I got the chemistry chair," Cullen replied, mustering as much confidence as he could that this was the truth.

You needn't be anxious, Black wrote in his last letter to Cullen, provided your course is better than Plummer's, which is impossible for it not to be.

Black's letters to him over the past few months of wrangling were careful. They gave the appearance that Black was in complete support of Cullen's bid for the chemistry chair over his own, but Cullen suspected Black harboured some disappointment all the same. He knew he would if the tables were turned. His former student made only vague allusions to an attack he protected the Earl of Hopetoun against, stating he'd explain more when they were next in the same city. It could be months before such an event occurred.

"I'm glad the Glaswegian side of the bargain is causing you less heartache," Leechman said. It was possible he meant it.

"It's an easy enough arrangement," Cullen explained. "The Glasgow Assembly aren't happy to see me leave, but they'll honour my recommendation for a replacement, because it saves them having to think or argue amongst themselves." After copies of Black's recent dissertation reached Glasgow, the faculty were begging Cullen to secure the young chemist's appointment. At least he didn't have to worry about a Town Council meddling in Glasgow.

"When is Dr Black returning?" Leechman asked. The sun was setting, bathing his parlour in a golden warmth.

"He was weighing up the benefits of going to London in his last letter. But even if he spends the summer at Hunter's anatomy school, he'll be back in Glasgow by October."

Cullen was halfway home when a liveried footman tapped his arm.

"Dr Cullen? I was asked to convey a message from my master, Lord Anglesbury."

"Really?" Cullen nearly tripped.

"Err, yes," the footman continued, taken aback by his beaming expression.

Belatedly recognising this twenty-something footman hadn't been tasked with delivering good news, Cullen reassumed a serious expression. Would it kill the Creator to bless him with a positive development today?

"My lord wanted to say...um... 'Lecturing in English, and your other theatrics, may be indulged in Glasgow, but Dr Cullen, I can assure you in that Edinburgh, where the brightest minds congregate, they won't tolerate such impudence.'"

Anglesbury wouldn't even stoop to putting quill to paper on

his behalf: didn't think him worth the exertion. Cullen folded his arms and affected a smile.

"We'll have to see about that, won't we?"

* * *

Entering the lecture theatre on his first day of class, Black found a room almost at complete occupancy, despite his early arrival.

This wasn't how they did it in Edinburgh. It was considered rude for students to enter the room before their professor arrived.

For the past five years, he'd been adamant he wouldn't shave his head and don the physick wig once he qualified to practise medicine. It gave Cullen, Monro, and like gravitas, but oversized wigs made him look ridiculous. Staring around the room, he was starting to doubt his decision.

He still looked like a student. How would he convince them he knew more than they did? Instead of looking like an infant playing with his father's wigs, he might look less like a peer and more like a figure of authority. It would have been another level of armour: the black robes covered his body, but left his head exposed.

The students were lounging on the chairs and desks, talking amongst themselves. They gave no acknowledgement of his arrival. His black academic robes felt cumbersome to move in, and he worried he would trip over the hem getting to the lectern.

Maybe their actions were a snub by Glaswegian standards, too.

After all, they'd been deprived of the university's most popular lecturer, and received a nobody in return.

"Good morning, Dr Black," one of the nearest students remarked in a heavy Doric burr. Black was tall, but this student outgrew him. His bearing and mannerisms suggested a prosperous mercantile upbringing, without encountering east coast snobbery to dent his ego. Oh, how familiar that appearance is, Black thought to himself. The student was about to return to his conversation when he noticed what was in Black's hand. "What's that there?"

Black had forgotten how forthright the Glaswegian students were in comparison to their Edinburgh counterparts. "This is a weighing balance of my own design." He set it on the table at the front of the hall.

Several nearby students paused their conversations to take a look.

"It's smaller than the one in my father's shop," an Irish student called out.

It was hard to tell if his intention was mockery, curiosity, or stating a fact.

"Quite so," Black agreed with a smile. "Yet my weighing balance is almost certainly more accurate."

There was an appreciative titter from the listeners. That noise was enough to silence most of the other students in the lecture theatre as they tried to work out what was going on at the front.

Black straightened. "In fact, this balance is here to act as the first demonstration of chemical and physical principles of the lecture course."

The merchant's son frowned. "We don't usually sit through lectures on the first day of the term, Dr Black. Professors here spend the first day collecting course fees. I didn't bring a quill."

The disturbance rippled through the auditorium. Students were looking at each other in confusion.

"Oh, I was about to clarify that I will devote the time to collecting your course payments...it is just that the balance will assist me."

Several students in the back row of seats were still talking, and the few paying attention were straining to hear him. Black took a deep breath. He lowered the pitch of his voice, letting it expand to fill the massive space.

"Concerns have risen among the faculty that counterfeit coinage is on the rise in Glasgow, after several noticed clipped guineas among their tuition payments last semester. As some of you might be aware, different metal mixtures possess different weights. Knowing the weight of a true guinea allows us to check coins for adulteration or clipping."

"And you can weigh a pile of guineas and tell it contains counterfeits?" a confidently periwigged English student with a Tory drawl asked, not bothering to move from his near-horizontal pose of recline across three chairs.

"Incorrect," Black replied with amusement. He paused. "I can weigh *one* coin and tell you if it's counterfeit or not."

A louder wave of noise crashed around the theatre.

"I certainly hope you'll forgive my caution," Black continued, turning his back on the students and moving towards his ledger and quill. "But as a new and youthful face in this university, I worry unscrupulous parties may take advantage of my trusting nature."

Black took his seat. He looked at the students surrounding him. Their faces betrayed a variety of emotions: curiosity, worry, fascination. But none of them looked bored. Tension, an electricity, filled the air.

"Professor Cullen never seemed concerned with counterfeit coins," commented the Tory student, now closer to vertical than horizontal.

What the students got from Cullen was the same thing they sought from all professors. They wanted to learn and feel intelligent instead of stupid. They wanted entertainment. They wanted spectacle.

A sly smile built on Black's face. He beckoned to the front row of students, who almost tripped over themselves to come forward with their purses. "Ah, but I am not Professor Cullen."

PART 3
EDINBURGH 1764 TO 1766

"It is said to be the manner of hypochondriacs to change often their physician...For a physician who does not admit the reality of the disease cannot be supposed to take much pains to cure it."

— WILLIAM CULLEN, FIRST LINES OF
THE PRACTICE OF PHYSIC (1777)

28

EDINBURGH

Cullen descended to the anatomy theatre like a modern Aeneas descending into the Underworld. No matter the season, a chill wind blew up the stairwell. Today, Cullen drew his academic gown around him in the hopes he wouldn't be seen shivering in front of Monro.

His bad mood started as soon as Monro's note requesting he stop by appeared in his own classroom a few days ago. Cullen didn't know what this meeting was about, but he knew Monro had already won.

A few weeks after he arrived in Edinburgh at the start of his first teaching term, Cullen thought he could ignore such petty notes; delaying the encounter until Monro was forced to seek him out. Over the years, Cullen instead learned that if Monro sent a summons, it meant he could afford to postpone the encounter where Cullen could not.

"Suffering builds character," Cullen muttered to himself, turning the final round in the spiral staircase. It's what his father always said after reprimanding him for arguing with his mother, or when he fell out an apple tree midway through attempted theft.

Postponing a meeting with Monro just gave his ill humours time to pool.

Monro always arrived at the college at some godforsaken hour of the morning, seemingly to get a few hours of quality gloating time to himself. As in their previous encounters, Cullen found the anatomy professor at the dissecting table, empty today, working through his papers.

The candles propped around the room caught under Monro's cheekbones and brows. He didn't waste his breath on greeting Cullen.

For his part, Cullen was getting good at maintaining eye contact with Monro while he crossed the classroom, even though there were uneven dais steps to navigate.

"Is this going to be like last month, when at first blush we were arguing about the oral examinations schedule, but it was really a spat over the disparaging remark I made about Boerhaave in '48? I enjoyed the thematic richness of that exchange."

Monro pinched the bridge of his nose. "Please. The subtext of that dispute was your remark from the spring of '46. Your 1748 Boerhaave comment can only be ascribed to puerile wit, and thus would be a waste of breath rebutting. However, your remark in 1746 came from a misunderstanding—certainly wilful—of Boerhaave's seminal thesis on the adrenal system, and should never have been propagated."

When he arrived in Edinburgh, Cullen expected the medical faculty to trade snide remarks and subtly undermine each other. There was nothing subtle about Monro's insults.

The anatomy professor flipped over his parchment and continued to annotate as he spoke, not looking up.

"I gain nothing from quarrelling with you about your medical theories, Dr Cullen. Your opinions are too entrenched, and I can't even claim following your circular rhetoric provides intellectual stimulation. What I need to tell you about is a topic I at least have a sliver of optimism I can persuade you to change course on."

"I wish I could share your optimism, Dr Monro," Cullen replied, unwilling to admit Monro had the advantage of him.

Monro flicked his quill onto the desk and gave it a contemptuous look, before staring Cullen straight in the eye.

"Last month a student named Quincy Mulligan approached you with questions concerning his dissertation thesis..."

Cullen didn't bother to suppress his groan of exasperation. Now he knew exactly why Monro was upbraiding him.

"...which he was writing under the supervision of Dr Rutherford, concerning a patient with febrile fever. Judging by your audible sigh, you recognise that your response to Mr Mulligan overstepped professional boundaries."

"Quincy asked for my opinion on the cause of febrile fevers." Cullen tried to keep his voice neutral. "Because I've discussed the topic in class. I certainly did not speak poorly of Dr Rutherford and his expertise, and if that's what you believe then someone has misrepresented my candid remarks."

As soon as Quincy opened his mouth Cullen knew the ensuing conversation would cause problems for him, but convinced himself the other faculty wouldn't find out. Rutherford subscribed to the traditional view of illness deriving from humoral imbalance, while Cullen argued disruptions to the nervous system were the cause of most sickness.

But as long as Quincy kept Cullen's remarks out of his dissertation, or addressed their theoretical disagreement with tact, his conversation wouldn't land Cullen in trouble.

Seemed Quincy didn't manage that.

Monro's expression remained the same: fixed.

"My least enjoyable conversations with you are when you feign ignorance about your inappropriate behaviour, so I will spell out your transgressions. First, you are tasked with teaching chemistry, not lecturing on medical topics."

"Unlike the late Plummer, I'm capable of covering chemical topics in a precise manner that allows me time to highlight other points of interest for a population of medical students." Cullen loathed feeling defensive about his teaching methods, or justifying himself to Monro, but pride made him speak out.

"Second, your nervous system theories are controversial and at odds with the prevailing wisdom. Which makes your espousal of them in the classroom problematic."

"As I've said, I don't contradict what the other faculty teach." Cullen couldn't remember if that's what he'd just said, but he believed he'd implied it. "I simply explain my own theories and the derivation of my ideas. The students can decide for themselves what they believe."

"Which leads me to my third point. Knowing the divergence of your stated doctrines from Dr Rutherford, you should have redirected Mr Mulligan back to his dissertation supervisor, instead of confusing him with your opinions. While some students are capable of discernment between competing dogmas, we both know Mr Mulligan is not one of them."

Cullen held this sigh in. Monro was right, and he knew it two sentences into his conversation with Quincy, by which point it was too late to stop talking. He enjoyed plenty of convivial discussions with his students in the classroom and tavern about medical topics: most of them understood he held a minority opinion, and therefore wouldn't repeat his theories in oral examinations or in their dissertations.

"Well, Dr Monro, I'm at liberty to teach what I like in my classroom, but I will add more disclaimers to protect the sensibilities of my good fellow professors." He wasn't trying to be sarcastic but nonetheless, sarcasm leaked out of every word.

Despite the darkened surroundings, it looked like Monro rolled his eyes.

"Again, the wilful misunderstanding. Dr Cullen." Here Monro's voice took on a sharper edge. "You've embarrassed Dr Rutherford by contradicting him—whether that was your intention or not—and hindered the education of a medical student. Mr

Mulligan has to rewrite his dissertation, and will certainly miss the June graduation date. A misfortune easily avoided, had you either declined to speculate on a patient case, or consulted with Dr Rutherford about how to counsel a student wishing to present competing theories in his dissertation."

"I'll speak to Quincy—I know he's a good lad—make sure he understands where Dr Rutherford and I differ in opinion," Cullen said quickly. He wasn't going to take responsibility for delaying Quincy's graduation—it was ridiculous to insinuate that was his fault—but arguing with Monro was a pointless endeavour and wasn't going to improve the man's opinion of him.

Monro waved his hand, not caring what wrongs Cullen was belatedly trying to right. "The problem with you, Dr Cullen? You don't behave as if we're on the same team."

Cullen had been ready to extract himself from the freezing anatomy theatre, but at Monro's remark his rage re-ignited and he flung himself back into the fight.

"It always comes back to this doesn't it, Alexander? The bewigged of Edinburgh sneering at William Cullen because he didn't study with them at Leiden; because he was slaving as an apothecary and village doctor when they were touring the Continent waiting to inherit their fathers' professorships. Because he doesn't talk their language of Boerhaave this, Boerhaave that. Because he stooped to teach in Glasgow, where they barely have a medical school." Cullen's voice bounced off the rafters, causing the shadows to vibrate. "In the end it doesn't matter what I say or do, because I'll always be the outsider, the usurper of damned Plummer, even though none of you liked him much anyway."

He'd tried to remain civil. Not letting Monro see how his barbs enraged him, and how deep some of his words dug. Cullen knew he had a reputation for rashness, and he'd tried so hard over the past few years to appear in control of his emotions. Now the rage tumbled out, proving the lot of them correct.

The echoes faded under the pounding of Cullen's heart. He sucked in cold air, staring at Monro and willing his foe to react.

All his got from Monro was a quiet exhalation and a return to his paperwork. "That summary of my sentiments is correct, but I've repeated it ad nauseam in one way or another, and am tired of retreading it." Monro didn't look tired; merely disgusted. "Believe it...or not...I meant something different with my observation.

"Dr Cullen, you operate as if you're a one-man medical school, and forget that you're one of ten medical professors that make up the Edinburgh College. No doubt you could strong-arm your way to what you wanted in Glasgow and force everyone else to accommodate your whims—you can't call what they have at Glasgow a medical school, and their senate was too awed by your popularity to oppose you. Here there's more than one great men, and the reason we have a great medical school is because none of those great men operate as single agents."

"I see nothing but inter-departmental vitriol here." Cullen said. He preferred it when Monro was contemptuous.

"Are you sure? You came all the way to Edinburgh just to condescend us up close?" Monro leaned forward in his chair. "I see a senate that gets things done. I see a system that prevents one medical genius from dominating proceedings and cowing his colleagues into serving his interests."

"Nothing gets done in the senate meetings," Cullen said. "Either departmental or university-wide."

"The smart men know better to than to bring crucial business to either of those fora. Planning the oral examinations is just one of those negotiating processes that takes place behind closed doors in a fraction of the time. When you decide to make a mockery of the oral exam scheduling, you insult the time of the other faculty, and reduce their likelihood of future cooperation."

"I know this admonition isn't welling from the fullness of your affection towards me, Dr Monro. Don't pretend lofty concerns of brotherhood motivate you."

A smile spiked from the corners of Monro's mouth.

"I do actually care about the running of this faculty. And since you are now part of this faculty, you become part of my concerns."

"Heartwarming." The cold cellar was giving Cullen a headache. Monro's presence was also giving him a headache. One of those headaches pressed in from the back of his skull, the other pressed from the front. "And incorrect. The dark chymists are why Edinburgh enjoys its pretension of status, and Dr Monro and Dr Rutherford's purpose is to give them everything they want, in exchange for humouring their fantasies of importance, and your little smallpox inoculation vanity project."

A icy fury crept into Monro's expression.

"Smallpox killed two of my daughters, Dr Cullen. You dare accuse me of being motivated by vanity?"

Of course Cullen wanted to provoke him, but as Monro's pupils constricted, he knew he'd struck too deeply. He was vaguely aware Monro lost four girls in infancy, but hadn't known their causes of death.

Monro drew a hissing breath in. When he spoke again his voice had returned to its measured hauteur. "The reason you're failing in Edinburgh, Dr Cullen, is the same reason you failed to succeed in Glasgow. It will be the reason you fail at any institution—high or low—you associate yourself with. The reason for your continued failure can be found in your own classroom, your own home. Any room with a mirror, in fact."

He should have stormed out of the room long before this. Wordless, Cullen retreated towards the door, refusing to turn his back on his opponent and give him the satisfaction of smirking at his back.

It wasn't as if Monro said something he'd not already heard a million times in his own head, late at night when Anna's snoring kept him awake. Coming from his enemy, actualised into spoken words, it still hurt.

"Damn it, Joe," Cullen muttered to himself as he stormed up

the stairwell towards daylight. "How did you survive in this pit of vipers? You made it look easy."

29

GLASGOW

A waterfall of dusty light spilled into his classroom. In the distance, Black could hear thrushes chirruping.

The room was usually cold, but right now he had a patch of sunlight warming the back of his neck. His chemistry class long-dismissed for the day, Black sketched a set of flasks he wanted his glassblower to make. They weren't of complicated design—this time—but Black didn't want any misunderstandings.

Unlike Cullen, Black didn't need to run around Glasgow in the afternoons seeing patients. His chemistry classes were at a size comfortable enough for him to live on, and consultation work from various linen bleachers and farmers allowed him to invest in newer equipment. Building his own medical practice was a blissfully low priority.

Speaking of Cullen, an unopened letter from his former professor sat on his desk at home. Black intended to bring it with him today, so he could read and respond to it between appointments, but it slipped his mind.

A couple of weeks passed since the letter arrived, and Black kept telling himself he'd get round to it, before forgetting.

He wasn't *trying* to ignore his former mentor...but the importance of those letters shrunk over the years. Once upon a time, Black would rarely wait a day before dispatching his replies.

Today for instance, Black had fielded letters from laboratory suppliers, a natural philosopher in Birmingham, two wealthy patients and the Secretary of the Faculty of Physicians and Surgeons, concerning the end of his second Presidential term. They all required prompt, thoughtful responses. He was busy every day with physician and scientific matters, but never overwhelmed.

All said, his commitment to the medical profession had yielded the perfect outcome.

"You cultivate such a scholarly appearance, Dr Black. I'm impressed."

Black looked up from his correspondence. A man his own age stood next to the benched seating, his flowing ministerial gown mirroring Black's own.

The door to his classroom was hefty oak, it required a lot of strength to open, and it tended to scrape against the flagstone. Yet he'd not heard anyone enter.

"I'm surprised to see you here," Black said with more honesty than he wanted to admit. For eight years he'd wondered about the fate of the semi-invisible assassin whose body he left in the wynd. When that young divinity student with the unnerving smile disappeared from Edinburgh around the same time, Black drew the obvious conclusion. It was a reassuring conclusion.

Yet here Holm was.

"I'm flattered to learn my absence in Edinburgh was noticed," Holm remarked, settling himself onto the bench. Four metres separated them. "But duty called. I've been tending a flock in the Hebrides these past few years."

"And what specific circumstances bring you into my classroom?" Black asked, pressing his elbows into the table as he leaned forward.

The manic glint in Holm's eye had faded with age, and he

carried himself with ministerial poise. But there was an undercurrent of something that caused Black's heart rate to rise. It was as if he were mimicking normal behaviour.

"Well, my wife and I are making our way back to Edinburgh, and we have to stop and rest somewhere along the way, I suppose." Holm flashed a disarming grin.

If this wasn't the man he killed, then who were they? Black wondered. He'd been so certain...

"There are numerous taverns that provide better hospitality than I am able to offer," Black said, rising. "I'm happy to direct you to them."

Holm stayed seated, ignoring Black's attempt to dismiss him.

Was there any way the assassin could have survived what Black did to him? He knew the force he'd lashed out with.

"State your business, Holm. I can't amuse you all day."

"It's Reverend Holm these days," Holm replied. He wasn't looking directly at Black, instead smiling to himself in a way that made Black nervous. "Unless with my friends. But I didn't think we were especially close, Joseph."

He was trying to provoke Black.

Instead of stepping forward, Black returned to his chair and started grabbing at his lecture notes.

"Well, until you have the mind to speak and conclude this encounter, I will return to my lecture notes." He didn't need to rewrite anything—his notes were updated last week. But Black still made a show of copying a note onto a new piece of paper. From where he was sitting, Holm wouldn't know.

There was a pause. Black tried not to look in the direction of his unwelcome visitor.

He saw the flash of dark movement. Holm was on his feet, rushing towards him, his face impossible to read.

Where once the art of summoning and discharging phlogiston required concentration, now Black found his body responded faster than his mind. Where it once felt like drawing a serpent through his veins, now moved as phlogiston part of him. He pulled the phlogiston into his heart and tensed, ready to strike.

His hand was half-raised when Holm froze.

"What the fuck was that?" he demanded.

Black let his hand drift down to the table. It was as if an invisible wall had descended between the two men. Holm was a few strides from Black, but seemed unable to move forward.

"I beg your pardon?" Black was temporarily too stunned by Holm's cursing to react any other way.

Holm's eyes and nostrils flared. Although his feet seemed pinned in place, the rest of his body started working.

The phlogiston was still raging through Black's body. The edge of fear had been taken away by Holm's strange behaviour, but on an intellectual level he recognised the situation had become a lot less predictable.

"God damn you, Joseph. It was that—I know it was…"

As abruptly as he rushed forward, then froze, Holm stormed out the classroom.

He was afraid, Black thought. Something terrified him.

He licked his lips. The metallic taste of phlogiston hung in the air, and it'd be hours before he got it out of his mouth.

Had Holm sniffed the air before he left? But that was impossible, Holm knew nothing of phlogiston: he didn't know it existed, so why did he act like he sensed it?

The immediate fear and adrenalin rush from the confrontation had dissipated along with the phlogiston, only to be replaced with a deeper dread.

That's something I'll have to ask William, thought Black. *When I next see him in person of course, since it's too dangerous committing the idea to paper. But I'll have to ask him—does he believe the dark chymists capable of raising the dead?*

30

EDINBURGH

"Where's the black-haired Irish weaver?" Cullen asked. "Did you move her to a different ward?"

Rutherford gave an exasperated sigh. "No, I sent her home."

"I'm sorry?"

"She was being disruptive and argumentative with the nurses. I figured if she was well enough to yell, she was taking up a bed another destitute soul could benefit from."

I'm surprised, Cullen thought. I know Rutherford too well to be shocked by his actions, but he has managed to surprise me.

"For every three steps she had to lean against the wall to get her breath back," Cullen said. "She was wrecked by consumption and it's honestly unlikely she managed to terrorise the nurses in her feeble state."

"Well, everyone's happier that she's gone. If you were here an hour earlier you'd have seen the state the wards were in."

"If everyone could have held their tongues, the Irish woman would have been useful to show my patients. There were a few interesting aspects of her consumption that I want my students to look out for."

"Patients with consumption are hardly orchids in Edinburgh, Dr Cullen. You'll get another case within a few weeks, I imagine."

He may or may not. There was never a guarantee a sick patient would come to the Infirmary when he had beds available, and the physicians always looked out for interesting clinical cases to present to their students.

Rutherford's excuse for removing Cullen's patient was just that: an excuse. It was another minor way Rutherford and the others sought to inconvenience Cullen. Too much expressed annoyance would convince Rutherford to pull this trick again.

It took several years before Rutherford even agreed to share his Royal Infirmary with Cullen, and that only happened because Whytt and Monro decided they wanted to conduct clinical lectures too.

By this point, students had begun to file into the Infirmary wards in preparation for the daily midday rounds. Cullen could do little more than scowl at Rutherford's back, and shepherd his students to the other room. It was one of the few rules of the Edinburgh game Cullen wholeheartedly subscribed to: keep your squabbles away from the students.

"Step this way, gentlemen. We'll begin in the west wing today…"

Having engineered the day's round to avoid Rutherford, Cullen took the short walk home. By four o'clock the sun had already dipped below the tenement lands, submerging the Cowgate in shadow. That said, the glimpses of sunset he got through spidery gaps between building was a pleasing golden hue. Cullen tried to focus on those pleasant beams, but he was still brooding over the latest slights from Monro and Rutherford.

Rutherford's dismissal of his Irish patient was probably retaliation for Cullen's role in Quincy's dissertation mess.

This was a repetition of the materia medica business. Almost as soon as he arrived in Edinburgh, Cullen's students clamoured for him to deliver a course on materia medica. The demand arose because Cullen took pains to explain to his new students why the chemistry he taught differed from Plummer's pharmaceutical preparation-based course. It was only natural the students would wonder how Cullen distinguished both aspects.

Since the students asked consistently over several terms—a sign they were serious about attending such a course and not merely feigning polite interest—Cullen decided to honour them. He delivered two courses on materia medica. The courses proved popular: several years later students still asked him questions based on those lectures. The Edinburgh faculty were furious, claiming Cullen hadn't followed protocol or obtained their blessing to teach the subject.

This seemed stupid to Cullen. He chose a lecture time that didn't clash with any of their courses—it's not like he'd have an audience if he competed with their classes—and it wasn't like Monro asked his permission when he split Anatomy into a morning and evening course.

They're jealous of you, he reminded himself. That's what this is about.

With the Earl of Hopetoun singing his praises and the dark chymists silent, it hadn't been difficult to establish a comfortable practice in Edinburgh. Nor had Cullen needed to encroach on the existing physicians' patient lists, because an increasing chunk of his income came from letter consultations.

Come to think of it, Rutherford hadn't—to Cullen's knowledge—extracted revenge for last summer's materia medica business. Or maybe today's incident was revenge against Cullen for not noticing Rutherford's previous attempt at revenge. Cullen needed a ledger to keep track.

There's never a moment in Edinburgh when I'm not doing something wrong. In walking up St Ninian's Wynd minding my own business, perhaps I have unintentionally failed to tip my hat to a strolling noble, causing deep offence.

Turning down the Cowgate, Cullen took a sharp left into Mint Close. Passing through a narrow gap between buildings, he came into the wide courtyard which housed the Scottish Royal Mint a few decades ago.

The one thing—perhaps the only thing—Cullen considered fortuitous about the move to Edinburgh was his new home. Anna and the bairns had struggled for a few months in rented lodgings, before Cullen learned the former dwelling of the Master of the Royal Mint needed a new owner.

Nothing about his new home was fashionable, but it was a more spacious and respectable home—the old oak panels and painted ceilings were charming to look at—than Cullen thought he'd find in Edinburgh.

He supposed that was another point of bad blood between him and the other physicians.

Cullen wanted to release the day's frustration by expelling fire across the close and letting the flames incinerate an abandoned cart, but he'd refrained from any phlogiston investigations while he's in Edinburgh for fear of the wrong person seeing them. Right now the courtyard was quiet, but most of the old Mint buildings surrounding him were occupied, and there was plenty of daylight remaining. He wondered if he could summon the phlogistic power back now it had lain dormant for several years.

It was a bitter pill to swallow; since moving to Edinburgh he'd encountered several students, Patrick and Nathanial among them, who Cullen thought would have the ability to wield phlogiston. It seemed cruel to deny them part of their natural talents.

But he couldn't risk exposure.

Black told him what he did to survive jumping out the collapsing tenement building, but he waited until Cullen visited Glasgow, almost a year after the fact.

"That would be a lot of force, Joe," Cullen had mused. By this point, Black buried his emotions regarding what transpired beneath a calm exterior. If the experience terrified him, Cullen wouldn't know. "Did you suffer ill-effects?"

Black had sighed, and Cullen knew it was a foolish question, because he'd explained that he remained on the High Street long enough to witness mangled bodies get dragged from the debris.

"There was some blood in my stool a few days afterwards. I had stomach aches and tenderness that faded within the week."

No one saw Black fall. He didn't recall landing at anyone's feet. He crawled away as the dust settled, invisible in the murky confusion.

Afterwards...nothing. No one questioned Black about his likeness. No rumours flew around Edinburgh regarding anyone's miraculous flight—Cullen was sure he'd know if they did. Talk of the tragedy morphed into political concerns: accelerating the proposed drainage of the Nor Loch and construction of a new town in the shadow of Calton Hill. The tenement collapse rolled into the mass of tragedies and deprivations that town leaders cited as one when justifying their civic expansion plans.

Black's escape and defence of the Earl of Hopetoun were all the graces the pair were afforded. A third instance courted damnation.

Cullen didn't have time to remove his hat before Anna's cough warned him against getting too comfortable.

"Visitors, love?"

While never gregarious, Anna adjusted to her role as Edinburgh physician's wife with less rancour than Cullen feared. She took a measured delight in being an attentive hostess to the endless stream of medical students, patients and university acquaintances that stopped by. She refused to elaborate on the state of her social circle, but Cullen suspected outside the house Anna experienced a degree of ostracism amongst women of her standing. She didn't take tea with Mrs Rutherford, that was for sure.

Awkwardly perched in Cullen's dining room was a tradesman with ink-stained hands, which he rubbed together constantly. Cullen resigned himself to bad news before the man opened his mouth.

"I'm sorry, Dr Cullen. I wanted to come and apologise in person..."

"Don't shake, Ewan. I understand how Edinburgh operates."

"The booksellers won't accept it. I talked to my connections in London and Dublin, and they were of shared opinion about the Philadelphia booksellers too."

"Did you send them the excerpts I gave you? They can see my textbook is not incendiary in the slightest."

"After consultation..."

"Yes, yes, the learned physicians, chirurgeons and apothecaries they consulted told them no..."

It was Rutherford's doing. Not that Monro wouldn't stoop to such behaviour, but Cullen's manuscript on the nosology of disease states was seen as an attempt to usurp Rutherford's standing as chief expert on medical practice in Edinburgh. That it was precisely what Cullen intended didn't help his case.

Black had talked him out of his proposed translation and commentary on Boerhaave's Latin aphorisms a few winters back.

If you can name one printer who you think will support you, I will assist with your translation, Black wrote. But any name eludes me.

Once the printer departed, Cullen sat in the dining room and counted to one hundred. Then he headed to the kitchen.

Anna was rearranging a stack of plates, no doubt waiting for him to seek her out.

"I'm sorry, love."

"It's not that big a problem," Cullen said, wrapping an arm around her waist. "Not in the grand scheme of today."

"Oh, it's that bad?" She didn't ask for more detail, and Cullen didn't offer it. They both knew what an average day heralded.

She pointed towards the table. A glass of wine was set there.

"Thank you, my love." This wasn't the first time Anna had anticipated his need for a drink at the end of a long day. He took a sipped and sighed.

"Are you sure you don't want to write to the Principal in Glasgow? I'm sure he'll be understanding..."

Cullen held up his hand.

"There's no need. I wouldn't want to burden you and the bairns with a return to reduced circumstances."

"It's not all about the money, William," Anna responded with a meaningful look, helping herself to a second glass of wine stowed near the plates. "And most of those 'bairns' are hardly helpless infants any more."

"Well, that's part of my point. Young Robert is on his way to becoming a fine lawyer, and Henry is still insisting he wants to be a physician like his father—proof if ever there was that intelligence and common sense aren't synonymous—not to mention how the girls are flourishing here..." Anna rested her chin in her husband's shoulder. He knew she knew all this. "I know you think I'm being mule-headed about this. If it were *just* a question of wealth, or *just* a question of our children's prospects...then maybe the choice between staying in Edinburgh and returning to Glasgow would be more self-apparent."

Monro claimed he was failing in Edinburgh. In some respects the bastard was right, but the family account books told of healthy class sizes and a stable, albeit not illustrious, physician practice.

"You're an ambitious man. I kenned that early on." Anna's eyes glinted. "No shame in that."

She might be the only person in Edinburgh who would claim that. But she was right: Cullen had always believed he was destined for more; that he could change things for the better. He thought moving to Edinburgh eight years ago was the first step towards fulfilling that destiny. From this vantage point, it looked awfully like it was fated to be his last.

"I know I should be grateful the dark chymists aren't peering over my shoulder, waving their daggers under my nose...but they aren't eradicated. Or else why would everyone behave like this?"

That was the smallest blessing: since moving here he'd never been threatened, nor left in fear for his life. Granted, some of Rutherford and Monro's malice was independent of their supposed patrons. But the men known as the dark chymists still lived, played and worked in Edinburgh. They kept mostly to themselves, but their reputation was enough. Cullen's appointment to the Chemistry Chair was the only defiance Edinburgh citizens were willing to express. People still largely did what the dark chymists wanted them to do, if only out of precautious habit.

"Why can't we just be rid of them once and for all?" Cullen sighed.

Anna raised her eyebrows. "Well aye, if we could click our fingers and the dark chymists vanished that'd be braw, I guess. But they've survived by being hard to flush out. Think of how they've married and incorporated their way across British high society."

"But there's only ten or so active players," Cullen protested. "The ones with the real power and access to Babylon."

He saw those men all the time going about their business, heading home from convivial gatherings, laughing together in the taverns. You could see it once you were close enough: who held the power in the room, who was watching each other for the cue to laugh. Lord Argyle and Sir Anthony were still on top of that ladder.

"How easily could you kill ten men?" Anna asked, still not taking him seriously.

Murdering in cold blood is what they do. We purport to be better than them.

He didn't want to concede his wife had a point. "Take away their library and I doubt they'd be so powerful."

Anna looked unconvinced. "How much coinage and power do you think they need to push Rutherford and Monro around?"

"Astoundingly little," Cullen admitted.

He'd not articulated these thoughts clearly in his head, but he worried about the same things Anna was worrying about. Would destroying their library be enough to stop the dark chymists? If Rutherford continued to bend his knee to them, what would change?

"It can't be long before Rutherford retires," Anna said, patting his hand. "You'll have your opportunity then."

For the dark chymists to remain cowed, I need to be respected enough that I can do what must be done. I need to be in charge. Cullen gave Anna's thigh a reciprocal squeeze. As far as he could tell, those two goals were one and the same.

Despite the chaos that was Cullen's professional life—rushing between international correspondence, patient calls, clinical rounds at the Infirmary, lectures and smaller gatherings with his students—he made a point of punctuality.

The other faculty couldn't conceal their surprise that Cullen appeared on time, and managed to leave in time for his next order of business without the appearance of being harried or rushing.

Knowing how intent the faculty and dark chymists were on inconveniencing him, Cullen strove extra hard to give the appearance of supreme organisation.

Maybe they thought he'd be too preoccupied burning Bibles, or whatever atheistic nonsense they ascribed to him.

31

WEST LOTHIAN

Seated on his favourite chair, positioned in the warmth of the afternoon sunlight, Rutherford drifted between wakefulness and slumber.

This week he'd allowed himself to relax in a way he hadn't in a while. In fact it felt like he was releasing many years of tension he'd forgotten he held on to. This little West Lothian farmstead wasn't much, but with a little more attention it would ripen in time for his retirement.

The first notions of retirement had come into his mind five or more years ago, and he'd not thought himself sincere in his desire until now. Before there had been doubts and hesitations. Concern about his legacy and leaving the medical school to the next generation of scholars. Of course Cullen's arrival forced him to delay his plans, but now Rutherford felt he knew what needed to be done, and his patrons were in alignment about his successor.

It was a tight knot he'd had to weave, but with the late afternoon sun warming his face he felt at peace.

A man's cough pulled him back into the room from his quasi-slumber.

"Dr Rutherford?" a stranger's voice asked. "Forgive us for disturbing you."

Us? wondered Rutherford, sitting up and focusing on the visitors.

They were strangers, though something about the man seemed familiar, but in an unfocused way. He was a minister, holding the hand of a diminutive country girl clad in rough cloth. That they were married was obvious.

"You have me at a considerable disadvantage," Rutherford admitted. He ought to rise and greet his visitors, who smiled politely and pretended they hadn't woken him, but he needed a minute before he was sure circulation had returned to his legs.

"For which is entirely my fault Dr Rutherford, and I beg for your forgiveness." The man spoke as if he was already known to Rutherford. He had to be in his thirties, a faint strip of sunburn across his cheekbones suggesting a rural life in line with his spouse's rustic appearance. "We enquired after you in the town, and were told you had retired your farm..." Rutherford felt a flash of guilt that the stranger seemed to know his thoughts, but he didn't mean retirement in *that* sense. "Given the hour and my own pressing business, I decided to repair to you directly without sending word. I imagine we can return to our town lodgings before sunset."

It would be a long day for the couple, Rutherford thought. He could make the journey from Edinburgh in half a day, travelling at the more sedate pace he could tolerate in his advanced age. To perform two hasty trips within hours of each other would exhaust most men, and who knows what it would do to a member of the fairer sex. If the wife had any complaint about the journey, she didn't show it. Instead, she modestly averred her eyes and leaned in to her husband.

"Oh, I quite forget myself!" Seeing Rutherford looking at his wife, the minister stepped forward. "Please allow me to introduce Mrs Cinead Holm to you, Dr Rutherford."

"My pleasure," Rutherford said, inclining his head. By this point he'd already pieced the fragments of memory together. It was the minister's use of the word 'business' that stirred his memory. Of course it was Malcolm Holm! The dark curly hair was concealed under a wig, he'd filled out from his narrow adolescent frame into a broader adult, but otherwise he'd barely changed. I must be old and half-senile if I managed to forget Malcolm Holm, Rutherford thought.

"I don't wish to detain you, given your long journey ahead of you, but I'm happy to offer you tea and dinner." Rutherford cursed himself for blabbering and offering such hospitality. He wanted his wife to come into the room, to be with him, even though she loathed the man.

With recognition came all the other emotions and memories Rutherford would rather suppress. The fear. Anger at himself for his cowardice. The way at the worst moments Holm's eerie smile constricted his bladder.

"I could not make such demands on your hospitality, Dr Rutherford," Holm waved his hand. "It would be unjust reward for my ill manners. And as I said, we must depart within the hour to be back in Edinburgh by nightfall."

"Well..." Rutherford needed a drink. His own wife had sidled into the room, clinging to the cabinet near the door. She didn't need to be reminded who this visitor was. "Love, please bring through the port."

He could think of no good reason why Holm would have rode out here with such urgency, especially when he told his acquaintances he would return to his city apartment Thursday.

"Given my rude intrusion into your charming dwelling, I should explain my purpose here without preamble."

Rutherford bade the couple sit. Holm gestured for his wife to sit beside him at the dining table, ignoring the port and glasses Rutherford's trembling wife placed in front of him.

"Don't worry..." Rutherford mumbled. He knew he didn't sound convincing.

"I seek your help as a matter of vital urgency. What do you remember of the night Lord Argyle summoned you to tend to me?" Holm asked. The tone was careful, as one might enquire about a recent illness that the subject appeared to have recovered from.

"Do you mean...?"

"It is okay for us to talk of these things. My wife has my full confidence." Holm smiled gently at his wife, who modestly looked at her knees.

Was it Gaelic he'd heard Holm speak a moment ago? Perhaps his wife did not even understand English. Rutherford knew many on the islands did not trouble themselves to learn the tongue of the country.

"I'm getting old and my memory isn't what it was," Rutherford said, shaking his head. "I'm not sure my recollections are to be trusted."

"Oh, but they are." Holm leaned forward with the sharpness that once characterised his youth. Rutherford flinched before he could stop himself. As if aware he'd made Rutherford uncomfortable, he settled back and smiled. "I don't wish to conceal my intentions from you, Professor Rutherford. I came here to ask you about this because ever since that night I'd settled on a particular memory of what happened to me. I constructed a story in my head you see, and its ink deepened in hue over time. But then very recently a chance encounter happened that threw my carefully constructed story into doubt."

"Perhaps some truths are best not dwelled on. Some of my patients were content not knowing the full extent of their maladies; being confronted with the ugly facts caused them much distress." Rutherford believed what he was saying, but he also hoped to dissuade Holm from entering into this conversation. He'd done all he could to banish the memories into that night into the recesses of his mind. Apart from the occasional nightmare, he thought he'd succeeded.

Holm smiled again. There was sadness in his eyes.

"Please, Professor Rutherford. Any insights you can share...I need to hear. Lord Argyle asked you to determine the cause of death?"

He spoke as if the dead body under examination wasn't his own.

He couldn't get Holm to leave. He'd have to go through this. Rutherford tried one last time to avert what was becoming the inevitable.

"Did you not speak with Lord Argyle?"

"Ah, our relationship cooled shortly after." Holm's gaze dropped to his dusty shoes. "My masters blamed me for failed business that night. It was a blessing, of course—to be freed from their clutches. I fear returning to their circle given how much I've worked to save myself: I'll face either cruelty or temptation."

It was hard to believe this was the divinity student who terrorised Rutherford and his family. It showed remarkable strength of character. Rutherford whetted his lips.

"The cause of death was inconclusive. I saw no knife or grapeshot wounds, nor any signs of strangulation. No broken bones, no injuries beyond light bruising on this limbs."

"It was a bloody business I used to engage in. Not a day goes by where I don't relive the horrors I inflicted." Holm pressed a hand to his mouth.

Holm's wife rubbed his shoulders and murmured something. For a moment it was as if the two had forgotten Rutherford was there—wrapped in their own world. Holm nodded and grasped her hand, and their foreheads almost touched.

It reminded Rutherford of when he first got married, those private moments with his young bride when nothing else mattered. It faded with time—it could never last—but the sight of it still made him nostalgic.

Holm turned his attention back to Rutherford, though his wife kept her hand on his shoulder and continued to look at him with warm eyes.

"The passage of time has blessed me with so many things, Professor Rutherford. Wisdom being just one of them. I should never have killed the Bennett boy. He was as innocent as as lamb. I knew as soon as it happened I had sinned grievously, that I could never wash his blood from my soul."

Rutherford never thought he'd see the day Holm repented for his depraved acts. He was cycling through many emotions—confusion, anger, terror—in such a short space of time. He gulped down another glass of port.

"Could I have been poisoned?" Holm asked, the suddenness of the question startling Rutherford as he swallowed a mouthful of port.

"What did you eat and drink that evening?" Rutherford asked. Being interrogated about medical concerns added another layer of confusion above the fear.

"No, no," Holm shook his hand. "That wouldn't have been possible. I meant was I exposed to a poison that had an instantaneous lethal effect?"

"I'm unsure of any poison that would act in such a rapid manner," Rutherford admitted. "You would have felt the effects of most common poisons, even if it felt like a sudden illness or stomach complaint. You felt yourself succumbing to poison?"

This process would feel less like guesswork if Holm told him what transpired before his apparent death. But he couldn't coax the details out of Holm—not that Rutherford wanted to hear them, really. Holm was in some altercation as evident by his bruises —to what evil the wretch intended who knows—and his memory of events was murky. Despite that, there was a lot he was concealing.

"But a man like Joseph Black would have access to all sorts of obscure pharmaceuticals, would he not?" Holm asked.

"Dr Black?" Rutherford's entire stream of thought was overturned by this abrupt change of subject.

"I mean men of the college," Holm said quickly. "Any philosopher with an interest in chemical pursuits might have the means to prepare subtle poisons?"

Holm appeared more agitated than he'd been since arriving. His wife took both his hands in her own, the Gaelic she muttered now discernible. She tried to command her husband's attention, but he appeared too distracted to be consoled.

Holm had let something slip he hadn't wanted to—he was biting his lip in concern now—but Rutherford realised he wasn't alarmed by the possibilities this inadvertent admission raised. There was always something unnatural about the young Joseph Black, wasn't there? Ever since he was a student Rutherford found him suspicious. The way he stared, but never reacted when you caught him staring. He never figured out what old Monro saw in the boy. Not with his slavish devotion to Cullen and inability to be impressed by anything.

No, Rutherford thought. Black and Cullen thought they could do whatever they liked, they always looked down their noses at the rest of the faculty. He didn't want to jump to the most obvious conclusion rashly, but now Holm's decision to approach him away from Edinburgh made sense.

Now he was thinking clearly, the edge of his nerves smoothed away by the port, Rutherford identified his absence of surprise as coming from another recollection, only now re-forming in his mind.

"It's interesting that you should mention Dr Black as an example, though," Rutherford began. Holm watched without blinking. "Because it brings to mind a fantastical rumour I once heard concerning the young doctor. It was shared with me several years ago by a consumptive water carrier I treated as an act of charity. He lived opposite St Giles..."

32

EDINBURGH

"You look troubled, Patrick. Care to tell me what's on your mind?"

Patrick hesitated, but Cullen used the pause to push a wine glass his way.

"Tell ye the truth, Professor Rutherford's giving me grief. I don't mean to speak ill of the fella..." Cullen waved his hand to calm Patrick's rising panic as he realised what he was saying. "But my chum and I can't make head nor tail of his lecturing. I practiced my Latin, getting good at reading it so I am, but he talks too fast in class for me to follow."

"You aren't the only one who's struggling, Patrick. I'll try to speak to Dr Rutherford in general terms about his lecturing style, and I won't mention any names."

Cullen's heart was low, because this wasn't the first time he'd tried to persuade Rutherford to either slow down his delivery, or switch to English. That conversation had gone as well as he expected: which was to say, terribly.

"Latin is the language of scholars, Dr Cullen. I once thought that by matriculating at Edinburgh, students were choosing to become scholars. When did I become mistaken?"

Patrick came from a town ten miles from Ulster. He was the first in his family to pursue a university education. Part of the reason he came through to Edinburgh was because Cullen treated his uncle back in Glasgow, and they'd struck up a conversation about his promising nephew.

In the evenings Monro used to round up his sons and the boys from other prominent chieftain families and spend an hour conversing in Latin with them. Patrick's father was a textile weaver who worked sunrise til nightfall and could barely read the bible.

Hours spent running around the countryside after his mother, the local wise woman and midwife, left Patrick with an encyclopaedic knowledge of botany and the components of many medical preparations. Last summer he'd helped Cullen revise his materia medica notes: Patrick didn't know the Latin names for many plants, but he recognised their etchings or cuttings.

Cullen wanted to defend Patrick's honour to Rutherford, but he knew Patrick wanted his name kept out of their arguments. Which was a valid desire. Rutherford's connections spread as far as several Irish cities, and he could inconvenience Patrick from as far away as Ulster.

There wasn't much he could do to help Patrick in that regard, and both of them knew it.

Still, he saw the boy had finished his wine and was looking out the window.

"It's shaping up to be a nice day, isn't it? We can go through some of the lecture material you're struggling with...or perhaps head to the Physic Garden and collect those plant samples we spoke about?"

It was a loaded question, because Cullen knew what Patrick would rather do, given the option.

"Let's head to the garden, Dr Cullen. I brought my list, by the way."

"Yes." Cullen smiled in spite of himself. "I suspected you did."

Cullen avoided telling Anna of his woes. She sniffed that

despite her womanly nature it was possible for her to understand the complex storm of civic and university politics her husband swam through.

That wasn't really the reason. Cullen wanted to come home to serene domestic bliss, escaping his daytime woes. Treating Anna as a confidant encouraged those woes into his households. He felt like a bad husband when he mixed the two facets of his life. Anna insisted she'd feel less stressed when she knew exactly what troubled him, but her assurances didn't help.

His assistant trailed Cullen through the university physic garden. It was a balmy May afternoon—a deceptively bad time to exert oneself outdoors for too long. The garden sat at the edge of the Royal Infirmary building, forming a neutral zone between it and the College grounds to the west.

While walking through greenery in the smoggy heart of Edinburgh should have been peaceful, Cullen found the garden more chaotic than serene. The older, more established Physic Garden on the north side of Edinburgh was being abandoned—the land around the drained Nor Loch basin was getting too swampy to cultivate—which meant the surviving plants were being brought here and crammed in to the available space. There once had been ordered beds and quadrants, but it was hard to find traces of them.

Usually this disorder would bother Cullen more than Patrick, since the boy grew up foraging in the country, but today he was unusually agitated.

Every so often Patrick would drop into a crouch and rub the leaves of the plants. Cullen focused on his own list of plants to identify and clip, but he noticed Patrick's frown was deepening, and he started to scurry back and forth among the sites he'd stopped at, peering under bushes and digging around in the soil.

"How are you getting on, Patrick?" Cullen asked, aware that something was amiss.

"If I'm honest, Dr Cullen, I'm a little concerned." He took an awkward hop-step towards Cullen and lowered his voice. "There seems to be..."

"Can I help you, Dr Cullen?" barked Alston, appearing behind him like a heat mirage.

The man was several decades' older than Cullen, but sprightly. The unruly grey tufts of his eyebrows clashed with the smooth, thick rolls of his wig.

"As a matter of fact, Charles, I hope you can." Cullen pretended that it wasn't an oversight of his that he'd not told Alston he wanted to collect samples from the garden he shared responsibility for. "Me and my assistant Patrick were hoping to sketch several herbs for my personal materia medica notes, and I'm having trouble finding..." Cullen fumbled with the list in his hands. There was quite a few plants he'd yet to find. "Wild rosemary, knot berry and..."

"I have a list of all physic garden plants in my room," Alston said. "Showing where I planted them in the garden. It's pointless you being out here without it." He turned and marched back towards the college.

The man did have a point. Cullen nodded to Patrick and the two of them trudged back towards the shade of the buildings.

"What were you about to say to me?" Cullen asked Patrick.

The young man shook his head and gave his professor a pained glance. "It was nothing, Dr Cullen. Forget I mentioned it."

Alston was within earshot, though he was doing a great job of ignoring them. Cullen decided not to push the matter at present.

Alston's teaching room was occupied with decades' worth of manuscripts and books with torn flyleaves. While Cullen and Patrick hovered awkwardly, he tossed aside dried plant matter, scissors and twine until he unearthed a green marbled ledger.

"Here, you see..." Alston came around the table and pushed the book under Cullen's nose. He started to show Cullen his notation and how the listings were organised. He never glanced at

Patrick: as far as Alston was concerned, the Irish student was a non-entity.

"Right, so wild rosemary would be..." Cullen could barely make sense of Alston's scratchy handwriting, and in speaking aloud he hoped his brain would have enough time to begin processing it.

"The categorisation is obvious when you think about it," Alston nudged the book into Cullen's hand.

Cullen was standing at the door, looking into the classroom. Over Alston's shoulder, Cullen could see Patrick creep up to Alston's desk and peruse whatever documents Alston had left there. Cullen saw what looked like shock flash across his student's face. Patrick dropped his face closer to one of the books and trace his thumb along the writing. With his back to the room, Alston could see none of this.

"While I'm here, Charles..." Cullen's imagination had gone perfectly blank. He tapped the book between his fingers. Alston stared at Cullen with annoyance, as if it was rude he'd been forced to share this limited quantity of materia medica expertise.

The only thing that came into Cullen's head was the letter he'd left on his desk at home before coming out to meet Patrick at the garden.

"I, err, received a letter from a gentlemen in Coventry who sought healing spa waters for his wife. He asked me where I'd recommend she seek treatment and um, I realised I knew nothing about the spas of Northern France..."

The wrinkles on Alston's face reformed from annoyance to incredulity. "You're asking me about the spa waters of Brittany?"

"Or Normandy, I suppose..." Patrick rifled faster and faster through Alston's notebooks, his expression no longer readable. "Actually Charles, I'm not sure who I should even pose such a question to—maybe you know of someone who has sought such restorative treatment abroad?"

"Dr Black grew up in Bordeaux, did he not? He appears the

obvious candidate to ask." Alston's contempt of Cullen's misguided questioning was plain.

"Right, yes, of course..." Cullen couldn't think of any other way to prolong the conversation. "Patrick and I best be getting on our way."

At the mention of his name, Patrick leapt like a startled cat and rushed back towards Cullen. He got several paces clear of the desk before Alston turned around. Alston gave the boy a disgusted look, but that was probably because he associated with an idiot like Cullen, rather than because he suspected him of reading his private papers.

"Return my book when you've finished with it," Alston said. "I'll be attending to business in my office for the next two or so hours."

"Of course, we'll return this to you in two hours," Cullen said, a hand on Patrick's shoulder guiding him out of the room so Alston couldn't see his guilty and panicked face. "My utmost gratitude to you, Charles."

Cullen indicated Patrick should retire with him to the shade of a sycamore tree in the corner of garden.

"Now that I was made to look like a fool in front of Dr Alston by the process of distracting him, could you kindly tell me what purpose my distraction served?"

"It's the plants, Dr Cullen. I'm sorry, I didn't mean for you..."

"Never mind about me," sighed Cullen. "Truth be told, I don't think Charles considers me more of an imbecile now than he did the hour prior. Tell me about the plants, lad."

"I visited the physic garden last week," Patrick said, hitching his knees to his chest. "You remember when we first spoke about this project it was a lovely day, so I went and looked for some of the plants we spoke about while our conversation was fresh."

Cullen nodded. This was typical sensible behaviour of Patrick.

"Well, today half of the ones I found are missing."

"Missing? They disappeared since last week?"

"Not just cuttings. There was a sizeable crop of purple saxifrage—I remember being relieved because it's so hard to cultivate—but it's all been dug up. Which seemed strange because most preparations only require a small quantity of it."

Cullen flicked through Alston's book. "Where would *Saxifraga oppositifolia* be? He told me his categorisation was obvious, yet it's not listed amongst the *Saxifragaceae* family..."

Then he paused. "Patrick. Are you insinuating what I think you're insinuating?"

"I don't know," Patrick admitted. He wasn't one for perceptive thinking. "But on Alston's desk there was correspondence and other ledgers. He's selling a lot of plants to the Dutch, the French and the American colonies."

Cullen closed his eyes. The sun felt pleasant on his face. It made everything else feel a little less horrible. "What quantities are we talking about?"

"I'm not sure, but there were some large sums of money mentioned in those letters. That's what caught my eye." Patrick fell silent. A bird chirped overhead. "But maybe the university knows about this..."

"Trust me, they don't." Cullen couldn't pretend he enjoyed much status within the faculty, but since the physic garden was on university property, he knew about its associated commercial dealings. Or at least the ones Alston chose to share with them.

"Not even Dr Monro?"

"If he knew, we'd know," Cullen sighed. "I think the eminent professor is too caught up in his inoculation project to pay close attention to his colleagues."

That was something most of the students had picked up on. There'd been a flurry of correspondence from the Arbroath parishes a few months ago following a smallpox outbreak, and Monro had met with local physicians to gauge their interest in a visiting the afflicted areas. Then came the silence. Cullen suspected this meant the project had stalled. Again.

Patrick leant against the tree, woes temporarily set aside to appreciate the stillness.

Cullen let his mind wander. "It seems Dr Monro is missing plenty of sensible solutions to his inoculation program woes. We could send our final year students out into the Highlands over the summer. Some of them grew up speaking Gaelic, I'm sure we can find others with family connections to specific rural locations. Surely that would be better than sending paunchy, bewigged chaps like myself from the lowlands? They get a bit of supervised physician experience, we get a few hundred more inoculations."

"What does Dr Monro think of this sensible plan?" Patrick asked slyly.

"He wouldn't call it sensible if he knew of it," Cullen laughed. "I can only speculate on other professor's projects as they appear to me."

"He'd appreciate you were trying to help him. Maybe he doesn't think enough students are interested in helping out."

"I've said too much," said Cullen. "There's a lot about Dr Monro's smallpox inoculation program known only to himself. And the patrons who support him, I suppose. He hasn't asked for my insight, and it's therefore boorish of me to presume it holds value to him."

Patrick didn't raise the matter again, and Cullen changed the subject.

33

EDINBURGH

"I hope your constitution is ready, Dr Monro." Argyle eased himself onto the seat next to the furnace pipe. "I am in the mood for a sweat."

"As am I, your lordship."

Monro was proud of the Royal Infirmary bagnio. He'd lobbied for years to secure its funding and construction, rallying board members to join his petitions.

As far as he was concerned, the Edinburgh bagnio was equal to those of London. Though if men wanted to procure the additional service associated with London bagnios—many no better than brothels—they'd be disappointed. The Royal Infirmary bagnio was purely devoted to rejuvenating healthy bodies.

It was a small space, but had been decorated with white and blue tiles in an Oriental fashion. Light filtered in through high windows.

The bagnio opened in 1757 and it still looked pristine. Argyle and his associates had come to support the venture, but Monro felt their support was more to humour him than because their personal convictions aligned on its merit. At this early hour, it was a quiet, private space to discuss gentleman's business.

For a while, there wasn't much to be had from Argyle beyond groans of satisfaction. Monro inhaled deeply, letting the hot, steamy air fill his lungs.

He wondered if Argyle indulged in the London bagnios when he last visited. Monro never had the time to visit when he was an anatomy student there. Anyway, he wouldn't have had the courage to seek out the ladies of pleasure who left calling cards in those bagnios.

Several years passed since Cullen's appointment to the Chemistry chair, and Monro was still in the dark about what transpired behind the scenes to enable that. Rutherford and he speculated a schism between dark practitioner families lay behind their confusing behaviour—minds divided on how to deal with Cullen. That would explain the uneasy aftermath: Argyle and the other dark practitioners became absent from Edinburgh in subsequent years: spending longer summers in the countryside, taking tours of the Continent or renting in Soho Square.

That said, their behaviour had long since resumed normalcy. Monro tried to gauge their opinion of Cullen on multiple occasions, but was waved off.

"The man's a thistle in the side," Argyle would respond. "Still, he seems to be behaving himself, doesn't he?"

That was true. Mainly because Rutherford assumed the mantle of thwarting Cullen's schemes. He complained it was like having a second occupation.

Thick wiry grey hairs erupted from Argyle's chest, making him look more like an ageing bear than a man. Monro didn't like to look.

They were on their second cycle through the heated rooms of the bagnio. The thick wooden sandals they wore to protect their feet felt hot against their soles. The cleats around Monro's midriff were as wet with the condensation as if they'd been soaked in a bucket. He focused on pushing the steamy air as deep into his lungs as it would go.

"How are the faculty doing, Dr Monro? I assume the Town Council is keeping out from under their noses."

Several years had passed since Monro received his honorary doctorate from the College of Physicians. Argyle never once slipped in how he addressed Monro; he never forgot the title. Most of the university faculty were the same. It was only Drummond's lackeys in the Incorporation of Surgeons who made a point of forgetting.

"All seems well," Monro said.

The surgeons built their own bagnio long before Monro's time. Even at its height of popularity, it was never more than a wooden hut adjoining the Surgeon's Hall. Interest in its use waned quickly. By 1721 it had long fallen into disrepair; stripped of its Turkish tiles and most of the interior furnishings.

"Professor, what are your sentiments towards Dr John Gregory?" Argyle asked.

Monro had to pause and think.

"You refer to Professor Rutherford's former student? I think he's teaching in Aberdeen."

"The very same." Argyle smiled, then let the silence drag out until Monro understood he'd not addressed his question.

"A competent physician, as I recall. Good head for medical theories. Generally agreeable company."

"You don't like him?"

"No my lord, it's not that," Monro protested. "I'm afraid I don't know him well enough to offer a strong opinion on his character and ability."

"That's an opinion in itself, I suppose," Argyle mused, leaning back against the tiles and inhaling.

Monro couldn't argue with that. How many years since John Gregory defended his medical dissertation? He couldn't remember. Rutherford always had a soft spot for the boy—Monro never understood what distinguished him from the hordes of otherwise similar students.

A shiver ran down Monro's arm. It might have been his body's reaction to the waves of heat, but his mind was already in motion.

"Does Rutherford want Gregory to succeed him?"

It was surprising. He thought Francis Aird—having missed the chemistry chair appointment thanks to Cullen's meddling—would be first pick for Rutherford's replacement. Even though Aird's nomination last time proved contentious, he was sure the faculty would rally around him eventually.

Argyle stretched his arms. "It seems a little eccentric of old Rutherford, does it not? I guess we are all guilty of little foibles..."

Monro wasn't a fool as to snatch that bait.

"I don't doubt there is some merit to the notion. After all, Dr Gregory is performing his faculty role satisfactorily in Aberdeen."

It didn't help that Aird retained warm ties with several Town Councilmen. Perhaps that was all it boiled down to.

Argyle hummed and changed the subject. The remaining time in the steam room was passed in meaningless conversation that faded into silence.

"Are you the kind of man that braves the cold plunge?" Argyle asked, with a barking laugh. "I find it invigorating to the spirits."

Men like Argyle are the sort who love to show off what's under their cleats, Monro thought. Even if icy water is the great equaliser of manhood. He gave a noncommittal nod. Argyle took it as approval—or a lack of disagreement—and rose to his feet.

They passed into the central hallway of the bagnio—similarly tiled—where a man-sized bathtub filled with ice sat under the window.

Outside in the entranceway, Argyle's servant Octavius sat patiently. He appeared unconcerned that he had to wait outside, looking neither bored nor distracted. Today he was dressed in an emerald green frock coat possibly handed down from his master. As far as Monro could tell, Octavius had moved past footman status in the Argyle household, now enjoying a status closer to secretary-amanuensis.

Monro saw this as proof of Argyle's sound judge of character. In many ways the African was the ideal servant: courteous, attentive, adaptable, honest. He seemed entirely without the stain of ambition, content with his role in life.

"Gregory said there are some leaps that test man's faith more than others. I liked the way he phrased that." Argyle spoke as if thinking aloud, intent on the ripples travelling across the otherwise still plunge tub.

Monro often wondered what life would be like for him if he stayed in London instead of heeding his father's call north. He read Donald's letters from the capital with envy, imagining it was himself idling in coffeehouses, or puffing himself up in Vauxhall.

He's already spoken with Gregory, Monro realised. Perhaps more than once. This meeting isn't about obtaining my thoughts on the appointment.

* * *

When Monro first assumed his teaching position, he was barely twenty-one, a decade younger than the other anatomy professors at the Incorporation of Surgeons. His father was a proud, forceful man: Monro wasn't in Edinburgh at the time to see how negotiations played out, but when he returned two anatomy professors tended their resignation in favour of Monro's ascendancy to the position. These professors had served for thirty years. They hadn't resigned willingly. Especially not Drummond.

Watching Cullen's usurpation of Plummer reminded Monro of his own fledging career. Old Plummer passed away only a few months after Cullen arrived in Edinburgh, so there wasn't enough time to see the proposed joint chemistry professorship compromise in action. The difference between Cullen and him was that he hadn't wanted the anatomy lectureship: he was only twenty-two, for heaven's sake. He wished to linger in London, but his father cleared a path and he had no choice but to walk down it.

John Monro was an untouchable figure within the walls of Edinburgh. His military service was impeccable. No one questioned his vision for a medical school affiliated with the university, or his suggested improvements for the Incorporation of Surgeons and College of Physicians. But many resented the younger Monro, who seemed to possess every privilege they struggled for. And Monro compounded their jealousy by becoming the most popular lecturer without any sign of struggle.

As his father aged, Monro feared waning protection from spiteful forces within the Incorporation and university.

The first few years of Monro's anatomy career took a physical toll on him. He was subjected to constant dizziness and headaches. Isabella acquired bruises down one side of her body because he thrashed around in the night. Monro couldn't remember his nightmares. He begged her not to flee to a separate bed, because he couldn't fall asleep alone. Mob protests outside the Surgeon's Hall became a weekly occurrence: they thought he was digging up their relatives from their eternal rest, or cutting victims up alive. Walking down the High Street he knew members of the mob recognised him as the target of their ire, but they were too isolated to do more than glare or spit on the ground near his feet.

He told himself it was because the ignorant fools did not understand science, nor the importance of anatomy to medicine. How could tomorrow's surgeons or physicians treat ailments, if they didn't understand how the human body worked? Anatomy instruction on human cadavers was a necessity. Many men in the mob—he recognised some of them—owed their lives and livelihoods to medical treatment underpinned by anatomical study in Edinburgh.

Then came the day Monro not only feared for his life, but said his prayers expecting at any moment to meet his Maker.

It was a sunny day, which brought more people than usual to protest outside the Surgeon's Hall. His dissection finished for the day, Monro waited several hours before departing, reasoning he'd given the rabble long enough to calm down and disperse for the taverns.

He hadn't.

"Murderer!"

A knot of protestors was still outside, loitering in the afternoon warmth. Crucially, there were enough journeymen and idling apprentices to confer mob-courage upon them. Monro tried to walk past them as if he wasn't afraid, but soon he was surrounded.

The men hesitated to do more than shout and jostle him. Monro kept his head high, desperate not to provoke them. But he knew at any second one of the street boys watching the ruckus might pick up a stone and toss it at him. Once that happened, an onslaught of projectiles would come. After that, anything would be acceptable.

He muttered prayers under his breath as insults were screamed in his face.

"Alexander!" Isabella caught his arm. She must have sensed the citizens of Edinburgh were in a bloodthirsty mood, because she'd run down the Cowgate to find him.

Had she arrived a minute later, the mob may have already have set upon a course of violence. As it was, they drew back with growled curses, their blood not yet raised high enough to strike a woman. She shepherded him all the way home, never once letting go.

The stress was too much, and as soon as their apartment door was locked, Monro burst into tears. He was wracked with guilt for days afterwards. As head of the household, it was his duty to protect his wife and children. A wife should never have to rescue her husband from danger. He couldn't shake the weight of his failure.

Aligning with the dark practitioners was a calculated decision to protect his life and his interests, which he knew were more in the service of the university and Scotland than anyone else's. In his recollections, the malice faded almost as soon as he accepted their patronage.

His maladies faded, and both he and Isabella managed to sleep soundly once more.

Cullen didn't even feign reluctance or mask his ambitions. He was unapologetic. He did what he wanted, and enthused about it. He stayed away from those he called 'dark chymists' and politely insisted he didn't need their support.

It drove Monro to fury.

34

EDINBURGH

To be on time to the medical faculty senate was to be late, Cullen thought to himself as he shouldered his way into the meeting room. He'd done his best, but young Hawthorn and Smith caught him in the Yards with a question about today's lecture, and Cullen considered it rude to brush his students off entirely. Few things would kill an inexperienced student's enthusiasm for medicine quicker.

"Ah, William decided to join us after all," noted Rutherford, looking up from his confab with Monro Senior at the central desk. "I suppose that's our signal to commence."

The ten or so professors in the room glared at Cullen as he awkwardly squeezed past them to take the last available chair. The table was too close to the wall, and the professors had to pull in their own chairs and hold their breaths to let him past. Most of the medical faculty were substantial men. Cullen muttered apologies and thanks as he passed, though they didn't acknowledge them.

At the head of the table loomed Rutherford, with Monro perched next to him taking the minutes.

"Gentlemen, with your agreement I'll start with an update on my conversation with the Lord Provost on the budgetary concerns we raised..."

As far as several men in this room were concerned, Cullen might as well have strangled old Plummer himself for how much they disliked him. But Rutherford really hated his guts because the dark chymists' beneficence dried up around the time of his appointment. Suddenly the medical faculty found their petitions for more funding falling on deaf ears.

Still, Cullen supposed it gave the venerable Rutherford an opportunity to work up some much-needed exertion.

"We had the Provost's blessing to look into alternative sources...ah, greetings, Charles!"

Alston slipped in to the room, shutting out the chatter from the quadrangle. The two Monros shuffled their chairs apart to give Alston room to pull a spare up to the table.

Several of the other professors smiled and waved.

"A thousand apologies, I hope I didn't miss anything."

"Not at all, old chap."

Cullen's eyes must have audibly rolled in his head, because Rutherford's next remark was directed at him.

"Is something the matter, William?"

Would it be churlish for him to say exactly what was on his mind?

"Not in the slightest. I was merely concerned that Charles would miss more of the meeting than me, but here he is."

It wasn't that Cullen laden his words with sarcasm, but his sarcastic intent wasn't lost on anyone.

Both Monros wrinkled their noses as if Cullen had tossed a lump of dogshit onto the table. Under other circumstances it would be comical.

"Ahem. As I was saying..." Rutherford coughed and continued his remarks, pointedly avoiding Cullen's corner of the room.

Cullen was initially too affronted to interrupt, but after that shock wore off he decided it was too late: the moment to re-interrupt had passed. He could see his colleagues smirk at each other, or wag their eyebrows at unspoken jests, no doubt uttered at his expense countless times before today.

They're going to think I'm being petulant if I raise the pilfered botany funds now. They'll think I'm motivated by a petty snub. If they want to complain about a leaky ship without actually plugging the leak? Fine by me.

He hadn't always been this cynical. Back in the mists of time, when he'd just moved to Hamilton, Cullen showed up at a Town Council meeting in his finest lime green frock coat. His intention was to raise a petition to facilitate market trading. He thought he cut a fine figure striding into the dusty hall.

Instead, the honest burghers had stared. "I'm not sure if sir understands the processes we go through here..." an elderly man said, voice thick with scorn.

"That's what I wanted to..." Cullen began. Then he caught a glimpse of how he must look to these villagers: a rustic bumpkin dressed in the ill-fitting finery of an urban upstart, looking like a parody of both. The men here were clad in thick wool coats in the darkest of greens, reds and browns.

He gave up and sank onto the bench, defeated.

"There's not much can be done at meetings like this," an amused voice said behind him. Cullen turned and squinted into the early morning sunbeams. An older man, leaning heavily on a walking cane, was set a distance from the proceedings by the wall. The tumbling brown curls of his wig—he was the only one aside from Cullen who bothered with one—marked him out as a set above the others.

"Your grace?" Cullen said, guessing correctly this was James, the Duke of Hamilton himself.

His lordship nodded, an acknowledgement of his identity, before shifting in his seat and grinding his cane into the floorboards. A few of his nearby servants discreetly looked the other way.

"I stop by here once in a blue moon to keep an eye on the proceedings; checking on the local sentiments, that sort of thing. But nothing is ever accomplished in these fora. An expanded trading license, did you say?"

"Yes, your grace."

"Well, it's easier for you to leave that with me." There was a conspiratorial glint in the man's eye. "I think I can move this forward."

Cullen handed over the folded papers with only a brief backwards glance at the ongoing meeting. He caught several dirty looks thrown their way: probably recognising he was taking his petition out of the council's mechanisms and giving it straight to the local noble, who'd ignore the Council and get his way.

Well, they should have thought of that before so rudely dismissing him, shouldn't they?

Cullen's first meeting with the Glasgow Principal proceeded far smoother. By then he'd been in Glasgow for, what, three years? Cullen had never articulated his goals beyond musings with his wife, nor had he asked anyone for advice. That was because—blessedly—the path to a lecturing appointment was simple and well-defined by countless before him: offer private lectures to local students, then upon gaining the requisite acclaim and reputation, the university offered an academic appointment. Well, 'acclaim' and 'reputation' made the process sound loftier than it actually was: the University of Glasgow offered him a lectureship in chemistry because he could bring them loyal students, ergo money.

Principal Campbell had waved Cullen into his office, evidently in a hurry between grander visitors. He'd taken in the walls covered in portraits of illustrious predecessors, all in hefty gilt frames. A portrait of the Principal—thirty years younger—draped in ermine and velvet occupied the back wall.

"This university needs a medical school," Cullen said, knowing time was at a premium. "I'm happy to teach whatever courses are necessary: botany, materia medica, medical theory, et cetera."

"We appointed you to the chair of chemistry," the Principal said. But it wasn't a rebuttal so much as a tired, harried man trying to keep track of accelerating events.

"Continuing to teach chemistry will not be a problem," Cullen replied, inclining his head. "The students are hungry for more medical courses, and we hemorrhage talent to Leiden." The students who couldn't afford to migrate to Leiden for a medical education made do in Edinburgh, but Cullen didn't mention that, because it'd draw attention to his own east-wards migration as a student. Not that he completed any medical degree at Edinburgh, but that wasn't the point.

The Principal nodded. Cullen had expected more resistance or questioning. But the Principal didn't care about his grandiose vision. He didn't care whether Cullen succeeded or failed, just that he got out of his office as quickly as possible.

"Whatever support you require, we'll be happy to assist you, Dr Cullen," he said blandly. Cullen had no intention of asking for help—which was just as well, because the Principal had no intention of providing it.

"I humbly thank you, Principal Campbell," Cullen said, scraping his chair and shuffling towards the door.

In those first few years, his freedom was glorious. The students would ask Cullen to lecture on a particular medical topic next term...and he would oblige. His flagship chemistry class swelled in numbers. When the university belatedly realised what he'd created, they scrambled to open more medicine chairs. Cullen didn't begrudge them: during a few semesters he barely saw his growing family. He was still on hand temporarily run those lecture courses while they waited for new hires to arrive, or when a professor vacated the chair. Far from resenting new hires permanently taking on the mantles of botany and the like, Cullen went out of his way to help them settle into the role, giving guidance as necessary on how he taught the material and the way to ensure a warm student reception to new courses.

No one higher up the administration grease pole complained, or even went out of their way to enquire about his plans. Suddenly, Cullen's annual chemistry class was the biggest in the university.

Far from shooing him out his office, it was other petitioners the Principal cleared from the room in anticipation of Cullen's arrival. It was Cullen who was offered a glass of his fine Madeira port. The Principal asked after Anna and the bairns, remembering their names and what was the last ailment they dealt with.

It should have felt like a roaring success. Cullen should have basked in the glow of his creation, like he basked in front of the Principal's hearth with a glass of expensive claret. But the hollowness never faded. It wasn't until young Joseph Black cautiously edged into his classroom that Cullen realised there was an absence at his core, and it was one he could name.

* * *

Anna Cullen hated feeling powerless. Usually she arranged her circumstances, however modest, to alleviate the lack of control. In the domestic confines of her home she was an attentive mother and competent wife. Her husband had never reason to criticise or question her managing of the household finances—not that he was critical towards her. She knew when to indulge her growing children, and when to reign them in. Amongst her female friends, she was a valued confidant. To her husband's guests, she was an attentive host who could engage them in lively discourse about topics pleasing to men's ears and egos.

But as she sat in the parlour painting watercolours and sewing, Anna knew that she was powerless, because she couldn't help her husband. She saw the lines on his face and sagging skin under his eyes; she heard him toss in the night; she watched him grimace at the dinner table because he had no appetite but didn't want to appear rude.

William had assured her the dark chymists were cowed, but his anxiety made her believe the dark chymists had in fact won. Her husband was the defeated man.

But when she tried to coax his ills from him, he'd brush her aside. Could she not see how well his private practice was doing? As if she wasn't conversing with his affluent clients. Didn't the steady flow of students into their house for formal and informal medical discussions speak to his success as a teacher?

"Then why do you look so unhappy, love? Why are you having trouble sleeping?"

"I've always been a light sleeper, my dear," Cullen insisted, kissing her forehead. "And I'm not unhappy—it's just that I'm busier than ever."

The man, bless him, was a terrible liar. As if the first few years' of their marriage weren't her struggling to adjust to his heavy snoring.

He pretended that the inability to publish his prized medical treatise was the sort of issue that plagued all professors; feckless, amoral printers getting more brazen than they used to. She could see the tense encounters between her husband and his fellow-professors on the street and at parties.

After a few years of this, Anna was convinced she'd go mad if she didn't do something. Heaven forbid she lose her temper with William, or make injudicious remarks in front of his associates.

What could she do?

Last week she'd walked with William to the market—it was her insistence he come out of the house with her, because he looked like he needed fresh air and sunlight.

They were almost at the Lawnmarket when her husband froze.

"Love..." Anna began.

Her husband grabbed her waist and pushed her into the narrow wynd. Anna let out a small shriek, too taken aback by the suddenness of what happened to take anything in.

She was partially pinned against the wall, with Cullen patting her mouth and making vague shushing noises.

He wasn't focussing on her. Anna followed his gaze and saw a couple walking down the Cowgate towards them: a young minister and his wife. They strolled along leisurely, the wife perched on his arm. They were silent, but companionable.

Anna peeled her husband's hand off her face. Her panniers were digging in to the small of her back and she worried they might break.

"Damn you, William. What madness?"

She was confused and scared. Her husband had never been rough with her, and she was taken aback with how much stronger than her he was.

"Please Anna..." begged Cullen, still watching the couple pass by. "Stay quiet."

Her husband was scared.

Once the minister and his wife passed without a glance in their direction, Cullen took a step back and lowered his hands. A whistling messenger boy squeezed past them, assuming the pair were engaged in amorous business. Or perhaps not, and he simply did not care to assist a lady under assault.

Cullen was staring at Anna, as if just realising what he'd done. He backed away, unsure if he should reach out to comfort her, or keep his hands away.

"We'll discuss this at home," Anna said icily. She offered her husband her arm. He took it, but it was like the limb of a tree under his arm. They said nothing on the way home.

Cullen explained who the man was. This was her first time hearing about the incident in Glasgow over ten years ago, which apparently haunted him to this day. Anna shuddered.

"Maybe his wife has had an improving effect on him," Cullen said. It was a struggle to get anything out of him.

"All matrimony does is speed up men into becoming what they are," Anna replied. "The bride of a good man will make him better. The sorry bride of a bad man will stoke his worse impulses." She wanted to demand why he hadn't told her about this until now. How long had he been suffering in silence? What else was he hiding from her?

"She looked to be a good christian woman," Cullen said.

"The goodness of the wife isn't a deciding factor, I don't think," Anna said. "They'll draw those impulses from their husband, intentionally or not."

But Anna wondered about the wife of Malcolm Holm. It was selfishness of her part, she couldn't deny it. But here was a pocket of Edinburgh there was the narrowest possibility that she could control.

35

EDINBURGH

There was a new patient in the Infirmary ward; an old woman shivering under the thin blanket. He begun his Saturday clinical rotations at an early hour of the morning, but Cullen saw the woman was awake. Given the rough snores, coughs and whimpers from the ward he couldn't blame her.

"Good morning, madam. I'm Dr Cullen. Let's take a look at your case history..."

The women shrank under her blanket. This wasn't an unusual reaction to a physician: partly because the poor of Edinburgh wouldn't call for one unless the situation was dire, and because physicians were associated with more discomfort—financial and physical. Cullen tried to put his patients at ease with gentle conversation.

"...Rather unpleasant weather for this time of year, is it not?" The woman had been admitted yesterday with a severe fever and placed on the standard regimen of purging and rest. "How are you feeling this morning?"

The patient resolutely stared at the wall, twisting her body as far as from Cullen as she could.

"There's no need to be afraid, madam—I'm simply here to

look at your notes, not prescribe new regimens." Cullen perched on the end of the bed. "The nurse will be around with a light soup shortly..."

His attempts to reassure the patient were getting nowhere. In fact, she seemed increasingly afraid.

"It pains me to see you distressed, madam. Is there anything I can do for you?"

"Please," the woman wailed, causing the slumbering patients around her to start and mumble. "I have no more money to give."

Cullen frowned, then smiled. "You don't need to worry with payment, madam. This is the charity ward—its for deserving individuals such as yourself."

"No," the woman buried her head in the pillow. "I gave the other doctor all my money. Please have mercy on my soul, doctor. I have nothing left to give."

"Doctor..." Cullen glanced back at the notes, fingers shaking. "Whytt?"

"I pray doctor, I have nothing more..." The woman shook and sobbed.

Cullen rose and walked away. There was nothing he could say that would calm the woman more than leaving her alone.

Besides, he didn't trust himself to remain temperate.

Cullen completed the round by pushing the conversation out of his mind, and distracting himself every time he felt it coming to the forefront of his thoughts. Whytt wasn't in the Infirmary today— thank Providence—it was only Rutherford, and of course Cullen wasn't going to engage him.

But by the time he was leaving down the Cowgate and spotted John Gregory, Cullen's self-control had eroded to the point where he felt ready to tell somebody, otherwise it would ruin his afternoon patient visits.

"A productive morning?" Cullen asked, when Gregory slowed to greet him.

Since moving from Aberdeen to Edinburgh last summer, Gregory had gradually developed his private practice out of the Stag's Head tavern. Cullen assumed Rutherford would be putting in a good word for his former student amongst his own patient group, because he'd stumbled upon Gregory's consultation sessions a few times and he never looked busy.

"Reasonable number of ailments," Gregory replied perfunctorily. "The cold spell brings out all the chronic complaints."

"That it does…"

Cullen didn't consider himself close to Gregory, but he was one of Cullen's few physician acquaintances in Edinburgh not tied closely to the dark chymists or the other faculty members. That made him a safe outlet, so to speak.

"I had a disturbing exchange in the Infirmary this morning; truth be told I'm still rattled by it. A charity patient told me one of my colleagues demanded payment for her admittance to the ward."

Gregory took a sharp intake of breath.

"Who was it? Did she say?"

His outrage seemed genuine.

"Dr Whytt was the one who completed her intake notes," Cullen replied with care. He knew Gregory held no affection nor discontent for Whytt, so it seemed safe to confide. "Truth be told, I fear it's not an isolated incident."

"It's not?"

"No, the signs were self-evident, I suppose…" Whytt hadn't been interested in ward privileges until Cullen began his lengthy petition process. He'd never shown much compassion for the charity cases, and often voiced his suspicion that most were just after a free bed and meal.

Gregory bristled. "Taking advantage of the most desperate wretches is beyond callousness. It puts the rest of us to shame. I should do something about it."

"You're quite right, Dr Gregory." Cullen ran through the list of possible actions to reprimand Whytt. They all involved alerting Rutherford and Monro. "Rather you than me in fact...err, if it's not too inconvenient?"

Gregory waved his hand. "The urgency is obvious."

There was an unfamiliar ardour in Gregory's eyes that worried Cullen. His impression of Gregory was of an average physician and unremarkable scholar, one who—if it weren't for Rutherford's personal fondness—wouldn't have managed to eke out a practice in Edinburgh. But it meant Gregory was of no interest to the Town Council or dark chymists, and Cullen viewed him as a safer pair of hands than most.

They parted shortly after—Gregory heading in the direction of the college or Infirmary, Cullen towards the High Street. As he plodded up the hill, Cullen realised Gregory hadn't confirmed what he intended to do about Whytt.

* * *

Anna told her husband what she wished to accomplish. While she was sure he'd refuse her, she decided she couldn't admonish him for keeping secrets from her and then behave in an identical manner.

Surprisingly, it took one conversation. Cullen was almost resigned.

"Her husband is a dangerous man, my dear."

"But what harm can his wife do?"

"We understand but a fraction of their relationship," Cullen said. But he wasn't losing his temper or pacing the room. Instead, he sunk further into his chair. "If you wish to speak to her, it cannot take place in our home. You cannot let her out of your sight, or let her touch you or your personal belongings."

And so it was agreed.

. . .

"I understand Gaelic to be your native tongue," Anna began. "Though I cannot speak the language myself, I can understand what is said almost perfectly."

"Is that so?" Mrs Holm asked coldly in Gaelic.

Once her quarry was identified perusing a herb seller's wares in the Grassmarket, Anna moved like lightning. As predicted, Mrs Holm didn't seem surprised by her hasty greeting. Anna introduced herself, but it was clear the woman already knew who she was. Begrudgingly, she acquiesced to tea in an oyster cellar, the nearest establishment to where they stood.

"I grew up near Oban," Anna explained in English, ignoring the deliberate rudeness. "My nurse and servants were all Highlanders. I heard more Gaelic than English in the first few years of my life."

Cinead sipped her tea as if Anna hadn't spoken. Anna thought she'd be more impressed with the effort she put into welcoming this Highlander.

"I am sure you try to be a good, pious woman," Cinead said in Gaelic after a frosty silence. "But it can't have escaped your attention that your husband is destined for Hell."

"Why?" Anna asked. "My husband has committed no sin worthy of eternal damnation."

It was late morning, and the cellar was almost deserted. Anna wondered if there were any Gaelic speakers among the cellar denizens, drinking gin with silent ferocity in the shadowy corners of the room.

"He sins against God every day with his actions," Cinead continued, settling in to her speech. "My husband sees how consumed with pride he is. It is a sin shared with many at the college."

Anna only dared approach Mrs Holm because she tended to go to the market without her husband. She wasn't sure what would have transpired if Malcolm Holm accompanied her today.

"For daring to help the poor in the teaching hospital he helped establish? For opening his house to students far from home? For waiving his course fees so the poorest students can still attend his classes? Tell me more about these sins of my husband, Mrs Holm."

This whole exchange was so preposterous Anna didn't know what to think. Why was she even bothering to defend her husband against this foolish woman? So much for extending warmth and friendship.

"You should be concerned, Mrs Cullen," Cinead said. "For your soul is tied to your husband, and you will share his final torment."

"Please, have more tea, Mrs Holm. If it gets cold it's wasted." She was within her right to storm off, but Anna didn't want to give this sanctimonious woman the satisfaction of knowing the extent of her offense. Let her drink more tea and suffer in this sinner's company a while longer.

Cinead obliged with a frozen cordiality, never breaking the intricate social rules that bound them in this conversation.

"I imagine it is a burden living in Edinburgh," Anna said after a long silence. "You will be far from your family, in a world you consider sinful."

"I lost most of my male relatives in the rebellion of 1745," Cinead replied, her upper lip curling. "I feared for my father, uncles and brothers when the uprising broke out, of course—but with such a large family it never occurred to me I'd lose them all.

"Lowland Scots, English—I can't tell them apart. They act like they know this land better than those who've lived on it for centuries. They try to tell us how to farm, fish and hunt...then blame us crofters when things go wrong. The Lowlanders whispered encouragement in the Jacobites ears, telling us our cause was as good as won. Then they betrayed us. As they always do."

36

EDINBURGH

As he was heading into his lecture theatre, Cullen almost collided with Monro.

Cullen swore and leapt back. Monro didn't even flinch.

"You have some explaining to do, Dr Cullen." Monro regarded Cullen with narrowed eyes, like he was an injured fox too demeaning for him to hunt.

Cullen turned to shut the door behind him.

"Well Dr Monro, please explain to me what I must explain to you."

"The medical miracle that is Joseph Black, who was seen falling from a sixth storey window on the evening of 11th February 1756 near St Giles, seconds before the whole building collapsed, and walking away with little more than a scratch. It defies everything I know about the human body, and I'm curious to hear if there is some gap in my anatomical knowledge."

Oh no.

"I would never stoop to pointing out gaps in your anatomical knowledge, Dr Monro," Cullen replied. "And given how flawed you consider my medical theories, I cannot understand why you seek my opinion."

"Black is your former student," Monro said. His voice was taunt. "What he didn't learn from me, he learned from you."

"This is probably an incident of unreliable sources." Cullen pushed past Monro towards his table in the middle of the room. "A claim of six storeys when in fact it was one. There was much confusion on the High Street that day, so I'm told. Heavens, they could have mistaken any falling body for Joe."

"I'm going to tell you what I think," Monro said, trailing Cullen to the table. "Because I don't have all day for rhetorical games and insinuations."

"Excellent. I love hearing what you think, Alexander..."

"I think you're dabbling in dark chymistry, Dr Cullen. Which is extraordinarily foolish before we even get to the fact you drew Joseph in to such research."

Cullen wished he had something in his hands to throw. He settled on smacking the table. "That is a dishonourable accusation, Alexander."

"And yet my actions are not nearly as idiotic or reckless as yours, Dr Cullen. I don't need to do anything more than say the name 'Donald Bennett' to you, I pray?"

"No," Cullen said, staring Monro back. "I know what those men are capable of, and how adverse to minor inconvenience they are. Which is why it's slander to say I would involve myself in their private arts."

A flush was spreading across Monro's cheeks, even as his eyes grew colder.

"You think that I'm the only one asking questions about you and Joseph? If word has reached my ear, you can assume it's reached theirs, too. You think they'll have trouble recognising dark chymistry?"

Cullen forced himself to stand still, to avoid pacing. "Well that's the thing—what dark chymistry could account for such a strange sight? Can dark chymists fly? Could they perhaps carve a sigil in the time it takes to fall six storeys? Or maybe someone had the foresight to draw a sigil in the middle of the High Street precisely where Joe landed? With your extensive knowledge, Alexander, perhaps you can tell me?"

Cullen was tired. He was tired in the immediate sense—he'd slept poorly these past few nights—and tired in the sense that this was the last in an endless sequence of arguments with Monro that he never won.

The pinkness in Monro's cheeks seemed to concentrate and deepen. The professor of anatomy didn't immediately respond to Cullen's heated questions, and by the time Cullen realised this was a bad sign, it was too late.

"It's not dark chymistry then," Monro said slowly. "Whatever you're playing with, it's something different." Without breaking eye contact, Monro started to circle the table. "Your aether theories. I thought you were spouting heretical nonsense, but if you take your arguments to their literal, applied conclusion then it's all about the generation of fire and force." Monro's words were rushing out. "You wouldn't need sigils, it's all about using natural resources within the human body to manipulate elements."

Cullen should have felt triumphant that someone finally interrogated his medical theories like he'd hoped they would. But it was tempered by the realisation it was Alexander Monro of all people who'd made the connection.

Monro stopped moving. There were more thoughts forming in his head, and Cullen had no idea what they were.

"You consider my theories on the nervous system erroneous, remember?"

"Anyone can see they clash with Boerhaave's observations," Monro replied distantly. His gaze drifted away from Cullen to some point outside the room.

"Well then..."

"...But maybe my lords will be the best judge of that." Monro spun on his heels and strode towards the door.

Two steps. Cullen grabbed Monro's arm. His colleague froze.

Cullen wished he knew what his plan was. He should do something to stop Monro from taking his accusations to the dark chymists, but he had no idea what. The two men detested each other. Monro would stick a knife in Cullen himself if he thought the blood wouldn't splash onto his coat. He had no doubt been waiting for the opportunity to hand Cullen to the dark chymists. Cullen couldn't think of any argument from his lips that would incline Monro towards mercy.

He could render Monro unconscious, or perhaps strike him dead, but that wouldn't be satisfying in the long term.

Actually, what would be satisfying...

"Want to see something, Dr Monro? Something you've never seen before?"

Monro didn't react. But he didn't continue towards the door, either.

Cullen shrugged off his cumbersome academic robe. Then he unbuttoned his coat and dropped it on the table. Disdain played across Monro's face, but he didn't try to leave.

Cullen rolled up his sleeves. He was being malicious and theatrical, but it felt good.

"Dear doctor, do you see anything on my arms? No sigils, charms or other arcane objects?"

He thrust out his arms.

Monro's lips curled. "Turn over your palms."

Cullen complied. After hesitating a moment, Monro took a step forward and took hold of Cullen's wrists. He swept his palms along Cullen's forearms as if he was inspecting for fractures. Satisfied Cullen wasn't concealing anything in his rolled up sleeves or the crooks of his elbows, Monro sniffed and stepped back.

Cullen kept his hands out. "Now, when you consider Stahl's phlogiston treatise, but place it in the context of the nervous system..."

"You suggest the human body is capable of regenerating any

phlogiston it lost," interrupted Monro. "Passive diffusion wouldn't account for it."

"Yes, but elastic nervous fluids generated within the human body would."

"You're saying phlogiston and aether are two discrete entities generated within the nervous system?"

"They'd have to be..."

"Because if you applied the principle of combustibility to animal heat, we'd permanently be on fire?" Monro's expression was guarded. "I'm familiar with these texts, William. We don't need to act out your entire Socratic dialogue."

"Fine," Cullen snapped. Two flicks of his wrist.

Cullen felt pleasure at the surprise on Monro's face seeing fire curl around his hands, even if it was quickly wrestled under control.

Monro blinked twice at the see-through crimson flames dancing between them. "That's it?" he asked.

Damn the man.

Cullen turned and thrust out his hand. An arc of fire shot across the room, shattering against the shutters. Fortunately, the wood was too old and worn to ignite under a brief burst.

"No Alexander, that's not all of it."

Cullen was about to grab his coat and storm out the room, before he remembered it was his classroom that he was due to teach in, meaning Monro would need to be the one to leave.

Fortunately, that's what Monro immediately did, not giving Cullen time to look at his colleague's face.

Alone, Cullen sagged against the nearest wall. For a moment he'd considered himself the victor of that exchange, only to reflect that Monro had threatened to out him to the dark chymists as a rival practitioner, and instead of protesting his innocence he'd gone and proven Monro correct.

However Cullen looked at it, things were about to get worse.

37

GLASGOW

"I believe what you're telling me," Black said carefully. "Is Monro Senior confronted you with allegations of our secret experimentation with phlogiston. Knowledge which, if exposed, threatens our lives. And rather than deny the allegations, you demonstrated their accuracy in front of him." He paused. "Interesting."

"Is that 'interesting' as in 'damned stupid', Joe? Or 'interesting' as a synonym for reckless?"

Black shrugged. "Just interesting—for now."

Cullen was back in Glasgow. The pretext was an overnight stopover on the way to see an urgently ill relative in Hamilton— hence the rapid departure from Edinburgh following his confrontation with Monro. Black invited Cullen into his chemistry classroom—Cullen's old room—for the discussion.

"He came to threaten me with the secret, I felt it deserved a strong response." Cullen found he didn't regret what had transpired, nor did Black seem particularly angry with him, but it cast a lot of confusion onto the board. Neither man was sure what Monro would do next.

"Actually, I suspect Dr Monro was *warning* you," Black said, twirling a broken quill between his fingers. "Or more accurately, trying to protect me."

"Really, Joe?"

"I correspond with the gentleman on a regular basis," Black responded with a sly smile. "I have some insight into his reasoning."

"Oh, you do?" Cullen felt faintly embarrassed he needed to have all this pointed out to him. He glanced around the classroom.

It had been years since he last saw Black in person. They wrote often enough: it was hard to notice how a person changed based upon their letters.

For someone learning that his life could be in danger, Black remained remarkably calm. He was frowning—there were more lines etched around his eyes and forehead—but with the air of a philosopher assessing an intriguing paradox. Black focussed on the quill in his hands—he was no longer the young man glancing at Cullen for constant reassurance and trying to gauge his mood.

"I wouldn't call our correspondence expansive or particularly intimate," Black added, still with a trace of amusement. "But we've exchanged opinions on medical matters, and he seems invested in my Glasgow career."

"I don't know how you manage it, Joe. Dr Machiavelli and I butt heads over everything."

"I talk with him, I ascertain what he wants, I articulate what I want, and we come to an agreement somewhere in the middle." Black set the quill down on the table. "How long will you stay on the west coast?"

"Not long," Cullen said, stretching his back. "I admit you've reassured me of Monro's intentions. Though Monro is probably right when he says that if he could connect the dots, others can too."

Black nodded.

"We need to stop the dark chymists once and for all. Cauterise the heads at the stump. I'm tired of them hanging over me, Joe."

When he came through the Edinburgh he'd allowed himself to believe the dark chymists were cowed into submission by Black's actions. Maybe they had been. But that didn't mean they weren't lurking in the shadows, still a ghostly presence in drawing rooms and private tavern rooms. They were probably propping up Alston and his illicit botany dealings.

"I intend to come through to Edinburgh once the term ends," Black said. He spoke calmly, but remained focused on the papers in front of him. "The Dean of Students role consumes a preposterous amount of my time. As you can image, it rises to its zenith about now."

The last few weeks before examinations and graduations. It didn't surprise Cullen. But he still felt his heart sink a few inches lower. Eight years ago, perhaps Black would have rushed to protect his old professor.

"The dark chymists are still out there, Joe," Cullen said, trying to sound more assured than petulant. "They may have been cowed, but who knows how long inaction will benefit them?"

Black didn't reply.

"I wish we'd figured out more about their secret library. Presumably they still can still access it." Cullen felt he was talking to himself more than his audience of one. "With your academic duties shelved for the summer, maybe we can form a proper plan of action. Find Babylon and destroy it for good."

The two sat in silence for a few minutes.

It was reassuring to see Joe again, Cullen thought. In many ways nothing had changed, aside from his former student looking older. Their conversation flowed through a familiar rhythm; reticent Black with his sly smiles, Cullen content to lead the conversation and posit.

But there was a moment when Cullen stood in the classroom door and watched Black leafing through his bookshelves in the corner. For a moment Black didn't notice Cullen was there, so engrossed was he in rearranging the latest volumes he'd ordered from London. There was a...poise to Black that Cullen hadn't noticed before, like freshly unfurled bracken. Then Cullen had cleared his throat and Black had turned around to greet him. His face lit up, but some of that self-confident posture faded in reflexive deference. But for a moment, Cullen saw Black as his colleagues and students in Glasgow must: a formidable scholar, at home among the city luminaries.

Knowing of Cullen's woes, Black kept his own updates diplomatic and brief.

"I'm contending with a lot more correspondence," Black admitted wryly. "Most of them want nothing more than a sample of my handwriting."

"Your latent heat experiments were astonishing," Cullen protested. "Don't undersell yourself, Joe."

It was polite flattery, because Black couldn't fail to comprehend the magnitude of his discoveries, or feign confusion as to why the natural philosophers in Britain and Europe wrote to him for advice.

"By the way, they finished renovating the west Cumbernauld road last autumn," Black said.

"They did?" That they'd begun the improvement works at all was news to Cullen.

Seeing his confusion, Black clarified. "I treated the Earl of Anglesbury shortly after I started in Glasgow. His dalliances with Venus unfortunately led to a longstanding dependence upon Mercury."

"Doesn't surprise me."

"Anyway, I took the opportunity during his recuperation to remind him of the road project, and he graciously agreed to fund the venture."

"Well...thank you, Joe." Cullen cast his mind back to find the year he first conferred with Leechman about the Cumbernauld road. "It was 1750-something I first raised the issue, wasn't it? Just think, if I'd followed Leechman's advice we probably would have got the renovation long before now. Shame I was too impatient then."

The quirk of Black's mouth suggested he considered his former teacher to still lack patience, even if he liked Cullen too much to consider him flawed. But Black didn't spell this out.

"It's a pity I couldn't stay in Glasgow for longer," Cullen said as the visit concluded.

"I agree." Black said it with sincerity, but there was a wistfulness in his response that suggested concealment of some feelings. Once Cullen made his excuses and departed, he'd no doubt greet the exit with relief: that he could resume normal business and get back to his reading.

38

EDINBURGH

It wasn't unusual for Nathanial to be waiting in Cullen's classroom when he arrived to begin the day. Months would go by without Cullen remembering he used to converse with Leechman in the Glasgow University tavern every morning, and how easily he slotted the rest of his day around those warm chats. But he still felt a kind of hollowness to his morning routine: when he'd bid Anna and the bairns farewell at sunrise, walk to the college, and immediately launch into the business of preparing for class it was like something was missing. Which is why he indulged Nathanial and the others in their company.

When Cullen returned to Edinburgh following his confrontation with Monro, it seemed nothing had changed. In the following weeks Monro avoided him, as had been the professor's modus operandi towards Cullen for years. The other faculty members treated him however they'd previously been inclined to treat him: everything from cordial indifference to barely concealed mockery.

The normalcy was what frayed Cullen's nerves. If Monro hadn't immediately rushed to the dark chymists to report the display of phlogiston, it meant he was holding the secret to use it to his advantage later. He might have gone so far as to have quashed whatever rumours prompted the initial confrontation, because Cullen didn't hear of them again.

He couldn't give Monro and his ilk the satisfaction of fear, even if it consumed him: images of Bennett's murderer breaking into his bedchamber while his family slumbered, or being tailed into a deserted wynd and never coming out plagued him.

Though once a month elapsed, Cullen found the edge of his terror worn off through the exhaustion of maintaining it. Perhaps he'd overestimated Monro's callousness? His medical practice wound on as before.

Today, his almost-former student was practically bouncing off the benches when Cullen came through the classroom door, licking his lips in a bid to control himself.

"Professor!"

"Good morning, Nathanial..." Cullen took a modicum of delight in pretending he didn't know what had got into the boy, so he'd hear the reason voiced. "You are looking awfully lively..."

"You've heard the rumours about Dr Rutherford, professor? That he's decided to retire this summer?" Nathanial's voice rose to a squeak.

"I didn't believe the day would come," Cullen said. "But I've heard it from four trusted sources and the untrustworthy professor himself." His trusted sources were the Town Councilmen tasked with filling Rutherford's chair once he retired. Autumn could not come quickly enough.

He hadn't time to bask in the news. The political machinations were underway, it was why the Town Councilmen broached Rutherford's intended retirement to him. They wanted to know if he was entertaining the chair.

Nathanial must have heard the news only a few hours after Cullen. As one of the current Medical Society Presidents he had the advantage of being well-connected.

"A group of us were supping together last night when we heard Dr Rutherford planned to retire. Naturally, we turned our conversation to how we should assist your campaign for the post."

"I'm touched the student body feels this strongly, but you don't need to involve yourself. This is a matter for rich, powerful men talking with the most respected physicians in Britain." Cullen was already penning letters to his most influential former students in London to appraise them of the situation and assess their willingness to speak up within their patronage networks.

"You told us that you consider me your friend," Nathanial said simply. "Was that not true?"

"Of course it was true, Nathan," Cullen said.

"Well, then let your friends help you. You cannot fight this battle alone." Nathanial's earnest face shone.

He was right, of course. Cullen shouldn't have been trying to shield his students from the political manoeuvring—they were smart enough to figure out what was going on.

"We spoke about you, Dr Cullen, and are drafting a letter in support of your bid for the Practice Chair. We think the *Edinburgh Courant* will be a good place to send it."

"Good thinking, lad." Cullen wasn't sure about the exact number of readers, but most fashionable coffeeshops held the latest issue, and the literary sect dissected its contents with the precision of anatomists. A number of men whose opinion mattered belonged to its readership.

"Besides," Nathanial continued. "It means we can petition for Dr Black to replace you in the chemistry chair."

Cullen couldn't argue with that. His former student's lectures were developing quite a reputation. He didn't mind admitting Black was probably a better chemistry lecturer than him.

Sensing his token resistance waning, Nathanial beamed.

"We're still working on the letter, but I'm not the only one pushing them to finish the edits before the end of this week. The sooner we make this campaign public, the more support we can hope to amass before Rutherford makes his case."

They were a smart bunch, Cullen thought. His heart swelled.

Nathanial paused and looked at Cullen, waiting to hear what he thought.

"Tell you what, Nathan...How about I take a look over the draft of the letter you have? I've no doubt it'll be a fine letter, but it makes sense for me to check there's not any compelling arguments you've overlooked..."

Nathanial lit up. "You'd look over the letter? Really? It won't be an imposition? That's wonderful Dr Cullen."

* * *

"I heard the rumours, my Lord," Monro said. "But what I don't think I've told you is when I was called to treat the unfortunate survivors on the High Street that day..." A curt nod from Lord Argyle indicated he was aware of this fact. "...I saw the broken remains of a young man who closely resembled Joseph Black. Very similar hair and frame. From questioning the wounded, I learned he was a lodger residing on the fifth floor of the tenement. When I heard the rumour this week about Dr Black, I realised this stranger was the source of the confusion, and wanted to ensure your lordships didn't waste their time on it."

Lord Argyle nodded again. "You may not be aware, but the rumour came from someone I consider a trustworthy source." He gave Monro a pointed look.

"Yes, having seen the unfortunate remains with my own eyes, I cannot fault anyone for this case of mistaken identity," Monro replied, his face empty. "Miraculous indeed."

"Indeed," murmured Argyle. "Thank you, Dr Monro. I will relay your account to my colleagues."

Monro was almost at the door when Argyle called him back. "Dr Monro? You didn't say what the lodger's name was."

Monro paused. "No, I didn't. The onlookers told me, but I'm afraid it slipped my mind in the intervening years. I'm sorry, my Lord."

Argyle was already buried in his ledger. "Rather unfortunate, but we'll do with the information what we can."

39

GLASGOW

Adopting a more deferential posture than he usually favoured, Black tapped on the chamber door.

"Ah, come in Joseph."

"Principal Leechman," Black said. "I hope this is a good time to speak."

Leechman waved him into the Principal's office. Following the death of Campbell after a brief illness, but long decline, Leechman was appointed with unanimous backing from the Assembly and faculty.

Cautiously entering the room and seating himself in front of the desk, Black could appreciate why. Leechman always projected a calm air, even though the role was a burdensome one. In the year he'd held the role, his complexion had lightened from grey to ashen white. Remembering Leechman from his student days, Black feared even a minor illness would spell the end of the former Moral Philosophy professor.

"I'm glad you stopped by so promptly," Leechman said. He didn't offer Black a drink, because the chemistry professor always refrained from wine and claret so early in the day. "You've beaten the crowds."

Always a popular and approachable figure on campus, Black could imagine Leechman was hounded at all hours in his capacity as university Principal.

"I came as soon as I received your note," Black said. The Principal's office was a soothing one to linger in; smelling of mahogany and fine port. He didn't often have cause to speak with Leechman, but could recognise an urgent summons when it appeared. "Whatever I can assist with, please ask."

"Oh, it's a puzzle." Leechman moved slowly these days, sinking into his chair as if he feared he'd never rise. "We've received a flurry of correspondence from Edinburgh these past few days, painting quite a contradictory picture, and I'm hoping you have a few pieces of the puzzle we lack to help us make sense of this."

Black's heart sank. "I haven't received any letters from Dr Cullen recently, if that's what you're alluding to."

"Ah, unfortunate. Well, I had to ask." Leechman creaked into a more comfortable seating position. "One of my colleagues came to me having received a vexingly opaque message from Dr Alexander Monro, asking about his interactions with Dr John Gregory from Aberdeen."

By now, Black knew Leechman wouldn't divulge his sources. He could usually guess their identities, though.

"But Gregory is in Edinburgh, is he not?"

"Yes. I'm not sure he's set foot in Glasgow." Leechman paused, perhaps to recover his breath. "My other correspondence informs me of an anonymous letter in the *Edinburgh Courant*, declaring their support for William Cullen to fill Rutherford's Chair."

"Oh." Black supposed if he were to walk out Leechman's office and collar the first person he encountered in the quadrangle, they would already know about this. But he'd arrived early enough on college grounds and gone straight to Leechman's office, so the news just missed him.

"Were you aware this letter also called for you to fill Dr Cullen's Chemistry Chair upon his promotion?"

"A promotion he's not yet secured. No, Principal Leechman. This was not something I was aware of."

"I didn't think so." Leechman sighed.

Silence filled the space between them.

"I don't have a particular interest in returning to Edinburgh," Black said, his voice calm. "And I can assure you I was not consulted on this *venture*."

Leechman waved his hand. "You don't have to explain yourself to me, Joseph. That aspect of the business wasn't what I called you here to assist me with."

Then what did Leechman need his help untangling? Black tried to cast Cullen and his letter aside.

"Does Dr Monro's letter mean Dr Gregory is a contender for Rutherford's Chair?"

"One would suppose so. I confess I thought Dr Aird was better-placed..." Leechman adjusted himself again, staring at the papers on his desk. "But if they didn't want him once, I suppose they're unlikely to want him again."

Black nodded. While there was nothing wrong with Aird as a physician, he didn't seem to excite anyone with his potential. In sticking around Edinburgh too long, he'd perhaps lost his lustre.

"What confused me, and this might be the infirmities of old age showing..." A flash of the younger man's twinkling irony flashed in the old man's face. "Is why Dr Monro needs to avail himself of Glaswegian opinion regarding a gentlemen who has spent the better half of a year in Edinburgh?"

"Dr Gregory studied in Edinburgh, if I recall," Black added. Despite his protestations, age hadn't blunted Leechman. "Could it be that Dr Monro has doubts about Gregory as a candidate, Principal?"

"That makes our pieces of the puzzle even more discordant." Leechman glanced at his side board where a bottle of claret sat. Black could understand the temptation. Behind him, the oversized portrait of Principal Campbell still hung. Leechman wasn't the kind to decorate the space with his own likeness. "Say what you like about the Edinburgh medical school, they are excellent at herding their faculty into conformity. I'm not sure I've ever seen a crack between Drs Rutherford and Monro in my decades here."

A pang of regret struck Black, that he hadn't kept in touch with Cullen over the years. The ground in Edinburgh must have been shifting for years, and only now was he made aware of it. Too late.

"I lack an intimate view of the situation, but I'm not sure there is much distinction between Drs Gregory and Aird in terms of their medical knowledge or aptitude for the Practice of Physic Chair." He knew the rest of today was a wash: he'd be wracking his brains coming up with plausible excuses for what was going on in Edinburgh, to present to Leechman. He feared the endeavour would prove fruitless.

"Two dismal choices, you mean," Leechman chuckled. "At least compared to William."

Black lowered his eyes. Next to any physician in Britain, none shone as brightly as Cullen, nor excited such ardent loyalty in their students. Yet there was no man in Britain who infuriated his fellow physicians as much, either.

Black could almost forgive Cullen for putting his name down for the Chemistry Chair without asking. While the anonymous letter in support of Cullen was unlikely to come direct from his quill, Black would be astonished if Cullen knew nothing of it beforehand. He also knew plenty of Edinburgh students wished he taught there—some had even pilgrimaged to Glasgow to hear him lecture—but none would dare sneak his name into Cullen's petition without the subject's permission.

If Monro wrote to who Black suspected, then he could make his own enquires about the letter's contents. He felt he knew Monro enough to read between the lines of any message he sent, to figure out what his former anatomy professor was trying to discern.

Gregory had always been Rutherford's protégé. He threw his weight behind Gregory when he moved back to Edinburgh, making his endorsement public. In that respect, it made sense Rutherford was more in favour of his replacement than Monro. But why was Monro concerned?

Leechman sighed, his gaze returning to the claret. "It's a shame Dr Cullen's campaign is over before it started."

"What do you mean?" Black leaned forward in his chair.

"That was spelled out in another letter I received yesterday, almost on the back of the first..."

40

EDINBURGH

Cullen knew, just knew, he operated from a sound theoretical basis. Letters to the broadsheets were precisely what faculty candidates did in these situations to improve their public standing.

Unfortunately, as he told his students, when theory collided with messy, imperfect reality, it was impossible to predict which theoretical lines of truth would hold.

A few days after Nathanial's missive went to press, Cullen stopped by Nicolson's Tavern on West Bow. He was on first name terms with the owner, whose friendliness increased when Cullen began bringing in current and former students for convivial gatherings almost every week.

"Greetings, Thomas!" Cullen hailed the man as he entered.

"Oh, um, good day William..." Thomas Nicholson's response was a little flustered, but Cullen barely noticed. Today was a lovely, brisk day. Sunlight made Edinburgh a tolerable place. Two of his former students from Glasgow—now physicians themselves— were visiting Edinburgh and promised to stop by. He scanned the familiar low-ceiling surroundings to see if Callum or Rob were here yet.

In fact, most people were congregated around the central

bench, pouring over something. Men at the back nudged each other in the ribs. High-spirited guffaws broke from the general murmuring.

"Oh, you got a new broadsheet?"

Cullen could usually find a week-old copy of the *Courant* or *Mercury* floating around Nicholson's. They ended up here once the literati in the coffeehouses finished inspecting them, and the news was stale enough to let the rest of society read. That a broadsheet would attract so much interest was a little strange, because by the time it reached this tavern, most patrons already had second-hand knowledge of its contents.

"Erm, William...?"

Thomas was trying to attract Cullen's attention, his voice oddly strained. Cullen hesitated in the middle of the room, halfway towards the crowd of engrossed readers.

"Is something the matter, Thomas?"

In the blink of an eye Cullen realised he'd miscalculated on two levels. The first was speaking in his normal booming voice; a voice recognisable to half the citizens of Edinburgh. The second miscalculation—as fifteen pairs of eyes snapped in his direction—was that the contents of the broadsheet concerned him.

"I didn't think you'd come in until later," Thomas said weakly. The primary emotion smoking off his sizeable frame was guilt. Like an unshaven, overgrown child caught stealing sweet-meats from the pantry.

Cullen drew his rapidly dissipating shreds of dignity together.

"Well, let's have a look at what they're saying about me. Then I'll let you all get back to reading."

Less than three days after Nathanial's letter proclaimed support of his candidacy for the Practice of Physic Chair, the *Courant* published an anonymous refutation. Except there was no mistaking the inky fingerprints on the second letter.

. . .

"That's what Rutherford called me in the papers? *Doctor Puff*? Well, that's certainly bold of him."

His wife looked uncomfortable. "Did you read the whole diatribe, love?" Through this morning's visitors, and her own coffeeshop trip, Anna had spent several hours getting up to speed on the spectacle. Had Cullen gone home before heading to the tavern, he might have caught wind of the situation in time to avoid embarrassment.

"I'm afraid I skipped several parts, though I fear I got the gist of it." Cullen had begun to read the letter in Nicholson's tavern, stopping before he flung the paper across the room, but after realising he was swearing aloud every time he got to a new bon mot.

No doubt Anna would rather be working on her embroidery, or preparing herself a pot of tea. Instead she was sitting patiently in Cullen's study. His former students hadn't turned up to socialise. No one had. He'd retired home before sunset. "The anonymous source—presumably writing at Dr Rutherford's behest—accused you of writing the first letter. They claimed it disagreeable that you would pretend the letter originated purely from your students. Hence the choice nickname."

"That's slander. I reviewed the contents of the letter—naturally, but the students conceived and drafted its contents."

Anna's expression shifted from one emotional state to another. "Ah, and did you suggest revisions to the letter prior to its publication?"

"Hardly," huffed Cullen. "I'd call them clarifications—strengthening the intended rhetoric, that's all." He paused. It wasn't worth putting up a front for his canny wife. "That was probably a mistake, wasn't it?"

"It gave Dr Rutherford enough pretext to discredit you," Anna said. "At least, that's how it appears."

"Not that Rutherford didn't have a hand in that anonymous refutation and commits the same puffery he accuses me of." But Cullen couldn't lie to himself. Rutherford made his accusation first, after Nathanial's letter claimed to have originated warmly from the student body itself. A counterattack now wouldn't help. "He complained I don't offer enough demonstrations in my chemistry course...after the faculty destroyed all my glassware? And I have a growing medical practice to attend to?"

Sensing her husband needed to verbally purge the chloric from his system, Anna murmured in sympathetic assent.

Cullen gesticulated, now warmed to his topic. "Or that I've not published my medical treaties? When Rutherford has forced the Edinburgh and London printers to turn away my business? It's ludicrous."

It was one thing imagining what Rutherford and his ilk said of him behind closed doors, or catching the rumours in other people's conversations. It was another thing to see their contempt in print for all of Edinburgh to see. It would be fodder for coffeeshops and dinners all week.

Cullen was sure he had the support of the students—he told himself that was the main thing after all—but how secure was he?

"His assertion that your knowledge of multiple disciplines made you less suitable for the Chair made no sense. Even I can see the opposite holds true."

Cullen sighed. "It doesn't really matter, love. No one cares about the specifics of what Rutherford says. The Town Council just want proof that opposition to my candidacy exists among the faculty and other medical professionals in the city."

Rutherford's letter was aggressive where Cullen's—Nathanial's, really—tried to be diplomatic and avoid attacking the other medical faculty. For this reason he knew the former would receive more attention among the Edinburgh literati.

"I suppose you're right." Anna looked deflated. "There's not much we can do."

. . .

"Sit yourself down and take a glass. We don't need to stand on ceremony, William."

Cullen sank into a thickly padded chair. It was a drizzly day outside, and the earl's study was reassuringly cosy. On any other day he'd linger.

"If I might enquire after your mother, my lord?"

"Doing as well as can be expected. Thank you. You're the first physician she's spoken about in a kindly fashion after the visit."

"I'm glad I could be of some comfort," Cullen replied.

He knew it would be gauche to immediately pivot onto the real reason for his appearance in the earl's apartment, but fortunately his benefactor didn't care much for pointless ceremony either.

The Earl of Hopetoun sighed in a very aristocratic fashion. Cullen recognised men like him had a whole symphony of sighs to convey the myriad frustrations and disappointments accumulated when dealing with their social inferiors.

"I'd ask what in Heaven's name you were thinking and hoped to achieve by that letter...but I fear I know the answer to that question, and that's in some ways worse."

"I don't expect you to make excuses on my part," Cullen said hastily. Not that the earl showed any inclination towards doing so.

He'd hoped—knowing it was a silly, childish hope—that somehow the earl wouldn't find out about the *Doctor Puff* letter. That it was a minor embarrassment, nothing more, and wouldn't disrupt the Town Council's manoeuvring. He held onto this stupid wish even as the week dragged on and the gossip refused to abate. Double or triple the usual number of *Edinburgh Courant* broadsheets snuck into coffeeshops and taverns around town. Not only that, but the copies he saw today were greasier, with more torn edges, than last week's.

"In entering such a public debate—instead of letting your friends speak quietly on your behalf—you've allowed all sorts of impingements upon your character and record to be aired." The earl drew a long sip of his claret. "Impingements with an unfortunate ring of truth to them. This puts me in a difficult spot. In private discussions I could perhaps convince others that these imperfections might be discounted or explained away, but broadsheet screeds don't lend themselves to that kind of nuanced defence. It doesn't change my opinion as to your suitability for the role, but it does change how much I can reasonably presume to influence proceedings."

In any other patronage relationship, the earl would be furious at his wayward supporter, demanding to know why he'd acted so stupidly. Frustration emanated from the Earl of Hopetoun, but Cullen recognised an element of self-chastisement in the display. The earl supported Cullen because he was a fiery disruptor of the old ways. Reckless behaviour was the opposite side of that cherished coin.

Cullen also recognised the self-directed frustration, because it mirrored his own.

"I know you agree with me, John, when I say the medical school needs new leadership. It's a corrupt mess that nobody else wants to fix. I feel like a madman: am I the only person who cares about not extorting charity ward patients, or seeking personal enrichment in communal botanicals? Well, I know *you* care..."

"But what you fail to see, William, is that it takes more than one man to move a mountain. I agree you would do a better job than most at leading the medical school...until today, when I witnessed a riot almost break out among my esteemed associates at the thought of appointing you to the Practice of Physic Chair." More lines appeared on the earl's face. He looked almost as tired as Cullen felt. "What use is having you in the Chair, when everyone else is opposed to you? How much good can you hope to achieve? The faculty are *afraid* of you. They're afraid of being ignored, of having their wishes trampled. Of you taking their private concerns to the court of public opinion, whenever you feel you're not getting your way. The Town Councillors doubt they can work with you. In one way you care deeply about the medical school, your patients, and your students. In another way...they see you as deeply selfish."

"It's a stupid letter, from a stupid, insecure man. Come on, John...my lord...you know that. This is all blown out of proportion." Cullen's fingers dug into the chair arms. "They're taking one mistake I made, and a letter from Dr Rutherford more scathing than substantive, and letting their nightmares run wild. I won't have them forget the good I can do."

If the earl slid any lower in his chair, he'd drop onto the floor. He covered his face with his hand. "I need you to understand something, William. Something I fear you'll never understand, but which I have to spell out or I'll scream. Getting involved in Town Council business has aged me faster than I thought possible. My hairline is retreating in disarray. My stomach plays up once a month, regular as clockwork. That's because leadership is *hard*. It doesn't all go my way. I've mourned the things I had to give up in compromises to get what I believed most important. I've watched the tide turn against me in those meetings, then had to grit my teeth and smile because I need to work with these men tomorrow, in the hope the tide will reverse, and I won't have embittered all my allies before it does."

"Well then let me help you, my lord."

The earl winced. Cullen let the rest of his protestation die on his lips.

"The trouble is...I'm no longer convinced you would make my life easier, or facilitate our shared goals. William, you need to know *why* you want to lead the medical school. Why it isn't enough to support from the side like Dr Monro, or to quit the system entirely. Because *leadership* is different from *change*: not all men can handle both. Not all men want to deal with both, if I'm honest. Sometimes I think all you want is change without the burden of leadership. Maybe I'm wrong in my assessment of you. Maybe I'm wrong to assume that's impossible...in this context, at least. But I'm doubting more and more that putting you in the Practice of Physic Chair is the right thing to do. My fear is it's not going to help anyone, least of all yourself."

"I understand, my lord." Cullen's chin was almost on his sternum.

The earl nodded more firmly, a signal that Cullen was dismissed.

"Pass on my regards to Joseph," he said as Cullen's hand brushed the door handle. "His last letter explaining his new theories of thermodynamics was such a treasure of riches I'm taking my time crafting the response it deserves. It will be a while before I'm in Glasgow again, but assure him I'm looking forward to our next meeting."

Cullen hoped the whirlwind of gossip would blow itself out shortly thereafter, allowing the Town Council to continue their deliberations in quiet. He wished he hadn't upset the earl, but supposed in time cooler heads would prevail. However, when he arrived at the College the following morning and found Rutherford seated in his classroom, Cullen realised he'd misjudged the speed of the reaction too.

"I received word from Viscount Salisbury on the Town Council..." Rutherford began.

"Spare me, John." Rutherford was ballooning with smugness. All Cullen wanted was to drag him out of the room.

"You are on friendly terms with Dr Gregory, are you not?"

That stopped Cullen dead.

"You can't be serious? They're appointing John Gregory?"

It was one thing to know he was no longer under consideration for the medical faculty position. It was quite another to know the Town Council had settled for Gregory so readily. That was insulting.

"Dr...Professor Gregory is a thoughtful and amiable young

man. Very promising, William. You can feign ignorance of the justified praise he earned from the faculty in Aberdeen, or the deserving poor he's treated in Edinburgh…"

"What, all three of them? Did the Aberdonian faculty even notice he taught there?"

"Childish petulance does not suit you, William." If Rutherford inflated any further with smugness he would explode. He clasped his hands across his belly. "Professor Gregory's youthfulness is not the detriment you think it is—the Town Council were quite receptive to it, going so far as to consider it an advantage."

"I hope you're feeling satisfied," Cullen said.

"My satisfaction runs deeper than you could know. Consider this a mercy," Rutherford replied, tidying his papers. "Despite grave concerns among the faculty about your suitability to teach at this college, we'll allow you to keep your Chemistry chair."

It wasn't that he struggled to hold back a retort. This time, Cullen couldn't think of anything to say.

Satisfied his message was received, Rutherford clasped his hands together. Wordless, Cullen watched him leave.

It really had been for nothing. He couldn't defeat the Leviathan that was the Edinburgh medical faculty. Monro Primus —damn him—hadn't betrayed him to the dark chymists, but knowing Cullen's secret was all the incentive he needed to block his appointment to the Practice of Physic Chair.

John Gregory was a non-entity! A healthy, forty-year old non-entity—which was even worse. He could occupy the Practice of Physic Chair for the next thirty years.

Rutherford had thrown up enough doubt about the suitability of Cullen for the role that the Town Council played along with it. In the end, the progressive faction cared more about getting rid of Rutherford than uplifting Cullen.

. . .

Anna and the children said nothing when he arrived home that evening, there was nothing to be said really. As soon as he walked in the entrance she set a glass of claret on the table for him. She'd probably not needed to leave the house to learn of Gregory's appointment: plenty of Edinburgh wives would've fought to be the first to South Gray's Close to break the news to her.

"Let's have an early night tonight, love," Anna pleaded. "Take a moment to breathe, please, For my sake?"

He'd nodded and promised, knowing sleep would elude him.

Cullen didn't know what would come next. His future resembled the grey stretch similar to his years Glasgow after Joe left: an extended period of waiting without an obvious 'next.' The thought was less comforting, because this time Joe had no limit on his tenure in Glasgow. He was settled and flourishing in a way Cullen was not.

41

EDINBURGH

Entering his apartment, Monro found a maidservant trailing just steps from the front door. Her eyes were red.

"I'm sorry, sir..." she whispered.

"Mistakes happen," Monro said, trying to sound generous. "Tell me the matter and we'll rectify it."

His maid Lizy shook her head and sniffed. "He's in your study, sir. I swear I tried..."

Sure enough, Monro found Holm in his study, the tortoise-shell cat already on his lap.

"There better be a compelling reason for such frothy, impudent behaviour," Monro said, shutting the door. "I won't have you threatening my servants."

"I did no such thing," Holm replied, unashamed. "Though your maid strikes me as a little sensitive."

Monro's temper was about to consume him, so he refrained from retorting. It didn't do to lose one's control around Holm.

"I visited your anatomy theatre the other day," Holm continued. "I made it as far as the door when I encountered a strange smell."

"There are many strange smells associated with anatomical

art," Monro said. A defensive coldness crept into his voice. "I confess I lose track of them."

"Well, this one stood out, Alexander. You'll recall my familiarity with the little phlogistic system William Cullen and Black are playing around with? No? Well, accompanying dispensation of their system is the most pungent metallic odour. I've not smelled anything like it—not in tanneries nor old Plummer's chemical storage. It lingers in the mouth for hours afterwards; quite vile."

Monro said nothing. Could Holm be bluffing about the Cullen's phlogiston experimentation, and claiming to know more about it than he did? Yet he'd wondered where the rumours about Black originated and how they reached his ears. Here was an unwelcome sign they'd passed through Holm's.

"So you can imagine my surprise on my approach to your lonely basement when I realise I can taste phlogiston in the area. I went away puzzled, wondering what could account for it."

"Any numbers of things," retorted Monro. "Dr Cullen is known to come down there to seek my assistance with faculty matters. It's likely I wasn't even in the theatre when you stopped by. I would have heard you." The elderly stairs betrayed even the softest footfalls.

A nonchalant chuckle escaped Holm's lips. "Oh, I think you were there, dear doctor. You may not have heard me, but I heard you."

"Well, it's a shame I can't indulge your idle speculation, Malcolm. I have no idea what you thought you detected." Monro folded his arms, then unfolded them. "If you've never smelled the like, how can you say it's one thing or another?"

"Ah, but I found a reference sample that was unquestionably concentrated phlogiston. Clever of me, wasn't it? Thinking like a natural philosopher for a day."

"And none of this has any connection to me."

"But that's the thing, Alexander. Several astute men in this town are concerned you've become...sympathetic to Cullen's doctrines."

"Absurd!" Monro slapped the table. "We've known for years his theories are riddled with flaws and hold no use."

"Quite so," Holm tickled the cat under her chin. "Yet the physicians in Edinburgh never seem satisfied with ideas unless they test, test, test. Most physicians would make terrible clergymen."

"Why would I waste my time testing Cullen's theories?" demanded Monro. He wondered if he should summon a servant to escort Holm out.

"Well, one of the lies Cullen spreads is that he's better than my masters and doesn't need their knowledge. I wondered if that might not appeal to you."

"No it doesn't!" Blood burned underneath Monro's skin.

Holm paused, his hand resting on the cat's back. "Something I wondered, that I always wanted to ask an anatomist...do animals feel pain?"

The tendons in Monro's throat constricted. "Yes," he said quietly, "we observe they experience pain as Man does."

"Interesting, isn't it?" Holm mused, scratching the cat behind its ears. "Men of the church and men of science pondering over the same questions: what makes us human, what makes us superior to dumb beasts—in rare circumstances coming around to identical answers. You dissect live dogs in your anatomy theatre, do you not professor?"

"It is important," whispered Monro. "Students must understand the sanctity of life, and what it means to give or take life away."

"A lesson taught on Sunday, and repeated on Monday." Holm's long finger tickled the cat under its chin. Purring ecstatically, the cat raised its head and closed her eyes.

"The dogs...they are strays off the street. No one misses them." Monro blinked rapidly, frozen where he stood. "Malcolm..."

"But with the kirk, the physicians and chirurgeons all teaching the same lessons, maybe the learned men of medicine forget their place in the natural hierarchy." Still stroking the cat's neck, Holm's other hand slid into his coat pocket. "Maybe the professors start to think themselves above God."

"Malcolm, I don't know what this is about…" Monro didn't know what to do. No matter how hard he tried to control himself, he knew every microcosmic action of his was communicating fear, and that Holm was drinking it in. "Malcolm, that's my wife's cat."

Holm wrapped his hand over the cat's head for a moment. The cat raised its paw in objection and struggled briefly, but a second later Holm resumed stroking its chin and the purring resumed.

"Do you know your place in the natural order of things, Professor Monro?"

"I do." Monro would have said anything at this point to make the ordeal end.

"I'm pleased to hear it. Though I worry such protestations won't satisfy everybody…"

Holm's right hand shot out of his pocket, but Monro was already lunging forward. He shoved the cat off Holm's lap, gasping as Holm's blade bit into his forearm.

The cat yelped with indignation.

Monro backed away from Holm, clutching his bleeding arm in shock. The pain was indescribable. Warm liquid seeped through his fingers onto the carpet.

The cat, already righted on its feet, shook its head a few times and wandered over to the bookcase. Holm had already stowed the knife back in his pocket. His eyes shone with vicious amusement, taking in his victim's fear and pain.

"Get out of my home, Holm," spat Monro. "Get out immediately."

Holm rose with an insouciant shrug, dusting cat hairs off his breeches as he did so.

"You should be more careful next time, Alexander. When I'm

out on my masters' business I'm in the habit of coating my knives with poison." With a casual hum he sauntered out the room.

The two Monros sat in silence. The only sound came from Monro Primus biting down whimpers of pain as his son stitched the wound closed.

After Holm sauntered away, Monro fled to find his son. As expected, Sandy was in the college anatomy theatre, finishing a wax cast of the lungs. Another man might rush over to his injured father who appeared clutching a blood-soaked arm to his chest, gasping and demanding to know what happened, if they were alright, et cetera. One sight of Monro Primus swaying in front of him, and Sandy rushed to prepare his surgical instruments and hot water.

By the time Sandy was ready to suture, Monro, grey-faced, had already cleaned up his wound. Wordless, Monro jammed a wooden stick into his mouth. Aside from the whimpers and twitches, he endured several minutes of the needle stabbing through his skin.

Once Sandy finished suturing, he grunted once and slid the vial of laudanum towards his father.

There was a mutual grimness to each man's expression. The younger Monro didn't need to ask questions, because he already suspected the answers.

Monro unscrewed the vial, but paused before swallowing any drops.

Sandy experienced a rush of emotions. Protective love for his father, combined with the horror and grief that came from realising how old and frail his father looked.

"This city is getting more dangerous, Sandy," Monro croaked. "We need to prioritise our own protection..."

42

EDINBURGH

By mid-afternoon, the College was as quiet as its library. Cullen wanted a break from his colleagues, so decided to track down a copy of the School of Medicine meeting minutes. Sandy Monro told him they'd left a spare in the senate rooms. The other professors probably expected he'd send a student to collect it, but Cullen felt the urge to get out of his chilly classroom. How many hours had he been stuck inside teaching?

Besides, Nathanial and his friends had been avoiding him since the Medical Institutes debacle. He'd tried to assure them they'd done nothing wrong, and he wasn't angry at them. But his protestations seemed to make their guilt worse, so he decided to leave them be. They'd come around eventually.

The senate rooms were on the opposite side of the Yards. Administrative offices and meeting rooms occupied this wing, though the majority of business was wrapped off by now. Nobody was using the senate rooms, and the minutes were on a bookshelf near the door, wedged under a dry inkwell.

Since there was no-one around and he was disturbing no meetings, Cullen began leafing through the minutes.

Then a murmur caught his ear. Someone must be using the

325

adjacent rooms after all. But now his ears were aware of the murmuring, they sharpened and bought the conversation into clearer focus.

The voices were all familiar too him, which was why they attracted his attention.

"My familiarity with the business is limited and affairs of the city have preoccupied my time..."

"Tell me when that wasn't the truth!"

Town Councillors.

Goodness knows what drew them to the college this afternoon. The Councillors flitted onto the grounds when the whim suited them. It sounded like there were three or four men in the room next door. Perhaps they'd reconvened after meeting with the Provost.

Cullen was about to slip out the door and turn right to avoid stumbling into the gentleman's line of sight, when he heard the medical faculty referenced. He paused. Was he about to hear his name?

"When he met with us last week, he was happy the five hundred be freed from the School of Medicine..."

'He' could only refer to Gregory. Cullen recognised this as a budget update, which was handled by Gregory as first port of call.

Except did he understand this conversation correctly? Rumours of the Town Council's windfall reached the college a few months ago, with much chitter chatter about how the generous budget would be allocated. The other medical faculty had clamoured around Gregory with proposals for the money: a new anatomy theatre, more botany supplies, a new professorship.

The Chair of Physic could not possibly wave away such a large sum of money. Monro would be spitting fury if he knew. He had to know...didn't he? But if this alleged meeting took place last week there was no whispers on campus.

Cullen leaned closer to the wall, until his ear almost touched the greasy panels. The voices in the next room rose and fell. Soft chuckles, a spirited assent, cleared throats.

"He left my apartment quite satisfied…"

"I expected a far more contentious levee…"

"Well waste not, want not!"

"Ha ha ha!"

Who on campus could talk sense into these snobs? It was two o'clock in the afternoon. Monro was indisposed. Gregory had pranced off into town. The remaining professors were at the Infirmary or calling on patients. Cullen paced to and fro, trying to recall his past hour—who had he greeted and spoken as he traversed the Yards? Surely a forgotten individual would spring from his memory and save the day. Someone who had the patience to deal with these braying fools without offending their delicate sensibilities. The only soul he'd seen was Monro Junior—nice enough lad, but hardly better than him when it came to…

Decades had passed since his disastrous appeal to Anglesbury in Glasgow, but the memory rose in Cullen's mind, almost as fresh as the day it was imprinted. A burst of cringing shame at the snub, and the anger that blossomed in its wake. Cullen hated feeling at the mercy of the rich and powerful, and he could think of several situations in the intervening years where he'd deliberately avoided a repeat of that encounter.

Hugh and the Earl of Hopetoun were straightforward: they already liked and supported him. Hostile aristocrats were another matter. Especially once they formed a sneering pack.

"Excellent. You and your lady will join us at Stanley's?"

Damn, they were adjourning; the conversation turning to their engagement diaries. Cullen pushed himself away from the wall, bunching his fists.

May God have mercy.

He barrelled into the senate room, flattening the creases in his coat.

He didn't have to cough, his entrance was noisy enough. Four beautiful, pale men paused and looked up.

Lord Carstaires of Invergoury wore a crushed red velvet coat with gold trimmings and buttons the size of guineas. For a moment Cullen wondered why his lips didn't curl in annoyance as soon as he entered the room, but then he remembered Carstaires was the Earl of Hopetoun's brother in-law.

"Dr Cullen? I'm surprised to encounter you on College grounds after noon." He turned to his cronies. "You won't find a busier physician in Edinburgh! Always calling on patients around town."

It was halfway between mockery and a compliment. Cullen smoothed his countenance.

"On the contrary, my lords, I am attending to an ailing patient as we speak. One greatly advanced in years and splendour, yet reticent to speak for herself in trying circumstances. This patient is unusual...in that she is a medical school."

"Ah, you were listening to our conversation?" Sir Neil responded, again with that infuriating neutrality between indignation and amusement.

"And I beg you let speak on behalf of this silent patient, who I have grown to care for deeply." Cullen clasped his hands in front of him in a gesture of supplication.

Viscount Fairfax laughed and nudged his friend. Cullen supposed he was the one who'd been so vocal a minute ago about moving the funds away from the medical school.

"My concern is Dr Gregory misunderstood the Town Council's intention when he spoke," Cullen said. "Or some other factor prevented him from full candidness with you."

"It was not our intention to deceive Dr Gregory. If you were in the meeting I think you'd agree I was fully transparent on the budget and its revised allocation." Fairfax gave Cullen a long look.

This was damn courtier politics. No one quite saying what they meant. Pristine manners hiding true sentiments.

"I apologise for insinuating wrong-doing on your part, my lord." Cullen swerved. "That was inelegantly expressed of me." *You know what I meant, you slimy fuckster. You're doing this to make me squirm.* "If you'll permit me to explain why the five hundred pounds should remain with the medical school..."

"Oh, you were listening closely!" Sir Neil laughed, a measure of admiration in his voice. "Pray, continue."

"For starters, Monros Senior and Junior are anxious to build a new anatomy theatre to accommodate their burgeoning class sizes..." *That's all the elder Monro is sniping about in faculty meetings, and it began to grate on my nerves about, oh, five months ago.* "...and with the recent split of botany and materia medica into separate courses the accompanying library shelves devoted to both deserve freshening..."

The Town Councillors raised sculpted brows and toyed with their kid gloves.

"I calculated the materia medica books would set the school back by forty-five pounds, and I imagine the botany textbooks total a similar value." Cullen didn't feel the need either point out or argue against his own personal investment in the teaching of materia medica—that was obvious enough and the men facing him were no fools. Hopefully they'd appreciate more than his selfish interest lay at stake.

Carstaires brushed a stray curl from his forehead with his index finger. "You make a compelling petition, Dr Cullen. But this puts us in a bind, as Dr Gregory assured us he had the unanimous agreement of his faculty, which you now suggest is not the case..."

It took everything in Cullen not to roar with frustration and throw his hands to the sky. Why would any professor turn down such a bounty?

"It appears there has been a miscommunication, my lords..." *Gregory's either a liar or an idiot.* "And I would beg a thousand pardons..." *Please God, give me just one week to sort out this mess.*

"Well Dr Cullen, your patient will sleep peacefully another

night." The men patted each other on the back, patting Cullen in the same manner as they ambled towards the door. "No documents have been signed, nor have any promissory notes changed hands. Perhaps you can call upon us tomorrow once this is cleared up."

Any relief Cullen felt as the door closed was swept under the greater wave of vexation at the realisation his work was not even half complete. He'd have to canvas everyone—even damn Monro—and get their affidavits through a repeat performance of this hoopla. Goodness knows what Gregory's motivations were for throwing away the funds. At best he was trying to appease the Town Council out of insecurity, at worst he was embroiled in a nefarious scheme for personal enrichment or protection and actively sabotaging the medical school. Did Monro and the others know he'd bargained away five hundred pounds? Cullen couldn't see these conversations producing anything other than acrimony.

Untying this Gordian knot seemed to be the kind of intellectual stimulation Black chased in Glasgow, and spoke about with the most excitement after his chemical experiments.

"You'd love this kind of challenge, Joe." Cullen sighed to the empty room. "I think."

43

GLASGOW

A thousand symphonies of silence occupied the mansions, homes and hovels of Britain, each one adding their own unique texture to the surrounding air.

The silence currently settled over this grandiose mansion on the outskirts of Glasgow was one of humming unease just beyond the edge of hearing. Even in the basement, servants moved with economy, fearful of disruptions rippling to the upper floors. They knew from painful experience what happened when the silence broke.

A single black-garbed physician making his way down the staircase and across the marbled entrance moved deep within that silence, his woollen coat making not a rustle.

One hand in pocket, the physician looked solemnly at the floor, as if the movement of his eyes had the capacity to disturb the stillness.

"Dr Black?" A woman hesitated in the doorway on his left. "Is everything well?"

"Lady Anglesbury." The physician pivoted on his heels, drew himself to full height, then regally inclined his head. "Your husband is in good spirits. He was desirous of rest when I left him."

The woman, well past her fiftieth year, was rake-thin and pallid. In fact, the copious lead powder on her face probably warmed her natural skin tone, rather than diminishing it. Her gown was expensive, but sat ill on her frame. Her hair was bundled into a bonnet. She shivered slightly, perhaps discarding a shawl in the parlour when she heard the doctor walk past.

"Very well." She nodded, bobbing her head. "Do you have pressing engagements you must attend to, Dr Black? Can I persuade you to take tea with me?"

The doctor smiled. "No pressing business calls me today, aside from some committee notes I must review this evening. That said, I would hate to impinge upon your time, Lady Anglesbury."

"Oh, no, no—you must never think of yourself as an intrusion, Dr Black. Please, I just had a fresh pot brought in."

The physician followed her into the reception room, silent as a shadow. There was indeed a pot of tea smoking gently on the table near the hearth.

"You are keeping well, Lady Anglesbury? I understand you just returned from Edinburgh."

"Yes, yes..." the older woman fussed with the tea, and made an impatient gesture to the serving girl stationed in the corner. "It's very kind of you to ask, Dr Black. I was visiting my sister. I found the trip quite rejuvenating to my spirits. They're been low this spring—I'm not sure why."

Upstairs, her husband slept off the ill effects of mercury treatment, an attempted cure for the multiple venereal diseases afflicting him. The physician merely nodded and leaned forward to better regard her, all sympathy.

If the woman had any complexion remaining, she might have blushed at this point.

"Your sister is the Lady Argyle, did you tell me that?"

"Yes, I suppose I must have done." The woman trailed off,

silver teaspoon clinking in endless circles around her cup. "She seems happy."

"I've only had brief acquaintances with the Argyles," the physician noted, a smile still on his face. "But I think of them often."

"Of course, you studied in Edinburgh didn't you, Dr Black?"

Nervous energy thrummed off the woman, though it had little to do with the handsome physician sipping her tea and watching her in an attentive manner. She stole glances at the door, as if expecting her husband to walk through at any minute.

"There was something I wished to ask you, Lady Anglesbury..."

"Oh?"

"If it's not an imposition..."

"Um, of course not, Dr Black."

"I heard Lord Argyle is entertaining quite a number of private parties this month. It was the topic of much petty chatter, because his gatherings used to be open to wider Edinburgh society. He and Lady Argyle's parties are much missed."

"Oh." His hostess lowered her gaze. A drop of tea splashed onto her fingers. "Well, I suppose men of the cloth don't make good party guests."

"I'm sorry?" The physician tilted his head and leaned forward. "I confess I don't understand your meaning, my lady."

"I apologise, it's nothing, really. I just meant Lord Argyle is mostly hosting men of the Kirk. Assembleymen and the like. They aren't what I'd call convivial gatherings, not with men of that stripe."

The physician sipped his tea and looked contemplative.

"Interesting."

"Abby says they're rather dull men." Lady Anglesbury leaned forward, with a conspiratorial air. "Very drab and serious."

"I can imagine. What can be the benefit of their company? Lord Argyle never struck me as particularly inclined towards theological matters, beyond natural piety."

Lady Anglesbury shrugged, and resumed stirring her tea. "I feel sorry for poor Abby, having to put up with all of them. It goes quite against her natural gaiety. She doesn't know what they're discussing until the wee hours."

The physician leaned back in his chair. In profile, his dark eyes glinted.

"Puzzling, indeed..."

44

EDINBURGH

The first rumours of death came onto the grounds not as words, but as a ripple of unease and tension. Standing in his open doorway overlooking the Yards, Cullen felt it sweep past. Students caught in whispering gaggles, faculty exchanged grim expressions and parted rapidly.

He'd arrived at the college too early, leaving the streets before the rumours circulated.

Cullen was sure his students would bring the news within minutes, but he happened to see Gregory hurry towards him along the side of the quad, clutching a stack of books with a pained look on his face. He was likely just coming back from a meeting with the Lord Provost.

Cullen stepped out of the door just enough to waylay his colleague.

"Good heavens, Gregory. I entered my classroom twenty minutes ago to sunshine and birdsong, and when I step out again its a deluge of misery. What's going on?"

Gregory glared at Cullen for a second, trying to deduce if Cullen knew the answer and was mocking him. A second passed before he decided the question was an earnest one.

"It's Whytt," he said simply. "God rest his soul."

"How can he be dead?" Cullen echoed. "Merciful heavens, what happened to him?"

"A sudden illness is what I heard." Gregory shrugged.

"I don't like this," Cullen whispered. He'd last seen Whytt puttering about the Infirmary earlier this week, a picture of vitality. Not that he was a young man, but age hadn't wrought much damage upon him until now.

Gregory looked away from Cullen, projecting his lack of care. "Now is not the time for your fanciful and quite frankly insulting gossip, William. I have to sort out Whytt's teaching for the next couple of weeks."

"If you need assistance…" Cullen managed, trying to keep his wits about him. He hadn't even thought about the havoc Whytt's demise would wreck on the teaching side of things.

"Don't." Gregory left, doing his best impersonation of Rutherford's dismissive glance. The inferior approximation would be funny if he didn't mimic his mentor so wholeheartedly.

Was Whytt's death a simple, cruel illness? Cullen couldn't imagine the dark chymists would wish to disrupt the balance of power in the medical faculty so soon after locking him out. But Gregory's cold reaction suggested there was more going on than Cullen was aware of.

After a strange, sombre lecture, Cullen found Anna and their maidservant waiting for him on Jamaica Street.

One look at his wife's face was enough to confirm she'd heard the rumours.

"It's been very queer on campus," Cullen said by way of a greeting. "The students are in shock, the faculty are very worried."

"They don't believe the cause of death was illness?" They started the slow procession home. Anna's face looked pinched.

How long since the last dark chymist-mediated slaying in Edinburgh, Cullen wondered. Not long enough: the faculty and older students still remembered those days.

"I gather Dr Gregory was the one who attended to Charles, and he's acting stranger than usual. I'm not sure what he knows, but I suspect it is more than the rest of us."

It wasn't that Cullen thought Gregory capable of killing a fellow physician. But he'd be the perfect tool to facilitate a cover-up at the behest of others.

"I know it's crude to think of these things so soon after poor Dr Whytt expired," Anna began. "But I imagine the tussling to fill his chair will begin around dinnertime today. You should prepare your case for the Town Council."

"It's best I don't, love," Cullen sighed. "The faculty has made it clear what they think of me, and I fear there's more viciousness yet they can unleash."

When Rutherford announced his retirement, he'd been foolish enough to believe his popularity among the students and Hopetoun faction would carry the day. He'd been cruelly abused of that notion.

It was his own fault, really. His pride led to that stupid broadsheet war, causing more harm to his reputation than good.

They reached the corner of the college, and turned downhill towards the Cowgate.

"This city would be a warmer place if you were leading the faculty," Anna said. She spoke breathlessly, hurrying out the words she'd held on to for so long. "I know you wouldn't indulge such bullying and mean-spirited attacks. The dark chymists have become more brazen since Gregory took charge, any half-wit can see that."

She bore a brave face, but Cullen knew the attacks on him hurt Anna as well. The number of her social engagements had dropped, and she offered resistance to dinners and parties she'd once been delighted to attend with him. As far as Cullen was aware—and he was certain he'd be the first to know if it wasn't so—she'd never said a word against him, or criticised him to lessen the pressure on herself.

He didn't deserve a wife this loyal. But she would scold him til his cheeks blistered if he claimed he was avoiding the Institutes Chair for her comfort.

"Let Aird or one of Rutherford's surrogates take the chair. They'll have no shortage of docile candidates."

Maybe Anna was right and he possessed the *ideals* necessary to lead the medical faculty. But time and time again he'd seen how little his ideals mattered when he hadn't the *skills* to attain leadership.

He'd already told Nathanial and the others not to push the matter, before they had a chance to open their mouths. That was a tough conversation. Nathanial turned red eyed, and he appeared wounded by Cullen's rejection of his pleas to help. It made sense that he'd feel betrayed.

Seems I've hurt everyone in this city, he thought.

Not that he doubted her, but it turned out Anna was correct when she predicted things would move fast. It was not yet four o'clock that evening when she her knuckles tentatively scraped Cullen's study door.

"It's Dr Monro Senior," she whispered. Seeing her husband's expression, she added. "I warned him you might be seeing a patient. He insisted he was not here to admonish you."

"Not that such a disclaimer ever stopped him before," Cullen remarked.

He'd not spoken to Monro since the demonstration of phlogiston in his classroom. Not properly spoken.

Avoiding Monro was always worse than speaking to him. He wasn't sure he had the strength tonight to deal with him anyway. But would he have more strength tomorrow or next week?

"Let him in, love. Don't bother with tea, though."

This was the first time Monro had been inside his house. He watched the Anatomy professor surreptitiously look around, taking in Cullen's bookshelves, paintings and furnishings. His expression hid judgement, but every item scrutinised added to the ledgers inside Monro's head.

Monro sat down before Cullen could either invite him to sit or snub him with a refusal.

They'd exchanged no more than a handful of sentences since Cullen exposed his phlogistic powers and Monro stormed off.

"You've no doubt heard the news regarding Dr Whytt..." Monro began.

"What do you want, Dr Monro?"

He snapped the question more harshly than he'd intended. Or at least he thought so. Monro looked taken aback.

"I was surprised to hear that you wouldn't be putting your name forward...."

"Get out of my house, Alexander."

For a moment Cullen felt a surge of satisfaction. He thought he'd be too weak to deal with Monro and his endless sniping, but he'd gone so far into tiredness and despair he no longer cared. It was worth it to see the shock on Monro's face, it gave him a twist of pleasure.

"I'm so tired of your gloating, your cruelty. Go find someone else to torment. I'm sure there's plenty of wretched souls in Edinburgh whose suffering you can derive pleasure from." Propelled from his chair, Cullen stalked back and forth across the tiny study. He could barely do that without stepping on Monro's feet. Perhaps if he got agitated enough he could do genuinely claim crushing his toes was an accident.

"I think you should put your name forward, Dr Cullen." Monro raised his voice to break Cullen's diatribe. His knuckles turned from yellow to white as he gripped the chair arms.

"And why's that?" Cullen only half-absorbed what Monro was saying. "Of course! It gives you and your cronies another opportunity to discredit me. Having trouble finding another "concerned citizen" to pen missives to the Courant? Curious to see how much mockery a man can stomach before he gives up?"

"They shouldn't have criticised your Latin," Monro blurted out.

Cullen stopped pacing. He turned to look at his colleague.

Monro seemed frozen. He stared at the point where the curtains touched the rug, lower lip clamped between his teeth.

For a moment Cullen was unsure if he'd actually spoken. He held his tongue, knowing anything he said would come out as a bark. Joe always urged caution when his emotions ran this high.

Monro's eyes were wider than usual. His mouth worked for a few seconds. Finally he swallowed.

"They slandered your Latin fluency and your decision to lecture in English." Monro's voice was clearer now. "And they were wrong to do so."

Cullen narrowed his face and sat down opposite Monro, who cautiously turned towards him.

"Latin is all very well for learned academic discourse with our colleagues overseas, and it's an important part of any gentleman's education, but I've never believed in excluding those from my classes who weren't fortunate enough to receive the proper grounding in Latin. Nor do I believe the teaching of medicine produces inferior results with English tongue."

Monro was shaking slightly, but Cullen realised it wasn't from fear. It was anger.

"Some of your medical theories are, well, a radical departure from what is accepted, but I can see you carry a lot of respect for the Boerhaavian tradition. And maybe Edinburgh isn't meant to become a perfect replica of Leiden. Rutherford is wrong to stand against you, and you have my backing for the Institute of Medicine Chair." Monro couldn't quite look Cullen in the eye, but he spoke with urgency.

Cullen smiled and shook his head. He returned to his desk.

"I didn't think I would hear such words from you, Doctor."

"Me neither."

Cullen leaned back into his chair.

"Do you still want to deny the validity of my aethereal theories?"

Monro swallowed. "No," he said after a pause.

Cullen waited to see if he'd say more about what he'd demonstrated—and what Monro had concealed from the dark chymists—but Monro didn't say anything further. He wasn't going to beg the man for secrecy, or rant about how his games terrorised him for months on end. Both admissions were weakness.

Monro gazed at his fingernails. "I'm calling upon my son this evening. He's his own man, of course, but he'll support you too. I suspect with less reluctance than myself in fact. After that we'll approach Drs Hope and Young." He seemed to be telling this to the room, rather than Cullen himself. "There's not much I can do regarding Gregory, but I don't suppose that will concern you. Apparently, he's meeting with Francis Aird a week on Wednesday."

"You've offered to do more than enough." Cullen assured him. The reappearance of Aird was annoying, but drearily predictable.

Monro rose. He worked his fists open and closed a few times. "Break them, William. You and Joseph: break their power. You two deserve to be here more than them." With a cursory nod he spun and departed.

45

STIRLING

Black looked around the sooty tavern with a mixture of curiosity and amusement.

"I've never visited Stirling before—it's only slightly larger than I thought."

"It's not quite equidistant between Glasgow and Edinburgh... but close enough, Joe." Cullen sat down and studied his measure of ale. The tavern maid's hand was less generous than the ones in Edinburgh, but it seemed pointless complaining.

In the haze, farmhands studied the pair from out of town, before grunting and returning to their conversations. Cullen decided it was good their business didn't look too intriguing.

"Are you sure Gregory is behind the death of Whytt?" Black asked. He ignored the streaks of grime on his wine glass.

"As certain as I can be about anything taking place in that snake-pit," Cullen said. Black nodded, thoughtful. "It was my own stupid fault, Joe. I complained to young Gregory about Whytt a while back—some business with extorting patients on the charity ward—and then Whytt passes suddenly and Gregory is looking mighty annoyed about the whole situation."

"I met Dr Gregory while I was a student," Black said. His tone gave no indication whether he agreed with his former teacher's assessment of events. But that he was still entertaining the topic suggested broad agreement. "He didn't strike me as a bad man... beyond a tendency towards trying to please everyone."

Cullen supposed that Gregory may have thought he'd please Cullen by confiding in Holm about his suspicions.

"Monro Primus offered me a deal," Cullen said. He'd waited until Black had brought the wine glass to his mouth to blurt this out. Black swallowed a quick mouthful, eyes widening only slightly. "He'll arrange my appointment to Whytt's Institute of Medicine Chair." He decided not to immediately mention the vacant Chemistry Chair he'd leave behind. Black was smart enough to make the connections, and he didn't want to rush the discussion.

Black took another sip of wine, swallowing it slower this time.

"Does Dr Monro share your suspicions about the late Dr Whytt?"

"Honestly, lad—I don't know." Cullen glanced around the room, but no one paid them attention. "Monro's problem is he doesn't care what the other faculty get up to. Well..." Black's eyebrows rose. "He cares up to a point that they're not disrupting the finely oiled machine that is the School of Medicine, but he doesn't care about the morality of individual actors as they go about their exalted business."

Was it naive to want a functioning, *ethical* medical faculty? One that didn't slither along on widespread corruption? Monro claimed to espouse Christian virtues—had he once felt torn between creating a productive medicine school or a corruption-free one?

The barmaid leant on the counter, eyeing the pair. She wasn't listening to particulars of their conversation—probably checking instead that those pretentious city dwellers didn't disparage her wares.

Black remained impassive, and continued to work through his

drink. Cullen could recognise a lot of thoughts scurrying across his mind. It cost all his self-control not to jump in, but to let the younger man think.

"Congratulations are in order, then." Black raised his glass with a slight smile. "To your promotion. I take it the news is not widely known yet?"

"If it hasn't reached Glaswegian ears, it means it hasn't reached Edinburgh ears either. But the reason I suggested we meet up, Joe, is because I'm worried about what will happen when the news *does* get out."

"Hmm?" Black must have worked out the Edinburgh chemistry chair was about to be dangled under his nose, and was perhaps disappointed Cullen hadn't yet mentioned it.

"If I'm right, and Whytt was killed, it suggests the dark chymists are resuming activity. That nasty piece of work Malcolm Holm," Black visibly flinched at the name "is strutting around Edinburgh like he owns the place. Maybe he does. To be honest with you, Joe..." Cullen lowered his voice. Black instinctively leaned closer. "Im concerned that the dark chymists are up to no good. They've been suspiciously quiet following news of Whytt's demise, and no one knows what they're up to."

"Secretly meeting with members of the Scottish Kirk, so I heard," Black said, shadows flitting across his face.

This was news to Cullen, and wholly unwelcome at that.

"Argyle has been hosting repeat gatherings at his house, I heard it from his Glaswegian sister-in-law."

Cullen took a sip of his ale, rubbed his forehead, then chuckled.

"Well, I suppose that's one way to take me out of the equation."

It was Black's turn to look puzzled.

Cullen set his glass down. Ideas poured into his head, like waves against the shore. It left a clear, and nasty, picture.

"For years the dark chymists and Town Council loyalists have been locked in a struggle for control of the college. It's not surprising that eventually they'd grow tired to trying to stack the Council with their own, and instead attempt to erase the entire edifice." He paused. "The high lords of Edinburgh always claimed to look down on their west coast counterparts, until they decide to emulate them."

The muscles in Black's face tensed. "But presumably they want to put their own spin on the Assembly-moderated Glasgow model. One with a much tighter grip on the faculty, no doubt."

"And if they needed to get their enemies in one place to snuff them out, how better than to use a contentious faculty appointment as bait?" Cullen always knew he would be the lit fuse. He didn't expect it to be in service of the dark chymists' long-simmering plans. He exhaled and shook his legs. A cramp was forming in his calves. "The college and Town Council will convene within weeks to nominate Whytt's replacement. It'll bring back a lot of nobles from their summer estates."

"So what will their plan be? Slaughter the Town Council when they convene? Will there be sigils in the meeting room?"

The tavern owner was loitering close to their table, no doubt sensing they were on the verge of requesting more drinks. Cullen obliged her. Once she'd been shooed away, he turned back to his companion.

"We'll have to warn them, Joe. Maybe get the Earl of Hopetoun to appeal directly—they'll listen to him."

"The situation must be approached with care," Black noted. "If the dark chymists learn about our warning, they will come up with a counterattack. Targeting the Town Councillors at the meeting is a risky preposition, because of how alert they'll be to this sort of interference."

That thought sat uncomfortably with Cullen, too. By this point, the dark chymist playbook was well-established.

"Unless..." What had Monro said the other day, just before he left? "There's another way to lure the Town Councillors into a trap. Perhaps tricked by someone they perceive as their own?"

Gregory was speaking with Aird this week. What if that meeting concluded with a suggestion—innocently delivered—that Aird meet with the Town Councillors in person to discuss the vacant chair?

Black's expression was turning darker by the minute. Cullen briefly explained his suspicion. He received a strained nod.

"Yes, Francis has always been seen as a Town Council man. The last thing they'd expect was for him to be luring them into a trap. Especially if he didn't realise that was what he was doing."

"Curse Gregory." Cullen didn't know if Gregory was aware of what he'd set in motion at the behest of his masters, but it didn't matter. The tragic end result would be the same. "Still, that's something we can work with. Figure out where Francis is leading his victims, unspool the trap, then finally...finally...get rid of the dark chymists once and for all."

He was tired of this malignancy in Edinburgh. Tired of what it did to onlookers and everyday citizens. Tired of their nefarious meddling.

He didn't have the full outline of a plan in place, but that didn't matter, either. He could figure it out. He might only have a few days, but that was better than nothing.

"I thought we'd cowed them for good, Joe. But since we haven't...well, it means they'll start back at us too. The dark chymists tolerated me these past years because they saw Rutherford keep his foot on me, making sure I wasn't a threat. He did an excellent job, if I saw so myself. If Monro is right and the medical faculty are moving to support me in defiance of his meddling...it means they'll view me as a threat again. We have to act before they do."

"I."

"Pardon?"

"*I* cowed the dark chymists, William. You were teaching in

Glasgow when the Earl of Hopetoun visited. Holm attacked *me*; and *I* dealt with him. I disarmed the dark chymists by removing their primary weapon." Black spoke calmly and kept his voice low, but there was force in every syllable. His gaze remained fixed on Cullen, daring him to look away.

Cullen had no intention of doing that. "You're right, Joe. And I owe you an overdue apology. That's part of the reason I asked to meet you." Black took another sip from his almost empty glass. But this time Cullen saw it was a way to temporarily break eye contact with him. "I know the rest of the medical school wanted you for the chemistry chair in 1756. I didn't induce the Earl of Hopetoun to petition so hard on my behalf, but I didn't do anything to discourage him, either."

This time Black didn't pretend to take more sips from his glass. He let it sit on the table, studying his hands for a moment.

"I felt it's my fault we drifted apart in the intervening years," Cullen continued. "I know I hurt your feelings. I mean, I know I hurt you. You had every right to feel hurt."

Black rotated the glass in his hands.

He was always so damn *self-contained*.

Cullen silently willed him to speak. He knew Black wouldn't back down from the upcoming fight—it would go against every fibre of his being, everything Cullen knew about the man—but he needed the words to be said.

"I understand. I think it was for the best, in the end," Black said after a while. "If you'd somehow persuaded John to abandon his petition, and if the Town Council decided to elect me instead of Francis or whoever else they called upon, I imagine the dark chymists would be double the strength they are today. To think I would have woken every morning knowing I remained in the same city as Malcolm Holm: what a terrible existence."

Cullen smiled. As Black spoke, his shoulders loosened ever so slightly. He looked relieved to be finally saying these words out loud.

"I possibly wasn't ready for Edinburgh back then," Black continued. "I was still in awe of Dr Monro, and barely knew how to navigate the university and its patrons. I needed to be away from my former teachers to grow on my own." He looked up. His dark eyes met Cullen's. A sly smile flitted across his face. "But I'm ready now."

46

EDINBURGH

Black pushed into Cullen's house without fanfare.

"I think I was followed here," he said without preamble.

So much for a pleasant reunion.

"All the way from Glasgow?"

Following their meeting in Stirling, both men had returned to their respective cities. A few days later, as promised, Black journeyed east.

"No, I think just from the High Street," Black said. He moved with stiff legs.

"Well, let them try and force their way in, Joe," Cullen said. "We can at least provide you with a drink after your long journey."

"It was reasonable enough," Black said, making his way into the parlour.

He didn't have time to sip his tea before the pursuer made themselves known.

Cullen exchanged a look with his wife. She nodded, and went to the door.

Black surreptitiously moved his hands from the teacup to his lap, palms up.

The two had a full view of the door, and could see who Anna let inside and invited to stand in the entrance before returning.

She couldn't hide her alarm. Her eyes pleaded with her husband.

"You don't have to retire to the kitchen," Cullen said after a moment's thought. He gestured to the chair by the window.

Anna immediately grasped his intention. The window overlooked the courtyard. She sat down to begin her vigil. The situation had become infinitely more complex and deadly.

Cullen led Octavius into the study, with Black following behind.

"What has prompted this?" Black asked. His eyes remained emotionless, his gaze intense. "Observers could be forgiven in thinking you enjoyed your unusual status with Argyle."

"I saw a man I thought enjoyed every confidence of my patrons in passing on the Edinburgh streets. He was seriously injured and scared. 'Did you see that man?' my master asked. 'Was there something amiss?' I lied and said there was no nothing amiss. Every action the dark practitioners take comes from Lord Argyle. He does not like to conduct business in the open and leave it wandering around."

"You saw unauthorised action against a dark chymist? And you fear for your safety?"

Octavius paused as if he wished to disagree with Cullen's assessment, but then he nodded.

"The Reverend Holm is a very dangerous man. He is not acting against my lord..."

"...Yet."

"His return to Edinburgh is causing disturbances." Octavius shuffled his legs. "Dr Black has an opinion about my conduct and morality; I have another. But I do not gain pleasure from the work I do, and know better to presume Argyle sees me as an equal. While the likes of Reverend Holm see me as part of Argyle as his coat buttons."

Cullen accepted the man may not come to him with the purest of motives, or it could be a trick. But at this point he hadn't exposed anything the dark chymists didn't already know.

"Then state your purpose, Octavius."

"I understand you are looking for information relating to Lord Argyle's private business, and I wish to offer a favour." Octavius appeared calm and collected, raising doubt whether this was a significant favour he offered or not.

"Why do you say that?" Cullen's hackles rose. Black's posture subtly shifted.

"I'm appointed the eyes and ears of my masters. It does not escape my attention when Dr Cullen departs with haste for the west coast, and is followed back to Edinburgh a few days later by Dr Black, that something is afoot on the tail of Dr Whytt's sudden demise." Octavius spoke calmly, though this conclusion couldn't have struck him more than quarter of an hour ago upon spying Black ride into town.

"A demise your masters had a hand in?"

A barely perceptible shake of the head. "My masters are under the belief Dr Whytt perished of natural causes. They cannot conceive Holm turning upon them, and I have my reasons for not wishing to point this obvious truth out."

Cullen didn't like the prospect of begging information off a man still in the employ of Argyle, however tenuously. But if Octavius was right, then the situation was even more precarious than they feared. Holm was crafting his own agenda. Anything could happen. Not least Holm taking control of Babylon.

"So what price will this favour render?" Cullen asked. The time to act was now. If they could use these scraps of information, so be it.

Octavius remained unperturbed. "I will take a ship from Leith to London, and make my living there as a free man."

"Slipping away from Edinburgh without your master's consent may sound easy," Cullen said, "But I can assure you,

Octavius, you won't have an easy passage. The Argyles will put advertisements in every British paper—I'm amazed you haven't heard about such things—warning everyone about their runaway slave. Young tall Negro male wearing a blue jacket with silver buttons and brown breeches, that sort of thing."

"I am aware," Octavius said. "I can read."

"Oh."

"So what do you propose?" Black asked.

Octavius made a show of inspecting a loose thread on his jacket cuffs. "Well, I couldn't help notice Doctor Cullen and his eldest son are about the same height as me and presumably own coats..." he paused to pick the thread loose, "...without silver buttons."

"I see." Cullen sighed and rubbed his eyes, which Black knew was a sign of capitulation. "Well, don't hold us responsible if you get caught. And goodness knows what we'll say if Lord Argyle starts asking us if we've seen his missing slave Octavius."

A ferocious glint flashed across the footman's eyes. "Well, you can tell him with hand upon your Bible that you've never seen a man who answers to that name. 'Octavius' was another mark they stamped upon me, a kind of joke, another chain of bondage when I was shipped to this country. Octavius was never my name."

47

EDINBURGH

"Ah, Francis. Do you have a moment?"

Aird looked from his broadsheet with a jolt of surprise. "Morning, Dr Cullen. I didn't see you creep in here."

John's Coffee House wasn't Cullen's usual haunt. He had to dig a lot of elbows into fleshy backs and ribs to reach the young doctor's perch. Next to the smoking hearth in the corner, another physician was inspecting a gouty patient, who'd removed his shoe and stocking.

"Can I join you, Francis? Shall I order another of what you're having?"

Francis visibly brightened. "A second Cauld Cock-and-Feather'? That would be marvellous."

Cullen wouldn't have offered quite so readily if he knew Aird was drinking John Balfour's signature brandy and raisin concoction. But this encounter hinged upon Cullen projecting easy conviviality, so he nodded and complied, doing his best not to wince or grimace when the sweet and spicy drinks arrived.

"Busy day ahead of you, Francis?"

Aird shrugged. "No rest for the wicked."

They continued in this vein of superficial pleasantries for a few minutes. Aird wasn't volunteering the information Cullen sought, so he waited until the banalities lulled.

"As it happens, Francis, I'm on the lookout for Lord Carstaires. There were a few items I wished to speak to him about. I know you enjoy warm relations with the man—do you know his whereabouts today?"

Aird's lips tightened a fraction, before the unbothered smile returned.

"As it happens, we'd arranged to meet at eleven o'clock today, perhaps I can convey a message?"

Cullen made a similar show of consternation.

"Hmm, it's a topic that requires some discretion on my part, or I'd take you up on that generous offer."

A few flashes of annoyance broke through Aird's otherwise sunny demeanour. It made his true feelings clear: he would be courteous to Cullen because that was his nature, but they were in competition for the Medical Theory Chair and he wouldn't forget it.

"Perhaps I can stop by your rendezvous, either immediately before or after, and beg a few minutes' of his lordship's time? I wouldn't intrude long."

Aird flicked a swollen raisin out of his glass with a fingernail, then popped it into his mouth.

He'd assume Cullen didn't know the true purpose of his meeting with Carstaires, ostensibly to discuss the Medical Theory appointment. Aird wouldn't want Cullen at that meeting, because there was a risk his rival would overshadow him. But Aird wasn't good at standing up for himself, and was baulking at a direct refusal. That's why Black insisted Cullen had a shot at getting the information from him.

"Well…" Cullen decided to try a tactic Black suggested. He bit his lip and fiddled with his brandy glass. "If I'm honest, the Lord Carstaires has been difficult to get hold of in recent days, and I worry he's indisposed."

Aird went fishing for another raisin. "I've not noticed any health-related impairments, if that's what you mean."

He didn't make eye contact, but Cullen sensed a subtle shift in his posture. The calculation changed if he believed Carstaires was avoiding Cullen. That suggested he *wasn't* the Town Council's favourite for the Chair.

"Just a couple of minutes of his lordship's time, then I'll make myself scarce," Cullen pleaded, hoping he sounded sufficiently desperate.

Of course, Cullen knew from Monro that he held the stronger position in the upcoming election. The Town Councillors remained more pro-Cullen than the faculty, even after the mess he made in the broadsheets. The only difference from the previous times was the dark chymists no longer cared what the Town Council thought or did: they were poised to make the whole institution irrelevant.

"I suppose you can try." Aird shrugged, probably to himself as he weighed up the benefits of disclosing the information to his rival. "Though if his lordship arrives late he might decide not to see you, I can't guarantee a conversation."

"Not a problem," Cullen assured him as fast as he could.

"We're meeting in Boyd's Inn. As I said, at eleven o'clock." Aird drained his glass. "Good luck catching your quarry."

A brief exchange with the tavern owner established that the Town Councillors had rented the upstairs dining room for a couple of hours. Him and the man knew each other on sight: Boyd's Inn was a couple of closes down the Canongate from Cullen's dwelling. It had a reputation as being one of the nicer coaching inns in the Canongate and Pleasance area, but that wasn't saying much. Besides, the Town Councillors probably agreed to it as a meeting point because it was out of the way and discrete, not because they desired luxurious surroundings.

With no coaches scheduled to arrive or depart until nightfall, the Inn was quiet this morning. A few stablehands leant on their shovels and gossiped in the courtyard, not paying Cullen any attention. Guests were no doubt sleeping off their arduous London rides in one of the pokey chambers on the top floors. A few stablehands puffed pipes in the main room, barely giving Cullen a glance. He imagined it wouldn't be difficult for a dark chymist to sneak in and set their trap undisturbed. The whole building smelled of horse and leather.

Not checking to see if he was being observed, Cullen headed upstairs. The narrow stairs creaked with every footfall. With a while before the scheduled meeting, the upstairs dining room was unlocked. No one was on the landing, and the only noises came from downstairs.

Cullen squeezed into a space that could comfortably seat ten, provided those ten were comfortable sitting on each other's knees.

Nothing struck him as unusual or out of place: the furniture was wonky and spindly, but the place had been brushed down in anticipation of the illustrious guests. The fire crackled, and plenty of sconced candles mitigated the murk caused by the small window.

Cullen had never knowingly set eyes on a dark chymistry sigil. Octavius claimed not to know what they were planning for the Town Councillors, and had no idea what sigils they'd chose.

"That information is not for the likes of me. I only know of the sigils I need to know."

How would the dark chymists even know when to spring their trap? They not want to risk being in the room—no, they'd need to be elsewhere so they could activate the sister mark without alerting their victims.

Had they rented another room in this inn? There were bedrooms further down the narrow, creaking corridor. Or maybe you could see...

Muffling his instinct to swear, Cullen dropped into a crouch.

Suddenly his saunter upstairs without bothering to check for watchers seemed dangerously foolish. What if a dark chymist was already in place, watching the room? It seemed unlikely—they were busy men—but not impossible.

Well, if they'd spotted him, perhaps he'd already be dead. Heart pounding, Cullen sunk onto his knees. The door was closed, and he was no longer visible through the window. He'd to start his inspection from the ground up.

Octavius had described where dark chymists commonly placed their sigils: often at ground level or on the ceiling, in spots where the marks were unlikely to be rubbed off.

"It depends what the sigil is for. Whether you are creating a man-sized portal, or something else."

Cullen found this lack of specificity frustrating. "But do you believe there's even a sigil capable of killing eight or ten men simultaneously?"

The footman looked him dead in the eye. "Without a doubt."

For a daytime job in the middle of a well-occupied inn, they were unlikely to bring in Holm. So that meant it was unlikely to be off to the side. You wouldn't know where everyone was placed, and they might be spread out. If you wanted to kill everyone at the same time without raising the alarm, then you'd need...

Wincing as a splinter dug into his palm, Cullen shuffled under the table. Although swept this morning, the floorboards were coated with grime from decades of spilled drinks, shit-caked shoes, and loose bladders. At least his black coat would conceal the worst of it.

Sure enough, a silver glint on a table leg caught his eye. Feeling his stocking catch on another splinter, Cullen moved close enough to identify the network of scratches and shapes on its surface.

"Blast it." He thought he'd be dealing with a charcoal marking, not a carved metal disk that was—yes—nailed to the table leg. Someone used to manual labour had done this job: the disk was firmly nailed in place, and Cullen couldn't prise it out.

Nor would he have luck moving the table: it was a hefty beast, requiring three or more men to lift. The last thing Cullen wanted to do was touch the sigil.

While he could—theoretically—come up with a scheme to relocate the Town Councillors to another room, Cullen found he couldn't in good conscience walk out of this room and leave an intact sigil that was capable of killing in there. Who knows what unfortunate soul might enter the room at the wrong moment? There were plenty of young maids and stablehands roaming the premises; women and their children used this coach and inn network.

He took another look at the metal disk. Probably tin, or another malleable metal like silver. Easy to carve meant...

Cullen looked at the hearth. He looked back at the sigil. Then he extended one hand towards the flames, and held the other inches from the metal.

Hopefully this wouldn't hurt much.

With a single twitch of his arm muscles, the comfortably sized fire vanished, and a white-hot beam was aimed at the centre of the sigil. Cullen drew his hand back as the tin glowed red. A pall of wispy smoke settled over the room. Fortunately, kneeling on the meant he wasn't breathing in the worst of it.

The phlogiston he'd pulled from the fire and concentrated onto the sigil lasted a couple of seconds, at best. But he could smell the table leg scorching, and see the carvings smudge.

Coughing from the hearth smoke, it took a Cullen a moment to realise the sigil was emitting smoke of its own: a thin wisp of whiter smoke. He could also hear a faint sizzling.

"Providence almighty!"

Throwing caution to the wind, Cullen scrambled to his feet and rushed to the window. His heart was jack-hammering in his chest, and his arms shook as he struggled to open the small window. Once unlocked, it took a couple of shoves to open fully. Cullen shoved his head out, panting like a dog.

There was a faintly acidic taste to the air in the room, blended with the woodsmoke. Cullen relaxed once he felt a steady breeze on his face.

When he risked sticking his head back in the room—breath held—he was relieved to see the sigil no longer sizzled, and the carvings were warped.

"I see what he meant about those bastards being dangerous to fiddle with." The sigil managed to do something in the process of being deactivated, and Cullen assumed it was a small-scale demonstration of its intended purpose.

Someone must have chosen this chamber, knowing its stuffy atmosphere and poor ventilation would be ideal for a gas-releasing sigil. Cullen could think of no chemical or reaction that would generate enough poisonous gas to incapacitate eight or ten men before one and time to open the door, but it was clear these sigils weren't bound to man-made rules.

Taking another breath, Cullen headed for the exit. The smoke should blow out before the hour was up, and nothing seemed to be on fire.

By the time the Town Councillors showed, Cullen intended to be well away.

* * *

With her husband out of the house, called away on this terrible dark chymistry business again, Anna Cullen retreated to the bedchamber and fumbled around in her armoire.

Buried underneath her ribbons, powder and jewellery was the note. It had already been crumpled tightly into a square before it came into her possession; crushed in someone's sweating hand over an extended period of time.

Anna meant to tell her husband about its contents, but he was preoccupied and tense all this morning. Since his tension didn't seem to be dissipating, she resolved to show it to him as soon as he returned, regardless of his mood or was else was going on.

She unfolded the note for the third time and reread it, checking she'd not misunderstood the wording or missed a key detail.

The writing was hard to decipher. It was written by someone whose instruction of English was limited to a few cursory years in a school, possibly the Church, for whom every letter was an effort of concentration. However, everything about the letter's furtive delivery implied it was drafted under intense stress and fear.

Plese com to St N log Close. S-thing <u>Wroung</u>

48

EDINBURGH

Black was in the process of swinging down from his horse when Isabella Monro angled into his line of sight.

"Mrs Monro, a pleasure to see you," Black kissed her hand, hoping he didn't smell too strongly of sweat. If he did, Isabella was too diplomatic to show it on her face. She was a noted dancer in her youth, and maintained that gracefulness despite her silver hair and translucent skin.

"Dear Dr Black—how fortuitous to encounter you. Will you call for tea?"

"Unfortunately this is a swift visit to Edinburgh and I regret to disappoint you," Black said with feeling. Isabella raised her eyebrows and cocked her head, alluding to the information her husband no doubt had spread about the imminent shuffling among the academics. "But soon, I hope."

"It cannot be soon enough," said Isabella. Like her husband, there was an air of brittleness to her, even though she was always hospitable to Black.

"Pass on my compliments to Drakaina Monro," Black said lightly. "I hope she continues to serve you well."

Isabella Monro laughed. "Oh, Drakaina is a respected member

of the household, but I can't claim ownership of that cat. Alexander is the one she favours. It's ridiculous: he's always nagging me in the winter months to check she isn't trapped outside for any length of time, or to call her in at night."

"I see," Black said.

He waited until Mrs Monro had departed in the direction of the market, before tugging his horse's bridle and urging him up towards the Lawnmarket. Once he obtained the key he'd need to move fast through the city, and a horse was the quickest way to do so.

It felt like the city had its eyes on him. Every glance from tradesman to guards seemed a piercing interrogation. A gaze that lingered was recognition and judgement all in one.

Given Octavius' information, Black expected to find Sir Anthony in John's Coffee House around this early hour, where he conducted business and scanned the newspapers. The crowd thickened as he approached St Giles.

"Sir Anthony will be the easiest to retrieve a key from," Octavius had told them. "He is the most brash and careless."

From the way the servant's lips pursed, Black suspected he was also the dark chymist Octavius liked the least. Recalling Sir Anthony's jibes at Octavius over dinner reinforced this impression.

Whatever personal animosity drove Octavius' advice, Black still considered it reliable. Sir Anthony always struck him as a boor, in contrast to Argyle's cat-like intensity. And now he knew Sir Anthony carried a key to the dark chymistry library in his left waistcoat pocket.

Black supposed from a distance he looked like an errand boy or servant holding his masters' steed. He wished he'd changed out of his physician's black, but he'd cleared his wardrobe of most coloured garments, and the ones he retained were for more formal evening occasions.

The last time he'd seen Sir Anthony, the man was dressed in a lavish frockcoat and waistcoast ensemble of emerald green. Today he was dressed in a soft brown overcoat with a shortened waistcoat hem. Black recognised his customary strut.

Then as Black slowed to a halt, thinking of where to tether his horse, the crowd parted. Grey looked up.

Their eyes met.

Black didn't bother to pretend he was interested in anyone else. He wanted Sir Anthony to stay frozen while he worked out his next move.

A second later Sir Anthony sprung into motion, dodging behind a pair of water-women and running.

Black hesitated for a second, his desire to chase so strong he contemplated just dropping his horse's reins and accepting the consequences later. He realised that despite his brash displays of affluence, the dark chymist could move fast and possibly outrun Black. He must keep up his physique with tennis.

There was nothing for it. Black swung onto his horse and kicked his heels in. Grey's brown coat fluttered around the entrance of Advocate's Close.

Was he heading to another apartment with a mirror way? All Black knew was that he couldn't let the man get away and warn the other dark chymists. A slight pull of the reins and his horse turned into the close.

Advocate's Close wasn't the narrowest close in Edinburgh, but it wasn't designed for horses.

Black squeezed his thighs into the saddle as tightly as he could, bracing for the scraping of flesh against brick. He ducked under a laundry line. An open window frame caught his arm.

His horse jumped over something, someone, blocking the close. There were screams and curses from doorways. Ahead Sir Anthony was pushing bodies aside and bellowing.

Black didn't have time to worry if his horse would lose her balance on the narrow, steep path, because after what felt like only a few heartbeats he burst out the end.

The city dwellings ended a few hundred metres above the Nor

Loch, a precipitous wasteland almost trodden clear of its grass and wildlife. There were several narrow pathways down the loch that plenty of washerwomen and wretches used to clean their clothes or gathering drinking water. Only the most desperate came down here.

Sir Anthony took one of those paths, looping back towards the North Bridge. He would probably try to lose Black in another close.

His horse slowed of her own accord, tossing her head and whinnying. She wasn't happy being forced on these narrow paths, and Black was worried the path wasn't wide enough to accommodate her.

He was only a few tens of metres away from Sir Anthony, so he leapt clear of the horse, landing more confidently than he'd expected.

His quarry glanced back a few times. He was starting to slow, and Black had the advantage of gravity pulling him downhill.

Sir Anthony may or may not have a pistol, but as soon as he got in range Black intended to strike. Trying to gain distance, his quarry dropped lower towards the edge of the loch. Only a few metres separated them now.

Until Black tripped, lost his balance and collided with the man. For a moment the two were suspended, slowing rolling in the air, then smacked into the surface of the Nor Loch.

It was deep enough to submerge the pair, though Black felt his shoulder and back collide with the rocks and detritus in the shallows. Before his opponent had time to kick or pin him underwater, Black refocused his energy on the man he was gripping.

The flash of yellow-white light was still clearing from his eyes as Black broke the surface, hauling the unconscious body of his target on the shoreline. It made no sense to kill the man, so he should recover his wits within a few minutes.

His sodden clothing was all stuck together, which made peeling through his pockets and layers all the more vexing. Not bothering to wipe the filth from his body, and ignoring the ache in his shoulder, Black inspected the odds and ends he'd recovered.

One of the objects was an ornate twisted piece of metal that resembled the abstract idea of a key. It was also carved on one side with a complex, asymmetric knot of shapes.

A few women were edging down the mound, not keen to be the first to arrive at the site of an apparent murder-robbery. Black rose and clicked his tongue to attract the attention of his horse, who'd followed them to the loch side and was drinking from a puddle. Black was unsure if harm would befall an animal who drunk the noxious waters of the Loch, but he hoped he horse would survive at least until he reunited it with her owner.

Where once was a broad web of possibilities, now the threads of action were tightening to a single braid. Cullen and him had an hour at the most—probably less—to reach Babylon before the other dark chymists learned a key was stolen. If Octavius had any sense he'd be on a ship that had already pulled up anchor.

His horse safely left at the White Horse Inn round the corner from Cullen's home, Black rushed into the South Gray's close. His larynx was raw, and hamstrings were burning, but he had to collect Cullen. Spinning through the narrow passageway into the close where the shadows closed in, he nearly collided with the barrel of a flintlock.

Before he had time to react, the butt of the pistol struck him across the temple, sending him tumbling down into darkness.

49

EDINBURGH

Cullen hoped against hope Black avoided the dark chymist's trap, but he was disabused of the notion when the prone figure of his former student was unceremoniously dumped into the chair next to him.

"Keep your eyes in front of you, and don't breathe a word to your friend," Argyle warned. "I'm not a medical man myself, nor are my assistants, but I understand head injuries are rather dicey things to inflict properly. Easy to kill a man, or permanently stunt his wits, with a misplaced blow."

Cullen didn't need the threat further enunciated.

Cullen's captor had lured him from home by pretending to be a messenger on behalf of Black. As soon as he was out of sight of his family and servants, the rogue had pulled his pistol. Several more men with hands in their waistbands had directed him to Argyle's Lawnmarket apartment.

In the initial confrontation, Cullen was too surprised to fight back. He also knew he didn't stand a chance against four or more men pointing firearms at him: he couldn't take them all out at once. The lead captor made sure to point out a man had hung behind at the mouth of South Gray's Close to monitor their journey up the street. The warning was clear: if the stopped cooperating, someone would return for his family.

The fact he wasn't shot in the wynd told him the dark chymists saw a benefit to him being alive, which he intended to exploit as long as he could.

Some of the captors had melted away when he arrived in the apartment.

"You aren't going to ask me what the meaning of this is?" Argyle asked, a narrow smile on his lips. He had a sword and pistol looped into his belt.

"I presumed you were waiting until Dr Black roused to tell us." As if hearing his name, Black moaned softly. The second guard in the room leaned over Black and whispered several threatening remarks in his ears.

Black made a few noises of confusion and pain, but otherwise remained still. The guard retreated. He drew his pistol and pointed it at Black.

Whatever Argyle knew about them and what they were capable of, he was assuming the worst. The other guard drew his weapon, though he didn't point it directly at Cullen.

"I am very grateful for your cooperation, Dr Cullen. You might think your politeness won't affect the outcome, but I can assure you it will."

That might be the difference between dying a drawn-out, painful death, and dying a quick painful death, Cullen grimly reflected. But he met Argyle's eye.

"I consider myself an honest and forthright man, my lord. But I expect the same from my acquaintances in return."

"As you should."

Argyle sat on his bed and stared at Cullen.

"My brother-in-law is a West Indian sugar trader. Remarkable, industrious man. You wouldn't know him, because he conducts his business out of Liverpool.

"Well, my brother-in-law and the company board of directors congregated in a dockside tavern many moons ago. It wasn't the type of establishment they would usually frequent, but the nature of their upcoming engagements required they meet quickly before necessity bid them disperse, and by all accounts they were well-protected.

"While these gentlemen conferred at their booth, they were approached by sailor. The man was deep in his cups, as hearty in temperament as his face was red. He saluted my brother-in-law by name, claimed to have been in his service for many years.

"Their business concluded, my brother-in-law thought it would be amusing to invite this fellow to their table, the cost of another bottle a pinching sum to pay for the remaining men's continued entertainment by this oblivious fool.

"And oh did this sailor entertain! Such wild, incomprehensible stories, delivered in the rudest dialect, sent the erstwhile board members reeling in laughter.

"His bawdy tales spent, and his audience crying for more wisdom, the mocked sailor cleared his throat and delivered his strangest tale yet.

"Several decades before, this sailor claimed to have served upon a ship called the Prince William, which departed from Portsmouth under auspicious blue skies to conduct business with the Spanish in the West Indies. He spun a yarn so incredible Gulliver himself would scoff at it, but the most pertinent detail was the presence upon the Prince of the young ship surgeon who spun fire out of the air in astonishing displays of power.

"Will Cullen, our sailor insisted the name was.

"This name meant nothing to my brother-in-law or his associates that night, but some time later he chose to share the tale with me, fancying nothing in its telling beyond piquing my amusement. For a time I thought no more of it, until I heard of a Dr William Cullen making a name for himself in Glasgow.

"Could our drunkard sailor have fashioned the name 'William

Cullen' out of whole cloth fabrication or confusion? Perhaps. Sailors are a fanciful, impressionable breed. I wouldn't put it past them to be bamboozled by parlour tricks contrived to entertain the ship crew on a tedious voyage. But what if there was truth in this wretch's tale? What if our august Professor William Cullen had secrets, and had accomplished even a fraction of what was claimed aboard the Prince? That would be an alarming situation indeed. For years I pretended to myself I was grasping a handful of coincidences...until I learned what Cullen's famous student could do, from the mouth of sources I considered trustworthy."

So that was it, Cullen realised. For a decade paranoia smouldered at the back of his mind, over his shoulder. Why were the men in Edinburgh acting like he was a threat? How could they have learned of his discoveries? Well, he had his answer now.

"You are an engaging storyteller, my lord. I wonder how you expect me to respond?" There was a chance, however small, that Argyle didn't actually have proof.

"What are you capable of?"

"What do you think I am capable of, your lordship?"

Argyle sighed. "You are a smart man, Dr Cullen. I'm sure you understand the consequences of crossing me."

"As yet, I don't understand how Dr Black or myself have crossed you."

Cullen's eyes hurt from straining to look at Black. His hands had been bound in white cloth behind his back—easy to see against his dark suit—and he was sitting up as straight as he could, given he must be suffering a blinding headache.

They'd kill Joe first. He was the dangerous one, Cullen was the important one, the one with more information. They'd calculate Joe's death or injury would be enough to loosen Cullen's tongue.

"If I'm not mistaken," Argyle said as someone knocked at the door and broke his reverie. "That will be the dark chymists and Reverend Holm."

Holm again. The man was a plague upon this city. He'd tormented Black and killed whoever was asked of him with apparent glee. As if a cassock would tame a man that amoral.

But when the door was opened Argyle gave a grumble of surprise. Instead of a mob pouring into the apartment, it sounded like only two men entered.

"Thank you for summoning me, my lord."

Forgetting his warning to stay still, Cullen's head snapped around. A pistol barrel jammed under his jaw forced his head back, but there was no mistaking who'd just entered the room.

"I hope you were not inconvenienced much by my missive, Dr Monro. But you don't need me to tell you how urgent the situation is."

"It's my honour to serve you, my lord," Monro replied smoothly.

"What is the meaning of this?" Snarled Cullen. The pistol dug into the back of his neck, this time making him cry out. It was a rhetorical question, he was pretty sure he knew precisely what was going on.

"Dr Cullen, you must be mad if you think I wouldn't act immediately upon discovering proof of your heresy. Everything I've ever done is in service of this city." He couldn't see the professor—he was standing near the door on his peripheral vision—but Cullen could visualise the crossed arms and curled lips accompanying Monro's derisive tone.

"You told me the proof against Dr Cullen was undeniable," Argyle said, sounding impatient for Cullen to shut up.

"He showed me part of the system he developed."

"What did he show you?" Argyle asked.

"Enough to make me gravely concerned," Monro said. Every word was icy, terse.

"As you should be," Argyle noted. "This is why I took immediate action to secure the pair. Thank you, doctor."

He should never have trusted that blackguard. Monro told him what he wanted to hear regarding the Institute Chair, and Cullen was foolish enough to believe him. Now he'd blundered straight into the serpents' trap. As if Monro would ever put in a good word to the other faculty on his behalf.

If he somehow survived whatever this was, he'd make the Judas pay.

"The others will want to hear your account, as you have told it to me. They will be here shortly."

Monro nodded. He remained standing, Argyle did not offer him any food or drink, and the third thug seemed to be watching him more closely than he observed Black and Cullen.

While Monro was not exactly a guest of Argyle, he wasn't treated as a dangerous prisoner.

Should Cullen point out Monro kept the information about Cullen's activities to himself for several months? The dark chymists wouldn't like learning Monro hesitated to come forward with such important information. But maybe that's why they were treating him with suspicion.

It was better he waited for the other dark chymists to arrive before incriminating Monro. The less time he gave that traitor to come up with excuses, the better.

"I expect my colleagues will be here within the hour," Argyle said. "They're busy men, after all. Of course, the Reverend Holm should get here sooner."

Monro swallowed. "Holm is on his way?"

"I assume so," replied Argyle. "It's his business as much as theirs."

"Right, right," Monro agreed. "Of course." Mention of Holm drained what little colour he had from his brow. He cradled one of his arms close to his chest.

It should have given Cullen pleasure to know Monro was as scared of Holm as they were, if not more, but he couldn't.

Cullen wished he could turn and get a proper look at Black. He'd always had a strange liking for Monro and his son—did he finally understand the man was not to be trusted?

A bottle of wine and cups were on the table at the other side of the room. After looking at the tableau thoughtfully, Monro walked over and poured himself a glass of wine. It was typical of the man—so entitled and convinced of his own superiority. The guard swayed on his feet; Argyle pursed his lips in displeasure, but Monro's infractions weren't egregious enough to stop him. Watching their reaction, Monro looked like he debating complimenting the host on the wine, then decided against it. Perhaps he thought he'd be less likely to be rough-handled if there was concern of him spilling wine on the furnishings.

Passing a step from Cullen's knee, the two professors made eye contact. Monro sipping his wine—it looked like he was barely touching it—Cullen trying to convey every iota of his hatred and loathing without making it seem like he'd succumbed to ungentlemanly passions.

A smile drifted over Monro's lips, like he his mind was elsewhere.

Then Cullen heard the whisper, so softly Monro's lips barely moved.

"Flamma fumo est proxima."

Flame follows smoke.

Then he trailed away.

Since the gravity of his situation wasn't sinking in, and he was never one for confronting unpleasant realities, Cullen found his spirit lurched lower at Monro's words.

This could not be happening...

Unfortunately, he knew enough about his colleague to see this abrupt betrayal and flagrant posturing in front of Argyle in another, less welcome light.

Monro hadn't said a word of criticism against Cullen's

doctrines since he learned of their existence. It had been several weeks during which he could have exposed their secrets.

A sense of honour had never motivated Monro, and though his professed duty to the city was a real thing, it was dwarfed by his pride.

Cullen stared at Monro, now traipsing away from them to the other end of the room, and concentrated all his proculopathic abilities on the anatomy professor.

"Damn you, Monro—you'll kill us. Stop whatever you think you're planning."

Monro paused for a second, as if he momentarily lost his bearings, then crossed the room to the four poster bed.

Monro didn't know about the existence of proculopathy, but it was worth a try.

Cullen craned his neck, trying to look at Black without their captors noticing.

"Joe. Joe. Joe! He's about to do something stupid."

As surely as he'd been convinced of Monro's turncoat behaviour a minute ago, now Cullen was sure he relished the opportunity to outsmart everyone and humble Cullen in the process.

He had to assume Black heard him, but his former student gave no indication. Instead, Black stared ahead with a look of cool detachment.

"Joe! What's he doing?" Cullen practically hopped up and down in his chair. The guard frowned, sensing his agitation but doubting if the cause was anything beyond realisation of his looming mortality.

Black's brow creased. *"Focus, William. Be ready."*

Ready for what? Was Black privy to Monro's plan? Or was he just really good at predicting what the cantankerous old peacock would do next?

Monro reached the four poster bed in the centre of the room

and paused. Argyle looked like he was running out of patience with his insolence.

"These curtains are particularly fine," Monro murmured, reaching out to touch the fabric. "My wife wants to replace our own bedchamber hangings, you must tell me where you bought these."

"I'm honoured by the compliment, Dr Monro, but I fear you couldn't afford the likeness."

"No," Monro agreed, a thin smile appearing as he stepped away, tracing his hand down the curtain. "Perhaps not."

A metallic scent flooded Cullen's nostrils, so pungent and sudden he was too confused to realise it was phlogiston.

Where Monro touched the curtains a second ago, flames licked the embroidered flowers.

With a flick, Monro sent the contents of his wine cup towards the kindling. Fire shot towards the painted ceiling beams.

Argyle yelled.

Black was already moving. Black brought both arms in front of him as he swept to his feet. The remnants of the cloth restraints still burning around his wrists.

For a second neither guard was focused on Cullen.

A single blast from Cullen's hand knocked Black's guard out before he had time to react.

Cullen started to rise from his chair when a pistol shot sent his knees buckling. Black dived to one side. He swung one hand out. A wave of force sent Cullen and the captor behind him flying sideways.

The second shot from Black's hand was on target and sent the captor crumpling to the floor.

Monro grabbed Argyle by the throat. Another pistol shot rang out. Since the pistol wasn't pointing in his direction, Cullen was able to make out a second flash in that corner of the room. A body slumped below the gunpowder haze, leaving Monro standing, clutching the wall for support. He looked like he'd been struck in the face: blood trickled from his nostrils and mouth.

Only Black, Monro and Cullen remained standing.

"You killed him?" Monro's eyes were unfocussed, so Cullen wasn't sure he'd get a clear answer.

"Is it possible to apply non-lethal phlogistic force?" Monro asked, blinking. "I didn't get those experiments to work." He looked at the body of Argyle at his feet.

Cullen doubted Monro tried too hard to explore non-lethal uses of phlogiston, but it seemed pointless getting into a theoretical argument now.

Black hadn't moved from the wall he'd tumbled against. Cullen saw his face creased with pain.

"Joe!"

Cullen peeled Black's left hand from his side. It came away drenched in blood.

"A pistol ball caught me," Black whispered. "I think it's just a graze...but it burns like Hell."

Monro appeared at Black's other side, and together they peeled off his coat and waistcoat.

"The ball's lodged in the wall," Monro noted. "Can you raise your arm?"

Black flinched at the thought. "No."

"You could have fractured a rib," Monro continued. "I can suture the wound shut. In the interim, if you apply pressure it should stop bleeding."

As Monro inspected Black's wounded side, his hand seemed to linger on Black's uninjured arm and shoulder. He better be feeling guilt for his actions, Cullen thought. The consequence of his triple-crossing was physical harm to poor Joe.

"We don't have time. I can handle this." To make the point, Black launched himself off the wall and strode across the room, still clutching his side.

From what Cullen had seen of the wound under Black's shirt

it wasn't a deep cut, but it seemed to curve halfway around his body.

Monro pointed Black towards the table, but the younger man was already dousing the side of his body with the remaining wine to clean the wound. His eyes flashed with tears at the stinging, but appeared to have retained his wits.

"What on earth were you doing to me after I first spoke to you?" Monro asked. "Aside from giving me the experience of death by apoplexy? I've never suffered a headache so painful just then."

"Trying to command you to stop your hare-brained plan using the power of thought alone."

"You should have just yelled. That would have been more subtle." Monro rubbed his knuckles into his temple.

So, he could detect proculopathy?

On the other side of the ruined, smoking bed was a tall mirror, with charcoal smudges at shoulder height.

Black swept one hand around the bed frame, removing the remaining fire from the smouldering remains. Faint flames circulated up his arm and dissipated into the air. The acrid burnt scent itched Cullen's throat.

"What possessed you to play such games with the dark chymists, Alexander? Joe and I could have been slain long before you had that opening for your distraction. Even then, they had time to grab their pistols."

"I had to do it this way, William." Monro looked even more pale and grey than usual. "Holm confronted me recently: he knew I found out about your fire-wielding, and slunk around my anatomy theatre looking for proof I was studying your techniques. But there was no reason for him to be anywhere near my classroom, he couldn't stumble into what he found by coincidence."

"You believe someone told him what you were doing?"

"Had to be Rutherford, by way of his current proxy. He had suspicions, shame I was near-sighted enough to miss them. The fact he was willing to betray Joseph and yourself to the dark chymists based on little more than a rumour was warning enough he'd betray me under the right circumstances. You must see why I had to offer you up, make it seem I was still in the dark chemist's favour before Holm convinced them to kill me too."

Cullen didn't see, but Black nodded with understanding, so he decided not to lengthen the argument. It appeared Black accepted he was collateral in this gamble and wasn't going to quarrel with the instigator of his woes.

Black picked up one of the dropped pistols and handed it to Monro.

Monro stared.

"Will that be necessary, Joseph?"

"You should hold on to that, Joe," Cullen said. "He said Holm is coming."

If the name struck fear into Black, it didn't reach his face.

"I can handle him. You need the weaponry more than me." Black spoke with total conviction, even as he held onto his wound. If you didn't notice the blood, he looked in slightly better shape than Monro.

Monro took the pistol. He seemed to accept Cullen and Black were better with phlogiston than him. Black nodded, then turned towards the door.

Cullen looked at the phlogiston vassal. Like the other set-up Black described, the vassal was next to the mirror.

"It should be charged, shouldn't it?" Octavius had explained how the vassals worked, but his explanation was cursory, and didn't seem to cover the myriad of scenarios Cullen now envisioned. He had no idea who or what would be waiting him through the mirror.

"You know how this device works?" Monro asked.

"Yes, it's fine. You can leave, Alexander. You don't want to be here when Holm arrives."

"Trust me, Dr Cullen—I know how...unpleasant that creature is."

"Well, good…"

"Which is why I'm coming with you."

Damn Monro. Always inserting himself into things.

"He'll be more use to you than here with me," Black insisted. "I can deal with Holm."

"Joe, you're bleeding. You should take Dr Monro home."

Black merely looked at Cullen. It was the cool, emotionless look that never let on what the man was thinking.

The vassal could hold the passageway open for more than a few minutes at a time, but Octavius warned him it became less reliable the longer it ran. The vassal might run out of phlogiston, or the sigil disintegrate. Knowing Black was on the other side of the vassal in case something went wrong gave Cullen the courage to step through it in the first place.

"Fine. But don't be a sentimental hero, Joe."

Cullen didn't think he had what it took to murder a man. Black did. Monro's cruel streak could come in useful. What the anatomy professor lacked in skill with phlogiston or a flintlock, he more than made up in vindictiveness.

There was a stick of charcoal on the dresser top. Cullen reached for it. The memory of what Octavius taught him faltered in and out of memory as he concentrated on it.

At the last second as he put charcoal to plaster, the movements reformed in his mind.

The vassal began to sing, a low humming that rose from nothing and soon filled his ears.

Cullen completed the last half-circle that Octavius told him would keep the passageway open until the 'close' command. The vassal glowed.

Monro moved closer. For a moment it looked like he wanted to clutch Cullen's forearm, but decided against it.

They looked at each other. Monro nodded slightly.

Cullen stepped forward, twisting his head to the side in reflex against banging his nose on the glass.

Instead the ringing noise forced into his eardrums. His eyes screwed shut.

He stumbled, less because of anything the act of stepping through the mirror felt like anything, and more because he had no idea what he was stepping onto.

For a moment there was nothing but the pressure of noise all around him. Then his calves slapped against wet heather.

50

ELSEWHERE

Cullen instinctively grabbed at his wig, as a sharp wind pitched him to the side.

Rain lashed his face. Opening his eyes he saw wet greyness, which grew in every direction until it encompassed everything.

"Curse this," Monro muttered beside him. He knocked against Cullen as he found his balance. "They chose to keep their secrets in the Highlands?"

They were balancing on a narrow trail running along a hillside. Through the dreich, Cullen made out a loch stretching below them, its surface rippled. Above them loomed crags, ascending beyond low clouds into the heavens. He couldn't see enough to begin to identify any mountain peaks.

Turning around, Cullen studied the glowing window that lacked a gilded frame, but held the same dimensions as the mirror in Argyle's room. It hummed faintly, though it was hard to hear over the lashing of heather and wind.

"That must be it." Turning his attention back to his partner, Cullen saw Monro pointing at a crude stone doorway against a bulge in the mountainside, perhaps twenty-five metres from where they stood. There was no other man-made construction within sight.

Annoyed he seemed slower than Monro at adjusting to his changed surroundings, Cullen grunted and moved forward. He had to concentrate on every footfall: the deer trail was pure mud, and one of his legs almost slipped out from underneath him.

They could be miles from civilisation. Or what passed for it. If the mirror passageway fades, Cullen had no idea how long it would take them to find a human dwelling, let alone which direction offered the most likely chance at salvation.

They were both under-dressed for conditions like this. Even though they were in the warmer months, allowing oneself to get this soaked in the Scottish outdoors could be fatal. In his eight years in Edinburgh, Cullen had known residents succumb to the elements of Holyrood Park within hours.

He fumbled in his pocket for the key, now clammy. Black warned him ahead of time that once he got the library key he would conceal it in his stocking. It seemed like an unnecessary precaution at the time, but in the end their gaolers had only searched their pockets for incriminating objects.

If Octavius told him anything about the working of the key he'd forgotten about it, so he hoped its receptacle was obvious.

They were staring at a stone alcove in the mountainside, made from carefully stacked stones.

Monro hung back, aware he had nothing to contribute.

There was a single iron nail at head height on the entrance stones. Octavius had called the object both a key and a pendant. There didn't appear to be anywhere else Cullen could hang it.

He could feel dampness spreading across his undershirt. It wouldn't be long before shivering began.

The key twirled, catching off a tiny fragment of mirrored glass jammed between two rocks on the opposite side of the arch.

That was it, the sigil was an inactive reflection. Its mirror form activated the door. Holding the key steady, Cullen directed the carved side at the mirror.

There was a deep rumble, a strong contrast to the high-pitched hum of the mirror. Instead of looking at an walled alcove, Cullen now stared at a descending passageway. The rocks he'd brushed against a second ago had vanished.

Cullen pocketed the key. Octavius assured him the library door was the one that would remain open without an external phlogiston source until it he activated the sigil a second time.

He ducked into the narrow passageway. Instead of darkness, there was a warm glow illuminating a well-formed stairway down into the earth.

"Vile, absolutely disgusting," Monro complained behind him, no doubt referring to the untamed nature he'd just been subjected to. He acted as nonchalant as he could about the magical alcove turning into a doorway, no doubt the mirror passageway had used up his capacity for surprise.

Descending a short flight of steps brought the pair into a cosy, circular room. Despite the rainstorm outside, here the air was warm and still as the College Library. There were candles in glasses on the walls, but the flames looked unnatural—frozen in place. Thick leather-bound books lined the walls from floor to ceiling. Cullen expected something more vast and impressive, but for a small group of individuals, there must be a lot of forbidden knowledge contained here that wasn't available elsewhere. If he stood with his arms outstretched, he'd almost brush the sides.

Monro tugged a blood-red grimoire from the shelf and leafed through it.

"Hmm?"

Every space in the pages seemed full of text. Cullen expected to see drawn sigils, but the sporadic geometric patterns bore little resemblance to the admittedly few examples he'd seen.

"Can't make head nor tail of this," Monro muttered. "It might be Latin or Greek, but it seems to be encrypted."

It was nice to hear the man admit there was something he *didn't* know the answer to.

"Argyle and the likes never let on how to untangle this?" Cullen was curious, despite himself.

Monro shook his head.

"My sentiment was they exaggerated the difficulty of translating the texts for new sigils. But perhaps not by much. They claimed individual grimoires had their own encryption, and sigil instruction could be spread across multiple grimoires." Both men glanced around the library. Despite its small size, there were hundreds of books here.

If the texts were as opaque as the dark chymists claimed, it could take a lifetime for a person to master just one of them.

"Seems a shame to burn them," Monro admitted, shelving the grimoire.

Annoyed at Monro for voicing a sentiment he too shared, Cullen shook his head. "Has to be done, Alexander."

He couldn't destroy their wealth, their enterprises, or their political patronage. But he could reduce the dark chymists to just another political faction in a country that was full of them. Get rid of their grip on the university and Edinburgh. Call a halt to the program of murder and terror they used to keep control.

Monro took a deep breath. A wall of crimson flame was hurled from his side with such force several books flew onto the floor.

Cullen cursed with alarm, which he had cause to repeat when Monro collapsed against him.

"Alexander?"

In the blink of an eye, a third of the books were on fire. Did the dark chymists have any secret defences against the destruction of their library? It didn't look like it.

Cullen was readying to set the rest alight when he realised it would basically trap them in the room. And now Monro was unconscious.

"Alexander!" Cullen wouldn't be able to carry him out. Not that Monro was heavy, but Cullen wasn't particularly strong. He was half-grabbed onto Monro's coat—enough to prevent him from falling all the way to the floor. A second later he decided to let Monro drop, kneeling himself to escape the thick smoke now gathering.

"For heaven's sake, Monro. What were you thinking? Discharging that much power could kill you. Have you even practiced?" Overusing phlogiston in the past left Cullen with cramps, headaches, and tenderness in the stomach. It gave Black nose bleeds. They risked internal hemorrhages pushing beyond those warning signs.

Was he breathing?

Cullen fumbled for a pulse, but could feel anything above his racing heart.

"Wake up, damn you. We need to get out of here." He'd worried incinerating the library would be time-consuming—Monro had set the whole thing ablaze in one minute.

Blood seeped from the professor's mouth. Cullen feared he'd choke on it.

The heat burned raw on Cullen's face. He screwed his watering eyes shut.

What if a burning bookshelf collapsed on them?

His shakes of Monro grew more frantic. The unconscious body was a dead weight. In a second, Cullen would need to choose between saving his own life—leaving Monro to burn—or in remaining here condemn them both to death. Maybe it was already too late.

He could barely see the entrance through the stinging smoke and heat. He kept coughing.

After a few more slaps, prods and entreaties, Monro groaned and rolled onto his side.

"Move, Alexander." Cullen practically screamed those last words. He started crawling to the place where the heat felt less intense, half dragging Monro with him. To his deep relief, the anatomy professor began to move of his own accord.

He almost sobbed in relief when his hand smacked a stone step. Lightheaded from the heat and half-blind, he hauled himself up. With every step the heat abated, and more air filled his lungs.

The twenty steps they'd descended without pause took what felt like hours to climb back up.

The two collapsed at the top of the stairs, letting rain coat their faces.

Behind them, the dark chymists' library became a blazing inferno.

Cullen couldn't fill his lungs deep enough.

"We better continue our infantile crawl out of here," Monro said, clawing against the wall and deciding that his legs couldn't support him yet. "I don't know how long the vassal will hold the doorway open."

"Oh yes," remembered Cullen, pitching forward and resigning himself to the feel of the damp heather soaked into his breeches, half-supporting Monro's arm against his shoulder. "That."

51

EDINBURGH

His head was a mess. Black's cerebral matter floated in pain, and he wasn't convinced he was thinking clearly. He tried to hold onto threads of thought, but it seemed he was dropping them, and he didn't trust himself to navigate any complicated thought processes.

Unfortunately, this seemed to be the only configuration that would succeed. Black knew he could stop Holm.

He could probably stop any dark chymists from a seated position. He wondered if he should lie on the floor pretending to be dead, if that would give him an advantage when they entered the room.

Probably not. He wasn't sure he could stay conscious in a seated or prone position.

Black made his way to the wall. The room widened out from the stairwell at the front, giving Black a corner to hide behind. He couldn't see the doorway, but there wasn't anywhere to view who was entering without exposing himself.

Black wasn't sure he was making good decisions, but his thinking was too blurred around the edges. If he hesitated, it'd make his headache worse.

Was it a headache, or just the noise of the vassal?

Propped against the wall, Black changed his mind. He needed to see the door. Holm could move quietly it was impossible to hear him coming. Black edged to the corner and looked around.

He had only time to register a glint of metal and duck. The gunshot consumed the apartment, seeming to come from everywhere. Black pushed himself into the wall, realising how weak and shaky his legs were.

"Joseph? Are you injured?"

Holm hummed to himself, a cheerful but discordant sound.

"He-he, the way I see it, we each have only one shot. Will see who can move the fastest, shall we?"

Black couldn't see Holm. He was standing in the doorway a minute ago. He has to be approaching the corner, Black thought. He'll strike before I have the chance to prepare myself. And why am I still bleeding?

The injury in his side stung. That whole side of his linen shirt felt wet and clung to his skin. As he leaned against the wall for support, the blood dripped from his shirt crease onto the floor; a noise louder than his own frantic heartbeat.

Drip.

Black tugged at his neckscarf, pulling endlessly. It started to run pink in his hands.

Drip. Drip.

Holm could hear him. He had to. The blood, the shaking, the way his hands trembled as he wrapped one end of his scarf around his right hand.

Drip.

Monro had warned him: Holm put poison on his blades. The pistol hadn't been reloaded—he would have heard that—which meant Holm would have drawn his dagger and be creeping around the corner with it.

Drip drip.

Black could step backward, retreating so there was a bigger

space between him and Holm when the man inevitably burst around the corner. But what if he intended to throw his dagger? Black would maybe have time to deflect it with a blast of force, but then he wouldn't be launching a killing strike.

Drip.

Holm would know where he was standing, he must hear the blood.

Drip.

Drip.

Black tightened his fists and raised them.

As soon as the shadow was in front of his, Black pushed his hands up. The neckscarf he held between his hands caught Holm's wrist, sending his hand and the knife blade flying upwards.

Both he and Holm tried to kick each other at the same moment.

Black pulled his hands together. Light shot out of them the same moment Holm recognised the action and dived to the side. He rolled and collided with Black, who crashed to the ground. A second knife was already in Holm's hand.

Less than two heartbeats. What erupted from Black's hands—closed together defensively—wasn't as powerful as his killing strike. Perhaps Holm didn't care and just wanted to take Black down as he himself perished.

But the yellow light Black managed was enough to sap the consciousness from Holm. He flailed and kicked, the pain in his side threatening to consume him, until he was crouching and Holm lay on the floor.

Black's arms were sticky with blood. He didn't know if Holm had managed to nick him with a poisoned blade. He focussed on breathing and re-gathering his energy.

I'll give it five heartbeats to recover my strength.

He wasn't going to let Holm live.

Then Black didn't hear a noise so much as a momentary

absence of noise, or change in the texture of something invisible. The phlogiston vassal stuttered.

Then it stuttered again. This didn't sound like the vassal in the tenement building winding down, this was a lot less controlled.

Black threw himself across the room without thinking. It wasn't that his priorities changed, it was that they subconsciously were already lined up in his head and he was simply behaving accordingly. He had to keep the vassal running.

Octavius had explained to them how the dark chymists recharged their vassals—an overnight process with multiple sigils and careful adjustment. He seemed sceptical of the professor's claims that they could draw phlogiston out of the air instantaneously.

Black grabbed the top of the vassal, through which the dark chymists poured the mineral mixture that held the phlogiston. He had no idea what was about to happen, if the vassal could withstand a fast charging, but the hum had lost all its harmonics and was about to make him scream.

Squeezing his chest muscles, Black forced the phlogiston out through his hands.

His vision greyed, and he had to cling onto the vassal for support, but the discordant harmonies slowly resolved themselves.

Sharp pains shot through his stomach and Black dared to pause. The vassal continued to hum for the heartbeats it took him to exhale and squeeze again.

He wasn't sure how many cycles of this he endured, letting the pain within him rise and fall, but the glow from the mirror flickered, and then the chamber was filled with noise and movement.

Monro and Cullen were soaked, he could see Monro's cream silk stockings were covered in mud, and it was only the dark colour of Cullen's fabric that prevented Black from seeing if he was the same. The smell of smoke within the room increased.

"Ghastly," Monro muttered to himself, letting go of Cullen's shoulder and supporting himself against the wall. Cullen bent over his knees and huffed.

"Doctor?" Despite their dilapidated and weakened state, both men appeared capable of moving under their own power.

"They put Babylon in the middle of the Scottish Highlands, Joe. It was a windswept abomination."

"But you destroyed it?"

"Yes," Monro said. "We did."

Panting and clutching his side, Cullen looked at Black.

"Holm? He didn't arrive yet?"

Holm! Black tore around, hands already raised.

The corner of the room was empty.

He could have been hiding, but Black sensed an emptiness in the room, the lack of a fourth heartbeat. He didn't need to check for a concealed enemy.

He'd allowed Holm to escape.

52

EDINBURGH

"You're early," Monro said. There was a note of surprise in his voice.

"It is a darker hour than I usually rise," Cullen admitted, stepping onto the anatomy theatre dais. "But I didn't get much sleep last night."

"No," Monro said, setting down his quill. "I can't imagine you did."

It was a departure from their usual pattern of behaviour—Monro hadn't even sent him a note—but it didn't seem worth the delay.

Black was recuperating in Cullen's home. Cullen left him that morning in some distress; blaming himself for letting Holm get away. Cullen tried to reassure the lad as best he could—in Black's position he'd have made the same choices. It wasn't clear if Holm would resurface, or where. To Cullen it seemed pointless losing sleep over it, else he'd spend the rest of his life terrified of shadows and stillness.

It was strange to think Monro would head here as if the world was carrying on as normal, but maybe he was waiting for Cullen. "I'd hate to impinge upon your valuable time."

"We don't have to converse long," Monro noted. "I'm sure there are points where we can condense the pleasantries."

"Well, as preamble I intended to thank you for saving my life. Though I suspect your focus was on saving Joe's life and I just happened to get caught up in it."

"Right—we've saved three minutes," Monro replied. "What were you planning to tell me next?"

"I would have expressed surprise that you helped us destroy their library, and risk your life against the dark chymists. That you sutured Joe up afterwards was less surprising, but I was impressed how steady your hand was under the circumstances."

Monro shrugged. "Consider it a favour from your colleague. Unfortunately," he added with a slight grimace. "They won't be available for much longer."

There was a pause.

Cullen knew that theoretically some faculty like Rutherford would retire early to enjoy a few remaining years of good health. Others, like Monro, would cling on to their medical chairs until they had no choice but to relinquish the role.

"It's bowel cancer, isn't it?"

To any other person, such a statement would be grossly insensitive. Not only was it unsolicited speculation from a man not operating in his capacity as a physician, but Monro was a fiercely private man, and Cullen knew he'd taken great care to conceal his symptoms so they'd go undetected.

Almost.

Monro nodded. "Astutely observed."

Cullen didn't need to say more. He certainly didn't need to point out that in observing the symptoms, he could speculate how much longer Monro would live. Both of them knew what the answer was.

"I know you're sorry," Monro added, breaking the silence. "You blink rapidly and bite your lower lip when absorbing bad news. Thank you. Genuinely—it means a lot to me."

"Do you even need me here to conduct the rest of our conversation?" Cullen asked, forcing a smile. "Or perhaps it's your turn to tell *me* everything I'm going to say next?"

"I'm alive now," Monro said. He took a breath. "How can we finish this business, William?"

"Gregory shouldn't be in the Practice Chair." Cullen should have couched this in tactful language. Arguing that Gregory was a pleasant fellow but too easily buffeted between Rutherford, the remaining dark chymists, or anyone else on the Town Council with a forceful opinion. That his lack of vision was harming the medical school, and he wasn't even the strongest theoretician or clinician.

"I agree."

But Monro knew all this.

"And I am here to ask my colleague..." Cullen barely hesitated over the word. "To help negotiate his resignation. In favour of me." He added the last part against the minuscule probability that Monro did not understand his agenda.

"I agree with that, too." There wasn't even his usual curled lip in proximity to Cullen. "While Gregory doesn't have a malicious purpose or strong conviction, he is rather content with the Chair and the benefits that accompany the role. He knows he's not a brilliant man; that makes him rather proud and stubborn. Threats and arm-twisting is entirely the wrong approach."

"'Nothing is so strongly fortified that it cannot be taken by money,'" Cullen mused.

Monro raised an eyebrow. "Cicero."

"That doesn't sound like an objection."

"I've not personally negotiated the buy-out of a Chair before, but I've heard enough from the Humanities school to know how they usually proceed. It's a simple process calculating missed earning potential; everyone knows the student numbers and course fees involved. My recommendation is to offer Gregory a low sum first. Not insultingly low, but low enough he'll argue for more and you'll cave. It'll give him enough sense of control over the situation that he'll leave the post without causing further difficulties for you."

"I hear smashing laboratory equipment is a common retaliatory move," Cullen remarked. There wasn't malice in the comment. Too much had passed for that.

Monro dropped his gaze.

"It would have been more productive manipulating myself onto your good side."

Cullen would have to ask Black if Monro had physical tells of his own. Did Monro's twitching vagus nerve signify remorse?

Cullen shrugged. "Hindsight is wonderful. Anyway, I think it taught me a lesson."

Monro permitted himself another smile, then scratched down a few notes.

"If you like I can speak with Gregory first, as forewarning. I'll appraise the other faculty members, but I suggest moving quickly before gossip has an opportunity to circulate."

"If you're talking to the other faculty members, you might need to warn them I'll be corralling the lot of them into a room, preferably a stuffy one, and not letting them out until we sort out a better way of splitting dividends from the Physic Garden. There should be no botanical shadow trade. There should be no incentive for anyone to siphon those profits."

"That sounds like a painful hour," Monro noted with a faint wince.

"The gamble is that drawing it out will hurt them more than it hurts me," Cullen said. "If it takes five hours negotiating before everyone is satisfied, so be it."

"But Gregory first?"

"Yes. We need to bring Joe along for that," Cullen commented. "It's better when I'm not the only one conducting the business dealings."

"It'll be nice to have Joseph back again," Monro replied, with a faint smile. "And I hope I don't embarrass myself to suppose the feeling is mutual. I don't think it'll take much persuasion to bring him back to Edinburgh permanently."

* * *

Cullen told Anna to stay home.

"Let Alexander, Sandy and myself handle this, please?" he said softly, with the kind of quiet insistence Anna knew not to argue against.

Holm's lodgings were deserted by the time they forced the lock. Holm's clothing and belongings were missing, but a lot of dresses, jewellery and make-up was left where it lay, which made Anna wonder aloud if Mrs Holm had taken any of her possessions upon their escape.

At this Cullen took Anna by the hand, and led her to the bedchamber away from the servants and children. His face drooped further with every step.

"Sweetheart, we must be prepared for the eventuality that Cinead Holm didn't leave Edinburgh with her husband."

"But then where...?" Anna began before trailing off. Cullen's grim expression was enough to make her understand.

"The only person Malcolm Holm cares about is himself," Cullen continued, his grip on her hand tightening. "And he may have learned his wife sent that note to you."

Seeing Anna's stricken face Cullen pulled her into his arms. "It wouldn't be your fault, my love. I promise you, *it wouldn't be your fault.*"

EPILOGUE

They found Gregory in his second floor classroom. Upon his promotion to the Chair of Physic, the professor swapped from a ground floor room into one at the end of the corner, in the quieter wing of the New Library. It seemed like a tactical avoidance to Cullen: making the de facto head of the medicine school physically hard to access. His legs noted a complaint ascending all those stairs.

"You were expecting us?" Cullen began, trying to sound light-hearted without slipping into mocking joviality. He didn't really know what to say. This was going to be one of the most difficult encounters of his professional career.

"If I wasn't, would it have stopped you?" Gregory remained seated at his desk.

Cullen paused. "Probably not," he said candidly. "We've delayed this too long."

No longer hesitating, he crossed the threshold. A second later, a footfall behind, came Black.

"Joseph too?" Gregory forced a note of sarcasm, but it was unsupported by his cowering posture.

"We thought it was best this way," Cullen said. "Since we all have a stake in this business." The two men settled into seats opposite Gregory.

Black's hand trailed into his pocket and stayed there. Cullen set his small black notebook in front of him.

"You've had time to consider our proposal? The numbers are to your satisfaction?"

Gregory grimaced and flexed his fingers. He obviously didn't feel in a position to object or argue.

"The students are excited to have you back teaching medical theory," Cullen said, making a few notes in his book. "I think they're right when they say your attention to theoretical detail far outshines my own."

"It's one hundred and twenty pounds?" Gregory asked, watching them closely.

"A third is coming from Joe directly..." Here Black nodded. "And I believe he has the ability to pay the sum in full now. I can pay you a third next month, and the remainder at the commencement of the winter term. I hope that will be agreeable."

It was only fair. Black was moving into the second chemistry chair that Cullen's promotion vacated. Most of the students considered them a package deal, too.

"I tried to do what was best," Gregory said, so quietly Cullen almost missed it. "There are few men that care more about the medical school than I do."

"We know John," Black said, before Cullen had a chance to open his mouth. "Dr Cullen and I know you'll continue to serve the medical school honourably, and we appreciate you more than we can adequately express."

Gregory nodded. This was the kind of soothing motions to his pride Monro counselled, Cullen noted. Black always knew when to apply the decorative touches.

"The type of power we're dealing with," Gregory began, his throat sounding dry. "It's stain can never be erased. A whisper of the power those men once held will be enough to entice others to search for its secrets again." He swallowed. "Those dark practitioners are never truly gone."

Cullen nodded. He hesitated before responding, not because he didn't know what to say, but because he needed the words to come out properly.

"If they try to return I'll be waiting for them, John. Protecting the Edinburgh medical faculty and students against them is my responsibility: first on the line and last man in the room, that's what I'll be."

Black's gaze didn't leave Gregory, but he turned his head enough towards Cullen so he could see his flicker of agreement.

The two men stood to leave.

They didn't need to rush Gregory out of his teaching room. He deserved a short time to himself, and the ability to change roles with dignity. Cullen closed the door behind him.

"You got what you wanted, William." Black turned to his colleague, his dark robes fluttering slowly in the corridor. A window must have been propped open to take advantage of the late summer warmth. "Congratulations. This has been a long time coming."

"Thanks Joe. I couldn't have done it without you." Cullen squeezed Black's shoulder and he felt for a moment his former student lean into him, like he was a boy seeking reassurance once more. Then it was gone. "Now, I think a few drinks at the Nicholson's Tavern is in order."

They exited the corridor, and their footsteps could be heard descending the staircase. After the sound faded, the university returned to its dusty serenity.

HISTORICAL NOTE

Today, William Cullen is recognised as a key figure in the Scottish Enlightenment—a period of great philosophical and scientific invention that brought about the modern world. Unlike his more famous contemporaries such as Joseph Black, David Hume and Adam Smith, Cullen's ideas and discoveries haven't withstood the test of time. His medical theories were an improvement on what came before, but were largely superseded, even in his lifetime.

Yet Cullen's importance to modern medicine should not be overlooked. His informal, holistic approach to teaching was ahead of its time, and his former students went on to remake the world. Looking at Cullen and his achievements gives us a sense of how individuals can drive progress; and what societal forces were shaping 18th century Britain.

Central to the development of this novel was *The Learned Medicine of Dr William Cullen* by Jeffrey Wolf. In addition to being an entertaining and well-researched read, it paints Cullen as a man of strong character: ambitious, headstrong, but generous to a fault. My other key reference was *Philosophical Chemistry in the Scottish Enlightenment* by Arthur Donovan, which digs into the decades of friendship between Black and Cullen.

The Scottish academic system ran on a complex network of patronage, politics and star-power. *Academic Patronage in the Scottish Enlightenment* by Roger Emerson delves into the messy process by which academic appointments, promotions and retirements were hashed out. They were every bit as fractious as depicted in my novel, though I've condensed the timeline of several squabbles as artistic license permits.

ACKNOWLEDGMENTS

My first thanks goes to you, the reader. Thank you for buying, borrowing, reading, reviewing or sharing *The Edinburgh Doctrines* series with the wider world. An author is nothing without readers, and I'm grateful to have you.

Early chapters of *Dark City Rising* were shared on Critique Circle: thank you to everyone who reviewed and took the time to offer their valuable insight.

As with previous books, I'd like to show my appreciation to the hosts and fellow participants of Shut Up and Write! and Writers HQ, for giving me a space for writing sprints. Too many baristas to name have helped fuel the creation of my books, by providing cakes and double espressos in Edinburgh and Philadelphia.

Thanks to the staff at the National Library of Scotland, whose collections I drew upon regularly when researching these novels, and whose materials continue to shape more books to come. Many historians, PhD students and scholars have created valuable source material for studying the Georgians, and I'm grateful for your expertise.

Thanks again to my family, for supporting my writing and saying nice things about my books.

ABOUT THE AUTHOR

CL Jarvis holds a PhD in chemistry and worked as a science journalist, healthcare copywriter, and medical writer before sitting down to write her first novel. She's held together by cat hair and double espressos, and lives in Philadelphia, USA.

You can learn more about her at: www.clairejarvis.com.

facebook.com/cljarvisauthor

instagram.com/cljarvisauthor

www.ingramcontent.com/pod-product-compliance
Lightning Source LLC
Chambersburg PA
CBHW011937210726

48290CB00011BA/2728